WHISPERS *of* INK *and* STARLIGHT

OTHER TITLES BY GARRETT CURBOW

Daughter of Light

Slayer of Gods

Father of Night

WHISPERS *of* INK *and* STARLIGHT

a novel

GARRETT CURBOW

This is a work of fiction. Names, characters, organizations, places, events, and incidents are either products of the author's imagination or are used fictitiously. Otherwise, any resemblance to actual persons, living or dead, is purely coincidental.

Published by Lake Union Publishing, Seattle
www.apub.com

Amazon, the Amazon logo, and Lake Union Publishing are trademarks of Amazon.com, Inc., or its affiliates.

EU product safety contact:
Amazon Media EU S. à r.l.
38, avenue John F. Kennedy, L-1855 Luxembourg
amazonpublishing-gpsr@amazon.com

ISBN-13: 9781662530081 (paperback)
ISBN-13: 9781662530098 (digital)

Cover design by Mumtaz Mustafa
Cover image: © djjeep_design / Adobe Stock

Printed in the United States of America

To Grace

Part One

House Fire

Chapter 1

She knows only the man across the table.

Father.

His cold eyes like drops of oil. Full cup of coffee, black. An impatient trimmed fingernail tapping a lace coverlet. In his other fist, he holds a glass vial filled with her blood.

She flips her hand to see the cut, but it's closed up now. Only a thin mark remains across the treelike lines of her palm. The head, the heart, the life, the fate. All bullshit, at least for her. She will never have love, a life, a destiny.

She will just have *him*.

"Very good." Father's voice is sleet on the back of her neck. He sets the vial down and wipes her blood from his knife blade with a napkin.

Her reflection swims in the vial's concave side. Violet bags droop low over her freckled cheeks.

She knows what he will say next so vividly, she could be an oracle.

Two consecutive blows, each worse than the actual incision across her palm.

Scrape. The knife slides across the table, its wooden handle pointed at her.

"Now, again."

Chapter 2

Fireworks rattle the old window, casting red and blue light across James's typewriter. In the square below, Lincoln's measly population is gathered like the townspeople at the end of a Christmas film with an unrealistically positive ending. The villain has a change of heart. Love never dies. Every cat gets adopted into a happy home. The people down there, aunts and cousins and past teachers and peers, gape open mouthed at the rainbow sparkles above the downtown gazebo like children mesmerized by a shiny necklace. *If they're the townspeople,* James thinks, *that makes me the grumpy hermit.* Glued to his work, cooped up in his mountaintop lair.

James tries to concentrate by pretending the crackling fireworks are jazz instrumentals. Nothing but background noise, like the hum of his teal Smith Corona typewriter. Like his parents and his sister, Midi, talking over steak and broccoli during Sunday dinner. Like everything he once loved seems to have become.

Background noise. Even writing.

His fingers poise over the keys, unsure how to continue. He promised his boss, Nancy, that he would have his assignment, about the new crosswalk beside the high school, finished for the paper's next issue, but the deadline is in two days, and so far he has written only three thin paragraphs.

Nancy doesn't *love* when he asks repeatedly for extensions, and she *hates* that he only submits finished articles on typewritten pages. She called him a "pretentious ass" once under her breath, but she desperately needed help at the underfunded *Lincoln Gazette*, and James needed a summer job. Thus began his dreary articles about painted stripes on asphalt. Instead of sunbathing on a beach somewhere, he devotes hours every day to a cramped newspaper office built in 1864. He doesn't hate the work—words are his passion, in any form or fashion—but he prefers to craft prose about dragons and murders and love affairs, not crosswalks.

James rolls the half-finished page out of the typewriter and stares at the shitty writing as if he can magically will it to improve. After a moment of consideration, he balls it in a fist and tosses it in a metal bin. Fireworks reflect against the window, crackling like gunfire. He replaces his fingers on the keys as his half-empty coffee mug goes lukewarm.

Downstairs, the front door of his parents' house creaks open, breaking his weak concentration again. Even his mom's mouselike steps make the century-old floorboards groan.

Her voice cuts through the bones of the house. "James!"

Sighing, he descends from his lair into the hallway that stretches from one end of the house to the other.

"Yeah?" He dreads his mom's worried tone when she asks why he isn't out with everyone.

She pokes her head in from the kitchen, her brown hair threaded with silver. "Uncle Benji's fireworks probably have about ten minutes left, then your dad goes on."

As much as James wants to say, *Sorry, Mom, I'm not coming out tonight*, he can't force it out. It's important to her that he stand beside his dad and sister, completing the ideal family portrait for the town to see, bathed in colors like they are caught in the cross fire of strobe lights. Is it important to him? No, but many things *are* that he would never expect his mother to understand. So he bends to her will, as he so often does, even when it breaks him.

"Yeah," he says. "I'm coming."

"Good. Help me carry some stuff out."

James schleps a red cooler across the manicured lawn and down the street to Lincoln's square. He drops it beside a gingham-covered picnic table laden with burgers and hot dogs. Firework smoke swirls with grill char, reeking of summer in the South. His dad flips burgers over flaming charcoal, a grease-stained apron tied around his waist. As the mayor of Lincoln, Peter Finch travels a lot, his arms tan now from a recent work trip to Savannah. His face is movie-star quality, his biceps push the constraints of his shirtsleeves, and he has an off-white, dimpled smile that puts people at ease. All genetic traits that somehow surpassed his only son, who hides his thin arms inside baggy blue sweatshirt sleeves, whose resting bitch face, hard brows, and sharp cheekbones tend to make people feel unsettled.

The First Lady of Lincoln, Teresa Finch, slinks an arm around her husband's waist and holds her light beer by its sweaty neck. She laughs at something pole-thin Aunt Patricia says. Children slither snakelike past the picnic table, shrieking laughter as they snag hot dogs and cups of homemade ice cream.

Despite his Grinchly attitude, James enjoys a burger and ice cream. He doesn't hate the fireworks. The kids pretending their sparklers are magic wands remind him of those golden years when *he* possessed the ability to cast spells and brew potions. Somewhere between the ages of twelve and twenty-one, he lost the superpower to make mundane things magical.

After Uncle Benji finishes off his three-hundred-dollar firework, James's mom tells him, "Your dad's on," dragging him across the grassy square to a circle of lawn chairs.

Midi and her friends note his presence with judgmental glances, then all return to their phone screens in unison.

He shoots his sister a bird, wipes the burger crumbs off his lips, and lifts his gaze to the smoky stars.

Nelle holds a corn dog in one hand and wipes away a tear with the other.

As if under a mass trance, everyone watches the fireworks explode like china cups against a stone wall. Nelle swallows a bite. Sweet and heavy with grease, but dry, coating her throat.

Hours before the fireworks began, Nelle planted herself on a bench in the sun to watch people in denim shorts and sundresses unfold tables and grill food, prepping for their celebration. They blew up red, blue, and white balloons that now bob in the breeze like heads swaying to music. She tries to forget about the cold, prisonlike bedroom she will return to when the night ends.

For now she is free to watch the stars. To smell smoke drifting across the square, over the heads of people talking and laughing and *living* together. Nelle doesn't need to talk to anyone or swing around a sparkler to enjoy herself, but she does wonder what it would be like to have friends. To live in a community, not a pen.

She soaks it all in, this world she has been walled off from for so many years. Glimpsed only occasionally, for a few short hours at a time.

Glass bottles and red cups are passed around, laughter growing more boisterous. A deep, twangy voice starts singing, accompanied by the strum of a guitar. When Nelle claimed her bench earlier, she never expected the night to become such a spectacle of beauty. Never expected to fall in love with the fireworks, with the people and food and music. She was naturally curious about the world outside her house, but she never anticipated this twisting ache in her chest, this desire to be a part of their world.

∞

James looks away from the fireworks and sees her.

An unfamiliar face in a town where everybody knows everybody. Watching the fireworks, her hair behind her ears, doe eyes reflecting the starburst. Her lips part. In her right hand, resting on her leg, she holds a half-eaten corn dog.

James's palms start to sweat.

"You see that woman on the bench." He leans toward Midi and her friends. "She's not in high school, is she?"

Midi's cheekbone highlighter shimmers as she squints across the crowd. "Her?" She frowns. "I've never seen her."

"Maybe it's someone's family from out of town," he murmurs.

"If you want to talk to her, talk to her," says one of Midi's friends—Mandy Tucker?

The rest of them glance up from their phones.

Before James can plot out every possible catastrophic event that might result from introducing himself, he jumps into the sea of people in the square, his stomach flipping like the kids cartwheeling across the green.

Her round eyes rise to meet his as he closes in.

"Hey." Maybe she won't notice him wiping his sweaty hands on his pants.

Her knees peek out from beneath the hem of an eggshell-white sundress. "Hi."

"I, uh, I saw you sitting over here, and I just thought, well, I thought that . . ."

"That I was lonely?" Before he can respond, she adds, "I *am*. Lonely. Most of the time. But not right now."

He tilts his head. "How old are you?"

"Twenty-one." Her smile hits his heart like a cannonball. "And you?"

He takes her question as an invitation and eases himself onto the wooden bench.

"*Also* twenty-one." James squints at the hazy sky. His dad's finale ended before he walked over, and the last sparks are sizzling out.

"The fireworks were pretty," she says.

"Yeah." The part of his brain that comes up with things to say sputters out. "And loud."

"The noise doesn't bother me. Do you have a name?"

"James," he says. "James Finch. What about you?"

She sticks out her hand. "I'm Nelle."

"Are you new in town?" he asks, shaking it. "I've never seen you here before."

Her smirk holds secrets. "Nope. Lived here my whole life."

"Cool." James pats his thighs and surveys the crowded square, cursing his inability to maintain a stable conversation. "Did you graduate with my class?"

She blinks like a cat. "Um, I think so, yeah."

Yet he has no recollection of her, and his graduating class could have fit on one bus. "From Lincoln High?"

She purses her lips. "I was homeschooled."

He tries to follow the path of her eyes as she angles away. "Are you looking for someone?"

Or are you trying to hint that you want me to leave? he thinks.

"No." She swings her feet, covered by ruffled white ankle socks and brown penny loafers. "Just looking."

James can see the curve of her lashes and the spattering of freckles across her nose and cheekbones, the kind of freckles that blossom in the summer and die when winter comes, only right now they are somewhere in between. A strand of dirty-blond hair slips over her shoulder, dragging James's gaze as low as her collarbone before he snaps it back up. His throat swells at the moon trapped inside her brown irises.

"Let's play a game," she says. "A question game. We'll take turns asking each other anything, but you have to answer honestly."

A box of butterflies opens inside him. "This your idea of fun?"

"Yes." Nelle folds her legs beneath her. "What's your biggest regret?"

"In a few minutes, probably agreeing to play this game."

She glares at him.

"Going to college somewhere I didn't want to."

He has never admitted that to himself, much less said it aloud. In September, he will enter his third year at the University of Georgia, studying boring biology. A path he took only because his parents laid it out for him. Twenty-one years old, yet his life has been decided, squeezed through a tube he didn't choose. He should be grateful to have his scholarship, to have been accepted into college at all, to be healthy and doing somewhat well in his classes.

Nelle hums at his answer. "Second question. What's something you've always wanted to do?"

"Move to New York."

His parents are just across the crowd. If they heard what he said, they would be appalled. He has never shown the slightest inkling that he wants to leave his home state. Of course they know he loves writing, but they don't understand how far his dream flies. How much he wants to see, to do, that can't be accomplished from a rural field.

"Last question," Nelle says. "It's a big one."

"Then it'll be my turn to ask you?"

"Yes."

James braces himself. "I'm ready."

Her head tilts like a doe in the woods. Wise, impossible to read.

"Why *don't* you go to New York?"

He doesn't want Nelle to recognize his lack of backbone, that he's too scared of the unknown, of failure, to pursue his passions, that he's convinced the support of his parents, both financially and emotionally, is the only reason he's still afloat at all.

"I've always been a very scared person."

She bumps his shoulder with hers. "You weren't scared to come up to me."

"Yes," he laughs, "I was."

Nelle nods to a middle-aged couple beside the firepit, elongated shadows in their cheeks, their foreheads orange. The woman's diamond-clad fingers glint. A teenage girl stands behind them with her friends, all dressed in baggy jeans and cropped baby tees. They pass around a phone, laugh over the screen, point with fake nails.

"They seem happy."

James tries not to laugh at the irony. Of all the people in the entire square, Nelle singles out the ones he *knows* pride themselves on appearing happy. And, for the most part, they are.

"That's my family. My parents and my sister, Midi, with her friends."

Nelle blinks, as if seeing him for the first time. "You're happy, too?"

He shrugs. "Sometimes."

Her shoulders relax, and she listens to the night air, to the rattle of insects in the trees dotting the green spaces.

"What about you?" James watches her breathe. "Are you happy?"

"I get to be right now." Nelle nudges his shoe with hers. "Your turn."

"Why do you only get to be happy tonight?"

She huffs, the sound raspy. "Because being home never makes me happy."

Not a detailed answer, but he will take it.

"Second question." He ventures for something lighthearted. "What's your favorite animal?"

Nelle's freckled nose wrinkles. "Horses."

"Why horses?"

"They're majestic, wise, and strong." A grin cracks her mouth. "They demand respect, but they love to play. What's *your* favorite animal?"

James shakes his head and laughs. "No, no, it's my turn to ask. Your turn to answer."

"Come on . . ."

"Fine," he says. "Cats."

"I knew it."

"You didn't."

"You're right. I would've said birds."

"Birds?"

"Like a raven," she says. "You seem like someone who's read too much Edgar Allan Poe."

An accurate assessment. "And you seem like someone who's read too much . . ."

Her dust-blond brows lift.

"Shelley."

"Percy?"

"Ugh, no," James says. "Mary."

"True," she says.

"Okay. Last question. You ready?"

Nelle shakes her head. "No, but ask anyway."

"When you grow up, what do you want to be?"

Too long a moment passes, enough for James to worry he has offended her somehow.

Then she grins, all teeth, and says, "A horse."

They talk and watch the people as the revelry winds down. Children whine through their sleepiness about wanting to stay. Families wave goodbye to each other across the square. When the courthouse bell rings ten, Nelle jumps to her feet, her white sundress aflutter.

James follows her up. "Is everything all right?"

"I have to go home." Her face falters. "But I want to see you again."

"I'll text you."

"I . . . don't have a phone."

How odd. "Well, where do you live?"

"Twenty-three Blackwood Road." Nelle spits the words out as if to expel them before they burn her tongue.

The address sounds familiar to James. "I can drive you. It's kind of a hike."

"I'll be fine, but thanks," she says. "Good night, James."

"Good night." He lifts his hand in farewell, too dumbstruck by her abrupt departure to chase after her, to insist she not walk two miles alone in the dark.

Cinderella fleeing the ball, a phantom between buildings, sinking into the shadows behind the courthouse. A white pebble dropped in a lake, visible for a moment before she is overtaken by darkness.

After he's out of his stupor, James tries to follow her, but she's long gone.

Chapter 3

James stops his razor mid-stroke, cutting a pale rectangle through charcoal stubble. His cheeks are hollow. Eyes sunken. Jaw sharp. Most of his diet consists of fast food and cases of coffee, so his problem could be a lack of nutrition, but he doesn't have the motivation to *fix* it.

He has wasted every night of the summer hunched over his typewriter, clanking out articles for Nancy. Attempted a couple of novels, too, but he has yet to breach a second chapter, and the stress induced by those scrapped dreams demands *more* coffee. Or whiskey. His traditional Southern parents don't approve of alcohol in the house, so he keeps a liter stuffed under the mattress.

His routine is simple. Wake up, go to work, go home, write, read, shower, sleep, then resist the urge to pound his head into the mirror as the cycle of what he will do tomorrow haunts him. Instead of harming himself, he finishes shaving, wipes his face, towels off, and steps back from the glass. Cold tile underfoot, he takes a deep breath. Come autumn, he will be back to textbooks.

That's it, he thinks. *After work, I'm seeing Nelle.*

That promise draws him to his dresser to find an outfit. Her address tickles the back of his mind, but he is not sure how he knows it. He has never had any friends who lived on Blackwood.

On his way to work, he stops at the gas station, buys two coffees, and pockets some creamer packets. When he started bringing Nancy the French vanilla she liked, she started being a lot nicer to him.

Inside the office on Lincoln's square, the smell of ink, paper, and old coffee grounds hits James's nose. He ducks through the foyer's cloud of dust—the building is a converted Civil War–era home—and into the back room. Nancy is at her desk, rapid-fire typing on her dinosaur of a computer. Over her glasses, she burns holes into his head until she notices the extra coffee in his hand.

James sets the packets of creamer on her desk, followed by his finished article. After his encounter with Nelle the night before, he was struck with creativity and cranked out the remaining eight hundred words as easily as exhaling.

"Done early?" Nancy raises her brows. "Can't wait to read it."

"I think you'll like it," James says. "It's my most inspired piece."

"Don't lose your inspiration." She leans back to open a filing cabinet and hands him a stapled packet. "Here's your next piece. I want it Thursday."

James drops into his desk chair, plugs in his laptop, flips through the packet, and starts researching the new auditorium under construction at Lincoln High School.

~

Nelle can't take another bite. She stares at her half-eaten oatmeal, the two remaining blueberries like Father's eyes, snake scales rubbing bare skin. She hates him the most when he sits across from her, puts his cold fingertips on her hand, and says, "Now, again."

She always loses her appetite after he cuts her. After he funnels her blood into the vials he keeps lined up in his study. Ready to dip his pens into.

Nelle shivers, thinking of the gashes in her palm knitting themselves back together, skin lacing skin.

But how can someone like me feel pain? Why does she ache for the outside world, full of rapists and murderers? Father warned her endlessly about the dangers of the world, but he never prepared her for its beauty. For fireworks. For corn dogs. For *people*. Laughter. Mindless, meaningless, beautiful chatter. Birds communicate for fun. People, too. Nelle wants nothing more than to be a part of their flock.

But in order to leave, she would have to write for herself, and that is the one rule Father's drilled into her skull harder than any other. If she tries to write for herself, she will die.

Her rendezvous with James was a once-in-a-lifetime opportunity. She had approached Father on a calm day and asked if he would take her to the festivities. He used to speak fondly of attending town gatherings with his wife and daughter.

His *first* daughter. Eleanor.

Father hates going into town now, so she expected him to say no. To admonish her for suggesting such a careless idea. But he said yes, he'd write for her to go until ten. By herself.

Nelle didn't ask why he wouldn't be chaperoning her and didn't want to poke the beast, so she waited until the Fourth before bringing it up again.

"You'll feel the pull to come back a quarter before ten," he explained before she left. Then his voice dropped lower. Colder. "Do I need to go over your rules?"

She hadn't heard them since her first trip to the library three months ago, but she knew them like they'd been branded onto her.

Don't look at anyone. Don't talk to anyone. Don't say anything.

So of course she broke all three at the first chance.

Nelle's fist curls under the table, silver spoon digging into her raw scar.

Father shuffles in the room behind her—the room he calls his study, the room full of bookshelves that hold the tales of her life—his pen scratching out what she will do tomorrow. When she was eleven, she caught a glimpse of one transcription: *Tomorrow, on the sixteenth day of May, Nelle will wake up at eight o'clock and make oatmeal. She will eat, then return to her room until three, when she will come out to play cards.* The memory makes her shudder. She always knew her actions were predetermined, but seeing it written altered her perception of reality.

Her life is meaningless. Governed by Father. *He* buys her the books and brushes and paint *he* approves of. He decides when they go to the library for the first time. He picks out her meals, her movements, where she goes, even *what* she does. As far as she knows, if he wrote that she stabs herself in the throat, she would have no choice but to obey.

She wouldn't die, though. Again and again, he has told her there are only two ways for her to die: if every last scrap of writing in her blood is destroyed, and if she writes with her own ink.

Maybe she should try it. Open her veins over a palette, mix the ink with paint, create a canvas of blood. Death doesn't seem too harsh a consequence. Some days even preferable to the torture she endures with her self-proclaimed father.

Yet she is still too scared of death to try to write.

At breakfast this morning, Father called her a burden. She has grown a second skin to fend off his insults, but this one stung. The Fourth of July was her first taste of freedom, of not being chained to his will, and now she craves more.

Since she was a child, Nelle has watched the horses in the neighbor's field, through the trees beyond her bedroom window. They gallop together, necks thrashing, manes luminous under the moon and sun. They are muscular, passionate creatures. They're *wild*, despite the fact that they're trapped, too.

If I'm a burden, why not release me?

But he won't. He can't. As her creator, he alone can write her instructions, and deep down, she knows that she needs him. His pen, her ink, and the shelves of leather-bound journals in his study. She *hates* that she needs him.

But without him, she would not exist.

ᯅ

The sun is hot when James gets off work. He climbs into his old truck, a hand-me-down from his grandma, and starts the cranky engine, wheels munching asphalt as he pulls off the square.

He takes a right down curvy River Road, where tree branches hang low and scatter shadows over the street, and then a left onto Blackwood. Mailboxes whiz by. It's a dead end, and the last metal mailbox has QUILL 23 printed on its side in tall white letters.

He rolls down the window, braking.

That's why he recognized the address. Old Wallace, the walking skeleton who rarely leaves his home.

In middle school, James and his friends would ride their bicycles here to throw pebbles at his windows. The curtains were always drawn, but they were terrified of a gaunt, pale face popping up behind one of the pollen-dusted panes. It never happened.

In retrospect, James shouldn't have been scared. *Old* was unfair for a man probably in his late thirties. And a man who had been through so much.

One unfortunate night twenty-two years ago, a faulty wire caught fire at 23 Blackwood Road. Within minutes, both stories were engulfed. Rumor spread quick. By the end of the night, everyone heard that the fire had taken two lives. Wallace Quill's wife and daughter were never seen again.

Then he rebuilt an exact replica of his historic home, painting it the same forest green. Afterward, he mostly disappeared. No one saw him at festivals or in the bookstore. Only at Tim's Market, every other Tuesday for groceries, though he moved like a ghost and never spoke. Rumors circulated that, along with his wife and baby, the smoke from the house fire had killed his vocal cords.

Did James mishear Nelle yesterday? No, without a doubt she said 23 Blackwood Road. Maybe Wallace moved. Or died. Then again, he isn't *that* old, and surely word would have traveled through town if he had left.

Guess I'll find out. James pulls into the gravel driveway.

A green colonial home peeks through the pine trees, camouflaged by the forest. Chopped wood sits stacked outside, half covered by a red tarp. A porch wraps the house, topped with a tin roof that reflects the sun, and a brick chimney. The only car is a 2004 Jeep beneath a droopy willow.

James swats through clouds of gnats and climbs the porch steps. The dead light by the front door is spotted with moths. His heart pounds, blood thrumming like static in his ears. All day, he has imagined this moment. What he will say. How she will respond.

Taking a deep breath to cool his wildfire nerves, James raises his fist and knocks.

⁂

Nelle forgets her unfinished oatmeal and the cut across her palm. She squints to make out the silhouette beyond the door, but the window is fogged glass, and all she can see is a dark head of hair. In her two decades, they have *never* had a visitor. Her throat tightens.

"Who's that?" Father calls from his office.

"I don't know," she says. "I can't see."

Then it clicks. Dark hair, broad shoulders, the only person she has ever given her address to. The boy she talked to on the square. The boy she hasn't stopped thinking about since. *James.*

Father locks his study door behind him and grumbles across the kitchen, past the table, to the front door—

"Wait," Nelle blurts.

She wishes more than ever to go where *she* wants to go. *When* she wants to go. Right now, she would go lock herself in her room for a week. Because when Father opens that door, when he sees James on the other side and learns that Nelle not only spent hours with a boy, but that she gave him their *address* . . .

She shudders, glued to her seat.

Father's ice-cold eyes narrow in suspicion.

The door screeches open, and James's smile drops on the other side.

Old Wallace Quill's black hair is combed behind his ears, his beard untrimmed, his irises dark like chunks of coal. Behind him, Nelle sits at the kitchen table, unnaturally pale, holding a spoon.

"Who are you?" Wallace Quill demands.

James extends his hand. Up close, Quill has a disturbing stare, though nothing else about him seems exceptionally off. But this is not the playful, intelligent Nelle he had the pleasure of being enchanted by last night.

"Hi, sir," James says. "Nice to meet you. I'm James. I met Nelle the other night at the square."

Wallace doesn't take James's hand. He swivels slowly to Nelle. She is trembling—silent, meek, forcing herself not to meet his stare—like a skeleton hung in the wind.

"You met her *when*?" he asks.

James isn't sure if Quill's grin is meant to be inviting or terrifying. "Yesterday at the square. At the fireworks show. Sir."

"Thanks for stopping by, but my daughter is busy with homework right now. Maybe another time."

"Oh, okay," James says. He waves to her as the door eases shut in his face. "See you later! And nice to meet you, uh, Mr. Wallace."

"Call me Quill." Quill grins again, that unnerving show of teeth, as the door clicks shut, leaving James with the dead moths, snared catching a pretty light.

Maybe Quill's not so bad. Odd, but not evil. Just a poor reputation with the neighborhood kids, the "wicked old man" back in the woods. Standoffish vibe. Tragic backstory. Lives alone, or so they all thought.

James tries to ignore the eerie rustling pines as he drives away from 23 Blackwood Road. Then he remembers Quill's words: *Homework?* Nelle didn't mention college.

Wait. *Daughter?*

Chapter 4

The pungent smell of vinegar barbecue hits the patio of Lindsey's Smokehouse, one of the only restaurants on Lincoln's square. James sifts through his pulled pork and tries to listen to his cousin Jessie talk about living in New York, the paid sponsorship she just got, the collectors buying her paintings, how glad she is that her sucky roommate's moving out next week, the friend she met who is unnaturally hot *and* smart and could possibly, fingers crossed, turn into more.

"Half the week I go to a little studio in Brooklyn to paint," Jessie says. "I swear it's like a scam. I get to do what I love, and these suckers are *buying* it." Her hair is frizzy from the heat and tied back in a ponytail. She wipes a smudge of hot sauce off her cheek. Two years ago, Jessie's artwork blew up on social media. Since then she has had an influx of commissions and people with too much money and empty walls scrabbling to clean out her shows, and brands constantly paying her to come to their events, to use their paint, to post a picture with their energy drink. "Every now and then, though, I pick up a shift at the place I worked in college. This tiny little bookshop, Shack O' Books. You'd love it."

"Mm-hmm." James leans on his fist, staring up at Lindsey's dusty storefront. A car vrooms behind him in the town square. It's been only two days since his visit to 23 Blackwood Road, and he can't forget the shell of Nelle he saw in that kitchen.

Jessie continues. "I also have my internship, which isn't great because it's unpaid labor, *but* I'm making unbelievable connections. Not just Lena, though she's definitely a perk of the job. She's really studious, which isn't normally my type, you know. But she just got a job working at some corporate law firm, so she'll probably leave the program soon, and when she's out, I'm out. I'm only doing it as an excuse to spend time with her."

"Mm-hmm." James tries to remember what she said, but her words are mush in his brain. He shoots in the dark with, "Then what?"

A crumpled straw wrapper bounces off his forehead.

"Ouch."

"Come back to earth please," Jessie says. "If you need to talk, talk. But don't leave me rambling. You know I'll go on forever."

"It's nothing," he says.

"My flight back is in eight hours, so you have about six left to receive my wise counsel."

He sets his fork down. "I met someone."

Jessie swirls her straw. "Intrigued."

"She was here on the Fourth of July, and on Monday I stopped by her house—"

"Where does she live?"

"Blackwood Road."

"Name?"

"Nelle. Nelle Quill, I guess."

Jessie purses her lips. "She lives here? I've never heard of her."

"Me, neither," James says. "She didn't give me a phone number, just her address. So I go see her, and Wallace Quill opens the door. He says she's his daughter, that she has to finish her homework, but I never heard about him having another kid after the accident with his family. And when I come in, he has this aura about him. Like he wants to pick apart my ribs and use each one as a bow for his violin."

"Gruesome, but okay. Don't most dads have that 'Oh, this is my daughter and you're not allowed to even think about her' look?"

"This was different," James shakes his head. "Nelle was in the kitchen. I could see her. But . . . she wouldn't move. She was trembling . . . and the way he talked about her . . ." Even in the ninety-degree heat, chills break out across James's arms. "I can't describe it, but I think something bad is happening in that house."

"Do you want my advice?"

He sighs. "Yes."

"Stay out of it," Jessie says. "If something weird is going on, trust me, you don't want to get involved. Call the police, and they'll take care of it."

"No." His heart hammers at the thought of abandoning Nelle in unknown peril.

"James." Jessie snaps her fingers. "Don't get hurt over someone you've only known for three days. If her dad is like you say he is, he might be dangerous, and you don't know what he's capable of—"

Straw to her lip, Jessie freezes, looking over James's shoulder. "Holy shit, he's here. He's watching you."

James whirls, knocking the table with his leg. Soda sloshes, pools around the base of the glass.

A 2004 Jeep zooms off the square, tires screeching as it pulls down the street.

❧

The evening is mellow, warm, sticky. Cicadas scream in the trees in front of James's house. He smacks a mosquito on his arm, leaving behind a trail of blood, and waves goodbye to Jessie as she backs out of his driveway in her rental sedan, off to the airport. It stings every time she leaves. He doesn't know when he will see her again, and he is jealous of the life she is flying away to.

He sighs. Is he stupid for thinking he, too, will one day get to live in New York? Being an author feels like a pipe dream, especially when his mom and dad slip med-school brochures under his bedroom door and shake their heads with disapproval every time he breathes Jessie's name. Aunt Patricia, in that classic mom way, calls her twice a week to guilt her into coming back to Lincoln.

The first firefly of the night blinks past. Pam, the town's mail carrier, pulls onto Anderson Street, bobbing her head behind her windshield. Her musical taste is vast and consistent: explicit rap Thursday through Saturday, worship songs Monday through Wednesday. When she pulls up to the house and waves at James, out spills a soulful lyric about sinking into the waves of God.

Wednesday. July 7.

Three days since he met Nelle.

Two since he went to her house and saw her sitting almost lifeless at that table.

James braces himself on the porch railing, his phone like a rock in his pocket. Just three numbers. He could dial three numbers, tell them he is concerned for Nelle, and be done with it. That is all he has to do. Anxiety eats at his stomach like a monster, stilling him.

Going back to 23 Blackwood Road terrifies him.

But Nelle might be in danger.

Shit.

He pulls out his phone, nauseous and trembling, and dials 911.

It rings for half a terrifying second before a woman answers.

"Nine-one-one, what's your emergency?"

"I, um . . ." James sucks in the warm air. "I went to a friend's house two days ago. Nelle Quill. She lives at 23 Blackwood Road. I met her father for the first time, or at least I think it was her father. But he seemed really strange. Scary. I saw him again today in town. I think he was following me. I'm just worried about her safety, so if there's anything you could do to check in on her . . . I know you probably need a search warrant for that, but—"

On the other end, a woman exhales strongly enough to cut him off. A pen scratches. "What's your name?"

"James. James Finch."

"Thank you for calling us about this, James. Where are you now?"

"Home."

"Stay there for now, 'kay, hon?"

"I can do that." Suddenly James's porch feels like a prison cell. All he wants is to break out and haul ass to Blackwood Road. Is sending the police a grave mistake? He leans against the chipped railing. "How soon do you think you'll send someone?"

"We can have an officer out there tonight."

James exhales and fishes his memory for Jessie's advice. *Stay out of it.*

"'Kay. Thank you for calling, James."

"Thanks," he says absently.

A frightened animal coils inside him, telling him to stop talking to Nelle, to disassociate himself, to resume life like normal and never think about her again. *Go back to school, graduate, get a job, stay in Georgia.*

But Quill is in that house with Nelle, and has been for God knows how long. James swallows.

Stay there for now, 'kay, hon?

He storms up to his Smith Corona and lets his fingers fly. Metal hammers clank down on paper. Fifteen minutes later he crumples a half-filled page and tosses it over his shoulder. It bounces off the trash can rim.

He rolls in another sheet.

Dear Nelle, I—

Should he ask if she's okay, if she needs help? If Quill is hurting her?

He feels like he's overstepping his boundaries as a stranger, but a bigger part of him can't ignore the uneasiness in his gut. The feeling of slime coating his skin that three showers haven't scrubbed away. Whatever is happening in that cabin at 23 Blackwood Road isn't good, that's all he knows.

And he needs to make sure Nelle's okay.

Something she said to him on the Fourth keeps coming back, echoing in his mind.

I get to be happy right now. Did her happiness end when she returned home? Chills spread like ivy up the back of James's neck. He slides his typewriter into position, ready to start yet another first line.

Dear Nelle . . .

❧

An out-of-breath panther paces Nelle's room, muttering to the floor, strands of black hair falling over his forehead. Her thin white rug slides crooked under his shoes, but he doesn't straighten it.

"I ask you to follow simple rules, and *still* you disappoint me."

Nelle checks the clock on the wall, a gift for her eighth birthday. Before, she used the stars to track time in this cage of a room. Since she got the clock, she has been tallying off the days on the baseboard under her bed using a hairpin. Almost five thousand little white marks now.

Father pokes her chest, hard, and she flinches, the quilt curling under her fingers.

"I'm the reason you have a beating heart under there, and breathing lungs, that you *fucking exist*. I *created* you." His words slice at her until she can feel the tendons of her love for him snapping. Only took twenty-one years, one too many tastes of freedom, and James Finch to get her to this point.

Up close, the liquor on his hot breath twists her stomach.

He growls and resumes his pacing. "All that work. Every day I slave over your life, writing for you. Don't you know what would happen if it weren't for me, Nellie? Don't you know?"

Nelle says, "I would be stuck here. I wouldn't be able to move. Or go anywhere. Or eat. I would be immobile." The words are a lifeless recitation.

"And you would rot," he says. "You would emaciate and rot until you were so weak you wouldn't be able to open your fucking mouth. I need you, my sweet girl, but you need me more. Without me, what would you be?"

Without him, she would be happy.

"I'm sorry." She uses the floor to hide her lying eyes. All she sees is his black crocodile loafers as he paces, back and forth, creak after creak. "I won't talk to him again."

His shoes stop—creak—pointed at her.

"Oh, Nellie, look at me." He touches the delicate skin under her chin, a hint of emotion in how he cradles her jaw. So rare for him. Maybe it is compassion. Or sympathy. Or maybe just a trick of the light. "I'm not trying to scare you, Nellie. I just want to keep you safe. That's all."

"I know." She waits for him to leave. When he doesn't, she decides to ask a question that has been trapped inside her for years. Best to test Father's limits right after he has thrown a tantrum, when he still feels sorry.

"Do you think I could try writing?" At his quick alarm, she adds, "Not with *my* ink—I know the consequences—but with a normal pen. I've been rereading *Little Women*, and Jo is . . . and I thought maybe . . . I want to write my own stories."

Father drops her chin, wordless. His silence scares her most.

"I don't need much. Just pen and paper." She twists a stray thread in the quilt. Even as a grown woman, he can make her shrink into a child.

"You know I don't think that's such a good idea, Nellie." He is gentler then she has ever heard him, swaddling her with his voice. "I can get you more paint if you're running low."

Empty canvases sit stacked against the wall, covered in dust. She hasn't painted in years. Father always kept strict rules on the subject matter of her art. She could only paint a bowl of fruit or the willow in the front yard so many times before she spiraled into insanity. When she was thirteen, she dared to paint without a reference, and Father retaliated by rampaging and shredding the canvas. She had painted a giant, naked woman squished into a tiny cage, legs and nose poking through the iron bars. He fed each scrap of canvas to the fire. Made her watch it burn.

She forces a smile. "I've got paint."

A knock echoes from the front door. Father swears as he storms out of the bedroom.

Nelle breathes through the spike in her pulse. If James has returned, she doesn't know what Father will do to him, or what he will do to her. She stares at the blank canvas and imagines it splashed with her blood and James's, black and red swirling together.

Nelle strains to catch every sound as the front door squeaks on rusty hinges.

"Hello, Officer."

Officer. Nelle freezes. *If James called the fucking police, I'll strangle him.*

"How's your evening, Mr. Quill?" asks an unfamiliar woman. Under her polite tone, Nelle hears suspicion, which means Father hears it, too.

"Oh, it's all right. Hasn't been the same since . . . well, you know."

"I'm sorry, I'm unfamiliar with what you're referring to."

His accent flares up, a sign he is either trying to confuse or charm. "My wife died a few years back. In a house fire."

Twenty-two years is more than a few.

"I'm sorry for your loss," the officer says. "Do you mind if we talk inside?"

Nelle hears a hard noise and imagines his arm lurching out across the doorway, blocking the officer's entry.

"Do you have a warrant?" Surprisingly, Father's voice sounds level. A general question, no hint of nervousness. But the question itself gives the impression he has something to hide.

"No, sir, I don't," says the officer.

Please, Nelle thinks, biting her tongue. *Come search. Find me.*

Though what would she do if they detained him? Only he can write her commands.

He is quiet for a moment, and Nelle can almost see his spiderweb smile curl from one dimpled cheek to the other. His charisma is his secret weapon. With a few words, a second to warm up, and a laugh, he can snare anyone.

"Come on in," he says at last. Two sets of footsteps move into the kitchen. "Would you like a cup of coffee? Fresh pot."

"No, thank you."

Nelle moves to lurch off the bed, to hide in her closet, but her legs are locked in place. He must have written for her to stay put. Her heart races. How will she explain to the police if they try to move her and she won't budge?

"I'm already on my third cup," he says. "Mind if I pop in the toilet?"

"Go ahead," the officer says.

The floor whimpers under his feet, closer and closer, until he slips into the bathroom across the hall from Nelle's room. A second later, she eases off her iron bed, springs groaning, and smooths down the quilt before situating the pillows. Making it appear unused.

She goes hazy with anger at her lack of autonomy, her body moving on its own, following the orders he has written for her. Her arms tremble as she pries the window free. She pulls hard, but it is glued shut from years of neglect. The toilet across the hall flushes, and she uses the sound to hide the *pop* as the glass pane jumps free. She hangs one leg out, then the other, and drops to the dandelions outside. Her feet ring at the impact, nausea filling her stomach. Then she tugs the window nearly shut, leaving a small gap so she can hear inside. She flattens herself against the house, struggling to breathe in the wet-blanket heat. A fly darts around her head and lands on her nose, tickling. She moves to swat it, but her arm is immobile now.

"What room is this?" the officer asks.

They're in my bedroom.

"This was my daughter Eleanor's," Father says. "After the fire, she moved to Scotland with her grandparents."

Lies, lies, all lies. Nelle can imagine him wistfully stroking the roses papered to the walls, the sparkle of a tear running down his nose.

Eleanor *died* alongside Bianca in the house fire. Nelle knows it to be true. She has watched Quill mourn her daily for twenty-one years.

The officer says, "She liked to paint?"

Nelle snorts and the fly speeds off. The dust-coated canvases and brushes will only serve to back up his story.

"'Liked' is an understatement," he says. "I keep everything she made from age two in the basement."

That much is true. For as long as Nelle has painted, she has given her finished pieces to Father to store for safekeeping. He never once hung one of them for display.

"My daughter loves art, too," the officer says. "You seem fine here. I got a distressed call from a young man earlier today. He was worried about a friend of his, Nelle Quill, but we have no record of you having a second daughter."

"It was probably a prank," he says. "The kids here think me the Boo Radley of Lincoln. My house gets TP'd about twice a year."

"I'm sorry to bother you, then."

Their footsteps fade.

Nelle releases an imprisoned breath as feeling returns to her face and fingertips. But it's not until minutes after the police car crackles away up the gravel driveway that she feels her body's tight hold unravel. A far-off command guides her around the house and to the front door.

Father stands in the kitchen, his back to her. The lights are off, so the room is shape and shadow.

"That boy is responsible for this," he says, his voice low and cold. Nothing like the poor, lonely man who spoke to the police officer moments ago. "*You* are responsible for this."

"I'm sorry," Nelle says. The apology leaves her lips like bubbling acid. She wants to spit it out, to sear his face with her words. Instead, she chokes. She tries to take a step forward, her thigh flexing with the force, but her legs are frozen in place.

A journal hangs limp in Father's hand. She can sense the switch in his aura, a cat going from cuddly to demonic in the span of seconds.

He flips on the stovetop, and a blue flame appears. The smell of gas hits Nelle as he scratches in his journal.

Her feet carry her to the stove, and she holds her hand over the flame. She no longer begs for mercy, not since she endured his hundredth form of torture—three hours with her head held underwater—and realized that he will never change.

Her hand inches closer to the gas flame. It starts hot and itchy, like her skin is peeling back. Her palm opens like a rose, but she doesn't dare look. Whimpers rip into sobs, and she relents to the fire. She scream-cries from the bellows of her gut. Years ago she gave up any hope that the neighbors were close enough to overhear her. The flame burns, but she heals fast, an endless loop of passing out and waking up over the stove to more indescribable torture.

Burn and heal. Over and over.

Again and again.

Chapter 5

James's typewriter hums under his fingertips as he finishes off the final draft of his sole fixation. Through the window above his desk, Pat the mail carrier's white vehicle hisses to a stop at the mailbox, blasting Nicki Minaj. Friday. It has been two days, and the letter is finally at a point where he thinks it makes sense. Where his questions for Nelle sound more curious and concerned than offensive. Where he is apologetic for sending the police and hopeful she is all right regarding that lapse in judgment. He signs the letter, *From your friend James.*

His next article for Nancy remains untouched, and yesterday was the deadline. Maybe, just maybe, if he starts working now, he can still beg her for forgiveness.

James folds Nelle's letter into an envelope as he steps into the dark garage to leave, but someone is already in there.

"Holy shit!" he shrieks, his caw bouncing between the garage walls.

His mom is seven feet off the ground, on a ladder, tinkering with the dome light.

"Please don't curse in front of me," she says. Then, straight to the point, "Where are you going?"

"To see one of my friends." He holds up the letter as proof. "I wrote her a letter."

"You what?" His mom frowns, either confused that her son is actually leaving the house for an innocent reason, or that someone in this day and age would send a letter. She climbs down the ladder, reaching for the envelope.

He snatches it back.

"Who's the girl, James, and why haven't you brought her to dinner yet?"

Her hands get all grabby, the baggy arms of her sweater swinging as she reaches for him. Reluctantly, he gives into her embrace, an iron grip around his letter.

"She's just a friend," he says.

"Sure."

When she finally pulls away, James tucks the envelope in his back pocket and wrestles with a question that has been on his mind. Before he started college, in the living room of their downtown house, eavesdropped on by his mom's hutch of antique dolls, his parents explained the financial burdens of life and how he would go under and be doomed if he didn't build foundations of support early on. His future could either be in medicine or law, no questions asked, and medicine felt like a subject he could study enough to be good at.

"Can I talk to you?" James asks.

His mom's teary-eyed pride transforms into a skeptical, furrowed brow.

Last December, in the sterile hallway of the science building, a brochure gave James an idea. It has stuck with him since, a thought cultivated into a dream, then into a plan. He already talked to his advisor and secured himself a spot in all the classes he will need. He has done everything to prepare for this change, save ask the people who will be paying for it.

Wincing, he drops the bomb. "I want to add a second major."

"What do you have in mind?" Her arms cross. "Political science?"

"What? No."

"Oh God." She pinches her forehead. "Please tell me it's not psychology."

"What do you have against psychology? You *go* to therapy."

"It's not a lucrative career path, James. Right now, if you don't get into any med schools, you can have a reliable job, like a nurse, but employers are not seeking out recent graduates from the Department of Psychology."

He laughs at his mom's odd prejudices. "It's not psychology. I want to add *journalism.* I love to write, you know I do, and this way, I can maybe make a living doing it."

"James—"

By her tone alone, he can tell it's a no, so he interrupts. "Please, Mom. I know it's impractical to you, but nothing else will make me happy. Journalism will at least . . . give me a purpose."

His voice cracks, and for a second he forgets about the letter.

"Don't you realize I'm settling here, too?" he continues. "Majoring in two degrees will add at least a year until graduation. It'll double my coursework *this* year, and though it's not writing novels in an English country house, being a journalist is a hell of a lot better than putting catheters into old men."

She sighs and flips on the light switch. The garage floods with stale LED.

"Keep dreaming. Money's tight right now, hon. With your sister about to graduate, we can't afford you to add a year. Trust me, it's smarter to focus on medical school. A journalism degree, there's no future in that, and the extra coursework would only distract you from making good grades in the classes that matter. Eyes on the prize, remember?"

"Yeah, I hear you." Her words fall through his head like air. All but two.

Keep dreaming.

∞

Now that he has met the man inside the house, the driveway of 23 Blackwood Road becomes the same terrifying mouth to the underworld that it seemed to James as a kid. Even as, through the rustling trees, sunlight flickers like a jewel off the tin roof.

He parks at the top of the drive, before the trees part to reveal the house. The July heat slicks up his back as soon as his shoes hit gravel. With every crunching step, the letter in his pocket grows heavier. He considers heeding Jessie's advice and remaining uninvolved. Turning around. It would be smart, but in his mind he sees Nelle staring at her oatmeal, so paper white she looked sick.

He circles the right side of the house, avoiding the front porch and Quill's Jeep.

Knowing that Quill is only a few walls away dries out James's mouth.

I'm here for Nelle, he reminds himself as he stands on tiptoes in patches of weeds and dandelions, peering through the windows. He first sees the kitchen, with its small round table and ceramic countertops. The next window is covered by tasseled velvet curtains. The last window reveals a room with rose-printed walls, an iron bed, empty canvases, and a shelf of books. *Little Women. Jane Eyre. Anna Karenina. Around the World in Eighty Days.*

James prays this is Nelle's room and taps the window.

Flattening himself against the siding, he waits. Sweat clings to his shirt and hair. He reaches up to knock again, but his knuckles don't hit the windowpane.

They hit air.

He spins around, fearing Quill's black glower, but instead he finds Nelle, the window budged open, her hair hanging in wispy strands. Arms folded. She wears an expression that suggests she has been waiting around for him all day.

Her mouth twists even as she hisses, "What are you doing here?"

"I wanted to see you again," he whispers. "Is that okay?"

"Did you call the police?" A creak echoes inside the house, and Nelle flinches.

"Yes," James says. "Sorry." He holds out the letter. "Read this. My address is inside. Write me back, and we'll talk that way. So *he* doesn't have to know."

"I can't write to you." She checks over her shoulder. "Come here tonight. You have to go now, though, I think he's coming."

As James slips away, he turns around. "I'll see you tonight."

But the window is closed, the white curtains drawn.

❧

Nelle snatches up the closest book she can find as her door bursts open.

Father's eyes are woven with red, a strand of sweat-slicked hair dangling over his forehead, a sheet of paper clenched in his fist. She recognizes his neat handwriting on the page: an account of what she will do tomorrow, ripped from one of his journals. No doubt what she will be doing for the following months, even years. All because of her mistake on the Fourth of July. She had one chance to see the outside world, to watch people and fireworks, and she ruined it all by talking to James. A choice she still can't make herself regret.

"Who were you talking to?"

She thinks about her painting of the caged woman, now shredded up and burned. *He'll never let me out again.*

Behind her back, she slides James's letter into the pages of *Little Women*. The corner of the cover scrapes the raw skin on her palm, still not yet completely healed from the stove two days ago.

Nelle knows better than to lie to him. At least fully.

She unveils the book in her hand. Four floating heads, the March sisters, against an emerald background. Staring at him with eight black dots.

"I was reading aloud." A hard bubble rises in her throat, her tell that she is lying.

He glares at the book. Nelle swallows.

"Let me see," he says.

She hands it over.

He runs a hand across the cover.

Nelle can't hide her pounding heart. Her ache to swallow again. If he finds that letter—if he reads it—what will she do? What *can* she do?

But he tosses the book to the hardwood with a thump.

Nelle presents a stoic expression to hide her relief.

"Read in your head from now on," he says. "Your chatter is distracting me." He holds the crumpled paper up as evidence of his hard work before storming out of the room.

Nelle waits forty-two seconds before crawling under the bed. The pages of *Little Women* split on James's letter, tucked into the scene where Laurie confesses his love to Jo. She has read it enough times now to know it by heart.

Cramped beneath her bed, next to her five thousand tally marks, Nelle reads James's letter, each word fuzzy in the dark. She finishes with a sigh. When night comes, she will tell him the truth. He might run off, terrified by what she is, but she doesn't want to keep lying to him. And even if he doesn't believe her, she wants him to know. Wants him to see for himself.

Nelle hides the letter between the pages and sits by the window. Maybe James *will* believe her. Maybe he will trust her.

She imagines herself taking off to New York with a finished manuscript and a typewriter case. She's Jo March, not a girl written into life by a man with ice for a heart. She makes coffee in her apartment. She picks up a paintbrush without it making her nauseous. She walks the streets she wants to walk. She learns to ride a horse.

***

Time drips slower than honey, and nothing James does seems to speed it up.

He buys coffee from the gas station, finishes his article, emails Nancy to let her know he will drop it off in the morning, and reviews his schedule for the fall semester. He is taking biology, anatomy, two science labs, and precalculus. The only class on his schedule that doesn't make him want to vomit is a once-a-week fiction workshop he signed up for electively, not for his major. His to-do list eats up only half the evening, and he promised Nelle he would wait until nightfall to come over, so he grabs his notebook and writes a vignette as the sky turns the color of a nasty bruise.

Only, now that night has come, James wishes he had more time.

His nerves skyrocket. In his letter he asked Nelle why her father acted the way he did, why she ran away on the Fourth, why she is his age and lives in this small town but he has never seen her. He wrote that he is concerned for her well-being, and he wants to make sure she is safe. He told her that he finds her interesting, and that if she wants, he would love to get to know her better. What was he *thinking* writing that?

James has no friends outside of books. Yes, Jessie, but she is only in town once or twice a year, and she is his cousin. Talking to Nelle on the Fourth awakened a part of him that has been hibernating for years. The part that *likes* people.

Or in this case, a specific person.

So when night finally comes, James shuts off his typewriter, closes his notebook of scribbled thoughts, and slips out of his parents' house.

Chapter 6

James stands in the bushes below Nelle's bedroom window, the forest buzzing at his back, his heart slamming against his chest. Again, he half expects to see Quill's face split the lacy white curtains.

You came back, he tells himself. *Don't give up now, baby.*

He sucks in a breath, then softly raps his knuckle against the window, ready to bolt at the first sign of Quill.

With a groan, a pop, the window lifts.

Relief.

"Hey, there." Nelle's aroma melds with the night. Sweet vanilla, like a bakery in the morning, tainted by a tinge of ink and colored with pine needles. James rests his chin on his arms, folded on the windowsill.

"Can I come inside?"

She pulls her vanity stool up to the window. "Too risky."

Cold water dumps into his bloodstream as he remembers that the subject of his fear is only a few walls away, possibly within earshot.

James scans the forest, the perfect place to hide.

"Why don't you come out, then? We can go to a diner or just ride around."

Nelle focuses on a noise behind her and picks at her nails, clearly frustrated, and James wonders whether her bedroom is locked or if Quill could barge in at any moment.

"I can't," she insists. "We'll have to talk here."

James wants to ask about the letter, but first . . .

"I'm happy to see you again," he says.

Nelle blinks, as if processing the words.

Too forward? he wonders.

Cautiously, she says, "I'm happy to see you, too, James."

"You, uh, had a chance to read my letter?"

"I did." She disappears into the room and comes back with the ripped envelope. She passes it through the window. "I need to tell you something. You don't have to believe me, but it'll be easier for both of us if you do."

He hates to imagine Quill hurting her, in any way, but all he has witnessed pushes his thoughts in that direction. He itches to know, yet he dreads the truth.

Nelle braces herself against the windowsill. "You're going to think I'm lying."

"Try me."

She sucks in a deep breath. "It might be easier to comprehend if I . . . show you."

Every idea James had evaporates. "Okay?"

"Do you have anything sharp on you? A pocketknife or—"

James jangles his keys. "This work?"

Nelle's arm, pale like an eel, reaches through the window.

He pauses before handing over the keys. "What are you going to do?"

"Just trust me for a minute. Don't make any loud noises, and *don't* try to stop me."

An uneasiness crawls into his stomach. "Nelle, if you're going to hurt yourself—"

"Give me the damn keys," she snaps.

James drops them into her outstretched hand. Her palm shocks his fingertips, like touching an electrical outlet. The warmth lingers. Nelle doesn't seem to notice. She pinches the house key, levels it over her palm, and digs it into her flesh.

"Stop!" He lurches toward the window. But she keeps digging the key in until—

Blood flows. She flips her hand on top of James's. Her blood falls steadily, filling the grooves of his hand like little rivers. Hot and black as drip coffee.

"Smell it," she says.

Horrified, he lifts his hand to his nose, and his nostrils burn at the smell. Ink. *Ink.*

"Good one." He shakes off his hand and wipes the ink residue on the grass, though his skin is stained a purplish color now. He laughs. "You got me."

"I told you that you wouldn't believe me." Nelle's jaw tightens like a windup toy. She shows him the spot on her palm where she supposedly cut herself. Her skin is unblemished, no incision. "This isn't a joke."

"You can let up now, it's funny."

"James, I bleed ink."

"No, you don't." He laughs again. "That's impossible."

"Go into the woods." She points to the tree line, branches and leaves lost to the shadows. "There's an old glass beer bottle over there. Break it and bring me back a piece."

James runs a hand through his hair. "You've got to be kidding—"

Nelle's expression is dead serious.

James decides to go along with whatever this is, this prank, this diversion from her real problem with Quill. When she's ready to talk about her issues, he will be here to listen. To help. Until then . . .

Pine straw crunches underfoot as he crosses into the trees. He swings his phone flashlight side to side until it illuminates a green glass bottle half hidden beneath a thornbush. He grabs it by the neck and swings it hard against a tree trunk. It doesn't break on the first blow, but on the second it hits a hard knot and shatters across the foliage.

Sorry for littering, James thinks absently as he carries a shard back to Nelle's window.

"Got it." He sets the emerald fragment on her windowsill.

Nelle picks it up.

"Look at my hand," she says. "And don't stop looking at my hand."

Exiled to the world outside Nelle's bedroom, James stares at her hand. But she doesn't do some drastic trick with the shard, doesn't move at all as she clamps her fist around the glass. She just whimpers, and her other hand lifts to her mouth, biting down to stop the noise.

"Nelle," he whispers. "Nelle, stop, what are you—"

"No, *look*," she exhales, opening her hand.

The glass drops onto James's shoe, but he is too captivated to notice the ink splattered across his white sneaker. His vision tunnels as the jagged gash across her palm leaks a pungent black liquid. She holds out her hand, and James takes it to study, the blood warm. When he pulls away, his fingers are smudged with fresh ink.

Ink. Not blood.

His brain spins. The *world* spins. He stumbles against the side of the house, painting the clapboard siding with her blood. Presses a hand to his heart—a black print on his white tee—to soothe the confused hummingbird in his chest. He remembers how the ink glistened inside her cut, and his nausea tidal waves.

"Okay," he manages to say, his mouth full of saliva. "I'm going to ask you one more time, and please be serious. How are you doing that?"

"Watch."

Reluctantly, he does.

Nelle's skin knits itself back together over the open gash.

James runs a hand through his sweaty hair, bracing himself against the wall. A firefly bobs near the trees. Another follows it. They float and blink, on and off.

"What . . . *are* you?" he asks. Oddly enough, he is not scared of her. Close to vomiting, yes, but no less enthralled. If anything, more so.

Nelle runs a fingertip along the windowsill. "I'm not a human."

"Oh," he says. "That's not what I thought you'd say."

"I'm an idea. A figment of someone's imagination."

James shakes his head. "You lost me. I don't imagine people."

"I didn't say I'm a product of *your* imagination."

She sounds real. She smells real. She *is* real. James has always had a wild imagination, but never enough to manifest entire human beings. He didn't even have an imaginary friend as a child.

"It started with Quill." Nelle glances over her shoulder, as if listening for a noise behind her. "Twenty-one years ago, he started writing about a little girl. A baby. And one day he woke up, and she was there, with him. A flesh-and-blood incarnation of the character he'd created. Living in his house. Screaming in the same crib his daughter had left empty a year before. It was iron, so it didn't burn with the first house."

James's head is a tornado. "I don't understand."

"I *am* that character. I'm Quill's daughter because he made me his daughter."

"So you're not real?" James asks. This has to be a prank. A twisted joke.

"I am real. I can think, I can breathe, I shit and sing and cry. I have a heartbeat and organs. And a mind that thinks on its own. A mouth that speaks what it wants to speak."

"How is that possible?" James asks. "I . . . I don't understand."

"It just is." Nelle hands him back his keys.

He studies her smooth palm. *Impossible.*

"It's easier if you accept it."

His shirt is drenched in sweat, and not from the humidity. "Am I going insane?"

"No."

"Well, in that case, I have *so* many more questions. Are you sure you can't come out with me for a bit? We can drive around and talk. Quill will never know you left."

She shakes her head, dirty-blond hair framing her cheeks. "I can't leave. I think what I want and do what I want, but I can't go where I want. I can only go where he writes me to go. And if he writes a specific command for me, then I have to do that, too. My body just . . . reacts that way."

"Seriously?" James asks, even as the pieces start clicking in place. "That's why you had to run home the other night. You could only be out for a certain amount of time."

Nelle nods. "And since he found out that I talked to you, he's decided that I'm never allowed to leave the house again. I haven't left my room since the day you came by, except to hide from the police. He's got me caged in here."

"Sorry for that, by the way." James glances at the trees, the grass, the pine straw. The broken glass littering the ground. Reminders of the real world.

"Sorry for what?"

He laughs until his gut hurts. Something about the hilarity of the absolute insanity he's found himself in. When he regains control, he says, "For calling the police."

"You already apologized in your letter."

"But again, in person, I want to say I'm sorry. I'm sure Quill didn't appreciate the visit."

"No." She curls her knees to her chest. "He didn't."

James hears the words she keeps inside, that her punishment for his poor decision was worse than his imagination could conjure.

"So you really can't leave?"

Nelle's fingers tighten on the windowsill. "No."

"We can always hang out like this, I guess."

"I'm just trying to be honest with you. I've never really talked to anyone but Father before," she says. "I'm not trying to scare you off."

"I'm not scared," James lies. He is fucking terrified. But when he looks at Nelle, he doesn't see a monster or a demon, only curiosity, excitement, and, further, sadness and anger. "I do believe you. I think."

Believing her makes him want to throw up the gas-station coffee he chugged an hour ago. His mom always called his stomach a beehive, reactive to every little poke.

Nelle drums her fingers on the sill. "In your letter you said you find me intriguing."

James's cheeks go hot.

"I find you intriguing, too," she says.

The moon emerges from behind splitting clouds. Nelle's freckles glow like stars on her cheeks and nose, her brown eyes are like melted chocolate, her lips so full he could write a poem about them.

"Do you want to come back tomorrow night?" Nelle asks.

James hesitates. Of course he wants to, but whether or not he should is a different decision.

"If you'd rather pretend you never met me, you can do that, too. I'll understand."

His lungs fill with summer air. How much longer can he survive doing what he should and never what he wants?

"Tomorrow," he says, unsure if his echoing is an agreement to return or merely an attempt to process what she said. *Everything* she said. The ink, the glass, the secret about Quill. The question itself: *Do you want to come back tomorrow night?*

Nelle glances over her shoulder again. "I think I hear him. Good night, James. *Tomorrow.*"

Before he can respond, she lifts her healed hand and pulls the window shut.

Driving home, the trees feel foreign. The town square smaller. The shadows in his neighbor's windows scarier. Under his too-hot comforter, as James falls asleep to the hum of cicadas and frogs, he wonders if his life has been irrevocably derailed.

Chapter 7

To make up for his late article, James is at the newspaper office on a Saturday. The clock slugs toward noon, until a mere ten minutes stand between him and his lunch break. Though it's not like Nancy regulates when he leaves his desk. Or the building. She is always in and out in a pair of chunky clogs, clutching a camera, her purse swinging like a pendulum over her shoulder, moving at a faster pace than everyone else in lazy little Lincoln. She once insisted they take a lunch break together and told him all about growing up in Chicago. When he asked her what she thought about New York, she shuddered and said, "Too many people."

After a bite at Lindsey's Smokehouse, James spends two mind-numbing hours scrolling through the layout for next week's issue. He adjusts and aligns gray squares where photos will be placed. Drags out text boxes and double-checks for grammatical errors before pasting them onto the page. Across the dusty workroom, Nancy drops into her rolling chair, acrylic nails clicking against her keyboard. If you're working today, then I'm working today, she texted back earlier. Thrown off by the change in routine, he forgot to bring her coffee, so she drinks from a ceramic mug, leaving red lipstick on the rim.

She scans the screen, probably planning editorial notes on James's latest article. Or flat-out changes she won't consult him about. She is the editor, after all, and she likes to remind him of that fact. She pauses for a moment, sips her coffee again, and brushes a frizzy, reddish-brown strand of hair behind her ear. Peacock feathers dangle from her earlobes.

James's focus crumbles as the words on his screen blur into the shape of Nelle's name, letters sliding away like streaks of her black blood, the ink on his hands, on the grass, on the side of the house, on his shirt, his shoe . . .

As he left her house last night, he resolved to never set foot there again. To move on with his life, finish his degree, possibly even go to medical school, and grind toward a reliable job.

All of which begins with forgetting about Nelle.

Which he seemingly can't do. He scrolls through a folder of images from an awards banquet at Lincoln High School, but all the students' smiling faces morph into Nelle's. He closes out of that tab and focuses on the newspaper layout, on transferring finished articles. But the words smudge like fresh ink and become *Nelle Nelle and Nelle went to the Nelle at the Nelle on Nelle—*

James slams his fist into his keyboard, and a spurt of random letters appears in the middle of the word *Saturday*. He deletes the error with six furious jabs.

"You good?" Nancy hovers over him.

James jumps, his throat tickling as a cloud of floral perfume encroaches on him.

"Just this damn article," he says. "Trying to get it done by three."

She leans on his desk. "You've been working hard lately, James, but don't spread yourself too thin. Take a break if you need it."

"It's okay, it's already half past—"

"No, a break *after* work." Nancy purses her lips. "Look at me, James."

He does, really *looks* at her, for the first time. She's not old, maybe twenty-six? Her glasses are red plastic, her lipstick the shade of fresh blood, her hair carefully curled. Black eyeliner wings cut into her temples. She is *pretty*, a fact that somehow James hadn't seen until now. Maybe it has to do with her looming above him.

"I have two tickets to a walking performance of *The Lion, the Witch, and the Wardrobe* at Riverside Playhouse, if you want to come with me. My date canceled." The perfume that previously suffocated James starts to smell like a field of wildflowers.

Her nails rattle against the laminated wood of his desk.

James swallows. All summer, he has thought of Nancy as his boss, his *elder*.

"How old are you?" he asks, immediately feeling a twinge of regret. *Not the right thing to ask a woman who just asked you out, idiot.*

"Twenty-five," she says, and to further prove her youth, "fresh out of grad school. Why, do I seem older?"

"No, no." His finger jitters on the space bar. "You seem, uh, very young. Not *very* young, but—"

Nancy peers down at him. Within seconds, her dusty-librarian aura became a sexy grad-student vibe, and James has lost all ability to speak coherently. Not the sparkly nerves he feels around Nelle, but adjacent. This is the anxiety he recognizes from *any* time an attractive girl has talked to him.

Can you go back to being my boss, please, so I can think straight? he almost asks.

But a night with a girl who *isn't* Nelle might be exactly what he needs to cast her and her craziness out of his life forever.

"What do you say?" Nancy jangles her keys. "I'll drive."

∽

When they arrive at Riverside Playhouse, a half-hour drive from Lincoln, the sun edges the field, painting the grass gold. James and Nancy trot down a gravel path to a check-in booth and hand their tickets to a man wearing a cashmere coat. Manure, sweet and putrid, rides the breeze from a pasture of grazing horses. Past the honey-thick haze in the air, a creek gurgles.

The show starts in a barn decorated to resemble the interior of the English country house where the Pevensie siblings stay at the beginning of the novel. James stands in the front of the crowd on a designated path, vaguely aware of his knuckles brushing the back of Nancy's hand. She sucks in a sharp breath.

When the four child actors discover a wardrobe built into the wall, James and the rest of the audience follow them outside into a field transformed from a hot July evening to a winter wonderland. Fake snow blankets the ground, the trees are frosted, and a horse-drawn sleigh gallops across the landscape. Stuffed snow owls hoot from high branches.

James finds himself sinking into the show, watching in awe and wonder, full of imagination he hasn't felt since he was a child.

The production ends with a battle and the Pevensie children returning to the mansion in the English countryside, far from Narnia and Aslan. James follows them through the hole in the wardrobe, though the snow has been stripped away now to reveal emerald grass and full trees. Back inside, the barn is a gray husk of what he glimpsed moments ago. He wants to go back.

When the show ends, Nancy asks him what he thought about it, but he can't find the words to describe how it made him feel. Like magic is real. Like *anything* is possible. Like for the first time in years, he is alive.

Immediately, he wants to invoke that feeling in someone else, to stoke that fire within himself. A poem, a novel, a lyric. His fingers itch to create.

"Yeah, I liked it. Thanks for inviting me."

They make small talk on the ride home—*Where did you grow up? Any summer plans? How's the layout coming along for next week's issue?*—but James is only half in the conversation. His other half is plotting a secret move to New York. He has some money saved up that he can use to help pay for rent if Jessie lets him stay with her. He will have to get a job to afford out-of-state tuition if he wants to go to school there. His parents would never help him be so irresponsible, even if they could, especially if he is going for a degree in the humanities.

Slow down, slow down, he tells himself. *Start by finishing a novel. Get a practical degree in the meantime. Then see if you still want to wreck your life.*

It's what his mom would say. And he can't argue that she would be wrong.

Half an hour later, Nancy parks her car outside the newspaper office.

She hesitates, hand on the door handle. "I had fun tonight."

The tension of a potential kiss dangles like a string above the center console, but he can't do it. He can't give her what she wants. He needs to feel magic, and there is none.

At least, not with her.

"Thank you," he says. "You don't know how much I needed this."

Nancy opens her mouth, a smudge of red lipstick on her front tooth.

"I think we should just stick to a professional relationship," James says as he opens the door. The dome lights wash out Nancy's confused face. "I really did appreciate this date. I loved the show. See you Monday!"

He waits in his truck for her to leave the parking lot, unable to wipe the giddy grin off his face as he backs out and drives off, out of the square. Not toward his parents' house on Anderson Street, but right toward River Road. Then down Blackwood.

To a house with a mailbox marked QUILL.

Nelle scrutinizes herself in her vanity mirror. She ties her blond hair up, pink bow dangling like bubblegum strings, then takes it down so it falls in thin, blond locks over her shoulders. She puts it up again. With a groan, she yanks the ribbon out and shoves it in a drawer. Silver glints beside it, a chain that dangles and shimmers when she plucks it up.

A glass pendant hangs on the end, holding soil from the lake behind Father's childhood cottage.

If she tries to write for herself, she will die.

But he never said what would happen if someone *else* wrote for her.

Nelle dumps the tablespoon of dirt into the drawer and pricks her finger with a sewing needle until a black bead blooms, and the little vial is full. Holding the pendant makes her feel powerful and guilty at the same time. Other than talking to James, siphoning off her own ink is the most directly she has ever disobeyed Father. Shaking, she hides the pendant beneath a sheaf of drawings in the drawer.

A muffled tap beats on the windowpane.

Nelle's chest swells with an uncharted emotion, a feeling she has read about but never experienced. She carries her vanity stool to the window and unlocks the pane, wincing at the resistant groan. James stands on the other side, beaming up at her. He takes off his red-and-brown flannel, revealing long arms, gold from the summer sun, a stark contrast to the gray of her own skin, lifeless from hiding in the shadows.

Her relief unspools. "You came back."

"I came back," he says through a smile. It's infectious, and suddenly she can't wipe a smile off her own face.

"I didn't scare you?" She doesn't want to tiptoe around the truth, not if this night is going to end with James telling her that he never wants to speak to her again. She wants to rip the rejection off like solidified wax, in one painful yank.

Hope inflates her as James says, "You *did* scare me, but here I am. For some reason, I believe you, and for some reason, I just . . ."

"What?" Nelle rests her arms and chin on the windowsill. The air outside is drenched in pine and manure. The smell of Lincoln. "You just what?"

"Want to be around you."

Nelle watches the bulb of his Adam's apple as he swallows. He is really here. He came back. For the first time in her life, she has a friend. She feels it with him. Trust. Connection.

And for the first time in her life, she might have a way out of this prison.

"Do you have any questions for me? About . . . you know . . . what I am?"

"You say you're not human, that Quill wrote you into existence," James starts. "What does that actually mean?"

"Father was married a long time ago. He had a wife and daughter that he loved." She looks above the spiky treetops to the stars. "Bianca and Eleanor. They died in a house fire. Like I told you, it started as a way of coping with his grief. He wrote about having an infant daughter. And one day, he woke up to find me in *this* room in a pink bassinet. Screaming and crying like a real newborn baby."

"So your creation was . . . accidental?" James asks.

The idea of Quill creating her *purposefully* has never crossed Nelle's mind. He only ever treated her like a mistake.

"I don't know if he wrote about a baby because he wanted *me*," she says, "and honestly, I don't want to know."

"Sorry if I crossed a line there."

Nelle shakes her head. "It just makes me wonder why he'd treat me the way he does if he *asked* for me. And I don't want to go down that road."

"He's an asshole, that's why." James sticks his arms through the sleeves of his flannel, and Nelle mourns. "Anything else I should know about your . . . condition?"

"I don't like when you call it that."

"Okay, your magic?"

She cringes. "Sure, magic. I can only go where Father writes for me to go, but I can *do* whatever I want. Unless he commands me to do something specific."

"So . . . you wouldn't be able to jump out of your window right now, even if you wanted to?"

Nelle stands and tries to push herself through the window, into the inviting summer night, but she physically can't. Her bones clench, her hands freeze on the windowsill. Her legs immobilize. Even her lungs contract. It's embarrassing, she realizes now that she is doing it in front of someone else, to strain like this without moving a muscle.

She withdraws back to her stool. "I can only go where he lets me go."

"And he writes for you every day?"

"With my blood," she says. "It really is ink. I have to fill up vials so he can write my daily commands. Even things like going to the kitchen and the toilet."

"Surely he can at least give you access to the whole house?"

"If he can, he never has."

James pauses. "So Quill *is* your real father? Are you safe here?"

Nelle's mental walls snap up, reliving every bruise and burn Father has left on her. The pinprick scar from the stove has nearly faded, but she can still feel the ghost of its burn, the smell of sizzling flesh stuck in her nose.

This is what you want, she reminds herself. Someone's outstretched hand.

"He's not my father." Her words are dipped in hatred.

Even the crickets seem to halt their chirping.

"Then . . . who is he?"

A tremor escapes her lips. He is only a few walls away. If he hears her, if he finds James, if he—

Another cooling breath in and out. The heat recedes from her face.

"My captor," she answers as a drawer closes from the other side of the house. She steadies herself against the window. "You should go, it's getting late."

"I'll see you tomorrow?"

Nelle nods, still focused on that noise. "Tomorrow."

She starts to shut the window when she remembers her gift for James. The key to her plan.

"Wait!" she hisses. He stops, and his hopeful blue eyes melt her insides. The curtains rustle as she sweeps away from the window, shuffling papers in her vanity. She returns with the necklace and unravels the silver chain into James's palm. After all she unloaded onto him, it is only fair that he gets to carry around the darkest part of her.

The chain spools around its vial, the size of a fingernail. Filled with black ink. *Her* ink.

When enough time has passed, when he really trusts her, then she will tell him what the ink is for. Then she will ask him to help her escape. She hates to hand him the reins of her life, but what other choice does she have?

"What's this?" he asks, holding it up to the bedroom light.

"For you to wear." She wonders how warm it is inside his tight grip. "So you can carry around a piece of me."

And so that maybe, one day, I can get out of here.

James switches off his bedside lamp, Nelle's necklace resting heavy over his heart. He holds the pendant until the glass warms.

Buzz. His phone lights up. He hopes, for a second, that it is a message from Nelle. But she doesn't have a phone. Or, at least, she said she doesn't. Curiosity wins and he flips it over to check the notification.

> Hi James, I'm glad you enjoyed the show tonight. See you at work.

James shuts his phone off and thinks, *I'll reply in the morning.*

But he won't. When he goes to sleep, all he sees is Nelle. When he wakes up and slides Nancy's notification away, all he sees is Nelle. When he goes to work and Nancy won't acknowledge him, he doesn't think about their date or his rudeness or whatever article he is supposed to be researching—

All he sees is Nelle.

Chapter 8

During the final hottest weeks of July, James spends more time at Nelle's bedroom window than his typewriter. He gets to know the buzzing crickets, the coin-thin split in the wooden sill, the dried-out ladybugs crusting the frame's bottom groove, and when the wind blows in, the honeysuckle from the bushes by the back of the house. He stretches back into the smell.

Nelle perches on her vanity stool by the window, chin on her knees, her eyes like a chinchilla in the dark.

"When was the last time you cried?" she asks. Her tone is bored, but James sees it for what it is. The effortless speech of the intimate.

He observes the wall of trees over his shoulder. A month before he met Nelle, he had a drunken meltdown during a two-hour bubble bath. He hated the pointlessness of his life, the school he had prayed to get into, his parents and their expectations, his lack of friends, his sister and her excess of them.

"I can't remember."

"Did you cry when Misty died?"

At some point over the last three weeks, he told Nelle about his family's golden retriever. Red blood matted in her fur. His dad burying her in the backyard. To James, losing Misty was like losing a sister.

"I didn't." He would do anything to scratch behind her ears again, to throw the ball for her. "Not in front of my dad."

"Why not?"

"Didn't want him to think I was weak."

The corner of Nelle's mouth twitches down. "I'm sad a lot, but it only sharpens me. You're better off for the shit you've been through."

"You think?" James touches the hollow of his neck, the vial on its chain halfway visible beneath the collar of his sweatshirt.

"You show your feelings proudly, James. At least around me," she says. "The smartest people *don't* push their emotions into boxes."

He laughs. "You sound like a tea bag."

Nelle's head gives a little shake, her face a question mark.

"The little paper thing attached to a tea bag." James motions with his hands. "Sometimes it has a saying on it, like a fortune cookie."

"What is a fortune cookie?"

"You've never heard of a . . . ? Well, it's like a wise phrase delivered to you with your food so you can think while you eat," James says. "At least, that's how I think about it. I'm not sure what the actual history behind it is. Why don't we look it up?"

Nelle sighs. "I can't go to a library. I can't *leave*."

"As much as I'd love to go to the library with you, I meant with my phone." He holds it up. A spiderweb crack laces its glassy back.

"A . . . cell phone?" Nelle reels back like he's holding a bomb.

"A smartphone." He types his question. "Wait, have you never seen a phone before?"

"Of *course* I've seen a phone," she says, a drop of Quill's Scottish in her American accent. "But it's big, with a cord attached to the wall."

"Welcome to the new decade." James reads the first article aloud. A full history of the fortune cookie with all its potential creators.

"Do you have an encyclopedia inside there?" Nelle asks.

"Think of it as a tiny computer," James says. "That you can also call and text people on."

"*Text* people?" She shakes her head again.

"Nothing nefarious." He rests his forearms on the window, fingertips dangerously close to Nelle's. "It's like sending a letter."

"Yours was the first letter I've ever received," she says. "I think I prefer that over *texting*."

"I think I preferred handwriting it, to be honest." James laughs. His voice rings out into the night, and he thinks about how late it is. How frequently he has come to visit Nelle and not once seen any sign of Quill, other than the car out front. Maybe it is worth the risk, just being close to her. Nerve worked up, he asks, "Do you think I could come inside?"

Nelle's fingers tighten around the windowsill. "You're the first friend I've ever had, James, and if Quill found you in my room, he'd kill you. Or he'd kill me."

He'd kill us if he found me outside *the house, too.* James respects Nelle's apprehension, but he longs to talk to her like on the Fourth. To feel her beside him.

He opens his mouth, "Maybe—"

"You remember how I told you an officer came to our house?" Nelle says.

James leans in closer to her whispering lips. "Because I called."

"I assume."

A rat of worry gnaws at his stomach. "Did Quill"—James licks his lips—"kill her?"

"*No.* But after she left, he made me pay." Nelle's glossy stare scorches his shoulder. "He wrote for me to burn my hand on the stovetop," she continues, fighting a tremor. "As punishment. Every time it healed, I'd have to burn it again." She's shaking now, like a tiny dog out in the rain. "For hours."

"Nelle, if I'd known, I never would have called the police. I thought I was helping, I'm so sorry—"

"Don't give me sympathy, James. I just want you to understand the kind of monster Quill is. Why you can't come inside."

He clutches his shirt, fist over heart. "I understand."

Low, like an animal, a long *creeaaaak* resonates through the night.

Nelle goes rigid.

Around the house, the front door opens, screen slapping. Footsteps move out onto the porch.

Every tree and animal freezes in the midsummer night as Quill bellows, "I KNOW YOU'RE HERE! I CAN HEAR YOU, YOU BLOODY BASTARD!"

The birds flap away. James, too, feels the instinct to run. If he goes into the woods, Quill will see him. If he stays, Quill will see him. If Quill sees him, he will hurt Nelle again. Worse this time.

"Let me in," he says to Nelle. He tries to heave himself up. *Shit, shit, shit—*

"James, run around the back of the house," she says. "I promise it'll be worse if you're in here."

Around the corner of the house, a yellow light bobs closer.

"Let me in," James repeats. "He'll see me, Nelle."

Hearing her name snaps Nelle out of her trance. She reaches out with clammy hands. James clasps on and folds over the windowsill, slamming the wind out of his chest before crashing to the floor in a pile of bony limbs. The world goes quiet.

While he gathers his breath, James takes in the room. A bedside lamp, its shade hung with tiny pearls, glows softly. Above the small brick fireplace, a line of tattered paperbacks holds court on the mantel. The walls are papered with two-inch pastel roses.

Nelle pulls the windowpane shut, locks the latch, and straightens the gauzy curtains.

"You can sneak out the back door," she whispers.

"I might run into him out there. Why don't I hide under your bed, wait it out?"

"No, no, no, if he finds you in here, he'll make *assumptions*."

"But won't he—?"

"Father—no, dammit! *Wallace* is not a reasonable man, James." The color leaches from her cheeks.

James hears pure terror in her voice, so he risks peeking into the hallway. Photographs line the walls. Quill holding up a book, Quill standing with a baby in a field of daises, Quill and a suntanned woman kissing on a striped towel.

"Down the hall. Through the living room. The door leads out back," Nelle instructs him. "Go through there, and you can run to the woods."

James, realizing that he is half a foot taller, kisses the top of her head. She blinks, flustered.

"Wish me luck."

Each whimper of the hardwood floor makes James flinch. Before he enters the living room, he checks around the corner. The furniture is old and floral printed, facing a blocky TV. Curtains pulled shut. Maroon shaggy carpet. Space heater filmed by dust. Fifteen steps to the door, burst outside, get out.

Click.

James freezes, staring down the barrel of a pearl-handled derringer, Quill's steady wrist at the other end.

"Hello, there." A disconcerting smirk twitches Quill's face. "I don't remember scheduling a playdate."

"You're sick."

"Really, Doc?" Quill doesn't lower his gun as he steps closer. Closer, closer, until that cold metal is pressed against James's forehead. Safety released. "But I feel fine."

"Don't hurt him!" Nelle yells from her bedroom.

Quill's eyebrow cocks. "She fancies you, does she?"

"She's my friend." He contemplates throwing a punch. "You piece of shit."

A growling laugh bubbles up in Quill's throat.

James glares at him. "What's funny?"

With that gun against his head, he's strangely not scared anymore. If he dies, he dies, oh well. But if he fights back . . .

"You're more amusing than I thought you'd be." Quill points his gun to a chair beside the fireplace. Within feet of the exit. "Sit down. It's story time."

He doesn't move.

"I'll make it quick," Quill says. "Promise."

With no other choice, James sits. Back straight, legs tense, ready to bolt at the first chance.

Quill crosses his legs on the couch, pistol resting on his thigh, pointed at James. He clears his throat and adjusts a framed photograph on the side table, a Polaroid of himself and Nelle when she was around twelve. She shows off a gap-toothed grin, her freckles pepper, her hair corn silk.

"I used to have a dream," he says, "which I carried with me from the time I was a child. To be an author."

James thinks back to his own childhood, mindlessly flipping through books and pretending he had written them. Signing sheets of notebook paper during math class until his signature was consistent enough.

Quill grins like the Cheshire cat. "You have a similar dream?"

James hates that he is that easy to read.

"I toiled throughout my teenage years, writing whiny, pretentious books. Then I wrote a tragic love story, as all are in the end, and my dream came true. Hallelujah, I had a book published! It was a hit. I was only twenty-five, and Bianca was pregnant with Eleanor—" Quill sinks into the couch cushions and sighs. "They were my world. It took only three months to know Bianca was the one, but I fell in love with Eleanor the second I knew about her. I read books to her, *Moby-Dick* and things like that, hoping she'd catch my wildfire for writing."

Quill stares off for a moment, smiling to himself.

"Maybe *Moby-Dick* wasn't the most inspirational choice for an infant," James says.

Quill's eyes darken into inkwells. "Our house caught fire when I was twenty-six, and they both died."

The gun tilts toward James now, but not precisely at him. If he can dart out of the line of fire, he might be able to escape.

"Before I made Nellie, I had stopped writing novels. I had enough money to last a lifetime, and I'd never been so miserable. I'd *lost* what

I loved the most in this world. So . . . I crafted a fictional daughter. On paper."

A mahogany grandfather clock stands in the corner of the room, ticking toward twelve o'clock.

"But for twenty-one years, she's taught me more about myself than I thought possible. Nellie is my little miracle. My baby. Don't you get it?"

"Get what?" James's anger slips out—only a hiss, not the whole boiling pot—through his gritted teeth.

"That she's *mine*." Quill stands and stretches to his full height. A tall, harrowing man.

James can't combat the instinct to shrink into his chair.

"And as long as you're around, you're a threat to her." Quill cocks the glinting pistol.

The grandfather clock in the corner of the room strikes midnight, clanging out a harsh tune. It shakes the floor, the walls, James's very bones.

Quill recoils at the sudden sound, and while he's distracted, James bounds toward the door. He swings it open and warm air hits him, treetops waving like fingers. But a hand from behind snags his shirt collar, yanking him back like a fishing rod. James doesn't hesitate. He balls his fist up and swings around, as hard as he can, and his knuckles explode as they collide with Quill's face.

The older man staggers, stunned.

James cradles his forearm, pain shooting from his elbow to his fingers.

"You little shit." Quill's pistol hand goes limp as he sleeve-swipes his bloody nose.

James darts past him, praying that any bullets miss their mark. He blurs through the living room, into the kitchen, to the front door, dodging the dining table.

Crack! The gun goes off like a cannon, and the window above the kitchen sink shatters.

James reaches the front door, cold knob in his grasp, and pauses. Now is the perfect chance to escape—to run away and never return—but he can't. Not without Nelle.

He spins around. The kitchen is empty.

Quill isn't following him.

ꕥ

Nelle glues the side of her face to her bedroom door. Feet scuffle, and a man yells out, but is it Father or James? A gun goes off and she winces. James, as far as she knows, doesn't own a firearm. Running footsteps, closer, closer . . .

The door opens into her chest, and she stumbles back into the bed's iron footboard.

Father barges in like a storm cloud, more animal than man now.

"You ungrateful little bitch."

Nelle jumps into his face. "He'll come back. He'll save me, and he'll kill *you*—"

Father's nostrils flare, and he strikes like a viper, his hand cracking her cheek.

Nelle drops to her knees, shaky fingers fumbling for the stinging hive on her face. Bile fills her throat, hot and sour, but she forces herself to stand. To shove aside the fear that makes her shrink, and to meet him eye to eye. His uncombed hair, his beard, his sallow cheeks—they all trigger her gag reflex.

"I hate you," she spits.

His face is impassive, fracturing her. Does he truly not care that she despises him? He has never shown her parental love like James described growing up with, but she always thought, somewhere in the caverns of his soul, that he cared about her.

It doesn't matter, because she still can't leave.

And after all she has said to him, what will he do to her? Her hands shake at the thought. She opens her mouth to fake an apology, to ask for forgiveness before her punishments increase tenfold, but her voice catches in her throat.

James is there, behind Father, peeking into her bedroom from the hallway.

She allows herself half a heartbeat to feel hope.

Father digs a pocketknife from his khakis and drops the blade. It clatters on the floor.

"Cut."

She picks up the blade, levels it over her palm, and slices shallowly. Fire dashes across her skin, but she is used to the pain. Some masochistic part of her finds it comforting. Father lowers himself to one knee, dips two fingers into her bloody palm, and writes on the white rug: *Nellie follows Daddy.*

Nelle's bones unclench, her brain a mindless soldier.

She takes Father's cold hand as he leads them into his study. Floor-to-ceiling bookcases cover the walls, ringing a massive desk, the shelves packed with leather-bound journals and novels and magazines and old newspapers. The heavy velvet curtains are shut, transforming the room into a silo.

Father locks the door behind them.

He writes in a journal before he retrieves two items from the desk: a box of matches and a bottle of whiskey. He twists off the bottle cap, flicks it aside, and swigs, throat bobbing, bottle sloshing. Gasping like he drank fire, he wipes his mouth and holds the bottle out.

"Want some?"

Nelle tries to move her arms, but he must have written for her to remain frozen in place. *Ugh.*

"No?" The side of his mouth droops. "Fine."

He circles the room, emptying the bottle across the bookshelves. When the bottle runs dry, he opens a hutch, clinks past crystal trinkets, and retrieves another, splashing it across more books and journals. The shelves are soaked.

As my final punishment, he's going to destroy me.

He takes a final swig before dropping the bottle, which shatters against the floor.

"Do you realize, my little Nellie, what happens if I burn all these journals. All of *you*?"

There has to be an exit strategy she hasn't thought of yet.

But there isn't. Because she can't move. Frustrated tears sear her cheeks.

"What happens?" she asks, playing the clueless child. Masquerading, hopefully for the last time, as naive, obedient *Nellie*.

"Poof." He bares his white teeth, maniacal. "You disappear."

⁂

James pulls away from the study door and weighs his odds of breaking it down. Quill wouldn't really destroy Nelle, would he? After all these years, all the work he put into her, all the effort to keep her hidden away, would he erase her like a typo? He doesn't want to find out. Panic builds in his chest. He tries the knob, but it's locked. The door is thick oak. He'll never kick it down. Feeling useless, he listens through the wood.

"You see, my sweet Nellie, I love you more than the world," Quill says.

Liar, James wants to say. *You love* controlling *her*.

"More than I love myself," Quill goes on. "More than I loved Eleanor. I am so, so proud of the woman you've grown up to be."

Nelle's words shake. *"Go. Fuck. Yourself."*

"You chose a stranger, a *boy*, over me, your father. You would leave me if you had the chance, wouldn't you? You would abandon your dad?"

Nelle doesn't respond. James's chest tightens, his heart pounding wildly. Time is running out, he knows that. Soon the fuse on Quill's anger will burn, and then he will explode.

I have to do something.

"If I gave you the chance, right now, to walk out the door, would you take it? Would you leave? Don't you want to see the world, Nellie?"

Quill's voice is manic. "Don't you want to experience life, huh? Love, happiness, heartbreak, anger, loneliness, death, depression? *Don't you?*"

Nelle chokes on tears. "*Please.* Just let me go."

"You could've waited for me to show you, but *no.* It has to be him, doesn't it? You know he will leave you."

Something crashes inside the room, and Nelle cries. An animalistic surge rises in James, and he slams his shoulder against the door, but that only shoots tooth-gritting pain through his collarbone.

"Don't do this," she pleads.

Quill's voice is thunderous. *"Don't* do *this? I have no choice!"*

James jerks the knob side to side and shoves with his shoulder again, but the door stands firm. Maybe he should've listened to Jessie when she told him to stay out of Nelle's life, but all summer, he has stood at a crossroads. Now it is time to take the road less traveled. To bury the old James and introduce the world to someone even *he* hasn't met yet.

Someone who fights for what he wants.

He finds the vial of ink tied to his neck.

Trembling, he empties it on the floor. It forms a small black mirror that reflects his hardened face. He drags his finger through the ink, harnessing the writer in his soul. On his arm, he writes a command in Nelle's ink, Nelle's *blood.* The black letters shimmer over his veins.

James waits and prays that it works.

∞

The match between Father's fingers teases its final wink when Nelle feels his control lift from her body. Her bones release like unlocked manacles. Like a tucked-in-blanket stripped off a mattress. There one second, gone the next.

In its place, there is a burning need to fight.

James, she thinks. If he has written for her, then every ounce of her that fills the pages of this room can be destroyed, and she will still be here. She will live.

If he has written for her, and it is *working*, then she is free.

"Burn it all," Nelle says quietly.

She wants to laugh, to fly. For twenty-one years, she was unable to defy Father. Twenty-one *grueling* years of pressure swelling. She was a star, working up to a supernova.

"I would rather die than live in this house with you." The words leave her lips drenched in fire. "Burn it *all*."

"I . . ." The match burns out. Father drops it. "You want me to . . ."

"Burn it!" Nelle screams. His dumbfounded expression gives her immense satisfaction. She chuckles lowly and glares at him. "*Burn it*, you miserable little man."

A quiet calm falls over him. He strikes another match, and it spits, catching fire. Without hesitation, he flicks it toward the circular wall of books, which ignites in a stinging blast. Nelle covers her face as white fire races around her, suffocatingly hot.

After the initial explosion, the fire calms and crackles along the shelves. It snakes across all of her journals until every wall in the room is up in flames. Her skin sizzles, hair floating with the billowing heat and smoke.

Seeing the pages that have made up her life flutter to ash should feel disheartening, devastating. Instead it's freeing. Nothing tethers her to Lincoln, to this house, to *Quill* anymore.

Father's heaving chest slows as he watches her, his coal eyes softening. He opens a drawer and slaps a manila folder on the desk.

"This is yours." He slides it to her. "I never intended to keep you here forever."

Nelle's immediate reaction is to reject it, but after a moment of consideration, she picks the folder up and holds it close to her stomach.

"Why don't I believe you?" she asks.

Then her mind, her body, her *bones*, feel an overwhelming need to leave. She walks backward, hits the door, and unlocks the knob. Facing Father, never turning away.

His gaunt face is splashed with shadows and firelight, a droopiness to his shoulders, a crack of defeat in his stature.

Nelle steps into the hall, hesitating before she shuts the study door. Father watches her go, and despite the fire wreathing him, no warmth touches his face. For a heartbeat, she considers saying goodbye. Then, on second thought, she slams the door shut.

James is already by her side, holding a chair. He wedges it underneath the handle, as if that will stop Father. Though he may not try to escape. Without her, what does he have to live for? She feels no remorse for leaving him to burn, instead relishing the idea of him melting while the pages of his precious Nellie crumble to ash.

A new Nelle walks through the house, chin held high, James beside her, strange folder held tight against her chest. She walks out into the sticky night, tears dry on her cheeks, fireflies blinking between the trees, and watches flames lurch off the tin roof, an artist stepping back to survey her canvas after brushing on the final stroke.

James starts his truck. Nelle climbs into the cab and feels along the cracks in the leather seat. He gingerly hovers his finger over the still-fresh cut in her palm.

"Is this okay?" he asks.

"Yes." She braces herself for the burn as his fingertips touch her open wound.

On the dashboard, he writes: *Nelle rides with James.*

A tight ball of yarn unspools inside her. As her cut stitches back together, Nelle watches the road and listens to her life crackle away over the sound of gravel under the tires.

Part Two

Wish Me on My Way

Chapter 9

Stopped at the one traffic light in Lincoln, James watches a stream of fire trucks and ambulances rush past, lights flaring red, sirens wailing. He cuts right onto Anderson and parks in his parents' uphill driveway. Through the bug-strewn windshield, their two-story house rises white and formidable. The sirens fade.

Nelle peers through the windshield. The moon sits over his house like a vintage plate hung in the sky.

"This is where you live?"

"Yeah."

James grips the steering wheel, and a clammy heat creeps into his face. What is common practice after leaving someone to burn to death?

"Do you think Quill will try to escape?"

"Maybe." She chews her bottom lip. "But if he could still control me, he would've. He kept my ink in the room he set fire to. It's long gone."

That's a relief, at least. Still, he isn't sure what to do. Nelle has nowhere to go. Will his parents take her in? Even if they do, he doesn't know what she will do in a few weeks when he moves back to college. He hates himself for the regret he feels. Every time he thinks he is getting out of one uncomfortable situation with Nelle, he finds himself in another.

"What's in that folder?" He gestures to the manila rectangle in her lap.

Nelle breaks the seam and cracks it open. A birth certificate. A social security card. All the information she needs to live. To travel. Even a passport, Nelle's teenage face staring up at them. All under the name *Eleanor Quill*.

"How did he get all of that?" he asks.

"I remember the day he took me to the courthouse for that picture. I didn't ask why, I was just happy to leave the house. The rest isn't mine." She passes it over. "It's his dead daughter's. He told the police officer that she didn't die, that she moved to Scotland to be with family."

"But she *did* die, right?"

"Yes. She died."

"But the government thinks she's alive," James says. "So, legally, you are Eleanor now. Maybe he wants you to be able to live on your own. Maybe . . ."

"He actually loved me?" Nelle says. "In some twisted way?"

"Isn't it possible?"

"You don't torture someone you love."

James flinches. "You're right."

"Thank you, by the way."

"What did I do?"

"You wrote for me," she says. "I gave you the necklace hoping that one day I could ask you to use it to free me. But I didn't have to ask."

He squeezes the empty vial, glass stained with her blood.

"What now?" he asks. "I don't want to leave you."

Nelle's hand sits on the folder. Pale, small, curling into itself. "What about leaving with me?"

James examines her in the dark. She's dead serious.

"You want me to leave *with* you?" That all too familiar anxiety creeps into his gut. "I can't. I have classes and my family and a job, and what would Nancy say if I just—"

"You're overthinking."

He looks at his house through the blue night, then back to Nelle, her one hand gripping her seat belt and the other on the manila folder.

Can they simply flit off without a plan? He thinks about the money he has saved, close to $6,000. Could that be enough for gas and food and hotel rooms? For how long? What about college? His parents?

"James." Nelle's voice fog lights through his thoughts.

Instead of counting costs, debating logistics, and stressing over reactions, he imagines the open road. The glorious unknown. A city of skyscrapers at the end of a rainbow.

"Wait right here!" He laughs as he leaps out of the car.

❧

Nelle stares at the social security card, *Eleanor Quill* in black letters glowing under moonlight. *This is really happening,* she tells herself. *You're free.* James's house towers above her. *Free-ish.*

He will have to write for her. Quill is gone, and yet Nelle's life is right back in another man's hands. A better man, but still.

She slides the documents back in the manila folder. She has no right to suggest that James uproot his life for her. But he does want to get out of Lincoln, to experience exotic places, meet memorable people, and *live.* How many times did he complain over the past few weeks about college? How many dreamy-eyed tales of his cousin's life in New York? Leaving Lincoln is a mutually beneficial decision, but guilt still nibbles at Nelle's conscience.

On some level, she orchestrated it all. *She* told James her address, *she* spilled the secret about her creation, *she* gave him that vial of ink. And although *he* was the one to find her under the fireworks on the Fourth of July, she took in his statue-cut jawline, his veiny typist's hands, and saw not only a beautiful boy, but a getaway car.

❧

James runs inside the house, down the hall lined with his and Midi's childhood scribbles, and upstairs to his bedroom. He shovels shirts and pants and a couple of jackets inside a bag. A new pack of toothbrushes and his favorite books. He crosses the hall to Midi's room—she's staying at Mandy's tonight, thankfully—and steals some clothes from her closet. Sweaters and shirts and pants. In the kitchen downstairs, he writes a note for his parents. *Hey, Mom and Dad, I'm going to see Jessie in New York until the semester starts. I have money saved up. Love y'all! I'll call you when I get there.*

He shoots Nancy a text, feeling a hit of guilt over her last unanswered message.

As he races down the porch steps, he can't wipe the smile off his face. He is being spontaneous, far outside his realm of comfort, and he loves the way it tastes. For the next few weeks, he doesn't have to worry about college or medical-school applications or the friends he doesn't have. The sad cloud that haunts his every waking moment has been broken by sunlight. His parents would say he is having a manic episode, but James thinks that maybe, just *maybe*, he is finally doing something right.

Chapter 10

How strange it is to be watched all night by the moon. From her bedroom window, Nelle could only see it for a handful of hours. Now it follows her like a spotlight, glistening on the waxy leaves that dangle over the curvy road, white-tailed deer frolicking in and out of the headlights, the bowl of stars.

James taps the steering wheel, shattering her trance. "So . . . you've been quiet a while."

The analog clock on the dashboard reads 3:02 am. Her butt is numb. She tries to stretch her stiff legs, but they can't unfold fully. Most of what she sees through the window are reflections. James one-handing the steering wheel, veins running from his shirtsleeve like rivers on a map. In her periphery, the moon now resembles Father's pale face.

"I think I'm hungry."

"I can stop. A gas station's coming up soon; hopefully they're open."

White lights glow over a hill. "They'll have food?"

He frowns. "Food-adjacent."

James parks beside a pump, and Nelle, still buckled in the car, squints through the glass at shelves full of food, candy, and drinks. She sleeve-wipes her breath off the car window.

"Want anything specific?" James opens the driver's door and grabs his wallet.

Panic squeezes Nelle's chest. "You're leaving me?"

"Yeah. Is that okay?"

She imagines Father standing behind her shoulder, nestled in the shadows. Following her. Waiting for the moment James leaves her alone to snatch her back. Every drop of her ink should have burned in the fire, but what if Father has more stored somewhere? He was always prepared. He *is*. Nelle hopes he burned alive, but there were windows in the study. She would be naive to believe that he won't be able to find her.

"I want to come with you."

James rounds the car and opens her side. "C'mon then."

"I can't yet," she says. "You have to . . ."

"Oh, right." He opens the vial she refilled earlier, dabs the tip of his finger, and writes on his arm, *Nelle goes into the gas station.* "There you go."

Inside she gawks at an aisle of neon candy packets and crackers and chips, overwhelming options that seem so sterile and plastic compared to her usual organic diet. Based on packaging alone, none of it remotely resembles food.

"Find what you want?" James comes up beside her, the bags under his eyes dark under the fluorescent lights. Behind the counter at the other end of the store, a man sits on a stool, his baseball cap hanging an umbral shadow over the top of his face.

"I don't know." She points to a jar of pickled eggs atop the shelf. "Maybe that?"

James makes a sour face. "Maybe not."

There are at least twenty-five different chocolate bars, over forty bags of candy, a rainbow of gum packs, tins upon tins of mints, and—

"I can pick out some stuff to try."

A minute later, she has a lime-green pack of candy, a bottle of black soda with a red label, and a crinkly bag of chips. James slaps a pocket-size yellow legal pad on the counter beside the snacks. The tattooed man scans each item.

"Do you have an ATM?" James passes over a stack of ones.

The man points to the far corner where a machine sits beneath a bug-plastered bulb.

Carrying their snacks in a translucent bag, Nelle watches the machine spit a stack of twenties into James's palm. She pieces together that it is money from *his* bank account, but he is able to access it here.

"What does ATM stand for?" she asks.

"Automated teller machine."

The twenties keep on coming.

"You don't need to take it all out."

"Don't worry, this is just what I've been saving for pocket money this semester." He folds the bills into his wallet. "My scholarship covers tuition, but even if it didn't, I'd rather spend my money on this. On *you.* I can always get another job."

With his back to the cashier, he uses his fingertip to scrawl a command in the new pad. *Nelle walks to the car.*

"What about your family?" They cross the empty parking lot. "Did you say goodbye to them?"

James sucks in a breath. "I left them a note."

"Is that normal?"

"Is what normal?"

Nelle shuts the car door and locks in her seat belt. "For your family not to care what you do?"

"No. They care *too* much." He cranks it, and the engine roars. "Ever since I went off to college, my mom's had an issue with letting go. She and my dad have all these rules for my life, like *they* know what's best for *me*. I want to make it clear to them that I'm an adult. That I can do what I want."

"Leaving in the middle of the night without asking permission? I'd say that sends a glaring message."

"Glaring, really?" James pales. He runs a hand over his face. "God, I know my mom will take it as a personal attack, but it's not. I just, for once, want to make my own decisions and fuck the consequences."

"And now that you're fucking the consequences, how is it?" Nelle opens her bag of candy and picks out a purple one.

"You tell me." He looks left and right, then pulls out, headlights swinging onto the tree-encroached road. "You're here, too."

Nelle pinches the tiny candy between her fingers. Holds it up to the moonlight. "I can't imagine fucking the consequences will make them disappear."

James blows air through his mouth. "You're right. When she wakes up, my mom will call me to chew me out. Or at least I'll get a victimized text. When she's *really* pissed she sends an angry emoji, no context."

"What's an emoji?"

"They're like . . . these little faces and pictures that convey emotion."

"Artwork?"

"Not exactly. It can be hard to convey tone through words alone, so people use them to add context."

"It's not hard if you use the right words," she says.

Nelle plops the candy on her tongue, shocked to find that it is coated in *acid*.

Her face twists up, and she spits the candy out before it can burn through *all* her taste buds. It leaves a violet stain on her palm.

James cackles. "Too sour?"

Nelle puts the candy back in her mouth and forces herself to chew, considering the spike of sourness, the fruity flavor, the sweet tartness that follows.

"I can't tell if it's good"—she eats another, contemplating. Less startling this time—"or disgusting."

For half a second, James's eyes flicker from the road to her. And for half a second, the follicles of her scalp send shockwaves to her heart, her navel, her toes. She rubs down the hair on her arms.

"Are you nervous about leaving Lincoln?" James asks, his voice dry.

"Yeah." She thinks about her rose wallpaper, her iron bed, her shelf of books, all sacrificed to fire and ash now. She thinks about the candy in her lap, the man beside her, the open road. Father was right about one thing. She is entirely unprepared for the world, and yet here she is, diving in headfirst. "I really am."

James glances at her again. "Say the word and I'll go back."

Nelle can't help but smirk. "No."

She will never go back to Lincoln, where that man who called himself her father tormented her, where she had no autonomy, no friends, no life, no freedom. "I'd have to be dead to go back there."

"How are you going to meet my family if you're dead?" James quips.

Nelle lifts a brow. "Who says I'm meeting your family?"

"Just an idea." He shrugs a shoulder. "We have a month of adventure ahead, and then, sadly, I'm shipping back off to school."

Unanswerable thoughts claw up Nelle's throat. *Who is going to write for me when James goes to school? Maybe I should've stayed with Father. He was a monster, but at least he shouldered my burden.* She shoves them to the recesses of her mind and tries to conceal her uncertainty.

"I'll never go back to Lincoln for myself," she says, "but if it's for *you*, I'll make an amendment."

They drive under the night sky. Fields stretch on either side, lined with forests. There are far fewer people than she thought there would be. She wasn't sure what to expect. New faces lining every street? Certainly not a desolate countryside with more deer, cows, and chickens than humans.

Nelle picks up James's phone from the cupholder. When she taps the screen, a photograph of a beach during sunset appears, the time hovering above it: 3:43 a.m. Straight out of a science fiction novel.

"I've never been to the ocean," she says absently. The back of the phone is shattered glass, dicing up her reflection. She watches the movements of her facial muscles: mouth open, eyes widen, frown deepen. Kissy lips. "I'm glad I never had one of these. I would've wasted so much time staring at it."

"Now that you're a member of society, you don't want a phone?"

"No."

"You can do so much with it, though. You can take pictures, call whoever you want, watch movies, listen to music, ask it questions."

"For some reason, I get the feeling that I'm better off without having constant access to . . . all of that."

Nelle feels a buzz. A notification covers the beach photograph.

"I believe Midi is trying to contact you," she says, holding the phone out to James.

"I can't answer while I'm driving. Can you open it?"

"Open the phone? Like a box?"

"No, no, no," he says. "Tap the button at the bottom. See?"

She presses a smooth circle at the bottom of the phone, and the screen turns on. A keypad pops up.

"Now press one, one, one, one."

"Cool password."

He glares. "Click the green icon that says *Messages*."

"What's an icon?"

"You're like a little old lady," he says. "Those floating squares. Click that green one there."

Nelle taps it, and words stream across the screen. "What is this?"

He glances down. "Those are my messages. Click on the top one, and read the last message in the gray bubble."

Nelle squints and reads out loud, "'Hey, dickhead, did you take my clothes?'"

"Huh," James says. "Yeah, don't respond to that."

Nelle tucks the phone back in the cupholder, her baby-blue sweater sleeve sliding up an inch. *Midi's* sweater. Guilt bubbles up in her at the realization of everything James abandoned in Lincoln. His job, his family, his savings. And didn't *she* con him into it all?

No, he made his own choice. To write for her. To free her.

James started the timer that blew up their lives. Nelle just planted the bomb.

Yet she is the one who told Quill to *burn it.*

"Did you steal her clothes for me?"

James's dimple creases. "Maybe."

Nelle eats a yellow candy, her tongue raw from the sour powder. For a while, they sit in silence, listening to the rumble of tires on unkept roads.

Then James says, “You know what? I’ll take you to see the ocean. And when we get there, I’m gonna throw my phone in it.”

“What?” Nelle chokes on a sip of soda.

“You’ve convinced me,” James says. “Life without a phone is better. I’m getting rid of it.”

She imagines the ocean, what it will smell like, whether the sand will be soft or rough under her toes, whether there will be seagulls.

“That’s very brave of you,” she says. “But is this just a ploy to avoid responding to your sister?”

“You know what?” James sits higher in his seat, boyishly energetic. “I can’t wait. I kind of want to chuck it out the window right now.”

Nelle grabs his arm. He shoots her a worried look, then relaxes his grip on the wheel.

“Wait for the right moment,” she says. “Trust me.”

Chapter 11

"I think I'm in love"—Nelle lifts her face to the sun, her freckles like flakes of pyrite—"with the sea."

Sand hardens in the cracks between James's toes. The water retreats, sighs, then races back up the shore, soaking his rolled-up jeans, cold on his ankles. Sunrise pierces through cotton-candy clouds the color of apricots. He catches himself smiling at Nelle, jealous of the wind playing with her hair.

His foremost reason for coming here was to show her the ocean, but he clenches his phone to remind himself of his other reason. Since his mom surprised him with a clamshell phone in middle school, he has been dependent on one. He checks it like clockwork every few minutes, scrolls for hours when he could be reading or writing or talking to another person *in person*. He looks at it now. Above him, the clouds are purple, red, and yellow. In the phone's reflection, they are black and white.

James flips it in his hand three times, spinning a yarn ball of courage, a batter rocking back and forth, ready to swing.

Then he chucks it. It slides from his hand too easily.

Nelle laughs, clinging to his shirtsleeve. She throws her hand up in farewell as his phone flies like a silver bird, far out into blue water. It disappears with a splash, an anticlimactic plop, then it's gone.

James watches the spot where it vanished until the wind dries his salty lips and a white boat appears on the horizon, breaking his stare.

Nelle tugs his sleeve. "How do you feel?"

He inhales the sharp brine. A hundred pounds slide off his shoulders. He feels, for the first time in years, weightless. Birdlike.

He exhales and spreads his arms. "I feel fucking great."

ꕥ

Nelle and James roam the pastel streets of Charleston until morning breaks into afternoon and they have to seek refuge from the boiling heat inside an ice cream shop. The AC hums, and the green and white tile clicks under their shoes. The place is lined with vinyl booths and smells like sugar. Nelle orders strawberry, James orders salted caramel, and they take their cones to a tree-filled park overlooking the harbor.

"Father used to tell me horror stories about cavities." The pink ice cream coating Nelle's tongue satisfies more than her sugar craving. Father tried to keep her healthy and pure, yet he punished her with violence. *Vengeance*, she thinks, *is best served in a waffle cone.* "Keeping me from this was his worst crime." A dribble of melted ice cream falls from her cone to the cobbles underfoot. "One time he caught me eating a peppermint and told me that my teeth would rot and crumble out of my mouth. I had nightmares for years. Look at me now, Father!"

She thrusts her ice cream to the sky like a middle finger.

"Why do you call him that?" James crunches the last bite of his cone.

Nelle shrugs. "Habit. When I call him Quill, it feels like I'm talking about someone else. A stranger."

Clouds pass overhead, graying out the park. Talking about Father makes even the sun want to hide.

"But he was no stranger to me. He showed me at a very young age just how violent a man he could be. But *Father*, well, that's just what I've always called him."

"It's too endearing a term for someone so horrible." James rolls up his sleeves, revealing the pre-notepad scribbles he has yet to scrub off.

Nelle leans against a metal railing and breathes in the harbor. As a kid, she wondered if the ocean had a scent. Now she knows; it is warm and sour, fish and sulfur.

"Does it bother you that you have to write for me all the time?" she asks, not sure where the question comes from, only that it has built momentum since they left Lincoln. Behind them, a little boy in the park opens his hand and lets his red balloon float up in the tree branches. It gets caught among the leaves, but it doesn't pop. Nelle is careful not to look at James, not until he answers.

"No," he says. "Of course not."

She isn't sure she believes him.

After lunch at an Italian restaurant, they pass a gift shop where Nelle stops and shields her face against the window. Beyond a rack of Charleston T-shirts and shelves of historic local books sits a display of leather-bound journals and a set of fountain pens, the old-fashioned sort with refillable ink barrels.

"Can I borrow a twenty?"

James digs out his wallet and hands over the money, no questions asked.

She almost reminds him that she needs his permission to enter the shop, but he is already unscrewing the vial at his neck, dabbing his fingertip against the ink, and smudging a message in the legal pad.

Once the ink is set, Nelle ducks into the store and dives for the journals.

Immediately, one stands out. Black and not too tall, and when she holds it, the pages fall open in her hands like the spine has been broken for years. She tucks it under her arm, along with one of the pens, and takes them both to the counter. After she pays, her legs carry her outside like they know where they're going, paper gift bag swinging in her hand, and she finds James leaning against a lamppost, a 1930s movie star with his sharp chin dimple, sleeves rolled back to his elbows, ankles crossed, brown hair curling behind his ears.

"What do we have here?" He pushes off the tree and peeks into the bag.

"I'll show you."

She cracks open the journal to its first blank page, the paper speckled with leaf-shaped shadows. She passes it to James before unscrewing the pen's glass barrel. Wincing, she digs the tip of the pen into her palm until she draws blood. Then, with the nib wedged between folds of her flesh, she presses the plunger down and begins the process of extracting blood from her hand.

It tickles in a horrible way. Like someone pulling a sheet beneath her skin, tugging toward that incision in her palm. Within a minute, the pen is full. A part of her hates that James has to see this, but she refuses to feel shameful about what she is. Who she is. She gets one shot now, and if she has to live afraid of herself, she won't be living at all.

❧

In the car, Nelle flips through the new journal. The road is dotted with red brake lights and gray puddles. She runs her finger over the half-filled first page. On their way from the park to the twelve-hour garage where they left the truck, they detoured at a coffee shop and an independent bookstore filled with putrid cats. James loved them and scratched each one between the ears. Nelle thought they were cute until a long-haired orange one hissed at her. She hissed back, which made James laugh.

The last line in the journal fuzzies up her stomach. *Nelle rides in the car.* With the road ahead of her, she can go anywhere.

She shuts the leather cover, slides it into the inner pocket of James's denim jacket, and reclines her seat until she's staring at the ceiling of the cab.

"Where's the next stop?" she asks.

"We can stop wherever you want. Whenever you want."

She studies the slope of his nose. The bags under his eyes, how his cheekbones sluice down his face. The brown curl tickling his brow.

"Thank you."

His head ticks. "Why do you say that?"

"I thought I'd be stuck in that house with Quill forever. I never imagined . . ." Her throat closes up, and she laughs at her own emotions. "I never thought I'd be here, in the car with someone like you, driving aimlessly."

"Welcome to freedom," James says.

So much beauty in the natural world. Craggy trees, wispy clouds, rain, stars, and seas. Cats and fireflies and rats. And the architecture. The art. The people, too. Random pedestrians, a shop owner, James—she falls in love with them just for being human.

"What do you want to see?" he asks. "I'd like to visit New York eventually, but we can go anywhere you want."

Anywhere I want. Nelle pulls her legs to her chest. "Paris. London. Scotland. Madrid, Hong Kong, Tokyo, Moscow, New York, Alaska, Boston, Vegas, Salt Lake City—"

"So . . . everywhere?"

She grins into her knees. "Oh, and Africa. I've always wanted to see a lion."

"We can go to a zoo."

"Not a lion in a cage," she says. "And not just in a book, either."

Tires roar on the interstate, eighty miles per hour breaking into ninety.

James blinks salt, his caffeine and adrenaline stores long depleted. "Shall we pull off?"

He takes the next exit. Nelle leans out the window, her hair a fiery blond tangle. The road curves into a forest, which opens up onto fields of sleeping cows and horses.

"This is amazing!" she yells, tasting summer's breath.

James pulls onto the side of the road in a stretch of grass by the tree line. "Aren't you exhausted?"

He cuts the truck off, and the headlights die, leaving them stranded in darkness.

Nelle gasps for air through her laughter, skin buzzing as her heart rate slows. "What are we doing?"

"Sleeping. You do sleep, right?" He grabs two rolled quilts from the back seat. At her nod, he says, "You all right with sharing the truck bed?"

"Yeah, yeah, of course," she says, though the thought of sleeping beside him makes her want to choke. She sits, still buckled. *Is he going to leave me in here?*

James pulls the pen out of his pocket, and her stress dissipates. He writes in the journal: *Nelle goes to the bed of James's truck.*

Her bones release.

In the back, he makes a bed. One quilt to lie on, the other to cover up with. She crawls between the heavy fabric, folds her arms behind her head, and stares at the stars. A ceiling of diamond teardrops, prettier than the popcorn paint of her bedroom.

"I'm so lucky," she says with a sigh. She notices him staring at her. "What are you looking at?"

"You," he says. "I'm thinking."

She laughs. "About what?"

He touches her nose with the tip of his finger. His hand snakes to the side of her face, across her cheek, and tucks a strand of hair behind her ear. Her mouth dries out. She feels the urge to vanish into his long body. She fights it.

James's thumb brushes the curve of her cheekbone. "That I'm so lucky, too."

All breath abandons Nelle's lungs.

"I was trapped," he says. "School and summer both leading toward a future I *don't want.*" He points to a star brighter than all the rest. "I didn't know it was killing me. You called me brave the night we met, but I'm not. Never have been. Until now. I finally feel like I'm doing what I want. I feel . . . weightless."

"Like you could float away?"

"Yeah." The corner of his mouth creases. "Just like that."

"Can you wish on any star, or only shooting ones?" She stares where he pointed.

He smirks. "I think any star is worthy."

"What about the moon?"

"Oh, of course, the moon." His voice is wood. Scratchy shell, soft heart. "What's your wish?"

She inhales and thinks, *I wish to feel this way forever.*

Instead she says, "If I tell you, it won't come true."

~

Nelle wakes up confused, sweaty, shaking, her body damp with a layer of early-morning dew. The trees along the road shiver with life. In a nearby field, a cow moans.

Father's voice rings out from her nightmare. He was following them, revolver in hand, murder etched in the hard line of his mouth.

She nudges James awake. He blinks at the cloud-streaked sky, his hair a tousled mess.

"Good morning." He smiles sleepily, then, seeing her, his expression drops. "What's wrong?"

Nelle's fingers curl around the cold quilt. "I think Father's following us."

"W-what?" James sputters. "Impossible. Even if he's alive, he can't know where we—"

"In my dream, he was trailing us. He will kill you if he finds you, James."

The thought of James dead kick-starts her tears, but she steels herself.

He starts folding one of the quilts. "You really think this was a . . . premonition? Not just a dream?"

Nelle helps him with the second quilt. She trusts her subconscious, especially when it comes to Father. Living alone with him for twenty-one years, never getting a break from his presence, formed a unique bond. And in a very literal sense, she is a part of him. She came from him alone.

Still, Father would have to be psychic *and* able to teleport to reach them, and no one followed them off the interstate last night.

"I think you're right," she says when they are back inside the truck. She watches the rearview mirror. "It was just a dream."

Chapter 12

The bars of DC come to life at night. James lopes down the sidewalk, a day of back-to-back tours heavy on his eyelids. He appreciates history, but he *hates* museums. Portraits of old dead guys, monuments of white marble, dim lighting, audio-visual supplements adding long, grueling minutes to each exhibit. They are a valuable resource in preserving the past, sure, but he finds them mind-numbingly boring. Here is an illegible piece of paper that was very important three hundred years ago! Great! Afterward, all the dusty, spotlit information becomes a nauseous blur.

But Nelle thrived off it. She drank in the history, the artifacts, the artwork as if they were nectar.

They pass a blacked-out storefront, music thumping within. The door spits out a trio of drunk girls in heels. Laughing, they cling to each other and climb into the back of a car.

Nelle grabs James's sleeve. "You know, I've never tried alcohol."

They pass a line of people in scant clothing, their makeup artfully done in every glittery shade of the rainbow. Nelle blends in with them, wearing a blue dress James picked out from a boutique in Charleston because it looked like it was made of sapphires. It is short, so he wasn't sure she would go for it. But when he pulled it off the rack, she squealed, tore it from his grasp, and ran off to the dressing room. Seeing it on her now, her slender calves unveiled, produces a reel of filthy thoughts in his head. Skimming his fingers up her inner thigh, his lips on her ankles, worshipping her legs until they part for him—

It saddens him to think that she spent so long smothered when she has the spirit of a wildfire. He clears his throat. "Not even for your twenty-first birthday?"

"*Quill* was drunk a lot, but he locked all the alcohol in his study, so I couldn't even go behind his back."

He shrugs. "We can have ourselves a little taste test."

Nelle points at a hot-pink light inside an alley. "How about here?"

James writes for her, and when the pen lifts, she is already dragging him toward the entrance. At the end of the alley, a staircase descends to the building's basement, and a sign on the wall says The Alley Cat in LED letters. A curly arrow points down.

Music pulsates through his organs as they descend.

Lights flash above a crowd of writhing bodies. Throngs of people hug the long bar, bottles upon bottles of liquor lining the shelves behind it. The bartenders shift around each other and pour drinks and take orders like worker bees. The floor mysteriously sticks to the bottom of James's shoes, he can't even hear himself think, beer and sweat clog the room, and yet he loves the place.

Or maybe he just loves how Nelle looks within it as she takes it all in. The dilation of her pupils, the lights illuminating her freckles and the glimpse of her front teeth as her mouth parts in awe. He falls in love with the adventurous stranger she has drawn out of him. The parts of himself that, growing up, he felt pulled to in books, in movies, when he saw heroes acting stupidly courageous. He wanted to be like them, but fear always beat him.

Until Nelle.

She has an inner compass pointing her in whatever direction is the most joyful. What better way is there to live than that? And what does it matter if she's not a human? She's still the most fascinating person James has ever met.

He orders four vodka sodas with limes.

"We're gonna chug the first round," he says, "to get a head start."

Nelle's nose twitches over the drink like a hesitant cat's. "How does it taste?"

"Pretty bad, but you get used to it."

They toast their plastic cups, then they chug.

Cold on the throat. Tangy from the lime. Ice hits the back of James's tongue, bitter and vulgar. He nearly chokes on it but forces a final swallow until it's gone.

A laugh bubbles up. He doesn't usually slam his drinks, but right now he *wants* to be drunk and careless. Coming off the craziest few days of his life, he's not ready for the high to end. He likes this new version of himself, the James who accepts no responsibility, no obligation.

Nelle chucks both empty cups into a big black trash can and passes him his next.

"Care to dance?" She guides him to the floor.

For once James doesn't think before he joins the throng of moving bodies. His limbs sway like a tree in the wind. Nelle spins, brandishing a mane of blond. They dance together until he forgets how many songs have passed, until his second drink is gone, until he is so full of light and energy, he feels like a firework that doesn't know its spectacle will soon end.

Nelle comes to a stumbling stop, breathlessly laughing, and tips forward into James's arms. Time moves slowly at first, then faster, gaining momentum. As the music picks up, two drinks grow into three, then four, until he is belting out songs he doesn't even know, and he is pretty sure he hasn't stopped touching Nelle for two straight hours.

Her arm loops around his shoulders, hot on his neck. Wet with sweat. She speaks, but James can only see her mouth moving. He leans in closer.

"I like the way you look!" she says.

He pulls back, surprised by her candor.

Nelle's brows curve upward, hopeful. Her frizzy hair is swept aside. Where the neckline of the dress he bought her dips, a triangle of freckled skin splits her chest.

Lowering his mouth to her ear, he says softly, "I like the way *you* look."

She shivers. Retreats an inch to peer up at him.

The song ends and the bar goes quiet. Something shiny glints near the ceiling: a mirror ball, suspended over the crowd, reflecting a thousand colors.

"I'm ready to leave," Nelle says.

Are you okay? he wants to ask, but she is grinning.

After James writes for her, they stagger down the street to a circular park. A ring of trees, waxy leaves black in the night, branches clinging to each other like desperate hands. Iron lampposts put off smeared, orange light. A sculpture of four women holding a bowl stands center stage.

James pulls Nelle into the shadow of the four women.

She spins, arms flung out, cutting wheels in the syrupy air. "It feels like heaven out here."

His hand slides into hers, stopping her mid-spin, and he pulls her in, chest to chest. Nelle's pulse ticks through her wrist, her sweaty knuckles interlocked with his. Their bodies were made to be pressed together like this, he realizes. Heartbeat to heartbeat.

"You're the most beautiful person," James says, the words falling out of him.

"And *you* are drunk." Nelle boops his nose.

A bright, white flash has both of them spinning around, searching for the source. At the edge of the circle, beneath the trees, a man stands with a camera. He lowers it and shrugs.

"Hope you don't mind. I'm writing an article about young love in big cities, and you two made the perfect candid. Maybe the cover shot."

"Really?" James wraps an arm around Nelle. "We can pose for another."

Nelle elbows his side. "We are not models."

"No," says the photographer. "That one was perfect, thank you. Would you two like a picture to keep?" He pulls a Polaroid camera from his bag.

"Sure, thank you," James says. Under his breath, "Shortest modeling career ever."

The man holds up the camera. "Say *money*!"

James turns to Nelle, but she is already facing him, nose pointed up. They lock in a stare as the world flashes like a strike of lightning, the camera purrs, and an image spits out.

Once it develops, the man hands off the photograph under the lamplight. Though a little underexposed, their faces are clear. Holding each other's gaze. Statue soaring behind them like a shadowy monster. Trees frame the shot. Nelle's sapphire dress sparkles, her hair is a wild mess, and James's baggy denim jacket, a hand-me-down from his dad, swallows him whole. And they are grinning like they just won the lottery.

"Thank you," Nelle says.

The man waves his hand—"No biggie"—and starts to pack up his camera bag.

In a tone so careless he surprises himself, James says, "Do you know any cheap hotels close by?"

Such an innocuous question, yet a month ago his anxiety would have shot it down.

The man pauses, closes his bag, and laughs. "It's funny you ask."

~

The photographer's suite in the Hay-Adams hotel is decorated in whites and creams, with an enormous bed and brick fireplace. He said that he paid for five nights but could only stay four because of a family emergency back home. If they wanted the room, they could have it.

Nelle shoots for the room's phone, probably grateful to see one with a cord. While James peruses the TV channels, she orders two cheeseburgers, two sodas, and ice cream sundaes. When she finishes ordering, he climbs off the king-size bed, choosing *not* to think about the fact that he and Nelle will be sharing it. A line of miniature liquor bottles teases him from the minibar.

"What'll you have?" He drops the bottles in a heap on the plush comforter.

"Quill's drink of choice." Nelle unscrews a bottle of whiskey and sips. She shudders, face scrunching. "He must've been truly miserable if *this* was his escape."

⸻

Room service plates dot the bed like lily pads on a monochromatic, cream-colored pond. James lies artfully among the plates and crumpled napkins, part of the pond himself. His sweater rides up his stomach, unveiling a dusting of cinnamon hair above his waistband.

Nelle yanks her attention away from that little detail and tilts the minibottle to her lips, downing the last drop.

James crawls around the bed to stack the plates and used napkins on the desk across the room. The plates clatter in place, and he spins around, bounding back to the bed like a puppy. Laughing, he rolls around on the mattress.

"You're such an idiot," she says, rubbing his tummy. "But you're a good boy."

"Too far." He sits up, breathless. "We need to implement safety words because the furry talk crosses a line for me."

"What?" Her hand is still out where his stomach was. "You were acting like a dog; all I did was play along."

"I'm kidding." His laughter dissolves into worry that he hurt her feelings. "I thought that was clear with the whole furry comment."

She hates feeling stupid, but for the thousandth time she has to ask, "What is a furry?"

"A person who—how do I put this?—*imitates* an animal, both in how they dress and how they act. And sometimes, not always, but definitely sometimes, people do it for sexual scenarios."

"Oh." New wires connect in Nelle's brain, an epiphany. "Humans are weird creatures."

James folds an arm behind his head. His white Henley wrinkles up his torso.

"I forget sometimes that you're not a human," he says, his face giving away no emotion.

"It's confusing," Nelle says. "Even for me. I'm essentially alone, the single member of the rarest species in the universe."

"You're not alone." James puts his hand over hers, rattling every molecule of her body. "You grow old, right? I mean, you were a baby, and you looked like a baby, and now you're twenty-one, and you *look* twenty-one, so by that logic, you do age. And you said someone *can* write that you die if you want to? So when you're really old, like ninety-nine, and your husband passes away, then you can have someone write for you to go, too. Maybe one of your kids? Unless you want to live longer, then by all means. But do you see what I'm saying?"

Nelle shakes her head, still hanging on to the husband comment.

"I'm saying . . ." James takes her shoulders. "You're *free*. Quill can't hurt you anymore, so do whatever you want. Go out, find love, make friends, break hearts, start a business, watch it crash, start another one, become a lawyer or a scuba diver or whatever it is you want. You may not've been born like the rest of us, Nelle, but you're no less human to me."

Nelle sways from a wave of dizziness, grateful for his grip on her. "Thank you."

"Why are you thanking me?"

"Because you're the reason I can be free." Nelle tries to ignore his throwaway comment about her hypothetical husband. If she thinks about how that word sounded on his lips, how amazing a partner he would be, she will rip off his pants with her teeth.

A firework goes off behind James's eyes.

"I have an idea," he says.

Nelle squints.

"I think you should try to write for yourself."

"I can't do that," she says.

James folds his arms behind his head. "Because Quill told you it'd kill you."

"*Yes*, precisely that reason."

"Did it ever cross your mind that he might have lied?"

Nelle's irritation spikes. "The first thing that crossed my mind anytime Quill said *anything* was that he was lying. But he never used my death as a consequence in any other regard, never included it in a lie, so I'd rather not risk it."

"But you could just *try*," James says. "You painted, right? That's basically the same, and nothing happened there."

"I didn't paint with *my ink*." Nelle has never been so exhausted in her life, and the bed seems to grow plush arms that pull her in.

"I think that if you try, it might work, and then you'll be really free." James clicks off the bedside lamp. A streetlight flickers into the hotel room.

Do you want to get rid of me? murmurs an insecure little monster in Nelle's head.

James shifts on his side, rousing the scent of sandalwood soap and bar sweat. "I hope I'm not sending the wrong message, but being able to write for yourself would change your life. It'd give you a choice. And *that's* what I want. For you to have a choice."

Nelle swallows. As she feared, she is once again forced to depend on another man. And writing for herself seems to be the only way out, though doing so may not bring the *out* she desires. She would rather have her pen tied to someone else's journal for the next eighty years than die trying to free herself.

I have a choice, she thinks, her eyelids shuttering. *I choose you.*

James wakes to a headache, ink in his nostrils. He wipes at his stinging nose, which results in a sneeze that jolts him up. He blinks at the daylight filtering in through the thin curtains. Memories from the night before crash into him one by one. The packed bar with the pink neon sign. Drinking too much. The photographer and his generosity. All the embarrassing things he said to Nelle.

The hotel suite is a wreck. Room-service scraps strewn among minibar bottles. Towels and blankets in clumps on the floor. Sheets of hotel stationery folded into airplanes and scattered on the fireplace mantel, the windowsill, under James's pillow, and, when he goes to brush his teeth, one paper bird half melted in the sink.

A few scribbled letters peek out from the paper's fold, so he opens it up. He apparently wrote that his dream was to have a book-release party in New York City. Nelle's was to visit all seven continents. *That's right.* Sometime during their drunken escapades, she decided it was a good idea to write down their goals. It was James's idea to send them flying.

After a vigorous face washing, he checks the time on the digital hotel clock. *I should really invest in a watch*, he thinks for the hundredth time since he threw his phone away.

Noon already. They slept through the morning, and despite his shuffling around the room, Nelle has yet to even wince. He watches her for a minute, endeared by the drool slugging from her parted lips, but she doesn't stir.

"Nelle," he whispers, "would you be mad if I left to pick up coffee to surprise you?"

Not even a twitch. He gently touches her neck to ensure that her pulse is still thumping, though she has said she can't die naturally. He yanks apart the curtains, hoping the blast of light will wake her, but all he manages to do is blind himself.

He grimaces at the street below. Someone whizzes by on a red bicycle. Cars wait for the valet. A man in a cashmere suit walks out of the hotel carrying a briefcase. *If he turns left, I'll leave, be gone for ten minutes, and surprise Nelle with coffee. If he turns right, I'll wake her up now.*

Nelle stretches like a cat, arms trembling across the cold bed. She yawns and rubs the crust from her lashes, trying to scrub her dream from her memory. In it, she was painting for the first time in years. An oil landscape of a cottage in front of a lake. But when she pulled away from the canvas, the cottage disappeared. In its place stood Father, his black stare boring into her.

Across the street, construction workers move ant-like along the twelfth-floor scaffolding. A drill growls like metal in a blender, springing up a headache to slash her skull in two. Groggy from sleep and cranial pain, Nelle flings the comforter away and pads barefoot to the bathroom, still in her dress from the night before.

God, the night before. The criminal behind this hellish headache. A flutter of pink feelings, a mirror ball, rattling music, the flash of a camera, drinking and drinking, eating greasy food delivered by a hotel waiter named George. The memories zip through her mind like a tape on fast-forward. She switches on the faucet and holds her hands beneath the icy stream. The drill outside stops, and without it, she suddenly feels the eerie silence of the hotel room.

James. Nelle splashes cold water on her face and towels off her last flakes of sleep. *Where is James?*

She frantically leaves the running faucet to search the main room, rechecks the bed, the closet, the bathroom. At the door she peers through the peephole at the fish-eyed hallway. She is about to pull away when something blocks the peephole.

It takes her a moment to place it—a pupil, an iris. Staring back at her. She leaps back, heart thundering beneath her palm. Behind the fire-escape map on the door, she hears someone breathing.

"James?" Maybe he got locked out. But why wouldn't he knock? Why wouldn't he—

The man in the hall chuckles. "Not James."

Nelle's blood goes cold. *Quill.*

"What did you do with him?" she asks.

"No clue what you're getting at," says Quill. "If James left you, he did so of his own accord."

"You're lying." Either James *did* leave for a good reason, or Quill took him, or . . .

He realized he was stuck writing for me indefinitely and ran off. Nelle shakes the thought, refusing to let panic set in.

"When James comes back, he will kill you," she says.

Quill's laugh cuts through her like a serrated knife through canvas. "You're being naive, Nellie."

Her molars grind until they ache. "That is not my name."

"What lies did you tell yourself to explain James's absence?" Quill asks.

"He's coming *back*."

"No, he's not, and I don't blame him." His voice gets closer, mouth brushing the door. "I think he woke up and realized how much trouble it is to take care of you. To write for you. To know that a single day won't go by that you don't *need* him."

"Shut up." Nelle stands, back to door. "Maybe you feel that way, but I know he doesn't."

"Where is he, then?"

She slides down, knees to her chest. The bathroom sink whispers through the wall.

"How did you find me?"

"We're soul-tied," Quill says. "I had a dream, saw you here, took the next flight to DC. Listen, Nellie, I'm not here to force you to come with me. I *can't* anymore. But I want to give you a choice."

Lies, lies, lies. She presses her fists into her eye sockets. *Don't believe a word he says. Just make him leave.*

"James left you."

No, whispers her heart, *he didn't.*

"He's not coming back," Quill says. "This is your one chance, Nellie. Come home, and I'll forgive you. I'll keep you safe, you'll see. You're too fragile for the world. It's too dangerous."

"Go away." It's feeble, but it's all she can manage.

"We will be different," Quill says desperately. "Nellie, I'll be a better father. I promise. No more punishments. And I'll let—"

"Fuck. Off." Nelle's fists clench by her sides.

After a minute, Quill's footsteps move down the hall.

She lets out a breath, and with it come the tears. Peeling herself off the floor, she only makes it as far as the bed before she crashes out entirely. Sobbing, sweating through the bedsheets, puffy and red, praying that James didn't leave for good. That she isn't stranded here.

When James returns, she is almost too numb to notice. She curls into his chest, under the shelf of his chin, sobbing.

"Quill was here. He came."

"What?" James's arms tighten around her. "He's alive?"

"He knew what room we're in," Nelle grits out through her tears.

His jaw rests on top of her head. "God, how did he even find us?"

"I don't know." She sees Quill through that peephole every time she blinks. "But I think he's been following us since we left Lincoln."

"Impossible," James says. "We would've seen him."

Nelle is still too frazzled to defend what she knows is fact. "Quill was *here*. How he found us doesn't matter. He did. And he will find us again."

Slowly, as James whispers his apologies, his arms tug her back to earth.

When Nelle finally pulls away, she fists the front of his shirt and growls, "Don't *ever* leave again without telling me first."

James kisses her knuckles gentler than a butterfly.

"I never will again." He holds out his pinkie. "I promise."

"What's that?" She watches his finger.

"It's a pinkie promise," he says. "Seriously, you don't—? Oh, why do I even ask anymore. It's like . . . a way to seal your promise. To make it official."

"Isn't the point of a promise that your word is enough?"

"Take it or leave it."

Begrudgingly, Nelle curls her pinkie around his.

"I promise not to leave you without your permission," James says. "*Ever* again."

As if he has performed a spell, her tight chest unspools. "Why did you leave, anyway?"

"I wanted to surprise you with one of my favorite things." He produces a plastic cup filled with brown liquid and ice.

She takes the cold drink as a peace offering. It's milky, bitter, and cuts through her in a way that jolts her nerves.

"What is this?"

"An iced latte."

James clinks his cup against hers. The ice rattles. She sits back against the creamy pillows, drinks her latte, and watches him watching her. How is it possible for someone to cure her anxiety so quickly? She knows it's an unhealthy habit to form, but right now, wrapped in his clean, intoxicating smell, she can't help but give in to her innate desire to relax beside him.

"You were sleeping so hard, I didn't want to wake you up."

"Oh no." Nelle wants to crawl inside herself and shrivel up. "I know I drool."

"After last night, I don't think we can afford to be embarrassed around each other," James says. "The karaoke competition?"

Memories hit Nelle's head like bricks. Singing off-key to songs she didn't know, jumping on the bed amid liquor bottles and sheets of paper, clutching the TV remote as her microphone. James was wild, too, screaming at the top of his lungs to guitar- and drum-heavy ballads. Honestly, they should have been thrown out for a noise complaint.

"I think I'll cross singing off my list of possible career paths," she says.

James drops his swollen duffel bag on the bed and digs through it for clothes. In the bathroom, Nelle showers and changes into a cropped black tee and denim shorts.

When she reemerges, James has changed into his Henley and baggy jeans. Despite the warmth, he tugs on his dad's weathered jacket.

"So, navigator," he says, "where to next?"

Nelle presses her hands to the window and looks out at the city, beyond the city, to the sky. The world out there waiting for her. Just as exciting as before, but it is tainted now by Quill. He could be lurking around every corner, watching, waiting.

"I don't know what to do about *him*." She chokes on the name *Father*.

James's sigh rattles with real fear. "Neither do I. What if he's waiting at the truck? Or in our *next* hotel room? I don't think he'll stop after today."

"I'm sorry," Nelle says.

"Why on earth—"

"For pulling you into all of this," she finishes. "I knew better than to mess with Quill."

"You didn't pull me into anything." James nudges her chin up. "I jumped in headfirst. And as for Quill, I think all we can do is hope he stays away."

She rests on his hand. *"Hope."*

"Where to next, Nelle?"

"I'm thinking . . ." She pauses, mostly for dramatic effect. "New York."

⁂

On the drive north, Nelle and James find a diner at 3:00 a.m. in a ghost town off the interstate. Its black-and-white checkered floor sticks to her shoes, but she loves the red-vinyl booths, the foggy plastic menus, the cloud of grease that wafts from the kitchen door with its circular window. James slurps a chocolate milkshake from a thick red straw, the glass as tall as his forearm. Nelle tastes hers.

"Have you ever had a milkshake?" James asks.

"Nope."

"Well?"

"Strawberry." Nelle sucks down another icy gulp. "Tastes like melted ice cream."

James laughs and pushes his milkshake across the table. "Try mine."

"Only if you try mine."

He plugs her straw into his mouth. Heat floods her cheeks, realizing that he has most definitely had a strawberry milkshake before. Probably a few. He hasn't been Rapunzel in a tower his entire life.

"Oh my God," he moans.

Nelle tries his. Chocolaty, but not as good as hers.

"Do you want to trade?" He's already wrapping his hands around her milkshake.

"No, thanks." She reaches across the table and swipes it back.

A childish voice in her head taunts, *Sharing straws, you're practically kissing*. She stares at James's dimple and jawline, how his throat bobs when he looks at her.

Back to her milkshake. "So you're a writer."

"You could say that."

"The only writer I've ever known was Quill," Nelle says. "What does that say about writers?"

"It says nothing about writers and everything about Quill being the only person besides *me* that you've ever met."

"Valid. So what do you write? Fantasy? Romance, or is that out of your comfort zone?"

James sits back, arches a brow.

"Sorry." She traces a line through her glass's condensation. "I shouldn't assume. It's just that, well, *do* you write romance?"

He crosses his arms. "No."

"Maybe you should try," she says. "I think you'd be good at it. Quill only ever found success as a writer when he wrote out of his comfort zone."

"Not sure if he's the ideal role model."

"As a father, no." Yet Nelle can't deny Quill's genius. "But he was a bestselling author. Think about pushing the boundaries of genre, that's all I'm saying."

From what she has witnessed, the last few days on the road have been as formative for James as they have been for her. He was living a life he hated in Lincoln. Now he is free to gallop.

"You have to try something new, too," James says. "Solidarity, sister."

Nelle scratches the sticky table. For twenty-one years, she has been locked away from the world. Now she can dig her fingers into all it has to offer. She wants to see every mountain, traverse every city, cross every river, dip into every ocean. She wants to talk to people, to take dance classes, to hold a brush again.

"I used to love painting," she says. "I want to do that, maybe."

"Oh my God, really? Jessie's an artist, too." James's grin is contagious. "I'm sure she will let you work in her studio."

Nelle once loved the smell of paint, mixing colors to unlock new hues, transforming an empty canvas into another world. She imagines herself in New York, painting in a tiny sunlit studio . . . Quill's beady eye blinking back at her through the peephole.

Her throat closes up. "Yeah, I think I'd like to try."

Chapter 13

James has heard horror stories all his life.

"Oh, the people are so rude; you don't want to be around people like that. The streets are filthy, and the crime rate, James, dear lord, you're just gonna hate it, son, you're going to hate it." He anticipated rats the size of cats and colonies of cockroaches.

After searching thirty minutes for open street parking, James climbs out of the car, writes for Nelle to do the same, and stands on the lamplit street lined with brick buildings. Not too different from those back home. Fire escapes scale the fronts, dotted with rugs and plants, a long-haired cat peeking through iron bars. Unlike little downtown Lincoln, these buildings hold apartments and sushi restaurants, cafés and improv clubs. Driving in, he saw people of all races, heights, classes, ages, and hair colors hiking up and down the sidewalk, all of them leaders of their own little worlds.

Nelle stands in a circle of yellow streetlight, hands in the pockets of her charcoal-gray pants. When she declared Midi's borrowed clothes too dirty to wear on the way out of DC, an hours-long shopping spree ensued in Baltimore. After trying on a hundred things, she settled on five neutral pieces. *I'm trying to pin down my style*, she said again and again as she ducked into dressing rooms.

"Is this the building?" She peers up at the fire escape. Sulfuric wind hisses down the street, twisting her blond strands.

"No." James squints at the street signs, not really sure where he is, and it's only getting darker.

A pair of students with dyed hair lurks on the sidewalk, both wearing crop tops. The boy's fingernails are painted black. The girl is smoking a cigarette. An older man in a leather jacket climbs on his motorcycle and revs the engine. A guy in a red tracksuit lingers on the corner after the light signals him to walk. He lifts his face, soaking up dusk.

"This is when we could use a phone," James says.

A bulb clicks on in his head, and he scribbles in the journal for Nelle to follow.

She turns after him. "Where are you going?"

He passes a closed coffee shop, and around the corner—

"Huh." He skids to a stop at the pay phone. "Didn't think I'd find one that fast."

Fifty cents. He digs through his jacket, miraculously produces two quarters, and dials a number he has had memorized for years. It rings, rings, rings.

"Please pick up, Jessie." The vastness of the city around him, the fact that he knows *no one* else for hundreds of miles, is starting to sink in.

Jessie answers, her staticky voice saving him from existential panic. "Hello? Who is this?"

"It's James," he says. "Remember that girl I was telling you about when you came to visit? Nelle? Well, we're in New York right now. I think we're pretty close to your apartment. You still live at 376 Bleecker Street, right?"

"Slow down." Jessie laughs. "You're in New York? Why? For how long?"

"All questions will be answered over wine and pizza, both of which we can pick up on our way."

"Wine I have. I'd love pizza, though," Jessie says. "No mushrooms."

"I need directions to your apartment," he says.

"From where?"

He reads from the street sign. Jessie prattles off convoluted directions to a 24-7 pizza place on the way to her apartment.

"The menu says the largest they'll go is extra-extra-large, but if you ask Kyle, he'll make what I like to call a 'big daddy.' He might resist a little, but tell him it's for me. He'll do it."

"Thanks, Jessie. See you soon."

James hangs up the phone. Nelle stands behind him, arms crossed. Behind her unfurls a New York street, graffitied brick walls, smooshed cigarette butts. A siren wails. Somewhere on this island are his favorite writers, the world's top publishing houses, the work of the most talented performers, painters, sculptors, some long dead. For the first time, it hits James hard enough to stop his breath.

I am in New York fucking City.

ꟹ

James knocks on apartment 3B, the pizza against his hip.

"Ding dong, the witch is dead," Nelle sings off-key.

She cradles a bottle of moscato in the crook of her elbow, adamant that Jessie would dislike her if she came empty handed.

"Was *The Wizard of Oz* on Quill's list of approved movies?" James asks.

"Yep. He always said modern films were too vulgar."

The door cracks open, revealing a slice of face behind a dead-bolt chain. A pair of eyeballs scans them. Nelle hears the scrape of a metal chain and, in that second, feels a classic *oh shit* hook in her stomach.

James hasn't written for me to go inside.

She reaches for the journal and pen in his back pocket, but the door opens, and her moment slips away like a wet bar of soap.

Jessie tackles James in a sideways bear hug, dodging the daddy-size pizza in his hands. Her red curls are fire next to James's walnut brown.

"Kyle didn't give you any trouble, did he?"

Nelle has no choice but to stare at Jessie while she hugs James. Her cheeks are lightly freckled, and her eyeliner sweeps out sharply, each point dotted with a stick-on jewel.

"I started the order by name-dropping you, so, no, no trouble." James gestures for Nelle to come into the apartment.

But she is frozen on the threshold. Trembling like a damn fawn. Realization dawns on James's face, followed by pale dread. He mouths, *One second*, before following Jessie.

Inside, he says, "Jessie, look at this pizza, oh my God."

While Jessie inhales pizza fumes at the kitchen island, James scribbles in the journal, then slips it into his back pocket.

Nelle can breathe again. She steps into the apartment and locks the door slowly to allot herself recovery time. Another deep breath. She exhales.

"I've never had pizza," she says, the words slipping out.

"What?" Jessie's concentration breaks. "You're kidding, right?"

"She grew up in a really strict house," James intervenes.

"My dad was really specific about what I could and couldn't eat. Nothing mass produced, only organic. He was mostly vegetarian, so I was, too."

Jessie uncorks the moscato. "You didn't go out to eat with your friends in high school?"

Nelle didn't go to high school. Father was her tutor in math, science, history, and literature. He claimed that it was a legitimate way to obtain an education, and at eighteen she received a diploma in the mail. She hung it up in her room, proud of her *normal* achievement.

"I didn't have friends in high school," she says. It's not *not* the truth.

Jessie passes out three ceramic plates. "Do you like cheese?"

"Yeah."

"Tomatoes?"

Nelle nods.

"Bread?"

"Yes."

Jessie lifts up a gooey slice. "Then you are going to *die*."

Doubtful.

She lifts a slice and nibbles at the tip. And she does, indeed, die. Of all the cruelties Quill inflicted, banning delicacies like ice cream and coffee and *pizza* may have been the worst. Tangy tomato complements the salted crust and melted parmesan. Garlic glistens in each bite. She stifles a moan. James offers her a glass of wine, but she shakes her head.

Jessie guides them from the kitchen, barely three feet of counter space with a two-eye stove and rounded retro fridge covered in magnets and photographs. She claims it's nice by New York standards, but the highlight, she says, is the wood-top island facing the living room. One wall of the room is exposed brick, the other two maple paneling. The couch is yellow and covered in quilted throw pillows. Threaded blankets are slung across the cushions.

Nelle's childhood bedroom housed her books and her art, but it was barely hers. *Owning* a place—growing into every corner and cabinet like kudzu—is such a foreign concept that Jessie's apartment feels massive simply because it's *hers*.

"It's very cozy." Nelle runs her hand over the back of the couch. Her feet guide her to a bookshelf on the far wall, beside a floor-to-ceiling window overlooking the street. She scans the titles, her finger whispering across the spines.

"Is this a balcony?" James unlatches the window, and it swings inward, inviting in the city air, rippling the sea-breeze candle on the coffee table.

"A small one, yeah." Jessie pokes her head onto the balcony, and a trash-rotten wind tousles her red coils. She swirls four servings of white wine in her bulbous goblet, stabbing James with her brown eyes, clearly pissed.

"Do you want a moment alone to catch up?" Nelle asks, hoping to dissolve the tension.

"Yes, please." Jessie sips her wine.

"Where is Nelle supposed to go?" James asks. "The fire escape?"

"I can wait on the balcony," Nelle says. She tries to step out into the night air, but her body freezes. *Shit.*

James's face goes blank with fear again. Panicky, he says, "Jessie, can I use your bathroom? It was a long drive."

"Down the hall, third door on the right."

"Thank you." He speeds off.

"Typical James," she says, plopping down on the couch. "Always running from conflict."

"I didn't think that was typical of him," Nelle says.

Jessie pauses mid-sip. "How did you two meet?"

Nelle keeps a careful hand on the balcony door. Any second, James will write for her to move outside, so she has to keep this conversation short.

"At the Fourth of July festival," Nelle says. "He came up to me, and we talked all night."

"And you've lived in Lincoln your whole life?"

"All twenty-one years."

"That's so strange, because I lived there until I was eighteen, and I never saw you. It's such a small town, and we're not that far apart in age, so you'd think that I would have seen you once or twice. Here or there."

"I was homeschooled," Nelle says. "And I didn't have any friends to go out with, so I mostly just stayed home."

"With your dad?"

"S-sorry?"

"You live alone with your dad?"

Nelle bristles. "Is this an interrogation?"

Jessie's face drops into a dead serious glare.

Nelle squirms, wishing she could walk out onto the damn balcony already.

Then Jessie laughs, snapping any tension like a bone. "Sorry if I made you feel weird. I don't always know when a bit's gone too long, that's my bad. Look, I don't know you, so having you here with James is a little strange, especially because he's never brought a girl around. But you seem cool."

Nelle relaxes. "You do, too."

Jessie pauses, studies her a moment, then reaches for the wine. She pours another glass. "Here," she says, passing it over.

Nelle takes the offering just as James barrels into the room, sweaty and obviously freaking out.

"What's the matter?" Jessie asks. "Did you see the ghost, because Lena swears she—"

"Can I speak with Nelle?" James says. "Alone."

"Sure. I'll . . . wait on the balcony."

Once Jessie is safely outside, he motions for Nelle to join him on the couch.

"What's wrong?"

"The pen is empty." He shakes it. "I tried to get some out, but it's all gone. I hate to ask you to—"

Nelle plucks the pen from his fingers. "Watch Jessie. Make sure she doesn't turn around."

"Wait, don't you want to go somewhere else to—"

Nelle gasps as the metal nib cuts into her palm. A bead of ink swells, as small as a black diamond. She fills the pen and gives it to James. He writes, *Nelle goes onto the balcony.*

"That wasn't so bad, was it?" She opens the balcony door, stepping into the summer night. A car alarm blares a couple of blocks away. The hot reek of subway steam wafts in her direction. Jessie looks up expectantly.

"You can go back in." Nelle lifts her wineglass in salute. "He's ready to talk."

∞

As soon as the balcony door shuts, Jessie whirls on James so violently that wine sloshes out of her glass. She doesn't even notice the Greenland-shaped stain it leaves on her faux cowhide rug.

"What are you thinking, running away from home with some girl you barely know? Do you know how many times your mom has called me, *inconsolable*, and I've had to talk her through it, to tell her it's all okay, and that you're not ignoring her texts because you hate her, which, by the way, I get why you'd ignore her texts, she is kind of annoying sometimes, but why the fuck are you ignoring *my* texts?" She gulps down six ounces of wine and holds out her phone. "Call your mom. *Now.*"

Her tone leaves no room for argument. James takes the phone with shaky hands.

His mom answers instantly. "Hey, Jessie, I—"

"Hey, Mom." Icy silence. "Sorry I haven't responded to your calls or texts. I . . . uh . . . threw my phone in the ocean."

"You *what*?" she says.

Jessie mouths the same thing.

"I haven't been answering because I threw my phone in the ocean," he says again. "I wanted to be free from technology, I don't know. It's been nice not to be distracted by it, but that's why I've been not answering. I haven't been receiving your messages."

His mom scoffs. "That doesn't forgive anything, James. You can't just up and leave on a random night—"

"I know, I'm sorry—"

"Your savings. School. Your job. You won't survive if you're not making mature decisions for your life."

He sighs. "I have considered all of that. Look, Mom, I love you, but I honestly don't care about school right now. I want to travel for the rest of the summer, so that's what I'm going to do."

"Whatever."

Oh, she is angrier than he has ever heard her.

"See you in a few weeks," she says, and hangs up.

"I hate you for making me do that." James throws the phone back to Jessie.

She hums as she sways into the kitchen, apparently proud of herself. While her back is turned, he whips out the journal and writes, *Nelle comes back inside . . .*

He continues the sentence, *with freedom to wander all of New York City.* As soon as he writes the words, they dissolve until the paper is blank. Next he tries, *with freedom to wander all of the West Village,* but that, too, fades. Finally, he writes, *with freedom to wander all of apartment 3B, including the balcony.* His chicken-scratch handwriting doesn't disappear.

As the balcony door squeaks open, street noise trickles in. Car tires *whoosh,* people's voices drift down like feathers from the rooftop bar around the corner.

Nelle steps inside, wineglass empty, more relaxed than he has ever seen her.

"It's so nice out there."

Jessie shoves her cheeks full of pizza crust, wipes her hands on a rag, and gathers up the plates. "Y'all want to see the roof?"

Nelle's smile rivals sunshine.

James scrambles for the journal and writes, *and the roof?* but the words vanish. He tries again. *Nelle goes to the roof.*

They follow Jessie into the dank hall and up a sketchy staircase to a door that can only be opened from the inside.

"What if we get locked up here?" James asks as they step into the sticky night.

Nelle bounces on her toes like a kid in line for a roller coaster. "Then we'll climb down. It'll be fun."

"Just enjoy the view, James," Jessie says.

Night hangs over the city, and skyscrapers light up in the distance past the comparably shorter streets of the Village. He leans against the half wall lining the roof, soaking in the view. A pigeon picks at a banana peel on the sidewalk. Trees hang over the narrow one-way street. Voices and car horns and the hum of the city underline the electric air.

A rumble of thunder shakes the sky. James flinches as water splats on his forehead. It ripples across the concrete, a hushed rainfall. The tree branches titter, droplets playing music on their thirsty leaves.

"What do you think?" Jessie wraps an arm around his shoulders. "You've wanted to be here your whole life, right?"

James sighs, unable to produce words to explain how he feels. A bubble starts small in his chest, engorging with every breath, filled with pink glitter.

New York. He made it.

∞

Nelle straddles the low concrete wall, her right leg hanging off the edge of the building. Her foot has gone numb. She trails her finger where people have carved *C+L*, *R+P*, and *G+G*, dodging smudges of black ash from crushed cigarettes and mysterious stains. She doesn't worry about falling into the street below because she wouldn't die. Would her bones break? Most likely, but only two things can kill her, and one of them is the black journal. The last words written in her ink. The last tie she has to the earth. With Father's study burned, she realizes that her life is literally in James's back pocket.

"Can I see your key?" she asks him.

He holds it out, then hesitates. "Depends on what you're planning to do with it."

"Nothing violent this time." She holds out her pinkie. "I promise."

Key ring wielded, she digs into the ledge, carving her initial. *N.* Then she scratches a squiggly ampersand, followed by a *J.*

N&J. Not plus. *And.* Nelle *and* James.

Thunder rolls through like an avalanche. Lightning forks over the city. Hot wind swirls around them. Leaves spiral down the street like green confetti. As the storm worsens, the illuminated skyscrapers hide behind pounding sheets of gray.

"Let's get inside!" Jessie screams over the torrent.

James starts to stand, but Nelle pulls him back. Shakes her soaked head. He understands.

"We're gonna stay for a minute!" he yells back.

"Suit yourself!" Jessie holds her jacket above her head and scurries to the door, propped open with a cinder block.

Nelle pulls James away from the ledge and leads him to the center of the roof. She raises his arm, her fingers wrapped in his, and spins herself around. He falls into her movement, assuming a dance neither of them has rehearsed. They waltz sloppily in the rain to an invisible orchestra, whirling and laughing as the water rushes over them.

Each raindrop hits the concrete like a note to a song only they can hear.

Lightning splits the black clouds, and the rain pours harder, but Nelle's not scared.

James sprints a circle around the rooftop, howling fearlessly into the night. His shoes splash in deep puddles, spraying rainwater. He is so much freer than the man she met under the fireworks last month.

Nelle chases after him. Warm water prickles her hairline, the tip of her nose, her parted lips, her neck, chest, arms, fingertips, toes—

She slows to a stop. Holds out her arms, extending her fingers, each tip sizzling as adrenaline pumps through her veins. She tilts her head back and opens her mouth. Water fills the back of her throat, dribbles over her lips, and spills out. When she breaks her pose with a giggle, James is in front of her. He leans in close, his lips brushing the lobe of her ear. She shudders. For the first time tonight, Nelle realizes that she's trembling.

"Did Jessie give you a talk when I was gone earlier?" James's voice is low, gravelly.

Nelle grins. "A little one."

"She's protective of me," he says. "But I can tell she likes you."

"I like her, too." She traces a finger along his scruffy jaw. "She has a nice book collection."

James touches her hand, stilling it on his cheek. "I never thought I'd be standing on a rooftop in New York during a thunderstorm. And I definitely never thought you'd be here with me."

Nelle has never wanted to kiss him more than she does now, in the darkness, rain-smeared neon blinking in the distance. His blue eyes burn into her like ice, his hair slicked back, his shirt soaked and pasted to his chest, his stomach.

"Here I am," she says.

"Here you are." His voice barely more than a rasp.

Her eyelids flutter shut, and she rises on her toes, holding on to James like he's a life raft. She has never kissed anyone, but she has read about it. Dreamed about it. Her pillow, her hand, and the shower wall have all substituted as men in her fantasies.

Crack!

White light blasts behind Nelle's eyelids. She opens her eyes, to see only rain and the ghost of a flash dancing past her vision. Too late. She missed it.

"Was that lightning?" James walks over and examines a black scorch mark that stains the concrete. "Holy shit, we almost got struck by lightning."

Nelle's heart hammers in her chest, whether from the near-death experience or the almost-kiss, she's not sure.

"I know this is stupid," she says, "but do you think that was a sign?"

"A sign saying what?" James asks.

"That we should wait . . . no, never mind, it's stupid." She shakes her head. For years, her first kiss was nothing but a wish. What better moment to make it reality than a stormy rooftop in New York?

"We should wait to . . . kiss?"

"Forget I said anything, James." She doesn't want to *wait.*

"No, no, I think you're right." He holds her hands. "You were right about me waiting for the right moment to throw my phone away, and you're right about this."

"But how will we know when the right moment for *this* is?" Nelle runs her thumbs over his wrists.

"We'll know." He brings their hands up and kisses hers. "Trust me."

Nelle doesn't want to wait, but she does trust him. With her life.

"Fine." She taps his nose, the bow of his lips, saying goodbye to her hope of tasting him tonight.

Chapter 14

The toaster spits up two brown slices of bread, which Jessie butters with a knife she inherited from her mom's first silverware set. A record crackles by the window, mostly guitar, drums, and a woman's soprano howl. Beside the spinning vinyl, a white moth orchid shivers in the northern sunlight. James's feet catch on the rung of Nelle's barstool. She follows the path from his ankles to his mouth until her feelings from last night come rushing back.

Last night.

Dripping on the stairs, Nelle and James stumbled down from the roof and into the unoccupied guest room, a glorified walk-in closet with a bed and a window, where they clumsily swapped their wet clothes for sweats. Once they were dry, they crawled under the comforter, side by side, tension stretching between their sleepless bodies. Nelle had never been so aware of him before. Neither said a word until, eventually, James started snoring.

"Appetizers." Jessie slides two plates across the tiny wood-top island. "There's a quiche in the oven." She sliced up strawberries alongside their toast. Almost the same shade as the fruit, her hair is pulled up in a small, spiky bun, exposing brown roots.

James gives a weak smile to show his thanks.

Nelle sighs. She has no patience for this. *He* is the one who rejected the kiss, so why is he pissed off? Is this weird tension now a permanent fixture of their friendship? Maybe last night was too much for him. What if it was too much for *her*?

"Coffee or tea?" Jessie asks.

"Coffee." Nelle fondly recalls the latte that resurrected her in DC. She accepts Jessie's mug and tries it black, fighting back a sour face. "Do you have milk?"

"Oat milk." Jessie grabs a carton from the fridge and pours a quick stream into the mug. "How'd you sleep last night?"

Nelle sips it. Scorching hot, but the taste is tolerable.

"Fine," James says, crunching on his toast.

Nelle fights the urge to kick him. "Fine, yeah."

Jessie flings a cabinet shut, and the *bang* makes Nelle slosh her coffee.

"Why are you both being weird?" Jessie wipes her hands on a rag before planting them on her hips. "Yesterday you were all like, smiley and heart eyes and let's dance in the rain. Now you're not speaking?"

Nelle squeezes her coffee mug until it burns her fingers. "I didn't sleep well last night."

Jessie frowns. Squints. "You said you slept fine."

Well, I did say that. "Um . . ."

"Nothing's wrong, we were just up all night," James says. His toast is half gone. "And we've been driving for days straight. I can't speak for Nelle, but I'm exhausted."

Jessie sets a timer on her phone. "You're giving me child-of-divorce PTSD. I'll be gone five minutes tops. Talk it out." As she pads down the hall in wool socks, she adds, "And don't let the quiche burn!"

Discomfort settles between Nelle and James. She dares a look at him, hoping to see the James she knows. He rearranges the strawberries on his plate.

Fine. If he won't talk, she will.

"What's wrong with you?" Nelle twists on her stool to face him. "Why did you shut down when we got back to the room last night?"

"I didn't want to talk." He sits a few inches taller than her, but he seems small.

"Why not?" Nelle purses her lips, her defenses up. "Because I thought—"

Jessie's phone timer goes off. James reaches over to stop it.

"Not because I don't like talking to you," he stammers, catching her tone. "I do, I love talking to you. It's just that . . ." He studies the ceiling as if he might find an explanation written there. "Oh, what the hell, I wanted to kiss you last night. On the roof and when we were in bed. It was all I could think about."

"*You're* the one who said we have to wait."

His dimples are dimpling. "I am very stupid sometimes. I have this idea of how things should go, and sometimes I try to . . . orchestrate them."

I wanted to kiss you last night. Nelle chews on a hunk of buttered toast to keep her focus off the animal inside her going rabid at his words. So far, she has kept it on a leash, scared of being hurt, scared of the real-world horrors Father warned her about: rapists, murderers, line cutters, heartbreakers. When she was seven, he sat her down on his knee in the living room and said, "People are the real monsters of this world, Nellie." She never forgot that, even if she doesn't agree with it. Now after feeling the world's texture for herself, she loves the people in it most of all. The only real monster in her world, she has discovered, is Father himself.

Nelle blinks from her reverie to find James staring at her lips.

"I don't have a frame of reference," she says at last, "but this doesn't feel like casual breakfast conversation."

"It's not." James pushes back his hair. "Sorry for being cold. It was all in my head, nothing to do with you, and next time I'm feeling anxious, I'll tell you the truth."

He leans in and kisses her cheekbone. Nelle shudders, her soul lit up like a glow stick. Grinning, James leans back on the island and kicks his socked feet out toward the living room. A bird chirps on the balcony. Nelle's throat goes dry. She hadn't realized that a peck on the cheek could be so sensual.

Jessie's door squeaks open. "Are we finished making out and making up?"

"Yes," Nelle calls down the hall, taking a plucky bite of toast. It is good, for being plain butter on bread. Maybe the flavor she tastes is freedom. Food made with the care and love of a sentimental hand-me-down butter knife. Food not prepared by a sociopath.

Jessie clears the air as she strides in. "All good now?"

"Yes, all good." James smirks behind his coffee mug. "Miscommunication is a bitch, you know."

The corner of Nelle's mouth tugs upward, as if James planted a hook where he kissed.

"Oh, I know, I—" Jessie cracks open the oven, and smoke spills out into her face, the dead smoke detector watching in amusement. *"My quiche!"*

Washington Square Park is a rare patch of green among the concrete, brick, and glass of the city.

James drops his empty coffee in a recycling can and finds a bench to sit on. Nelle settles in beside him. The last sentence in the journal reads, *Nelle roams freely around the park.*

After Jessie went to work, they spent the morning and early afternoon testing the boundaries of Nelle's existence.

"Father already experimented with how much I *can* be controlled," Nelle said before they left the apartment. "Time to figure out how I much I can't."

Though her independence doesn't stretch beyond Jessie's apartment door, James successfully wrote for her to roam all four floors of the Union Square Barnes & Noble. Why she can traverse one multifloor building and not another boggles him, but who is he to question the fickle rules of magic? Bryant Park also proved to be a success, so long as she stayed within its border. Central Park was a failure.

James discovers that he can write for her to *go* places by herself, like Quill did on the Fourth, but doing so requires a written command to return. They tried it with the coffee shop on the corner, and Nelle came back with two iced lattes, smiling brightly. James mirrored her glee, but in truth her joy only made his chest ache. Having been imprisoned by Quill her whole life, a simple solo walk down the street was a miraculous experience for her. And James takes it for granted every damn day.

He knew New York was a walking city, but holy hell, his legs are tired. He sits and digs two battered paperbacks from his back pockets, both from Jessie's bookshelf, a romance and a thriller. In his left hand, a half-naked man and woman sit enraptured on a cliffside, wind thrashing their orgasmic expressions. In his right hand, a rain-streaked window looks out on a lamplit street.

"What's this one about?" Nelle asks as he hands her a book.

"I think it's a murder mystery." He cracks open the romance novel, research for *trying something new*. The dedication makes him smile: *To my cat.* Three pages in, he is walking in the author's world. Two chapters later, if the two leads do not end up together, he will riot.

He looks up during the book's turbulent midpoint, startled to see that his shadow has grown longer. People gather around the fountain, tossing pennies into its rippled water. A woman in a flat fedora strums a folk song, an open guitar case at her feet containing two crumpled dollar bills.

"Do you like your book?" Nelle asks.

"I do," James says, flipping it over to examine the cover again. "It's like if a strawberry milkshake was a novel."

She jabs his side. "Inspirational?"

He thinks about the beats of the plot, the character-focused scenes, the banter between the two love interests. Would it be refreshing to take a break from castles, dragons, and battles to write about something softer? Something slightly more real?

He pulls out the pen with Nelle's ink. "Want to grab another coffee before we go back to the apartment?"

"Sure," Nelle says, "but I have another idea for after coffee, before home."

~

Fresh cortado in hand, ice rattling, James steps after Nelle through the door of an antique store. Dust coats every shelf, yellow-paged book, and creepy doll. He gags on the smell of mildew as the doorbell tinkles. The old man behind the narrow counter smokes a cigarette and flips his magazine page.

"Nice place," James mutters, steering clear of a supersize teddy bear covered in brown stains. "Are you looking to buy a demon-possessed Barbie?"

"No." Nelle scans every shelf, low and high. "Just looking. How cool is this?" She plucks a gold locket from a necklace rack, the smooth oval engraved with a rose. Inside are tiny empty frames, waiting to house two floating heads.

James watches as she clicks the locket open and closed. "We should get it."

Nelle double-checks his face. "Really?"

"Yeah." He holds it up to the dim light. "We can put our faces in it."

"I'd love that." She spears down another cluttered aisle. "But we need to find a souvenir for you, too."

He waves the idea away. "I don't need anything."

She gasps. "James!"

He ducks around the shelves and finds her kneeling on the floor next to a small suitcase.

"Isn't this *gorgeous*?" She unbuckles the case and opens the lid.

A red manual typewriter sits inside. James examines it. Fresh ribbon of ink already installed, the keys intact and functional, as far as he can tell. The carriage lever slides smoothly.

Nelle searches for a tag. “How much is it?”

“Doesn’t matter,” James says. It’s coming home with him. His hands tremble as he carries it to the front counter. “Is this still functional?”

Chapter 15

For two weeks, James swims in his story. He writes all night, and when he is out to eat with Nelle and Jessie, or walking through a park, or in line for coffee, he is *thinking* about writing. The story—these characters—consumes him.

Fingers cramping, he finishes typing a sentence and stretches his arms behind his head. Outside, the city buzzes. On the bed, Nelle curls like a question mark with her back into the pillows. She goes to sleep hours before he does. Hours before Jessie, too. Some nights, James tiptoes into the kitchen to find his cousin at the island, hunched over a bowl of spicy ramen, huddled in a duvet cocoon, watching trashy reality TV.

James has been writing for Nelle for weeks, but now he has rediscovered how much he loves to write for *himself.* That red typewriter unlocked the floodgates. And the words have yet to stop rushing in. He drinks three more cups of tea and finishes typing another seventy pages before the sun rises.

Nelle stirs awake, her face cute and puffy. "Did you sleep?"

James's fingers freeze on the clacking keys. "No, ma'am."

"You wrote all night?"

"I've only stopped to pee. And to get more tea." His eyes are so dry and tired, he can barely keep them open. But more adrenaline pumps with every word he types. "It's like something's fueling me, but the fuel isn't running out. I think it's being here, in this place."

Or it's you, he thinks.

"This apartment?" Nelle asks.

"No, New York." He spins toward her in the desk chair. "I've never been *this* inspired in my life."

"What time is it?" Nelle grumbles.

James glances at the wall clock. "Half past six."

Nelle's head hits her pillow, and soon a new line of drool dribbles out of the corner of her mouth.

James stands in line with bloodshot eyes for fifteen minutes at an artsy coffee shop on Seventh Avenue, rereading the pages he wrote the night before. He stapled them together to carry around, and they are already riddled with wrinkles, coffee stains, and red ink. He orders an iced latte and a cortado and carries them back into the morning sun, down the street and around the block. With full autonomy throughout Jessie's apartment, Nelle gave James the permission to leave her there under the stipulation that he come back with coffee for her.

He doesn't bother being quiet when he comes in. Jessie works afternoons in a bookshop sometimes, interns part-time at a personal-injury law firm, and spends her other days with a group of artists in Brooklyn, often not returning until well past two in the morning, also often stoned out of her mind. Last night, she went across the river and has yet to come home.

James carries the drinks down the hall into his and Nelle's room and sits on the bed beside her sleeping body.

"Nelle," he coos. "It's not half past six anymore."

Nothing.

He clears his throat. "I have coffee."

Miraculously, she stirs, stretches out a lazy arm, and takes the cup from him. She plunges the straw into her mouth like it's her life support.

"Thank you," she says when she finally detaches herself.

"I thought you might need a little energy after the weekend."

On Friday and Saturday, they visited all the touristy places they wanted to see. Rode the elevator to the top of the Empire State Building. Took a ferry ride to the Statue of Liberty. Spent the evening at a Broadway production of *Wicked* in the nicest clothes they could find, James in a rented tuxedo and Nelle in a green satin gown. After that they joined Jessie at a bar in the East Village where they got so drunk, James could barely walk home. Seeing the city's tourist attractions so late was an unspoken way of putting off leaving the city. Now that they've experienced New York as visitors, he knows that Nelle wants to move on. Only a couple of weeks until school starts, anyway. But James isn't ready.

Her sleepiness fades as she hungrily drinks her latte. "Where do we go next? Paris? Tokyo?"

Can she read my mind? "Why don't we stay here a little longer?"

"Why?" She sits up. "We've seen New York. I want to see the *world*, don't you?"

"We can see the world, but . . ." How can he put his feelings into words?

"We've been here over two weeks," she says. "And when August ends, you'll be back at school."

He doesn't want to think about returning to his premed classes, his lonely one-bedroom apartment, his college town, full of football games and frat guys playing beer pong on their front lawns. He reaches out, but Nelle retracts her hand. The rejection twists his heart.

"I like New York," he says. "Being here makes me happy."

Nelle sets her empty cup on the nightstand. "I like it here, too, and we can come back when we're done."

James's face burns. This is what he feared. She wouldn't love New York, he would love it so much that he would go back on his promise to show her the world. Maybe it's the same fear that made him stop their kiss, weeks ago. Even though he wanted to kiss her. Even though her lips are all he can think about at night, every night, when he finally pulls away from his manuscript.

"Will you *ever* be done, though?" he asks, voicing his fear aloud, hoping for reassurance.

Nelle glares at him, which is fair. Silence rings through the apartment until a couple of angry cars honk at each other and normality resumes.

"I'm sorry," James says. "I'm being selfish, I know. A few more days? That's all I ask."

Nelle picks a book off the nightstand and stares at the page. "A few more days."

"Are you mad?"

She looks up. "I just don't want you to forget why we took off in the first place."

He hasn't. His manuscript has consumed him. He'll admit that. Since he started it, he has been a lousy friend. Nelle deserves more attention than what he has given her.

The typewriter whispers to him, but James perks up and asks, "How about we explore today?"

Nelle dog-ears her page. "We've explored enough here. Write if you're inspired, James."

"Tonight, then? Dinner, just me and you."

"I'm going to ask Jessie if I can go to her studio."

James lights up. "How long's it been since you painted?"

"Years." She shakes her head. "I don't even know if I remember how—"

The apartment door swings open with a bang, and Jessie enters, rambling about some insanely sexist joke one of her colleagues made. James slides down the hall in his socks. When Jessie doesn't return from her studio until daylight, she always has a good story to tell.

"I hate that you don't have a phone anymore," she says. "I was halfway home, stopping at the takeout place, on my third attempt at calling you, when I remembered you *chucked your phone into the ocean*. So I hope you don't have a problem with Charlie's Kickin'

Chicken, chow mein, and egg rolls, because that's what we're eating, you primitive idiot."

"You do realize it's nine a.m.?" James says.

"And I'm coming off an all-nighter, so for me, this is dinner." Jessie drops the takeout on the coffee table and storms down the hall.

Nelle creeps into the living room, glancing back at Jessie's door. "Is she okay?"

"She's always exploding. When she was in fifth grade, I was in kindergarten, and we had recess at the same time. There was this kid in her grade that started to pick on me, and when Jessie found out, she *destroyed* him."

Nelle's brows fly up.

James shrugs. "No one bullied me after that."

Jessie pokes her head out of her room. "I'm hopping in the shower, but I'm not shaving, so it'll take five minutes flat! Put on a show for us, and don't touch the food, or I'll cut your fingers off."

She ducks back inside, and James peels open the plastic bag, ready to sneak an egg roll so his growling stomach will shut up.

"Don't," Nelle says. "If she cuts my fingers off, I'll bleed ink, and how will we explain that?"

James laughs and takes the egg roll anyway.

Nelle sniffs one of the takeout containers. "Huh. What exactly is *in* Charlie's Kickin' Chicken?"

~

"This is the studio." Jessie jiggles her key in the metal door and kicks it twice with her boot before it gives. Flakes of rust fall onto the threshold of the moonlit loft.

Nelle needs a moment to compose herself after she steps inside. The farthest wall is all floor-to-ceiling windows exposed to the East River and the glittering Manhattan skyline. Another wall of windows faces south, so light can spill in during the day. The walls and floor are covered in scattered artwork: watercolors, pottery, acrylics, sculptures made out of cans and baby doll heads and light bulbs, pencils, charcoal, paper, glue. The expressions of many artists all mixed together.

"This is my latest piece." Jessie bounces over to a surrealist painting of a blue woman with an ass the size of a glacier and a head the size of a grape. "It's a self-portrait."

Nelle spots a stack of blank canvases, and her throat closes up. She is back in her bedroom in Lincoln, choking on the thick dust accumulated on her easel, her canvases, her favorite brushes. Crying to the fireplace while her best painting blackens and curls.

"You good?" Jessie asks.

"Yeah, sorry." Nelle blinks back her tears. "It's been a while since I painted."

Jessie chews her lip. "Wait here." She disappears into an adjoining room.

Nelle watches the street below. A cat bounds down the sidewalk, claws stretching toward a fluttering pigeon. Jessie returns a minute later with a cup of steaming coffee and flips a switch by the door. Twelve hanging lights, all hand blown and shaped like fishbowls, flicker on.

Nelle accepts the coffee, hints of cinnamon and vanilla pooling on her tongue. "Thanks."

"No problem." Jessie leans against the wall. She is a beautiful woman, Nelle realizes. Her blue eyeliner and sparkling eyeshadow are creatively applied, her hair short and lightly curled, her face heart shaped. She gestures, her fingernails individually painted with different flowers, and says, "This is your spot, whenever you're ready. I'll be here all night."

Nelle stands in front of an easel. With shaky hands, she picks a square canvas off the stack. The material is familiar, rough, terrifyingly empty. Her heart pounds as the white square seems to grow, a monster intent on swallowing her whole—

"Want to hear a story?" Jessie asks, her strawberry earrings glinting.

Nelle tears away from the canvas, grateful for the distraction. "Please."

"Follow me." Jessie disappears through a curtain of tinkling multicolored beads.

Please work. Nelle sends up a prayer to whatever magic controls her life. She is already stretching the boundaries of what she can do by leaving the apartment without James. The first time she went to the café by herself, she nearly burst into tears while ordering a latte. Still, her ink has limits, and James only wrote for her to go to Jessie's *studio*. Nelle has no idea if her body will allow her to cross into the room where Jessie disappeared to. She might freeze on this side of it, and how would she explain that?

Sorry, Jessie, but I actually have a phobia of beads. Can you tell your story in here, far away from those little bastards?

Her heart pounding, Nelle sucks in her breath and plunges into the beads. Strands of rainbow orbs cling to her as she passes through, and she sags in relief.

Paint-splattered furniture seems to be the theme in the room she steps into. Three strangers sprawl across the couch, two playing a video game on a flat-screen TV, the other thumbing through an oversize magazine. Their hair is dyed various shades—pale blond, rose red, black—and when Nelle enters, they all stare at her.

"Want a turn?" The redhead holds up a game controller.

"I'm good, thanks," Nelle says.

Jessie presses a button on a single-serve coffee machine, and it starts to hum. She leans on a colorful island, reclaimed wood muralized by myriad hands. Nelle spots a painted mermaid with seaweed hair and small breasts. Beside the couch, a lamp sculpted into a black cat. Across the hardwood floor stretches a warm, polychromatic rug that appears handmade in the best way. Uniformity has no place here.

"I came out when I was sixteen," Jessie says. The coffee machine beeps, and she spins around to retrieve her cup. "Leaving out all the gory details, my parents were not proud. They forced me to withdraw from my art classes, and after that, I kind of withdrew from life. Got depressed. James was there for me, even as a little kid, but I couldn't talk to him about wanting to die when he was eleven. I stopped painting. Is that about where you're at?"

"It's about where I was. Before I met James."

Jessie blows softly into her coffee cup. "He's helped you then?"

"We've helped each other," Nelle says.

Jessie smiles, her upper lip lingering above the rim of her mug. "Before senior year of high school, I knew I wanted to study art in the city. I got a part-time job, did what I could to have the best grades possible, and saved up for therapy. Then I got medicated, and *then* I decided to start painting again. It was frustrating at first, but after a few weeks of relearning the basics, I was all in. Sometimes painting was even more therapeutic than talking to a professional. I didn't have to try, it all came spilling out."

"And here you are," Nelle says. "You did it."

"I did." Jessie looks at the little kitchen, the other artists on the couch, the adjacent room. "The first painting I finished when I got back to it was my submission for art school."

"Really?"

"Yeah. But I wouldn't be here if I hadn't tried again."

Nelle finishes her coffee while chitchatting with Jessie and her friends. Meg is the redhead, Luke the blond, and Denise is the pixie-cut diva with neon-green makeup and black lips to match her hair.

Nelle brews another cup and pads back into the studio to stare at the canvas—that unforgiving white. It mocks her. Haunts her. Inhaling, she pulls up a stool and lifts a thin paintbrush.

Quill's house burning.

Riding, windows down, on the highway.

Sending paper wishes across a hotel bathroom.

Dancing through puddles on a rooftop.

Jo March picking up her pen again in chapter forty-two.

The horses through her window.

The city night twinkles in through floor-to-ceiling glass. *I remember.*

An artist with a vision, Nelle dips the brush into her coffee cup.

⁂

When she emerges from her frenzy, Nelle first sees the sun over Williamsburg. She steps back, flexing her fingers, to observe what she created. A watercolor done with coffee, the overlapping shades of brown burnished gold by dawn.

It's a palomino with wings, soaring above a sea of skyscrapers.

"Wow," breathes a voice behind her.

Nelle jumps and whirls. A gorgeous stranger looms over her, transfixed by her painting. She smells like apricots, sweat, and weed. Black hair curls over the nape of her neck.

"This is incredible," she says. "You painted this with coffee?"

Nelle glances at her work—far from the best she has done—then back at the woman.

"Yeah," she says. "Sorry if it was your brush I used. I'm not sure—"

"Don't stress over it." The woman laughs. "You must be new to Jessie's little clubhouse. I'm not an artist. I'm Lena. Jessie and I are in the same internship."

Nelle peers over Lena's shoulder, but the rest of the studio is empty. Sculptures and sketches have been shuffled around, but she had been too absorbed by her painting to notice anyone else through the night.

"Jessie's in the kitchen making breakfast." Lena reads her searching expression. "Well, she's moving it from to-go containers to paper plates."

Jessie emerges from the kitchen holding a tray stacked with bacon, eggs, and pancakes.

"We are celebrating today, my beauties!" She places the tray on the coffee table with a flourish. "Nelle, I—no joke—shit my pants when I saw your piece. It's my favorite of the year. I shouldn't have doubted you. James knows not to date a bad artist."

"We're not dating." Nelle sits on a pillow at the coffee table. "And at what point during your motivational speech last night did you doubt me?"

Jessie forces down a half-chewed bite of egg. "You're not dating?"

"No," Nelle says.

"Have you fucked?" asks Lena.

"No," Nelle repeats. Her cheeks go hot. "Anyway, what are we celebrating?"

"Your rediscovered artistry," Jessie says through a mouthful of bacon. "After this, we're going out for bottomless mimosas."

Panic sets in.

The studio and back, that's what James wrote for her.

"Thanks." Nelle looks at the painting, the horse galloping midair, feathered wings flung wide. "Can we stop by the apartment and pick up James before mimosas?"

Lena perks up. "James? I want to meet James!"

Jessie drizzles syrup across her pancakes. "Fine, we'll get James. But you better be on your best behavior," she says to Lena. "And before we leave this room, you have to define our relationship."

"What do you mean? We're seeing each other."

"Not good enough." Jessie shrugs. "I only let family meet girlfriends."

"All right, all right." Lena softens as she shapes the word, more intimate whisper than voice, *"Girlfriend."*

A short, silent conversation passes between Jessie and Lena, then Jessie laughs and leans over to kiss her new girlfriend.

Nelle eats without saying much. She is desperate to see more of the world before James goes back to school, but she can't deny how happy she is here, surrounded by people who love each other, who are nice to her. Painting her heart out with the view of the borough across the river, the morning light like fallen coins across the water.

She sits back with her coffee and listens to Jessie and Lena bicker about meeting each other's parents, pretending that there is no ink, no journal, no Quill.

For a few minutes, she is a woman. Nothing else.

Chapter 16

For years, James has dreamed of typing two little words.

The End.

Eight slow jabs, one held breath, ducts bursting with tears that have waited a decade for this.

Carefully, as if it might spontaneously crumble to dust, he rolls the final page free from the typewriter and places it atop his *completed* manuscript. Two hundred and forty-two pages of *his* words. He scoops the stack of paper up and flips it over to chapter one.

I did it.

Immediately, he wants to type the manuscript on a computer and upload it to the cloud. But he left his laptop in Lincoln, and dropping a grand on a new one would make a hazardous dent in his savings account, which he needs to travel with Nelle. With the completion of his first draft, he finally feels like leaving New York wouldn't be *The End.*

There is a whole world to roam, and he's lucky to have a partner to roam alongside. They might be leaving sooner than he's ready, but he's not sad about it. No, the next two weeks will be a golden period. His imagination churns out a slew of images: floating on a gondola in Venice, climbing the Eiffel Tower, hiking the Scottish Fairy Pools.

He started plotting their first kiss, but nothing is set in stone.

Nelle is normally nestled in bed at this time of night. The empty sheets hold her shape. So caught up in the last few chapters of his book, he forgot that he wrote for her to go to Jessie's studio. She has been back three times this past week to paint, even without Jessie. James has yet to see any of her finished pieces, but Lena and Jessie both say they're remarkable. He believes it. Can't really imagine Nelle being *un*remarkable.

Holding the manuscript like a small cake, James carries it down the hall. Jessie is frying an egg in the kitchen, a dishrag slung across her shoulder.

"Guess what I did?" he says.

As if handling a newborn, Jessie takes the manuscript and flips through the first few pages, disbelief written across her face.

"Holy shit, you finished a freakin' book."

"I've been talking about it long enough."

"Have you told Nelle yet?" She turns to page one. "Is this because of her? Is it *about* her?"

"No, no, and no." James takes back the manuscript into his own care. "And it's nowhere near ready for reading."

Jessie picks up a spatula. "Elevator pitch me."

"It's romantic, but not really a romance. And there is a curse. And two main characters."

"Oh really? Main characters? Let me guess, it has a beginning, middle, and end, too. Your pitch is going to need improvement if you want to sell the thing, James."

"I haven't had time to formulate a detailed summary as I finished it literally minutes ago." His mouth wrestles with a cheek-aching grin. *I finished it.* "I need a favor."

"Sure." Jessie frees a tea bag from its packaging.

"Will you keep my manuscript safe while I'm traveling with Nelle? Just until school starts, then I'll come back for it. I'd hate to lose it, and I don't trust anyone else."

"I'm honored." Jessie scoops her eggs onto a plate and steeps her Earl Grey. "Don't worry, I'll be the best guardian. If the city issues an evacuation notice, I'll grab it before my phone."

"Thank you," James says.

Jessie's finger goes up. "Under one condition."

"No." He shakes his head. "You're not reading it yet."

"*Fine.* Does it have a title?"

"An excellent question." James refills his water bottle, savoring Jessie's anticipation. "For now, I'm calling it *The Summer Curse.*"

"That doesn't sound romantic."

"It's not supposed to sound romantic. It's a title, it's just supposed to sound cool."

Jessie reels backward like a psychic slapped with a premonition. "I'm having a thought. You need a celebration."

"You're always making an excuse to throw a party."

"This doesn't need excusing. This is a big deal, James!"

"I know," he laughs. But does he? Finishing *The Summer Curse* feels both momentous and insignificant. Within a month, he scaled the impossible cliff, only to reach the top and realize it was never as difficult as he thought it would be. Which means he can do it again and again, producing a lifetime of books with his name on the spine.

Jessie blows on her tea. "Last November I slept with the owner of this cute bar on Carmine, so I can probably get it rented on short notice. Does Friday work? Or Thursday? I know y'all are leaving soon. Where is it you're going again?"

James knows better than to argue with Jessie once she has her mind set, though the idea of a room full of people celebrating *him* makes his skin crawl.

"I need to ask Nelle again, but last she said, Paris. And don't you think Thursday's better for the party? School starts in two weeks, so we'll need to fly out as soon as possible."

Jessie already has her phone out, and she's tapping away. "Thursday, say . . . seven?"

"Seven's perfect." James stands. "Until then, I'm going into hibernation."

He can barely get the words out through the sludge of his mind. When *was* the last time he slept more than a few hours? He stumbles down the hallway, fatigue slamming into him like a bag of bricks, and crawls into bed. Cool sheets on his legs. A fan stirring the air in the room. His pillow whispering sweet nothings.

ꕥ

Nelle is restless, sitting at the desk, watching James. She once begged Quill to let her into the front yard to catch fireflies. She was eight at the time, and he said no. But James doesn't care where she goes. Even celebrates what she does independently. Earlier in the summer, he wanted her to write for herself. Until she told him that it would kill her.

But what if Father lied?

Nelle hungers for the pen. She started spiraling about Quill's honesty while mixing paint in Jessie's studio. Struck by a sudden compulsion to write for herself, she abandoned her half-finished painting and stormed out. Vibrating, she hiked over the Brooklyn Bridge and up Broadway through Lower Manhattan. When she returned, panting, to the apartment to find James unresponsive, Nelle was guiltily grateful. She won't have to debate with him. This is something she needs to do—to try—even if it kills her.

But if she does it, she wants a new journal. If James has to live with those pages as his only memory of her, she doesn't want them to hold the sentence that killed her.

Nelle nudges James as she slides on his denim coat. "Can you write for me to go to Shack O' Books?"

He cracks open an eye, then writes so sloppily that Nelle is shocked her ink recognizes it as language. As soon as the journal closes, he is snoring again.

Twenty minutes later Nelle crosses the street to her favorite bookshop in the Village. The air holds hints of fall. Back home, it'll be in the nineties. She feels in James's coat pocket for his wallet. Still there, palm-size and leather. She pushes through the shop door and goes to a section of journals near the back. She grabs the first one she sees.

No hesitation. If she stops to think, she will never go through with it.

Quill's biggest fear was losing control over her. He lied to her about the world being full of dangerous people. He lied when he told her that only *he* could write for her. He lied when he called himself her fucking father.

Nelle pours her change into her coat pocket, and takes the red-cloth journal out onto the sidewalk. People zip around like gnats. She has considered New York's citywide egotism a flaw until now, when anonymity is what she needs. She drops to the concrete and bites into the meat of her hand. Hard, until bitter ink stings her tongue. Spitting, she flattens the journal open on the stained concrete and shakily touches the wound below her thumb. Ink glistens on her fingertip. *Her* ink.

"Is it worth it?" says a voice above her.

Nelle squints up, as if emerging from bathwater, mistaking the newcomer as an angel.

Quill crouches beside her. How uncanny to see him here, in this setting. She has only ever seen him in their house, except through the peephole in DC. Never on a street, in broad daylight, surrounded by people.

"The risk," he says. "Is it worth it?"

Nelle's adrenaline melts away. "How'd you find me?"

Another drop of ink hits the page and runs to the journal's spine.

"I don't have to search," Quill says, as if this should reassure her. "I close my eyes, and I know where you are. The farther you go, the clearer you get."

Nelle looks between him and the journal. She came—literally—from his mind. The way he feels her . . . she feels him, too. His presence. Like a cold lizard perched along the back of her brain. She ignores it most of the time, but the farther she gets, the more the bond strengthens. She feels his anger, his sadness, his patience.

"Are you going to follow through with it?" Quill nods to her bleeding hand.

Nelle shrugs. "One way or another, it'll put me out of my misery."

Except I'm not miserable. For the first time in her life, she has friends. She has James. They have plans to leave New York, to see more of the world.

Nelle hesitates. Legs whoosh around her. A black droplet grows heavy on her fingertip. Swelling and stretching, until—

The drop hits the page and splatters, black and spiky, like a spore.

I can't do it.

Quill touches her shoulder, his fingers like a raven's claw. "It's okay, Nellie."

"Move your hand." Nelle twitches. "Or I'll bite it off."

He recoils. "You scorn me again and again, but you'll understand when you're older. You'll realize how grateful you should've been for your father."

"This is the last time I'm going to say this," Nelle says. "I'll call the police if I have to, and I'll tell them the *truth*. Stay away from me. I don't want to see you *ever* again. I don't want to talk to you. I want nothing to do with you. Don't you realize how fucked up you are?"

Quill blinks at her.

"You *tortured* me. You kept me captive for twenty-one years. I have every right to hate you until the day I die."

"The question is . . ." He stands up to his full height. "Is that going to be today?"

Nelle waits until he's around the block to hurl the journal in the nearest trash can. She shoots up the street, back to the apartment, hand dripping blood.

She must be visibly rattled when she barges in because Jessie pauses the TV. "Are you okay?"

Nelle checks her hand to make sure the cut has healed over.

"Fine," she says, heading to the kitchen for a cup of herbal tea. Her fingers tremble as she tears open the purple packaging and unravels the tea bag. The little paper tab hangs over the ceramic lip.

"What's your fortune?" Jessie says from the couch.

Nelle reads it, and, for the second time this afternoon, feels the prick of tears.

"It says, *Look how far you've come.*"

&

"Bring it out!" someone says from a booth. Before long, everyone in Pinkies, Jessie's ex-lover's bar in Greenwich Village, joins the chant. "Bring it out! Bring it out!"

Candles hang from the thirteen-foot molded ceiling in handblown glass spheres, barely illuminating the maroon and wood decor, the original marble floors, the crowd of people in the tiny establishment. Nelle thinks she hears Jessie and Lena's voices above the others.

"Bring it out! Bring it out!"

Whiskey sour half lifted to his lips, James asks, "Are they all pumping their fists at me?"

They are, definitely, all pumping their fists at him. Nelle feels their supportive energy, but her body flinches at the thunder of voices.

"I think they want you to bring it out," she says.

"Bring *what* out?" He shakes his head slowly. "My manuscript? I left it at home."

Before he can fall into the depths of full-blown panic, a warm orange light swings around, and the people all part to form a path to James and Nelle. Their chant dissolves into cheers, which then fizzle out, too.

Jessie and Lena follow the path, carrying a fully lit cake. As they approach, Nelle sees the words *The Summer Curse by James Finch* in blocky icing. The sides of the cake are decorated with a deckle edge.

"Holy shit," Nelle says. "You guys made this?"

"We did," Lena says.

Jessie doubles over. "All *I* did was sit at the counter and blow motivational kisses."

"It's perfect," James says. Tears fill his eyes, shiny blue pebbles in the candlelight. "Thank you so much, Lena. Jessie. For the party, the cake, for letting us stay with you." Nelle leans into the curve of his shoulder, his fingers on her wrist. "I don't know when, but I'll be back. For good. Don't worry, though, I'll get my own place."

Nelle's pulse thumps into the pad of James's thumb. Where will she be then? With him? Cast aside somewhere? She can't imagine him abandoning her, but she can't force him to stay and write for her forever. Only Quill was willing to do that.

Jessie snivels. "Live with me if you want." She presses her teary lashes into her balled-up sleeve. "I don't care. I love having you here. *Both* of you."

"Okay, okay," James laughs, "but eventually I'll get my own place."

"Sure," Jessie says. "And contrary to what I said about wanting you to stay with me forever, I'm sending you away."

She holds out an envelope. James accepts it like it might explode.

"What did you do?" He hooks his thumb under the paper lip and peels it open. Two tickets slide into his hand.

Nelle reads the blocky text. *JFK To CDG.*

"Is this what I think it is?" James asks hoarsely.

Jessie shrugs.

"Oh my God." He practically falls on her with a lanky bear hug. "Thank you, thank you, thank you."

Nelle squints at the paper with all its unrecognizable abbreviated jargon. "What is it we're thankful for?"

"Don't worry, my vision's shit, too," Lena says, light catching her pearlescent teeth and silver earrings. "I refuse to wear glasses *or* stick my fingers in my eyes. They're tickets to Paris, babe. Your flight leaves tomorrow."

"*My* flight?" Nelle takes in the cake and its crowd of flickering candles, the bar and its crowd of sweaty revelers, the plane tickets clutched like gold in James's fist. Her heart skips.

Lena lifts a Polaroid camera. "Get together. One last picture before you go."

James slinks an arm around Nelle, but his touch doesn't feel right. They are heading off for two more weeks together, and they have barely spoken about what will come afterward. Or even *during*. He hinted that he wanted to kiss her, but it has been weeks since that first night on the rooftop, and he has done *nothing*. She was patient during his writing frenzy, but now with the congratulatory cake in front of her, she wants James's feelings clarified.

She steps away before the photo is taken. "I want you and Jessie in it, too."

Chapter 17

Five years old, inspired for one of the first times in her life, Nelle searched the crayon box for Midnight Blue. She settled for turquoise, leaned as far as she could over the kitchen table in that house on Blackwood Road, and colored in the sky behind the tower. She liked drawing the moon and stars more than the sun, but daytime would do. Blue for the sky and black for the tower. A girl-shaped smudge stood at the top, holding the hand of a man.

"What's that?" asked Father, his voice like snow sluicing off a roof. Dripping down her neck.

Nelle held up her drawing. "It's for you."

He inspects the page. "Where've you seen that before?"

Nelle pointed to the top of the tower. "That's me there, and that's you beside me. See?" Hands trembling, she set the paper back down. "Will you . . ." She paused to twist her ankles, gathering courage. "Will you take me there one day?"

This was one of the unfortunate mornings she encountered Quill's inner monster. He snatched up the drawing, slashing her trust in him alongside her dreams. He may as well have yanked out her heart.

All she could do was squawk in protest as he tore it to pieces, scattering featherlight fragments across the ground. She didn't cry, though she wanted to. She didn't scream, though she was steaming like a kettle. She sat back and faced the fact that she could do absolutely nothing. She couldn't even rise off her chair without his permission.

"You will never see this place." Quill was nearly growling. *"Ever."*

Nelle stared at him, then at the blue and black scraps scattered over the hardwood, and blinked.

"You're the meanest person in the world," she said.

The words must have stung because he locked her in her room and banned her from reading or painting for six months.

ꕥ

Nelle clutches her armrests as the plane shudders.

"After that day, he changed," she says. "The punishments got worse."

James turns from the window, where his favorite city fades beneath the clouds. "No amount of anger justifies that kind of treatment. *Nothing* justifies it."

Nelle shrugs. Talking about her past puts her in a somber mood. "His wife and daughter haunted him."

"Like . . . actually haunted him?" In this new world where women can be created out of ink, who's to say ghosts can't be real, too?

"Metaphorically." The plane shakes again. James takes Nelle's hand, and her fingers dig into his palm. "He created me to fill the void they left behind. I guess what he didn't realize is that, more than he missed them, he was angry that they died. I reminded him of what he'd lost."

Imagining how horrible Quill was to Nelle makes James want to tuck her in a blanket and tell her that she's safe. But is she? Quill found her in DC and again on a random street in New York. James barely slept the night she told him about the encounter, knowing that anywhere they go, Quill is likely lurking behind.

"You're right." Nelle relaxes her grip. "It's not justified, but don't get caught up on it. Look where I'm headed now."

"To Paris." James lifts his airplane-supplied cup of champagne.

Nelle echoes, "To Paris."

ꕥ

The silver waters of the Seine tremble under Nelle's swinging feet. She sits on the cobblestone walkway and takes in the architecture sweeping above her. Across the wide river and the Pont d'léna, past a white yacht, and surrounded by luscious green trees, stands the Eiffel Tower.

Sitting in its shadow is an out-of-body experience, a dream she never imagined would become reality. Sitting here with James is even harder to comprehend. A breeze in his brown hair, the morning sun illuminating his face. The last hour of their flight was nauseating, and they arrived to baggage claim to learn that the airline lost their luggage. James suggested they go with just the clothes on their back, so they left the airport in a taxi and went directly to the Eiffel Tower. Beneath the iron behemoth, people chatter, carrying coffees and lightweight coats.

"Is it everything you thought it'd be?" James asks.

Just like her drawing, the Eiffel Tower is like a spoon swirling the clouds. Iron lacework peaking to stab the blue. The only piece missing is the girl at the top.

"More," she says.

James guides her to her feet and writes for her to follow him toward the bridge. "I thought we could spend the day drinking coffee and browsing bookshops. How does that sound?"

Not for the first time, Nelle has to tackle the urge to slip her fingers in his hair and kiss him, but his voice on the roof in New York rings back to her. *I'm getting tired of waiting*, she thinks.

Another urge follows, surprising her. She used to be fluent in seeing the angles and colors that make up the world. Painting came as natural as breathing, but somewhere over the years, she lost the joy in it. It deteriorated from disuse, but now that she has dipped her brush back in, she sees color in blades of grass, periwinkle clouds, a magenta scarf. They reach the stone steps up to the street and Nelle stops, unable to leave until he writes for her again.

"Thanks for planning the day." She beams up at James as he splays open the journal, scribbles, and her locked bones release. She trails him up the steps, holding his hand. "I also want to buy some art supplies."

"Sure," James says. "You gonna paint while we're here?"

"No, I want to sketch."

James stops an old man and his dog to ask where they can find paper and pens for sale. The man furrows his shaggy gray brows and gesticulates angrily, snapping in French.

"I think he said that way." James points. "Also, not to kill the mood, but the pen is running low on ink."

Nelle touches the spot on her palm where she draws from, tired of breaking her flesh with the fountain pen's dull tip. Quill may be a monster, but he only cut her with the sharpest of blades. She knows better ways to get this done.

The first papeterie they find, a shop with wood-paneled walls and books and knickknacks, has a letter opener for sale beside the counter. And a small pad and art pencils. Two birds, one stone. The uniformed crone at the register glares up through a pair of magnifying spectacles.

While James counts out a handful of euros, Nelle slips off to the toilet with her new knife. She winces at the touch of the tip to her palm. The blade isn't as sharp as a usual knife, so it takes some force to break skin. Still, it works better than the pen nib. Her blood drips to the tiled floor. *I'll get more precise*, she thinks, shuffling to the sink.

Once the pen is refilled, Nelle sticks it in her back pocket and catches a glimpse of herself in the mirror. Her skin has a honeyed touch. Untamed sandy-blond hair frizzling down to her waist. Maybe it's the white blouse James bought her from a boutique called La Maison du Fil, or the thin silver chain hanging daintily on her collarbones, but for the first time in her life, she is happy with her appearance. Or maybe, for the first time in her life, she is just happy.

She ducks out of the bathroom and scans the empty papeterie for James before her feet carry her out the front door. Narrow Rue Raynouard is framed by gorgeous Parisian architecture, balconies and windows covering stone facades down the street. Cars slink along the sidewalk, bumper to bumper, until they curve out of sight.

James appears like a mirage, leaning on a lamppost, holding a bouquet of flowers wrapped in a green ribbon. He flourishes the bouquet with a balanced bow.

"For you, my lady."

Nelle runs the scarlet petals under her fingers. "I've never seen flowers up close. Quill didn't have them in the house. Other than the roses on my wallpaper. What are these called?"

"Dahlias," James says.

Struck by their smell, she brings them closer. Not perfumy, but wet dirt, still morning air, and a mystery note, distinctly plantlike. Both repulsive and wonderful.

"It's what I want to name my daughter one day," he says. "Dahlia."

She looks up from the flowers, taking him in. "Really?"

"Yeah." He clears his throat. "Since I was sixteen."

Nelle lifts on her toes to press her lips to James's cheek, her heart swollen with feeling. He will make such a better father than Quill, but it will never be with her. She can't get pregnant, has never even had a period. Quill taught her about them when she was eleven but told her she wouldn't be affected. Created as she was, she can't reproduce.

James turns around to write in the journal.

She peers over his shoulder. "What is it?"

"Do you trust me?" His pen hesitates. "I thought our next destination could be a surprise."

Nelle softens. She *does* trust him. "Lead the way."

James takes her down the lamppost-lined street as evening burns.

Eyes closed, Nelle feels a magical string tug from her chest, reminding her of her lack of autonomy. Despite her dependence on James, she doesn't feel like she did with Quill. Not constricted, even if her movements are predetermined. Even if, *still*, she has no true free will.

She spends the next half hour tripping over the back of James's feet.

"Okay," he says, "some stairs coming up here."

After a few minutes ascending, Nelle's calves are burning.

"Just a few more," James assures her. "Okay, stand here."

Balmy air caresses her cheeks as he steadies her shoulders.

Nelle plants her feet and hears the chatter of people around her, their words lost in the wind.

"Now," James says, his breath hitting the fleshy shell of her ear. "Open them."

Yellow and pink clouds bulge across the sky like cotton candy. The streets and alleyways of Paris stretch out in all directions, a sea of white stone, curved roofs, and chimney smoke. Below, the Champ de Mars spreads out like a green lake. Behind Nelle, the Seine mirrors the sky, only grayer.

Atop the tower with them, people are taking pictures, laughing, kissing.

Unable to contain the emotion blooming in her like dahlias, Nelle feels hot tears spill down her cheeks. After Quill tore her drawing to pieces, she never let herself dream of this. Nearly a thousand feet high, atop the Eiffel Tower, leaning out over the world. Her chest seizes, and she laughs, still crying. James's hand finds hers. Their fingers intertwine, knuckles locking like puzzle pieces.

"It's beautiful," he says, watching her.

Nelle takes in the city putting on its nighttime attire. Shops closing up. Bars opening doors. Music getting louder and lights brighter. To the west, the sun sets.

~

Nelle soaks in Paris with watery eyes, her lips parting, rosy with gloss. Back in the airport, James wrote for her to explore a beauty store—Jessie's friends inspired her to try makeup. She came back with a single tube of lip gloss and James with a new book. When Nelle saw the cover, her face dropped. *Ravel* by Wallace Quill. They are both haunted, and being hunted, by Quill. James at least has to know if their stalker is a good writer, or if Quill only wrote one good thing in his miserable life: a woman made of laughter and fire and ink.

Even in James's lightest moments, the book in his back pocket weighs him down.

He shoves Quill from his thoughts and steps closer to Nelle. "Do you think this is the right moment?"

That breaks her trance. Nelle's hand trails up his shirt.

"Every moment's been right enough for me," she says.

The inch between them disappears. Feather soft, a breath passes back and forth. Nelle lets out a little half gasp, half moan, and James is undone. Crushes his lips against hers. Tastes the salt of tears on her tongue as it flickers against his. His hand curves up her back, fingers entangled in her hair. He dissolves into this kiss—into her—until time ceases. He doesn't care how many people are around. If they can't full-on make out atop the Eiffel Tower, then what's the city of love for?

❧

Nelle nearly dies a little death. So *this* is kissing. Her internal organs become hot goo as James grips her hip, fingers digging in. His kiss is gentle but strong, and his mouth tastes like coffee and mint. She is on the beach again, watching the waves crash, losing track of time.

He breaks away, lips swollen, cheeks flushed gold in the setting sunlight.

Nelle holds the back of his neck, his curls like satin between her fingers. She wants to taste him again, to put her mouth all over his precious little face.

"Do you want to know a secret?" James asks, his voice low.

She rises on tiptoe, bumps the tip of her nose to his. "What?"

The corner of his mouth lifts, dimple creasing. "You're my best friend."

Nelle's heart sizzles. "You're *my* best friend."

He runs the pad of his thumb over her brow, down her temple, to her ear, his brown hair mussed from her fingers. "Do you want to kiss again?"

"I fear . . ." She moves closer, until she can taste his breath. "That I may never want to stop."

ℴ

After they stepped into the hotel room, Nelle kissed James good night and crashed. Now he sits on the bed beside her, unsure whether she is still awake or if she actually snapped into unconsciousness that fast.

"Nelle?"

"Hmm."

"If you're going to sleep, would you be okay with me going downstairs to see if there's a computer I can use?"

"Sure," she murmurs. "Have fun. Watch for Quill."

He dips down and kisses the warm pulse of her temple. "Good night."

Four floors down, the hotel business center turns out to be a glorified closet off the lobby, crammed with three dinosaur computers. Through the wall, he can hear the concierge arguing with the guests. The overhead light is out, so once the computer boots on after three minutes of low humming, James sits in the dark in front of a shaky electronic glow. He signs in to his student account, the keyboard gentle and foreign after weeks of using a manual typewriter.

Five unanswered emails ask him to pay his fall fees. Two of his upcoming professors have already sent out their syllabi. He takes a deep breath. Upstairs, Nelle is asleep, oblivious to his inner turmoil. Ten days until the fall semester starts. The two months he has known Nelle have felt like two days. What will the next ten feel like? A minute?

A few poems spring to mind, all about making choices, none of them helpful. He knows which path will make him happiest *right now*, but who knows how he will feel in seven years. Still, the old James would gawk at where he's standing now. The decision before him, so far beyond simply adding another major. Return to hell, or to keep flying with Nelle?

Fingers trembling like twigs in a rainstorm, James logs in to his account and withdraws from all his classes. He sends the school an email informing them that he will be dropping out for a semester, but that he hopes to join them in the spring. It's a lie, something to soften the blow. He will never go back.

He logs out and shuts down the computer. For a few minutes, he sits in the quiet darkness of the lobby. How long has he been drowning in the quicksand of school, knowing that his time with Nelle would then end prematurely? Now it's clear: he doesn't want to go back to no friends and endless studying. Yes, money will be an issue eventually, but Jessie's gifted plane tickets bought them at least a few weeks. A month if he's frugal. And afterward, he envisions a life in New York, working to rent his own place. Maybe a place he can share with a certain ink-bleeding girl.

He goes back to the hotel room, clicks on the lamp, and sits at the edge of the bed. Watching Nelle sleep soothes him. The breath flowing in and out of her parted lips, hair stuck to her forehead with sweat. A subtle reminder that although her origin is unusual, she is real.

Her dahlias, tinged with brown decay, sit on the table beside the king-size bed. James kicks off his shoes and, swearing to start pinching his pennies tomorrow, orders a room-service burger. A sense of calm settles over him. Finally, he feels weightless.

He doesn't remember falling asleep, but when he wakes to pale morning light and an uneaten burger outside the door, he comes back to bed and whispers to Nelle. She doesn't stir. He rubs her shoulder for a minute or two before she squints angrily at the light.

"Is it morning?" she groans.

"Yes," he says. "And I have good news."

She sits up against the headboard, hair frizzy. "Why are you this perky without any coffee?"

"I'm no longer a student," he says.

Nelle blinks. "You're no longer . . . what?"

"I unenrolled. We can keep traveling, no time restrictions."

"Jessie's gonna kill you."

She's shaking her head. *Why is she shaking her head?*

"What about your career?" Nelle asks.

"I told you, I don't *want* to be a doctor, and Jessie will be okay. She will understand, especially when I tell her—"

"Your mom? Your dad?"

"They'll be all right, too. This isn't about them, it's about me. It's about us."

"Are you sure?" Nelle asks. "You don't have to drop out. We can go back now. You can go to school next week, and I'll—"

"It's already done," James says. He adds, with real confidence, "I know I made the right decision."

Nelle's worried face cracks. "Really? So this means you want to keep traveling the world with me?"

He stands and holds out his hand. "Coffee first, then the world."

Yet he can't ignore the sinking in his stomach. Part attraction, part warning. It is the feeling of tumbling through the unknown and having a blast while doing it. But as with all free falls, the landing will be rough. He dreads having to tell Nelle the truth. His money won't last forever, and at the end of this rainbow, he wants to stay in New York.

Chapter 18

Legs sore from the twelve-hour southbound train, James relishes the walk from Nice's city center to the Plage de la Réserve. He follows a staircase down to the pebble beach, seawater stinging his nose. Nelle's white cover-up billows off as she hops over scorching pebbles to the aquamarine shallows.

Without warning, James bolts to the water, Nelle's laughter trailing him like popping bubbles. He barrels into a wave, spray splashing cold on his chest, salt on his lips. When he turns around, Nelle is gone. He scans the crowded beach for her, but he definitely heard her running after him. His heart races, jumping from thought to thought, bouncing back and forth between the beach and the water. Suddenly, the roiling waves are menacing as they swell and sweep into the ocean. The undercurrent's fingers curl around his ankles.

He's about to dive under to search when Nelle shatters the surface wearing a pearly grin. James tries to hide his panic as she grabs on to him, laughing, her hair wet and slicked to her neck.

"I've never swam in the ocean before. It's so . . ." Nelle licks her lips. "I knew it was salt water, but I never knew you could *taste* the salt."

James's panic eases like the shifting tide. *This* is why he loves traveling with Nelle. Everywhere they go, every experience, is new to her. New car, new road, new city, new food, new views, shiny new seawater. Every time she is awed by something James finds mundane, he steps back and appreciates that thing anew, and in that moment of disassociation, he realizes: *Yes, it* is *incredible that you can taste the salt in the ocean. It* is *incredible that I am on a beach on the French Riviera with the girl I love.*

He freezes, repeating his own thought back to himself while Nelle dolphin-dives in and out of waves.

The girl I love?

She wades to him and wraps her arms around his neck, dragging him down to her level, chin-deep in the water. His toes dig into the rocks and sand as she fits her body to his, soft in places he is embarrassingly hard.

Her eyes widen. "Is that . . . ?"

Fire engulfs his cheeks. "I'm sorry, I—"

"You don't have to be sorry." She shifts against him, and for a split second, he worries he's going to come in his swimsuit.

"Your freckles are starting to show more," he points out.

Nelle squints down at her nose, searching. "Do you like them?"

"Love them," he says, testing the word. It flies out effortlessly.

She laughs, a sound like silver wind chimes.

"Thank you for bringing me here," she says.

"Thank Jessie, not me." His chest tightens with the need to say three specific words to her. It feels like a lie to keep them in. He needs to know whether she feels the same way. Whether she, too, needs to wrap her arms around him and never let him go, to know how his skin feels under her tongue, to study him like a poem so she can remember the lines of him forever.

"James," Nelle says, her lips a shivering inch from his. She takes on a serious tone. "I need to do something, but I don't know where to go."

He bobs in the water. "Whatever it is, do it here."

She shakes her head. "I *can't*."

"Why not?"

"Because . . ." She drops her voice. "Because I need to pee."

"I feel dirty." Nelle climbs out of the water and finds refuge on her towel. She folds herself on the red-and-blue striped rectangle and hugs her wet legs, craving a scalding shower.

"It's completely normal." James picks up *Ravel*, bookmarked halfway. "Everyone does it."

"Everyone does *not* pee on themselves."

He glances up from his page. "It's not really peeing on yourself if the water is cleaning you off while you do it."

"Would you clean yourself off in the ocean any other time?"

"Well . . . no."

"My point proven." Nelle picks up her own book, a mystery. "You wouldn't, because it wouldn't clean you at all. There are probably urine particles on my legs right now. Still inside my bikini, too."

At the mention of her bikini, James's cheeks go apple red.

Nelle's lips become the south pole to his north, aching to connect. Heat swells behind her pelvis.

"Think of it this way." He nudges his book against her stretched legs. Not even skin-on-skin contact, but it sets her aflame. "Peeing in the ocean is yet another new experience."

When he returns to his book, his hair hangs over his dense eyebrows. A droplet of seawater slides down his temple, his chin, and he wipes it away with the back of his hand.

Nelle runs her fingers through his wet, silken brown hair. Almost black. Touching him is the most exhilarating thing she has ever done, more than traversing New York, more than tasting salt in the sea, more than leaving Quill. Somewhere in her chest, a dam breaks, releasing a deluge of golden magma. She wants this feeling to bury both her and James, to hold them there forever, hardening under her lava.

Nelle has been alive for twenty-one years. Between the Technicolor men on the boxy TV she used to sit cross-legged in front of and the men in the pages of her books, she has grown familiar with her sexuality. But she has never felt this before. This pining, more powerful than lust. It is new, electrifying, and the moment she feels it, she knows what to call it.

She never felt love with Quill. Only fear. What she has with James is freedom. It's an old country road, laughing late at night, drinking coffee, kissing in the sea.

"Why'd you do that?" He touches above his ear, where she ran her fingers to the nape of his neck.

Nelle sucks in a breath, winded by her own epiphany, and lets out the easiest words she has ever said. "I love you."

James opens his mouth like he's going to respond, then shuts it. He bridges the space between their towels and kisses her. Sunbaked salt. The flick of his tongue and the seam of her opening lips. Wetness and his hands finding her waist, holding her in place.

He hums against her mouth. "I love you, too."

❧

The bus from the beach rattles as its six wheels hit potholes like they are picking guitar strings. James sways in his seat and traces circles over the back of Nelle's hand. His clothes scratch his reddened skin, and he smells of sand and sunscreen, but he doesn't care. He is in France. In France with Nelle.

And, since the night he dropped out of school in Paris, he has been keeping a surprise up his sleeve. Well, actually up his pants.

James unravels his fingers from Nelle's, digs into his pocket, and pulls out an envelope. When he made the decision to buy the tickets, he knew exactly where *he* wanted to travel to, a place where, coincidentally, Nelle likely has living relatives. Still, he doubted his choice, banking solely on Nelle loving anywhere she has yet to go. He unfolds the crackling envelope, passes it over, and waits a minute for her to open it, pull out the slips of paper, process what they are. Silence stretches between them like a heavy rope.

Nelle squeals.

Train tickets to Edinburgh, leaving tomorrow. They dented James's dwindling savings account, but he still has enough for a couple of weeks of frugal travel and plane tickets home. Enough to give Nelle a fortnight of freedom, and then what? What *is* his home? Without college tying him down to his old life in Georgia, he can go anywhere. Be anyone.

New York whispers in the back of his mind like a drug. *Come back.*

Nelle kisses his cheek, his temple, his neck. "I love you, I love you, I love you."

Chapter 19

Windmills stand sentinel across green pastures sliding by out the window. The fields resemble the squares of a quilt, stitched together by seams of low stone walls. Sheep cluster under a gray sky. All of it puts James under the illusion that he is living a past life. A life without social media and technology. A fantasy world where he can fall in love with the girl sleeping on his shoulder.

He resumes reading. The train rattles, and Nelle's head slips off his shoulder.

She snorts awake, squinting at him in confusion.

"Where are we?" Two blond hairs are pasted to her cheek by a line of drool.

James wipes it away with his sleeve. "We should be getting close to Edinburgh now. You were sleeping pretty hard."

"I was dreaming about a story Quill told me." She yawns and stretches, oddly catlike. "You know he grew up here?"

"Yeah. His accent gave him away."

She laughs. "I'm not sure where in Scotland he's from, though."

"Do you feel comfortable sharing it?" James asks. "The story?"

Nelle taps the window as if putting in a code to unlock her memory. "He grew up in a cottage. I think farther north."

James sinks down into the train seat. Across the aisle, a middle-aged woman with a sleeping baby shoots them a dirty look.

Nelle whispers, "He had a brother, Sam. Their family didn't have much money, so during winter when they couldn't afford gas, their mother would make Quill and Sam a pallet in front of the stove."

"So he wasn't *raised* by a monster," James says. "He just became one."

"It's no excuse for how he treated me." Nelle traces circles on the thigh of her tan pants. "But he dealt with a lot of loss in his life."

"Oh." A pit opens in James's stomach. "This story has a sad ending, doesn't it?"

"*Listen* and you'll find out," she says. "Quill's mother, Lily, adored words. In her free time, when she wasn't taking care of the house or putting together scraps to feed them, she'd analyze literature and write poetry. She had a few collections published. Quill kept copies in his study, but he never let me read them. Anyway, when Quill was lucky, his mother would sit him on her lap and read to him. Old myths and folklore. He claimed his passion for stories bloomed in those misty highlands where every moor was a blood-soaked battlefield, every forest a fairy kingdom.

"His father, Thomas, was a carpenter from the States. He had a close relationship with Sam, his younger son. Would ask him to come to work with him, chop wood behind the house, or feed the livestock. But he never asked Quill. As the years went on, it became an unspoken rule: Quill belonged to Lily, Sam to Thomas. When he asked his mother *why* his father hated him, she assured him that Thomas merely showed his love in strange ways. Quill knew it was bullshit, though. He saw the way Sam was treated. He saw through Lily's delusions. His father didn't love her, and somewhere along the way, he'd stopped loving Quill, too."

"Damn." James purses his lips. "So that's why he's an asshole."

"That"—Nelle nods—"among other things. Story's not over. On one of those harsh winter days when the loch beside the cottage was frozen over, Sam and Quill went out to skate. Quill threw a rock across the loch, testing the ice's stability. It bounced and skidded across. Safe for skating. So they went out. Quill said he felt like a bird, his arms spread wide. About an hour later, face red and wind chapped, Quill heard a sound that would haunt him for years. The groan of continents wrenching apart. The ice under Sam caved in, and Quill had to watch as his little brother fell into the water. He saw Sam's hand pop above the ice, his face frozen in a scream, then he was gone. Maybe taken by a creature, possibly shocked by the cold. Quill never found out."

Nelle picks at a thread in her shirtsleeve.

"Leaving didn't seem like an option—what if Sam resurfaced and needed his help climbing up?—so Quill screamed for their parents until his voice gave out. Jumping in after Sam didn't cross his mind. That water was death. When Quill eventually returned to the cottage, he told his mother that Sam was dead. She didn't cry. When his father came home, tired and sweaty, she broke the news to him. Quill stood behind her. His father dropped to his knees in the doorway. It was the first time he'd ever cried in front of them. And Quill hated it. The *last* time he saw his father cry was a year later, at his mother's funeral. On that awful day, he remembered thinking that maybe, *maybe*, his father really did love her, somewhere beneath his own layers of ice.

"A week later, Thomas claimed he had nothing to live for in Scotland anymore, so he moved them to Georgia, where he had family. *Living* family. Quill never saw that cottage again, nor the lake that would forever serve as Sam Quill's grave."

James blinks as he processes all this. "That's an awful story to tell a child."

"Quill didn't talk to me like a child. Unless he was being condescending." Nelle watches out the window at the stone city rushing past. "He's a twisted man, but I know he wanted me to understand why he did what he did. Why he was who he was to me. But it still makes me wonder why he told me about the cottage. Why I'm dreaming about it now. When he found me in DC, he said he saw me in a dream. What if I'm supposed to find the cottage? What if he meant for me to?"

The cold determination in Nelle's jaw makes James's stomach drop.

"He never told me any other stories about his childhood. *Nothing.* Think about it . . . why would he have given me a birth certificate? A *passport*?"

James doesn't believe that a man who only allowed Nelle out of the house a handful of times in twenty-one years would *ever* send her alone on a scavenger hunt through Scotland.

"I can't explain it." She sits up straighter. "It's just a feeling I have. I'm supposed to find this cottage. That's all I know."

James sighs. In the short time he has known Nelle, has she given him a reason not to trust her gut? If she wants to dance on a roof in a thunderstorm, they do it. If she is ready to leave New York, they do it. If she wants to track down her dad-captor's childhood home, then damn it . . .

He gives Nelle's hand a supportive squeeze. "Let's do it."

Chapter 20

As the train eases to a stop and the doors slide open, James writes for Nelle in the leather journal. She notes that he is carrying the blue backpack they purchased in Paris, stuffed full with their clothes, as she follows him off the train into the heart of the station. Edinburgh Waverley is a mammoth of concrete and glass and people milling in all directions. Nelle looks through the ceiling at the overcast sky as they weave through the whirlwind of families and suitcases. Sharp, heavenly espresso hits her nose, but she doesn't suggest they stop.

For the first time in weeks, something takes precedence over caffeine.

The cottage in the mists of her mind, hovering like a bad memory. A stony house on a hill. Flagstones crisscrossing up to the stoop. A lantern hanging from a post, a ring of gold light. Footprints in the snow. A lake, as clear as a mirror, undisturbed behind it.

When she woke on the train, she knew she had to find it. As natural a need as her next breath. She hoped that telling the story to James might help her understand *why* she woke up with this powerful instinct, but reliving Quill's past only soured her mood. On top of that, she can sense James's skepticism through his optimistic acquiescence, and she can't even blame him.

Out on the street, they blink at the dull evening. The road is lined with gray sandstone and limestone buildings, detailed with touches of medieval and Victorian architecture, crowstepped gables and palatial turrets.

"Where's the best place to start our search?" Nelle asks.

James stands like a pillar among the people entering and exiting the station.

"A library."

They walk farther into the city, people drinking at sidewalk tables, smoking cigarettes over dinner. With every pub they pass, Nelle's stomach growls. The meaty, starchy, homey smells pouring out of the old oak doors whisper to her, but James leads them confidently, and if he can help them find the cottage, she isn't going to suggest a pit stop to refill her stomach.

A cool, wet wind cuts through Nelle's sweater.

"How's that one?" She points to a granite building, *National Library of Scotland* in silver across its facade and a stone-worked Royal Arms over the entrance.

"Almost too perfect." He writes in the journal, and they dive into the sprawling, well-lit complex.

Historical artifacts line display cases between shelves upon shelves of books. People putter past, speaking low. James leads her, speed walking through the fiction section. She has never seen so many novels in one place. Thousands of worlds awaiting her visit, a treasure trove under one roof.

James finds a desktop computer and starts typing. "What was Quill's middle name?"

"Jeremiah." Nelle pulls up a chair. "Wallace Jeremiah Quill."

James types the name in, and thousands of links appear. Headlines about Wallace Quill and his bestselling debut novel, outselling some of the big-name authors of the year. Announcements for film options that never came to fruition. Die-hard fans theorizing about why Quill suddenly disappeared from the publishing world, never releasing another book.

Nelle knows why. He stopped writing after her accidental conception, at least for publication. Is it possible that he feared creating something, or someone, else?

She points at an article. "'Wallace Quill Sells His Soul to the Devil' is a funny headline, but not helpful. Nothing here connects him to the cottage. He never talked about his childhood."

James scrolls through an interview. Another. All surface-level questions with surface-level answers. Nothing about Quill's past, where he grew up, his family, his love life. Nothing. Half an hour passes, then a full hour. James huffs and brushes back a wayward hair.

"It's getting late." Nelle squeezes his shoulder. "Maybe we should find a hotel."

James's blue eyes snag on the screen, confusion and intrigue crossing his face. Nelle has begun to understand his expressions like a secret language.

"What is it?"

"I'm on a message board about *Ravel* and this guy says he knew Quill when he was a kid." James poises his fingers over the keyboard, then starts typing rapid-fire.

"What are you doing?" She marvels at the speed of James's fingers as they fly across the keys. His nails are clean and short, and she can't help imagining where else they might be put to good use.

"I'm replying to him. Asking if he's local so we can meet up and ask about Quill."

"We can't randomly invite him to meet us, right? We're two strangers. We need a reason."

"Aren't you supposed to be the one without any social training?"

"I'm a fast learner."

He pounces on the keyboard. "We're writing his obituary, and we need as much personal information as we can get. I'll add that, uh, he's an A-list celebrity in our town."

"But Quill's alive," Nelle says.

"This guy doesn't have to know that," James says. "We can ask him more specific questions about Quill's childhood, his upbringing, *where* he grew up."

"Seems risky. And wrong."

"I never claimed to be right."

He finishes crafting their lie and hits "Send."

"What if he doesn't respond?"

"We'll come back tomorrow," James says. "Or use the hotel computer. However long it takes."

"Thank you. There's still one little problem." *We don't have a hotel.*

His hand falls to her waist, finger through her belt loop. "What is it? Oh, shit. Is it your period? We can stop at a pharmacy—"

"James, James, stop." Nelle puts her hands on his arms. "I don't have a menstrual cycle. I don't . . . I can't . . . reproduce."

He blinks, processing.

She scratches her arm, trying to decipher his reaction. *I do* not *need to stress about this right now*, she tells herself as her stomach goes ice cold. She only wanted to ease his cute, momentary concern, give them something to laugh about. She considers saying, *It's okay; we can adopt*, but she settles on pushing the subject aside entirely.

"The problem is that we don't have a hotel yet."

James recovers fast. "I think we can solve that."

~

Nelle studies the boring, smooth hotel ceiling. Twilight bleeds through the curtains. Scotland doesn't get dark until midnight during the summer. She tries to sleep on top of the comforter, annoyed by the suffocating blankets. James's soft snores are the only sound in the room, aside from the clock above the door. Outside is an occasional voice or burst of bird caws.

When her life was confined to a bedroom with rose-printed wallpaper, she never felt this, but since she left, storm clouds brew over her heart every time she settles in one spot. They have barely been in Edinburgh for a day, and she is already anxious to move on. Maybe scared that her past will catch up to her.

That *Quill* will catch up to her.

She wants to see Japan and Morocco and Fiji, every continent and island, only now a roadblock stands in her way. The cottage.

Her gut instinct practically *demands* she find it. As primal a need as eating, and it's only intensifying. Was the dream sent to her by Quill, or by some higher power connecting them? If he orchestrated this, then she could be heading into a trap. But her need to find the cottage doesn't feel ominous. It feels . . . right. Her skin itches thinking about it.

She flips her pillow, uncomfortable but content to watch James sleep. His rigid jaw and nose. His fluttering lashes. That one piece of hair that falls away from the rest.

Nelle pushes it back. At least one of them will be well rested in the morning.

A car honks in the street, and James is back in New York. He stirs awake, thinking about his novel, the characters he created, the life he left behind. He sits up and the moment shatters. He's in Edinburgh. Nelle is asleep on top of the blankets, her brows drawn together, a deep crease between them.

He kisses her forehead and her freckled cheek, writes a note to let her know he will be back in fifteen, grabs his coat, and ducks out into the drizzly morning. He finds a coffee shop down the street filled with people going to their early jobs and jogs.

He returns to the hotel room bearing two hot lattes and a blueberry muffin.

Surprisingly, it only takes him touching Nelle's shoulder to wake her. Normally, that is only the first step in a ten-minute routine to drag her from sleep. She blinks at him, like she does every morning, as if unsure whether he's part of her dream or reality.

"Coffee is served, Your Highness." He bows his head.

"Your *Highness*?" she mutters, always a bit cross when she wakes. "What is that about?"

James kisses her forehead, wrinkled with sleepy annoyance.

"Because," he says, "you're my princess."

"That'd make you my . . ." She tilts her head, hair mussed. "Servant."

He climbs off the bed before he ends up kissing her all morning, picking up the blue backpack. They have other things to do today.

Nelle sits up. "And where are you going, servant?"

"If Your Highness permits it, I'm taking a shower. Once I'm clean, we can shop for clothes and check on our lead."

"Hmm, maybe library first, shop second?"

James catches a glimpse of her as he steps toward the bathroom. Cross-legged on the bed in her little shorts, thighs tanned from the beach in Nice, hands wrapped around a hot coffee.

He stops and gives a short bow. "As you wish."

❧

James logs onto the library computer. A red dot alerts him of a notification.

"He responded."

Nelle nervously picks her nails, leaning over James's shoulder. "I could shit myself right now."

"Whatever the response is, it's okay," he says. "We'll find the cottage."

"No matter how long it takes." She pulls her chair in closer.

James bites his tongue. They *do* have a time limit, ticking down with every dollar they spend. His savings are half of what they were, and most of what remains he has put aside for plane tickets back to the States.

He clicks on the private message, ears thrumming as he reads.

> TerryNolan1981: Hi, I did know Wallace Quill when we were children. I'm very sorry to hear that he's passed away. I'm sure his obituary will be in good hands with you. He was a friend to me when we were

> boys. I can try to answer whatever questions you have, though I'm not sure how much help I'll be. I live in Edinburgh, so if you're ever in town, we can meet up for lunch and a chat. Thanks for getting in contact. —Terry.

James drafts a message asking how soon they can meet, emphasizing that they are available today. Nelle reviews the response and presses "Send."

While they wait, James taps the mouse in time with a beat in his mind. Nelle paces, weaving her long blond strands into a braid. James refreshes the page.

"I can't stand waiting," she says. "I need to distract myself."

"We're sitting inside a haven of distraction," James says. "Go ahead, wander around. I'll wait here."

Per the journal's instructions, Nelle has free rein of the library. She beams as she vanishes into the bookshelves.

James closes out of the messages tab, leaving an empty search bar. A blinking, taunting cursor. Without thinking, he types *New York City.* He scans through apartment listings, jumping through street views, noting cafés and bars and bookstores he wants to visit.

Another search. *New York University.* He scours the university's website for the creative writing program. The deadline for undergraduate transfer applications isn't until the end of September. He has the rest of the month to decide.

James starts an application.

An hour later, he has submitted his SAT scores, resumé, and impromptu essay responses. He feels guilty for not telling Nelle, but he doesn't have to talk to her yet about the possibility of returning to New York. He can bring it up after they find the cottage. *I'm thinking too far ahead.* Right now, he doesn't even know if he will be admitted. And if he is, he might not even *enroll.*

He closes out of the New York tabs. The damage is done. Application sent.

He opens the previous message board and freezes. There is a tiny red dot.

> How's tomorrow at noon? I'll message you café details in the morning. Cheers. —Terry.

Every thought of New York drops out of James's head. He opens his mouth to yell out Nelle's name, remembers where he is, and stops himself short. He retreats to the keyboard.

> Sounds great! See you there. —James.

Chapter 21

Walking to the café, the butterflies in Nelle's stomach turn into hawks, growing talons that yank her intestines like loose threads. The red nylon hood of her new coat is pulled over her head, halving her view of the rain-soaked street. Cars slosh water onto the curbs, steam floats off the concrete, heavy-duty rain boots shuffle on the sidewalk. Finding Quill's childhood cottage could easily be a fool's journey, but she's not ready to face that possibility. If this lead ends up a dead end, who is to say she will find another?

"It should be around here somewhere." James holds up a map of Edinburgh, wet from the rain and crumpled from his back pocket. "He said it was called the Underground Café."

Nelle squints through the misty drizzle. In this part of New Town, every building is tan and rectangular and smooshed up to the others in rows. Picturesque, with window boxes full of wet flowers and ivy hanging off trellises.

"Let me see the map," she says. "You probably took us down a wrong—"

"No, it's right here." He pauses beside a building with a hot-pink sign on the window that says Eye Care.

Nelle peers up. "I don't think this is it."

He points. "Down there."

She follows his finger to a descending staircase at the base of the building.

Hence the name, genius.

James takes out the journal and scribbles, and Nelle follows him down into the belly of the building, steadying herself on the cold iron railing. At the bottom of the staircase, yellow light glows through the window of a blue door.

The Underground Café is all wood tables and warm, cushiony booths. A few patrons are scattered across the establishment, though most of the tables are empty. Along the back wall is a long, lacquered coffee bar with a silver espresso machine atop it. Behind the bar, hundreds of mugs hang on hooks. The walls are exposed brick, decorated with colorful surrealist art. Nelle is captivated by a painting of a red sky over a glass tower. It reminds her of New York.

They find a back corner booth, the lantern over the table catching them in its honey glow.

A waitress comes by. "How can I help you today?"

James taps the table absentmindedly. "We're meeting a friend. Any chance you know a Terry Nolan?"

The waitress's smile vanishes and she screams, *"Terry!"*

A head pops up behind the coffee bar. A wiry man with a thick red beard holds an espresso shot with his long fingers.

His brows twitch. "Yes, dear?"

"Visitors," the waitress says in a knife-sharp tone. She plasters back on her smile. "I'll bring your menus."

Nelle reaches under the table for James's hand, grateful to be sitting on the same side of the booth.

Terry downs the espresso shot in one swallow, shivers, and circles the bar. He removes his apron and folds it as he walks, tucking it in the back pocket of his khakis before he slides into the booth across from Nelle and James.

Her heart pounds as James sticks out his hand. "Hi, I'm James Finch, and this is my, uh, associate, Nelle . . . Finch."

She blushes. *What's the implication there?* she wants to ask. *That we're siblings, cousins, or married?*

Terry lifts a dust-red brow, his eyes like blue lagoons. "Young for reporters."

An observation, not a question.

"We're actually aspiring reporters," James says. "Wallace was my distant cousin. When I heard about his passing, I took it upon myself to write his obituary, seeing as he has no immediate family."

"Ah, yes," Terry kneads his hands on the table. Nelle's chest seizes . . . is he going to buy it?

"I was sad to hear about his passing. It's been so long since he was in the media. I heard about what happened to his wife and daughter all those years ago, though. Tragic stuff."

Nelle tenses. She pulls a miniature yellow legal pad and a normal pen from her coat pocket, ready to take notes, to distract herself from thinking about Quill and the lovely family he had before she came around. The daughter he devoted his life to doting over.

"He wrote one hell of a book, though," Terry says.

James clears his throat. "I want to ask you a few questions, if that's all right. Whatever you remember about Quill—Wallace."

Terry blinks at the quick turn of the conversation. Even Nelle is taken aback. Of course they want answers from Terry, but he won't give them valuable information if he is uncomfortable with them. She places a hand on James's thigh, smooths it down to his knee, a signal she hopes conveys, *Chill out.*

Advice she should probably take herself. Her hummingbird heart hasn't stopped since they left the hotel this morning.

James sweeps in, "Sorry for my curtness. It's only that, well, the paper printing his obituary wants it done as soon as possible."

Terry shrugs. "Sure, I get it. Deadlines."

The waitress returns, and Nelle lifts up her head, hoping to quench the grumble in her stomach.

But Terry waves her away. "No time for food, they're in a hurry. Three coffees should suffice."

Nelle's shoulders sag. Her stomach might start eating itself soon, but at least she will get coffee.

"Ask away," Terry says.

She poises to take notes.

"How did you know Quill?" James asks.

"We were boys together." Terry's voice scratches like sandpaper.

"Where?"

"Scourie," Terry says in a tone indicating that James should already know that.

Nelle scribbles on the legal pad to disguise her nerves as the drinks arrive in red mugs, the same bright scarlet as her coat.

"Oh right, you're from Wallace's dad's side," Terry says. "American. Scourie is this little village on the northwest coast. We went to school together as lads. Wallace was my only friend, really."

"How much time did you two spend together?"

"Every afternoon we'd swim in the pond behind his house, play with the animals, climb trees. Anything to pass the time after school. Quill was always reading, though I didn't care for books much, or learning at all, to be honest, so he didn't really read much around me."

"You went to his house a lot?"

Nelle stiffens. *This is it.*

"Sure," Terry says. "His folks were a little strange. His da, Thomas, was American, no offense, and always gone. Lily, his ma, usually had her nose stuck in a book, though sometimes she'd smoke pot out on the patio. But it meant we got away with anything, really. Little Sammy, bless his soul, would follow us around everywhere. He wanted to be like the big kids."

"You knew Sam, too?"

Terry sighs. "Devastating stuff. Sammy and their mother buried not even a year apart. Though Sammy's grave is more for memory's sake, innit. They never did find his body, even after the ice cleared."

"We'd like to see where Wallace grew up. We think it'll help us feel more connected to him as we write."

Terry sips his coffee. "Naturally."

Nelle's heart screams with anticipation. *Tell us where it is!* Her face feels hot, but she keeps her cool, glued to her pad as she writes every word Terry says.

"But . . ." Terry lets out a long, wistful sigh before he drops the bomb. "You can't. Just before I moved to Edinburgh, the house burned down."

Nelle's heart falls through her rib cage, hits every bony rung, and splatters in her stomach.

"It . . . burned down?" She can't feel her face or her hands or her feet. "Completely?"

"The chimney's still standing." Another sip, then Terry wipes his red mustache on a cloth napkin.

"Oh." James stares in shock.

Nelle can't stand it. She needs to excuse herself to cry, to remind herself that it's okay, that she doesn't *need* to go to the cottage. That this pressing compulsion is an illusion she conjured in her head.

But it isn't. It's as real as she is.

She swallows and taps James's leg under the table, trying to get his attention. She needs to leave, and he needs to write for her to do that. If she stays here another minute, she is going to burst into rage tears. Her pokes turn frustrated. If she goes any harder, Terry will notice her odd convulsions under the table.

But James is still staring at Terry, ignoring her. He pulls out his map of Edinburgh, flips it over, and flattens it out. On the back is a map of Scotland.

"Show me how to get to Scourie," he says, ever the man on a mission. "Nelle, your pen?"

She passes it over—not the one filled with her ink—and Terry draws a jagged line northwest into the highlands, following a major road. Then he veers off toward the coast, where he sketches a small star.

In the corner of the map, he writes out a phone number. "If you have any other questions, I'm always happy to answer." He slides the map across the table. “Good luck to you both. I’m truly sorry for your loss.”

“Thank you,” James says as Terry walks away, tying his apron back on.

Nelle feels her tears subside as she stares at that little star.

Scourie.

Chapter 22

The road to Scourie is winding and grassy, the hours of driving punctuated only by an occasional highland cow. Finally, when the sun is nothing but an orange smear behind the hills, James sees the road sign for the village. SCOURIE: 5 KILOMETERS. Driving on the left side of the road is utterly foreign, but with the windows down, he barely notices the abnormality of it, his attention stolen by the beautiful highlands. The brown and green hills, chalky cliffs, and fields of wind-rustled flowers all plucked out of a fantasy world. He catches himself distractedly veering more than once, grateful that traffic this far north is next to nonexistent.

Nelle stares out the window, silent.

James doesn't have to ask what's bothering her. They are nearing the village, and she is scared to face the burned ruins of the cottage she has so desperately sought.

"It doesn't seem right," she says at last.

James goes left down a narrower road, dropping his speed to thirty-five kph. The air swells with salt. Between the hills ahead, a black ocean sits underneath pink skies.

"When I close my eyes, I *see* the cottage," she says. "I've never been there, but I can see it. *Intact.* Like a memory."

"You might have a vivid imagination."

She cuts him a look. "I am a walking, breathing, literal *product* of someone's vivid imagination, am I not?" Her voice takes a frustrated edge. "It was more than that. You know when you're dreaming about someone you know in real life? Like your mom or a friend?"

Or you, James thinks. Sometimes he lurches up in the dark, drenched in sweat after watching her catch flame and burn like paper, other times his favorite dreams of her rouse him awake with wet, sticky briefs.

"That's what this cottage feels like. Not imaginary, not made up. I can envision it as clearly as Jessie's apartment, so it doesn't make sense that it burned down. How can I see something that's not there?"

"Maybe . . ." He pauses and rethinks what he wants to say. "Maybe it has to do with what you are."

As soon as the words come out, he knows he made an asshole mistake.

Nelle's nostrils flare. "*What* I am?"

He watches the road, thankful to have a reason not to look at her. "The way you came into this world." Desperate to clarify, he pulls the journal from his back pocket, the pen-scarred pages falling open. "I just meant that maybe *this* is connected to you seeing the cottage from Quill's memory. Because he created you."

"Oh." She stares glumly. "Maybe."

"But if your vision does have something to do with that," James adds, "it only makes it more meaningful."

Nelle sits up straighter. James reaches across the console for her hand when he realizes that she's perking up because they are here. He slows as they roll through town. He wants Nelle to ease into this, yes, but he is also scared of what they will find at Wallace Quill's childhood address.

Scourie is nothing to boast about. A stone house here and there. A filling station. A general store. A small police station. The twisty road climbs back up into the hills, lined with more houses and dark-green backyards. James studies the landscape as they ascend, searching for a lonesome chimney, a heavy stone pulling his stomach down, down, down.

Icy air cups the nape of Nelle's neck, so she unties her hair. It cascades over her shoulders but does little to protect against the biting wind. Neither does the red coat she pulled on when she stepped out of the car.

Though maybe she's not cold. Maybe all the blood has just left her body.

Terry was right. Only a chimney rises from the dead grass. Like a boring brick tree.

Nelle sags. "This is so fucking pointless."

"Hey now." James brushes his thumb over her knuckles. "Think about everywhere we've gone. Everything we've done. Absolutely no part of *this*," he stretches his arms out to the hills, now bluish in the evening shadows, "could ever be pointless."

She can't help but love his buoyant attitude, even as she sinks inside.

Down the hill, behind what was once the cottage, a small pond glimmers like an amethyst. No bigger than a pool, but to Quill and his little brother, it must have felt like a great lake. Stagnant water full of weeds and grass. Nelle imagines it during the winter, ice-skate lines crisscrossed over it like a toddler's scribbles.

And buried beneath years of silt, Sam's decomposed skeleton.

Nelle runs a hand through her hair and stares at the chimney one last time, as if the house might materialize from its decimated past.

"C'mon," she says. "Let's go home."

James shakes the fountain pen, writes in the journal, and Nelle feels that all too familiar release in her limbs. She climbs into the car and buckles her seat belt, sinking back into the headrest. *Let's go home*, she said. But where is home? Lincoln never was. New York doesn't feel like it yet. Scotland sure as hell isn't.

So home is the road, she supposes. Why hasn't the car started?

She finds James through the window, tall in his heather gray sweatshirt and jeans, hands in his back pockets, talking to an old woman at the edge of the property. Nelle can only see her back. Her hair is tied in a waist-length braid, white wisps spiraling around her ears. She wears a long wool cardigan, a cotton dress printed with flowers peeking out underneath.

Nelle presses her nose to the glass, waiting for James to let her out. Waiting and waiting for him to remember that she can't leave until he writes for her. One minute stretches into an irritating two. Then the woman shifts on her feeble legs, revealing her face, and Nelle forgets her irritation.

Set into the woman's wrinkled face are Quill's black eyes.

❦

The rail-thin woman in a baggy cardigan seemed to appear from nowhere, little embroidered flowers scattered across her cotton dress like beads of water. James grew so accustomed to people ignoring each other in New York, such a natural fit for his social anxiety, that an approaching stranger feels wrong now.

"Hi," he says, to be polite.

She surveys the dead plot, snow-white wisps curling around her face. Despite her age—she must be eighty, pushing ninety—there is a youthfulness to her.

"Do you know whose house this is?" she asks.

"Wallace Quill, I believe."

The woman shakes her head. She's missing a few teeth. "*Thomas* Quill."

"Wallace's father."

"You're a fan, I presume."

He clears his throat, praying he can lie his ass off. "I'm actually a distant cousin of Wallace's. He passed away recently, and I'm doing some research for his eulogy. Where he grew up, what his life was like before he moved to the States. The people he . . . impacted."

He forces himself not to gag on the words. Giving that much respect to Quill is almost too nauseating.

"What's your name?" the woman asks, hands behind her back as she observes the chimney.

The shape of her nose, or maybe her cheekbones, rings familiar.

"James Quill." His voice wavers.

The woman turns, those eyes pierce his, and the dots connect like a twisting knife in James's gut.

"Penelope Waters," she says. "My daughter was Lily Waters. Her *husband* was Thomas Quill. Now, I've studied the Quill family tree, extended cousins and all, for many years, and I've never spotted the name *James* among its many branches."

James stands, speechless, licks his lips. "You're Wallace's grandmother?"

"Yes," Penelope says. "And since I'm generous, I'll offer you one more chance to tell me who *you* are."

At this point, the truth is his only option, though it makes him feel shameful for having lied to her in the first place. She peers at him with the guilt-inducing, disapproving look of a trained grandparent.

"My name *is* James, but I'm not related to the Quills. I'm also not writing a eulogy for Wallace Quill because, for one, he's not dead, and for two, I would never. If honesty's what you want, then know that I hate him with every fiber of my being."

Penelope beams at him, life igniting the coals of her eyes.

"I didn't come here alone. I, uh, brought someone who'd probably like to meet you. Or rather, she brought me." He bends toward the car, away from Penelope, and quickly scribbles a command in Nelle's journal.

She cuts him an irritated glance as she climbs out, but he is too excited to care. This is exactly the sort of discovery she hoped to encounter in Scotland, some real insight into Quill's life, and therefore *herself*. Meeting an actual blood relative of Quill's, not to mention someone who probably knew him closely as a child, will exceed her wildest dreams.

But when Nelle charges up to her great-grandmother, she leaves no room for introduction. "You're related to him."

Penelope extends her shaky hand, tracing the curve of Nelle's face.

Nelle flinches at the touch but doesn't pull away.

"So are you." Penelope's hand stills. "Why don't you both come back to my house instead of wasting money on a hotel? I'll make tea and snacks, and I think I have some old movies, though the Lord knows the DVD player's likely too ancient to function. And I'm not sure where the remote is. Never mind that, I have books. And cards. And tea."

Nelle wells up as she watches Penelope hobble down the street to a parked car.

James feels something so pure, it makes his chest ache.

Though they met only minutes ago and barely exchanged five words, Penelope held Nelle, recognized her as a granddaughter, and accepted her without question. A sort of unconditional love that, in twenty-one years, Nelle never received from Quill.

Penelope Waters lives two kilometers down the road in a small house with a sheep pen in the backyard. Her living room has pink and eggshell striped wallpaper, a brick fireplace, and books crammed into every free space. On the table, in the hutch, and along the mantel sit ceramic cats. Nelle sinks into a plush pink armchair by the unlit fireplace, her hands warm around a cup of tea, black.

Across the living room, perched on the edge of a white sofa next to James, is her great-grandmother.

Nelle tries not to stare, but it's surreal to be in the presence of a relative. She obviously knew that Quill had parents and grandparents, but the idea that any of them were still alive, or that she would ever *meet* them, seemed like a childish wish.

When they first arrived, before they even left the car, James had to write for Nelle to have access to the entire house, which thankfully worked. Inside, Penelope prepared the tea while James set up the DVD player per her fuddled instructions. Nelle pulled back a curtain behind the couch. It was still light out, but dim, and the lamplight inside turned her reflection orange. She moved to the nearest shelf of books, skimming through the pages of a thriller, until Penelope swept in from the kitchen with a tea tray that she set between the couches.

Now they stew, wordless. A film called *The Princess Bride* plays on the thirty-two-inch TV.

Penelope finally speaks. "Need any milk?"

"I'm fine," Nelle says. "Thanks."

James waves a hand. "All good."

"Good, good." Penelope purses her wrinkled mouth.

"Do you have a cat?" James asks, cutting pointed glances to the larger cat sculptures tucked around the room.

"Yes, Ptolemy. But he hides from new people."

After another pause, Penelope says, "So you're Wallace's . . . ?"

"Daughter."

"Daughter," Penelope repeats. She sips her tea.

"I'm sorry if he never told you about me. He was a secretive man." Nelle sets her tea on the coffee table. "If it's any consolation, you're news to me, too."

James interrupts the next awkward beat. "So, have you always lived in Scourie?"

Penelope smiles sympathetically. "You must be fatigued from the drive up, if that's the best small talk you can muster. No judgment here, though, I'm exhausted just from going into town."

She gathers the teacups, though they have only taken a few sips each, and carries the tray away.

When she returns, she says, "We adhere to the sun's bedtime around here. When she goes down, I go down. Take the guest room if you're sharing. Second door on the left down the hall. Toilet's attached."

Nelle and James say their good nights and shuffle to their room. He digs their toothbrushes and clothes from the backpack while she takes stock of the room. Iron bed with a white quilt, one shuttered window, a slim door to the bathroom, blocky mahogany nightstands holding opal-glass lamps, wallpaper dotted with tiny tulips peeling at the corners.

"Are you going to take a shower?" she asks.

"Wasn't planning on it," James says, rinsing his toothbrush. "It feels a little weird, doesn't it? To shower in a stranger's house? I mean . . . we talked for a total of ten minutes."

"I guess." Nelle washes her face, towels it off. "She doesn't feel like a stranger to me."

They climb into bed, pitched into darkness.

"Do you care if I turn on the lamp?" she asks.

"Not at all."

She clicks it on, and the room becomes a watercolor of incandescent yellow and shadows.

"I hope tomorrow's not as awkward," she says. "I didn't know how to act. What to say."

"You did great." James rolls onto his side. "I promise. I think she was nervous, too. Maybe it threw her off that Quill never told her about you."

"Maybe, but I don't want her to dislike me because of that."

"If she does"—James kisses the tip of her nose—"then she doesn't deserve to know you."

A ripple of pleasure spreads down to Nelle's toes. She cups his neck and pulls him to her. Lips brush. She savors the anticipation. This tantalizing exchange of breath. His bare toes skim hers, stoking the animal within her.

But James loses control first, dipping down to pull a kiss from her. She lays everything she is at the altar of his lips, offering her body up. As they kiss, she feels subsumed by this celestial, glittery state.

Her pajamas are silky and small—a button-down shirt and shorts—and James's fingers feel like bolts of lightning along her exposed calves, her thighs, her neck. She arches her back, pushing into him, needing more.

"Touch me," she gasps, barely able to get the words out. "Touch me, James."

He works at the buttons of her shirt, grazing her breast. One by one they release, until the fabric splits like stage curtains, unveiling her naked torso. Blood rushes south. Pulsing and hot and wet for him.

The hunger in James's voice is almost unrecognizable.

"You're beautiful." He licks his lips.

Nelle isn't scared, though some part of her feels like she should be. "Take off your shirt."

He pulls it over his head and tosses it aside. She studies the rigid lines of his stomach, his slender muscular arms, the dust of hair trailing down to his sweatpants.

Nelle sits up, level with his sharp collarbones, and lets her mouth guide her where it wants to go. Her tongue swirls his right nipple, and he lets out a little groan, hands grappling for the back of her head. She sucks on it and lets go, then teases the other with her teeth. Her own nipples harden like pebbles in sympathy.

"Stop, stop," James says as Nelle tugs at the hem of his pants.

She looks up, breathless with lust. "Why?"

"Not yet," he says.

It's hard not to roll her eyes. "This again? There is no right moment, James. There's just *this* moment."

"Was the Eiffel Tower not the right moment for our first kiss?"

Nelle slumps back against the pillows, feeling no vulnerability, even half naked in front of him.

"You know I'm right about this," James says.

He's not *wrong*. "Fine."

"But," he lights up, "there is something I'd like to do to you. If you'll let me."

The creature inside Nelle, starving for him, goes wild. *"Anything."*

James cradles her left breast and skims his lips across her right. Soft breath brushing the milk-white curve, each kiss making it harder and harder for her to breathe. God, she wants him. All of him. Wants to wrap her hand around that hardness between his legs, to feel him inside her. But not tonight. Soon, but not tonight.

He sucks and bites her nipples before marching his mouth down her stomach.

His fingers curl over the waistband of her shorts.

"Is this okay?" he asks.

"Yes."

Slowly, he peels the silky material down her thighs, over her ankles, and tosses them aside. No underwear.

Nelle spreads her legs, inviting him in.

James crumbles between her knees. Desire races through her, begging for release as his lips move along her inner thigh, scorching every spot they touch, until his breath hits that throbbing between her legs. His kiss, at the apex of her sex, brings the sensation of being submerged in the roaring ocean. Her brain goes numb, giving complete control over to her body.

James curls his tongue upward, encompassing all of her in one fiery stroke before homing in on her swollen bud again. She shudders, thoughtless, fingers grasping to keep her from floating away. The bedsheets, James's hair, the iron headboard. If she's moaning, she doesn't know, and, frankly, doesn't care. Surely Penelope, if she has ever experienced something like this before, will understa—

"Oh my *God*," Nelle groans.

James's tongue flickers faster. His hands slide underneath her, cupping her cheeks and lifting. That's it—she's done. Undone. *Fuck.*

With one more stroke, his tongue slides into her, and Nelle's pulsating pressure explodes. She is a red balloon, a golden bird, a flying fucking horse—

Her thighs clamp around his head, and distantly she has the thought that she might be suffocating him as she rides out the waves of pleasure, rocking against the mattress. As her body sizzles, she finds James watching her, head propped on his hand.

Nelle kisses him and, exhilarated, tastes herself. "Why haven't we been doing this the whole time?"

⁂

The next morning, the glint of Penelope's black eyes tells James that she knows exactly what they did last night. If so, then she must be choosing to reward rather than scold them because she offers to buy breakfast at a café by the bay. And to his dismay, she offers to drive.

James throws on his denim jacket, journal and pen in the pocket, and as they're ready to walk out the door, he excuses himself to the bathroom to scribble, *Nelle rides with Penelope to the café.*

Nelle sits in the passenger seat on the bumpy ride into town. James isn't paying much attention, preoccupied with his memories of last night. Nelle's wetness on the sheets, how hot she throbbed against his lips, how she tasted. It took *all* his self-control not to give in to their mutual impulses.

The "café" is a charming food truck parked beside a cluster of picnic tables. In the back seat, James pulls out the journal and writes for Nelle. They find a table while Penelope orders. James taps his shoe to Nelle's.

Her lips twist. "What?"

"I wanna kiss you."

"Which part of me?"

James adjusts his pants before Penelope sidles onto the bench beside Nelle with a tray of food. The right moment better come *soon.*

Breakfast is delicious: hard-boiled eggs sprinkled with pepper, beans and toast, juicy slices of bacon, and some sort of onion-pepper-potato hash. He doesn't realize how hungry he is until his plate is scraped clean and his stomach growls for more.

"How often do you come here?" Nelle asks.

"Every day," Penelope laughs. "The last thing I want to do when I wake up is *cook.*"

Nelle squints at the bright morning. "It's a nice view, too."

Green hills swell alongside the black water. A breeze hustles in from the vast Atlantic, raising goose bumps on James's arms. He drapes his jacket over his shoulders. Far across that water are his parents and Midi, going on about their lives without him. He misses them, but not Lincoln. That town might be too sleepy to ever draw him back.

He thinks about Jessie, and his heart clenches as it strikes him, not for the first time, how badly he misses New York.

Chapter 23

Four days later, Ptolemy reveals himself during a heated game of rummy. A white ragdoll with blue eyes pointed in different directions, he waddles out from under the couch and leaps onto the coffee table, scattering the cards. Nelle fawns over him. James mourns the ruined game. Penelope cackles, scooping Ptolemy into her arms like a baby. He only allows it for a moment before he squirms away and retreats to a corner of the couch.

"Does this mean he likes us now?" James asks, gathering the cards.

"Tolerates you," Penelope corrects. "Now that he's met you, he will decide if he likes you."

"How will we know?" Nelle asks.

"You'll wake up with him on your chest, staring at you like you committed a crime."

"Seriously?"

Penelope nods grimly.

"Sleep with the door shut," James says. "Noted."

"If you do that," Penelope adds, "then he will never like you."

Nelle leans back, eye level with the cat. "Is that true, Tom?"

He hisses, mouth pink and fanged.

Penelope takes the cards from James. "He hates nicknames. Trust me, I've tried them all."

"You have a very particular cat," James says.

"What can I say?" She pats Ptolemy's round head three times and he blinks, blinks, blinks. "He gets it from his mommy."

Ptolemy meows, then jumps off the couch. He circles the coffee table once before walking away, brushing his duster of a tail against a door James assumed was a closet.

"Is that Ptolemy's bedroom?" Nelle asks.

Penelope's face goes sheet white.

"No." She forces a smile. "Just a broom closet."

The cat rubs his body against the door, tail straight up.

"He must really like brooms," James says.

Penelope laughs, but he hears the falsity in it, lower than her typical cackle.

She shuffles the deck between her knobby fingers and clears her throat. "Another round?"

Later in the night, James wakes in a sweat. After peeing, he tiptoes into the living room, wincing at every pop of the hardwood floor. The broom closet calls to him. Checking over his shoulder for Penelope, he jumps at a pair of icy-blue eyes. Ptolemy, watching him. No, watching the closet door. James tries the knob.

Locked.

~

"You can go inside to pee, James." Nelle's hands are buried in the sheep's tufts. "I could stay out here with Clifford forever."

James squints up at the September sky. He doesn't want to leave her out here alone. "But it might rain."

"I don't mind," she says, more absorbed with the animal than with him. For the week they have been at Penelope's, Nelle has spent an hour after lunch every day in the backyard with Clifford. Her ink restricts her from accessing Penelope's entire property. She can roam the fenced-in yard or the house, but not both.

"I'll be right back," he promises.

Nelle pulls a carrot from inside her jacket and guides the sheep across the yard with it, wind ruffling his white wool. "Cliff will keep me company."

He bleats for the carrot, and she laughs as she feeds it to him. Clifford, it would appear, doesn't mind nicknames.

James slips through the back screen door. It shouldn't scare him so much to leave her out here. He left her in Jessie's apartment all the time. She went to the studio night after night, alone. But that was in the city, and contrary to popular opinion, James feels safer surrounded by people than he does in the middle of nowhere. Imagining her out there, exposed to the cloudy sky, the sea, the hills and all their wildlife, sends a spidery chill down his spine.

On his way back, he opens the fridge for a drink. With a carton of grapefruit juice angled over his glass, he pauses, hearing the front door open. Penelope back from her daily trip to the store? But where is the familiar rustle of grocery bags?

"She's not *aware*," Penelope angrily whispers.

A droplet of juice falls into his glass. James swallows, silent, listening.

"No, I don't think she will," she says. "They have a system worked out."

She's on the phone, James realizes. He keeps his juice ready to pour, prepared to appear innocent the moment Penelope sees him in the kitchen. Definitely not eavesdropping.

"*He's* smarter than you give *him* credit for," she says.

The living room floorboards groan. She's pacing.

Penelope scoffs. "What would you have me do, Wallace? She trusts me."

James's fingers slacken. The carton slips from his hand, knocks the glass to the floor.

"Shit, shit, shit." He snatches it up, but half the juice has already glugged out in a sticky splattering across the linoleum, and the glass shards are an even bigger mess.

Wallace fucking *Quill.*

James is too confused to be angry. Why is Penelope in cahoots with him? A week ago she acted like she never knew about her great-granddaughter. He glances out the window. Nelle is still chasing Clifford around like he is a floating cloud.

"You good?" Penelope comes into the kitchen, phone dangling in her hand. "James?"

Nothing devious about her. White hair braided back, tasteful sweatpants, fur-lined boots, and a cashmere sweater.

"Sorry," he says, "about the mess. I lost my grip."

"I'll say." Penelope hesitates. "No worries, I'll clean it up."

This is my chance to see inside the broom closet. "I can do it."

"No." Her tone is final. "Go outside with Nelle. I'll take care of this."

James considers insisting, but if she is working with Quill, he doesn't want to mess with her. She could be as dangerous as her grandson.

Out of politeness, he offers again, "I really can clean it up."

Penelope shakes her head. "You're my guests. I'll take care of it."

James wipes his sweaty palms on his pants and hurries outside. He beelines toward Nelle, and she must see the shock and fear on his face because she leaves Clifford, even as he bleats at her.

"What is it?" She grabs his arm.

Maybe she doesn't have to know. She can live in peace, believing that Penelope cares for her, that her great-grandmother is honest, trustworthy.

"James, talk to me." She gives him a nudge. "What's wrong?"

Inside the squat house, Penelope's white head bobs past the window, sweeping.

"I was in the kitchen just now, and I overheard Penelope on the phone . . ." He recounts what he heard, as close to verbatim as he can remember. At Quill's name, Nelle's face goes ashen.

"You're sure that's what you heard?" She watches the house over his shoulder.

"Without a doubt."

"Maybe Penelope knows another Wallace?"

"Then why would she need to bring up that *you* trust her?"

"She said my name?"

"Well, no, but—"

"It could be completely misconstrued," Nelle says, hope visibly flickering.

"I don't think so," James says. "I think Penelope's working with Quill. The last thing I want is for you to distrust her, but I know what I heard. I like Penelope, I do, but I won't let *anything* happen to you, Nelle. I can't."

Clutching his shirt, Nelle watches Clifford mope along the fence line.

"Tonight," she says, looking back at James. "Tonight, let's break into the broom closet."

❧

Nelle's chest winds up like a jack-in-the-box, her heartbeat ticking like a crank. Any second, she will explode, either in tears or projectile vomit.

James jiggles a hairpin in the lock. His brows are furrowed, tongue poked between lips. Then, with a slip of his fingers, he drops the pin. Nelle squeaks, her nerves getting the better of her, but James keeps his cool. With a glance down the hall to ensure Penelope's not coming, he goes back to work.

"Where'd you learn to do this?" Nelle whispers.

"Scouts," he says. "Not an actual sanctioned lesson, but one of the older guys knew how to do it and showed me on a camping trip." He fiddles with the lock. "Been a while, though, so I'm a little . . ."

Click. So soft, Nelle nearly misses the sound.

"Rusty." James pockets the hairpin. "You ready?"

It's 12:00 a.m. Penelope should be well into her deep sleep cycle by now, and she has no reason to suspect them. Nevertheless, Nelle feels like she is standing at the lip of a crumbling ninety-foot cliff, wondering if the view is worth the risk. She twists the glass knob, and the door opens, thankfully, without a creak. The room beyond swims in darkness. She paws at the wall until she finds the switch, flips it on, and lets her vision adjust.

Amber light flickers through the room. A tasseled shade on the mantel, an iron lantern hung above a blue velvet chaise, a green banker's lamp with a pull chain on the desk. All wired to the switch that Nelle's finger lingers on.

The room hums to her. Not audibly, but her blood sizzles, her bones rattle. Looking at this room is like looking at the sun, only she can't stop. Books crowd the walls, stacked on every flat surface, wedged like bricks in the fireplace. Leather bound, paperback, hardcover, manuscripts both typewritten and scrawled out longhand.

Do you feel that? she almost asks James, but she knows this soft buzz, these whispering books, are for her alone.

"Definitely not a sex dungeon," James says.

"What's a sex dungeon?" Nelle hesitates at the doorway. The room feels sacred, untouched. She thinks twice before stepping in and defiling it.

Then a throat clears behind them, and she has no more time to think.

"That's what you thought it was?" Penelope crosses her arms over her nightgown, her hair in a silk cap.

Nelle can approach this in two ways, and she hopes James will play along. She can either use Penelope's conversation with Quill as her excuse for breaking into the room, or she can play dumb. Maybe she can't explain *why* she distrusts her great-grandmother, but she knows how to distract Penelope.

Just tell her the truth.

"I know it's late," Nelle says, "but . . . there's something I want to talk to you about. Secrets I've been keeping from you about *who* I am. *What* I am." She reaches back to find James's hand.

Penelope eases the library door shut. "Go sit down. I'll put on tea."

Twenty minutes later, Penelope not only listens intently to Nelle's story—how Quill created her and imprisoned her for twenty-one years, how she escaped and has been exploring the world, Quill's unexpected and unwanted visits, the vision of the cottage—but accepts it as fact. Maybe she *was* talking to Quill. No sane person reacts to a story like that with calm understanding. Nelle shivers.

Penelope pours herself another cup of tea and stirs in a dash of cream. The spoon *tinks* against the rim of the cup. She sips, and Nelle sees a response formulating under her methodical movements.

"Wallace has his mother's curse," Penelope finally says. "His father, Thomas, didn't want to admit it, but I knew."

"All I know about Lily is that she wrote poetry," Nelle says, concealing her suspicions. She needs proof if she is going to risk ruining her relationship with her only loving family.

"Wallace and his mother were both writers. And avid readers." Penelope walks to the doorway of the magnetic room. "This is my library. All of these were Wallace's and Lily's. Their personal collections and their own works." She pauses as if thinking twice, then nods into the room. "Take all the time you need."

Nelle hesitantly enters the small library. She spins once, twice, before sitting back on the chaise, overwhelmed by the sheer volume of books. It'll take her days to peruse them all, if she even *wants* to. Quill only ever brought her misery, so reading his and Lily's—her *grandmother's*—writing might take Nelle to a dark place. Maybe to the place she has sought after.

Roots curl into Nelle's chest, locking her to this room. These people.

Penelope sighs. "I'll make something to eat. Take all the time you need."

Then, with the soft click of the door, Nelle is alone.

She picks a random shelf and finds a soft leather journal, the inside cover signed *Lily Waters*. She takes it to the chaise and begins to read. Her grandmother's poetry streams fluid, natural, without a structured rhyme scheme, carried beginning to end by a linguistic musicality.

When she is finished absorbing the first journal, she finds another, bound by navy cloth. Then another. And another. Hundreds of poems, each like a shard of Lily's stained-glass mind.

She finally works up the courage to pick a book with Quill's name on it.

Thin, hardback, handwritten.

The first line sucks her in.

⁂

"She's been in there for an hour," James says over roasted rosemary chicken and peas, served on a hand-painted cat-themed plate. Two a.m. and his eyes are salty with sleep, but Penelope insisted they wait for Nelle. "Shouldn't we ask her if she's hungry?"

"I suspect she'll be in there for a few more hours, at least. Maybe a day. Who knows how long it takes?" Penelope wipes her mouth with a napkin. "Though she may like a plate brought to her."

"How long *what* takes?" James asks. "What're you expecting her to find in there?"

"Answers."

James scoops food from a Tupperware onto another cat plate, heats it in the microwave, and brings it with a glass of water to the library door. He knocks twice with the toe of his shoe.

"Coming in."

Nelle is reading in the corner, swaddled in a blanket on the chaise, a book open on her lap. Too engrossed to notice his entrance. When the plate clinks on the table beside her, she doesn't look up. Doesn't say a word. Whatever she's reading has sucked her into another dimension.

He backs out and eases the door shut.

⁂

Nelle slides another volume of Lily's poetry onto the shelf, the words ringing in her head, a welcome break from Quill's moody, brilliant prose.

As she reads, the pieces of her family history begin to form an intricate conglomerate. Hints found in lines of Lily's poetry:

> My olive skin, obsidian eye, shining star
> And you who walks alone, cursed with red, little
>   moon

Two brothers. Wallace and Sam. The star and the moon. One favored by their mother, the other by their father.

Nelle reaches for another of Quill's books. Leather, thick, with a buckle strap. *Wallace Quill* is carved into the cover in a slanted, professional script. Must have been expensive. The leather is worn but carries a cool, fresh aroma, and the spine crackles as she opens it to the first page.

The Cottage on the Hill, a novella by Wallace Quill.

The next page: *For Mother and Sam.*

Nelle sits and starts to read. The words resonate in her like the hum of a coming storm. These are not just words, they are the words of the man who wrote *her* into existence. These stories, these characters, are her family. Her blood. The ink on the page in front of her is the same ink thrumming beneath her skin. Stories about a mother—*Nelle's mother*—stories about brothers—*Nelle's brothers*—stories about love—*Nelle's lovers.* All written by Quill, including her.

She closes the book. Through the window, night has given way to the soft blue of early, early morning. Maybe 3:00 a.m. Her exhausted eyes burn. Her cheeks are sticky with tears.

A painful resolution settles into Nelle, as final yet infinite as a funeral.

Her quest is not yet complete. The truths revealed to her in this novella, in these stories and poems, fictional and autobiographical, have shown her that much. That magical rope tugs her from the inside.

Trust yourself.

∽

"So you're a writer." Penelope bends over a chessboard on the coffee table. She moves her rook. "What are you writing?"

James sets aside his cup of tea and concentrates on the board. "Are you trying to distract me?"

"Not necessary," Penelope says. "You don't stand a chance."

He finds a square for one of his knights. She laughs, and her rook takes the knight, swiping his piece onto the rug.

"So what are you working on?"

"The dreadful question." He moves his queen. "Not much."

"You're lying. Writers write. So either you're keeping whatever it is secret, or you're not truly a writer."

James locks his nervous fingers together. "I just finished a novel, actually. My first. *The Summer Curse.*"

"What's it about?"

He scrutinizes Penelope's eyes. They are a mug of tea on a rainy day, not the harsh ice of her grandson's. He wants to trust her—he *likes* her—but how can he after what he overheard?

"The bones of the story are about our journey together," James says. "Mine and Nelle's, that is. But the meat is different. I guess I'd been marinating the idea for a while, then, when we went to New York, I was on fire, and I wrote it in, like, two weeks."

"How honest were you?" Penelope asks. "Is your story more a memoir or a novel?"

James purses his lips. "It was closely based on us, until the characters arrive in New York, then the plot spirals off in a different direction, because I obviously didn't know what would happen to us. The characters took on their own personalities. It all felt very natural."

"And Nelle's character is . . . the same as she is?" Penelope asks.

"Yes."

"I'm not a writer," she admits, "but I was married to one, and raised another, so I know a thing or two. From what I've gathered, there are different types of writing: the kind that lets you breathe but should never be seen by anyone else, and the kind that is crafted to share with the world. Most of what's in that room is the former. Which kind of story is yours?"

"You don't think I should try to publish it," he says. "To protect her, right?"

"What you have to ask yourself"—Penelope sips her tea—"is whether or not there is a cost to publishing this story that you're not willing to pay."

James has never considered the possibility that his book could harm Nelle. But if anyone found out, her life could be over. If word leaked that Nelle isn't a human, what would the government do? Sweet Jesus, what would the media do?

"I would *never* reveal to the world what Nelle is," he admits. Which means he may never publish this book. Like Penelope said, some writing is just for wringing out the soul.

"And if she wasn't here to be harmed by your honesty, if your story could really be considered fantasy?"

"Then yeah, technically," James says, "but I don't want that."

Penelope grunts and stands, shuffles into the kitchen, and returns with two more cups of tea. James takes his mug with both hands. It's painted blue, with the faces of two palm-size fairies bulging out with little noses and lips. Jessie would obsess over it.

The floorboard creaks, and James snaps up from his tea.

Nelle steps out of the library, a satchel full of books hung from her shoulder.

"Take me," she says to Penelope. "Take me to the cottage."

James sets down his cup. "It burned down, we saw it—"

"No." Nelle doesn't break her stare. "Take me to the cottage. Now."

"Write it down for her," Penelope says.

The words don't register in James's head, too befuddled by Nelle's sudden entrance and insane demand.

"Write it *down* for her," Penelope repeats, and this time he catches her urgency.

He scribbles in the journal, *Nelle rides in the car.*

Penelope takes Nelle's hand, and together they disappear out the front door. James stares in disbelief at the rectangle of night. Insects vibrate. A wet chill splices the air.

Then he snatches up the blue backpack and races out the door after them.

Chapter 24

The vacation cottage is carpeted in dust. Every corner hosts dried-up insects strung wall to wall by thoughtful spiders. James's flashlight swings onto a tattered couch facing a brick fireplace and a slanted bookshelf. In the adjoining room, there is a gas stove, an empty refrigerator, and a stained coffeepot.

The first bedroom was, without a doubt, Wallace and his brother Sam's. Two twin beds, a shelf sagging with books, and an oak desk. A wooden castle and a collection of untidy toys are half hidden beneath one of the unmade beds. James feels a pang, imagining Midi ripped from his life in some violent, sudden way. He would never touch her room again.

Already well past 3:00 a.m., Penelope advised them to spend the night at the cottage before she left, so James votes to sleep in the master bedroom. Unlike the kids' room, it doesn't have the uneasy energy of a morgue. A California king bed fills the space, leaving a few feet for the dresser, the vanity, and a beautiful armoire, its doors carved with the outlines of woodland creatures.

After they probe the house, James sits on the sofa, years of cigarette smoke wafting out of the cushions. Nelle has been quiet since they got in Penelope's car, steeped in concentration. She weaves in and out of the cottage's rooms, opening cabinets, rummaging through drawers. James doesn't know what she is trying to find, and he is starting to doubt that even *she* knows. But she must have learned something important about this place from the books in Penelope's house. Something Penelope must know, too. He drums his fingers together, perturbed to be out of the loop.

"Aha!" Nelle rings out from the room with the twin beds.

James jumps up and barrels in, only to find her sitting on the floor, prying at the boards with her fingertips, sweating as she pulls to no avail.

He drops beside her. "What did the floor do to offend you?"

"It's hollow." She grits her teeth. "Help me get it open."

James digs in the gap between boards, but his fingers are bigger than Nelle's, so the attempt is futile.

He sighs. "Still got that letter opener?"

She passes it, polished wood handle out, from her jacket pocket. He presses the blade between the floorboards. Breaking a sweat himself, he jiggles the board free and wrenches it up, victorious.

In the hollow underneath sit stacks upon stacks of paper.

Nelle reaches in and withdraws the top sheet. The paper is bluish in the moonlight, and she squints to read it. James shines his flashlight over her shoulder.

"This is Quill's handwriting," she says. *"Twenty-first of September. Today, I will eat breakfast at nine o'clock, work on my novel on the porch until two o'clock, eat lunch in the kitchen with my mother, then read in my bedroom until five o'clock, when I will eat dinner with my family in the kitchen, and then I will read again in my room, and then go to sleep at nine o'clock. I will wake at eight tomorrow."*

"He kept daily logs?" James peers into the floor cavity. From what he can see, the papers all record daily itineraries, handwritten in lists. *I will do this at this time, then this at this time, then this at this time.* Over and over and over again, endless lines of instruction.

"No, no, this is more than that." Nelle's holding two pages, crinkled between her fingers. "Quill was like *me*."

James shakes his head, unsure what she means.

"He was created like me." She points at the papers. "Look at all of these. Quill created me. Quill's mother, Lily, created *him*. Penelope's late husband, Samford, created *Lily*. Do you know what this means?"

"What?" James asks, trying to wrap his mind around the succession of writers. Did that make Nelle any more or less human? He shakes the thought away. Just his anxiety talking. She has proven to him—though she never had to—how much she can feel the weight of sadness, and stress, and fear, and guilt, and hope. However she *became* human doesn't matter because she *is*.

"I can write for myself." A grin splits Nelle's face. Her body seems ready to spring open. "I don't need you to do it anymore, I can do it myself. I found Lily's old journals. She wrote poems to dictate her life. It's why everyone thought she was crazy, you see? All her mystic statements and rhymes, her distant stares, the irregular pauses Quill wrote about in his short stories. She was a poem, through and through. Quill wrote basic, daily instructions for himself, like he did for me. But I'm made of fucking ink, dammit, I can write my own story."

The papers drift from her hands.

James offers up the journal and pen, but Nelle has already peeled a splinter from the old floorboard to prick her finger. A bead of ink settles at the tip. She brings it to the floor and writes: *I run into the lake.*

She shoots James a raw smile.

Then she takes off through the cottage and out the back door, across the stone patio, and into the night, howling like a wolf.

Once again, he is drawn to her like the tide to the moon.

When he emerges from the back door, Nelle is already halfway down the hill, her clothes strewn among the weeds. The pale curve of her back flashes before she crashes into the surface of the loch, then twists and slips backward, disappearing under bubbles and murk.

Like a lost cub chasing after his pack, James runs down the hill, kicking off his shoes, pulling off his socks, shimmying out of his clothes until he is naked and free and gaining momentum, the wind hitting his balls like ice—

He cannonballs into the water and plummets to the reedy floor. Freezing, electrified, rippling skin. A gong rung. His body undulates with feeling and sound.

It's September, and he's skinny-dipping in a small Scottish loch—*what is life?*

He kicks off the muddy bottom, breaks the surface, and slings water from his face. The cold racks his body with shivers. So far from the city, stars glitter like cinnamon on the water.

Nelle splashes at him. A freezing blast, startling him from his reverie.

He chases after her, but she paddles back toward the shore, a sea creature stroking on her back, exposing her breasts. Each sliver of skin James glimpses sends his blood rushing southward. Memories of the other night flash through his mind, fueling his desire.

Nelle walks to ankle-deep water, naked amid the reeds. She lifts her arms to wring out her hair, exposing the side of her breast, the outline of a pointed nipple, her back dimples.

James swears and averts his gaze to the cluster of gnats under the alder tree, whose branches twist over the water.

Out of his periphery, he sees Nelle staring at him.

"Look at me," she says. Commands.

All he needed was permission.

"James," she says, softly. An invitation. A plea.

For a few seconds, he studies her. Committing this to memory. Collarbone shadows, her nipples tight, her soft stomach curving into a V toward her thighs. He wants to feel every inch of her, first with his hands, then his tongue. Or vice versa.

He walks out of the waist-deep water, taking pleasure in her eyes roving down his chest. Lingering with the same magnetism he feels, the silvery force bouncing off their bodies, drawing them closer.

Nelle steps forward, rises on her toes, and kisses him. Her cold breasts brush his chest, her skin dripping.

Mouth to mouth, she says, "Bite my lip. I'll heal quick."

He hesitates but kisses her again, skimming his teeth on her bottom lip.

"Harder, you baby."

Ever so slightly James bites down, drawing blood, the ink bitter on his tongue. Nelle reaches up to touch the wound. He is sure he hurt her, but instead of crying out, she takes her ink-covered fingertip and traces it across his chest. Halfway through, she taps her lip again, reopening the cut. When she finishes writing, she steps back to admire her work.

Nelle makes love to James is scrawled in a sloppy line beneath his collarbone.

"Ignore the handwriting," she says. "Haven't had much practice."

"Are you sure about this?" he asks. "What if it's not the right—"

Nelle grabs his jaw and kisses him. "Fuck the *right moment*, James."

She pulls him uphill, only he must be heavier than she expected because her feet start sliding on the grass. Laughter bursts out as James wraps his arms around her waist, wheezing in camaraderie.

Back in the cottage, their footprints tracking wet grass across the floor, James lifts her up. Her legs lock around him, wet skin to skin, as he walks them into the master bedroom and lays Nelle on the bed. She stares up at him, brown eyes like opals in the shadows.

His lips brush the nook behind her jaw. "I've wanted you for so long."

He trails down her collarbone while he awaits her response, his tongue grazing the curve of her breast, and she lets out a ticklish gasp. She is cold and wet. A dessert he can't get enough of but wants to savor.

"How long?" She lifts her neck.

"Since New York." He kisses where she wants, right behind her ear. "Since the rooftop."

His mouth slides to the shadow of her navel, farther, featherlight brushes down the slope of her pelvis. He holds her waist with one hand, her breast with the other, as his tongue finds her center, flickering over flesh.

"Holy shit." Nelle's back arches, her fingers curling into the bedsheets.

"How long have you wanted *me*?" James's hands tighten on her thighs, lifting her.

"Since the night I fell in love with you." Her nails dig ten indentions into his scalp, and she tilts back into the pillows.

James wants her so bad, he can't stand it, a coil so tightly wound inside him, he is worried it will unravel prematurely. He didn't know it was possible to love someone with such conviction.

"What night was that?" he asks as her fingers curl through his hair. *Touch me more.*

"The night of the house fire," she whispers. "The night we ran off together."

He loses himself in the taste of her and nearly comes himself when she does, thighs like an iron vise around his head. She shudders, digs her heels into the mattress. Breathless, James wipes his mouth.

Without warning, Nelle grabs the back of his neck and pulls him up, eye to eye. Her lips are lake water and salt and ink, her tongue like a live wire.

"I can't imagine ever having not loved you," he says.

Nelle flips him onto his back. She kisses his jaw. His body arches upward into her touch, a need to feel her skin burn against his. Her tongue on his neck. Nelle kisses his throat, the curve of his chest, down his stomach. He sees her hair and the dark bedroom before his world splits into oblivion—

She doesn't take him but kisses him. Featherlight, treating that part of him with the same adoration she has shown the rest of his body. As she looks up at him from between his legs, her back arches, tan from the beach in southern France. He glimpses the smooth curve of her ass. Blond hair draping his inner thighs.

Her voice is low. "I want you, James."

"Fuck," he whispers, pulling her up against him.

Chest to chest, he turns her onto her back and positions himself.

"I know you said you can't get pregnant, but—"

She rolls her eyes. "Based on my predecessors, there's only one way I can procreate, and it's not this."

"Right, but shouldn't we be safe?"

"I *can't* get pregnant, James."

"But how do you know for sure if you've never tried?"

Nelle's brows furrow. "Are we having sex or an interrogation? I *know* the laws of my existence."

"You're right," he says, his mountain of worry dissolving like a sandhill. "I believe you."

He dips down, his top lip brushing hers.

"I love you," he says.

A leg folds around his ass, nudging him in.

He hesitates, teasing her wet entrance. *This*, he thinks, *is the right moment.*

She takes him slow at first, nails digging into his neck. Further in, a whimper.

He loves her wondrous spirit. The strength she grew to survive her childhood. Her brain, how it ticks and plots and argues and wishes. How she dreams.

Their stomachs connect in a touch of hot skin. Her other knee bends around his waist, locking him to her. Nelle's jaw gleams as her head falls back to the pillow. Her hands lock around his neck.

James knows he won't hold out for long, so he makes his second, his third, his fourth thrust intentional and slow. He tries to ground himself in the motion of his hips, but he is already spearheading into oblivion.

Nelle rocks against him. "Faster, James."

Sheets hiss. Throats make involuntary pleasured noises, back and forth, until they blur into one. Sea, skyline. East, west. Five seconds or an hour, he doesn't know. But he can feel the cliffside now, edging.

"I wish," he says, breathless, "that we could stay this close forever."

Eyes lidded, Nelle cries out. Her calves tremble as her claws sink into James's shoulders. Her abdomen arches up, hot against his. He slows his pace, but it's too late. He's already gone . . .

Fireworks crackle through his body.

His brain, *off.* Darkness, hot pleasure, and Nelle.

Her fingers fall from his sweaty hair to his lips, lingering.

"I love you, too," she says. The words hang, light as a glass ornament.

He slides out, utterly out of breath and amazed and in love and ready to duck between her legs and pleasure her again. His lust must read on his burning face, because Nelle's hand tightens on his jaw.

"Can you hold me?" A tear spills down her cheek.

Hovering over her, he leans down to touch the tip of her nose with his. "Always."

⁂

Nelle is giggling under the bedsheet with James like they are at a sleepover, flashlight holding them in a dome of light, when she hears a groan from the living room floor. Too loud to be an old-house noise. Too precise. She snaps her finger to her lips, slicing James's whisper mid-word.

With a trembling hand, she pulls the bedsheet down. James cuts the flashlight.

In only his T-shirt, she grabs her journal and pen and slides off the mattress.

James stands, shirtless, in only his boxers. "What are you doing?"

Nelle writes for herself. "Checking on that noise."

"I didn't hear a noise."

"Then why are you standing up?"

"Old houses make noises," he says. "My parents' house literally screams at night, I swear."

Nelle shakes her head, a deep pit of dread gnawing at her stomach. "I'm serious, James. I need to make sure everything's okay out there."

"All right," James says. "Let's go."

She glares at his sudden persistence to join. "Why don't you stay and protect the bed?"

He glares back at her, placing his hand over hers on the doorknob.

"Move," she says through gritted teeth. "Please don't be stubborn right now. I *can't* die, James. *You* can."

"I want to go out first," he says. "You can come right behind me."

"What if it's a bear?" She has seen videos, and she hates their enormous heads, their tree-rattling roars, their black-as-ink eyes. "I don't want you to get mauled."

"I promise it's just the pipes. Or the fridge, maybe. Old fridges always make weird noises."

Nelle gives up. He's right, it's probably nothing. "Fine, go ahead."

He opens the door, sliding outside first. Nelle creeps on his heels, an inch behind him, so she sees the man in the living room as soon as James does. Sees his soulless, deranged smile and his pearl-handled pistol.

Wallace Quill, acclaimed author, disappointing son, and god-awful father, in all his glory.

"Having fun?" he asks. "Enjoyed fucking in my dead parents' bed, did you?"

"Yeah, we did," James says, clenching his fists.

What is he going to do, punch a bullet? Nelle wants to tell him to back down, to cool off, not to make Quill angry because that will only make him pull that trigger. But she's scared it's already too late. That he is already fuming.

Quill takes aim.

Nelle grabs James by the shoulders and shoves him back as hard as she can. As he stumbles, she darts to get out of the way herself.

When the gun goes off, it sounds like a wooden balloon popping. She hears the blast, then only silence and her muffled heartbeat.

She can't see, she realizes. Or hear.

The back of her head rings. Her body floats in a dark pool. And she has this deep feeling within herself that things aren't going well.

ꟹ

James drops down, Nelle in his arms. He can't hear her cry, but he can tell by her contorted face that she is in terrible pain. The ragged bullet hole inches from her heart, the exposed purplish muscles above the bone, the ink streaming out in hot pumps . . .

He tries to remember what he learned in school, but his mind is blank. *I'm no doctor.*

Hands pressed above her heart, his only course of action is to use his cotton briefs to stem the bleeding. Nothing matters, not his nakedness, not Quill standing across the room with a gun that is most likely still loaded. All that matters is keeping Nelle alive. She said she can't die, but what if she's wrong? Surely she has never bled like this.

James screams for Quill to get help. In his own ears, his voice is muffled, but he hopes that Quill feels it like a slap to the face.

The front door slams shut.

James steadies Nelle between his legs and does not dare let go of the fabric against her chest. Instead, he eases them both backward until his back meets the wall. He keeps one hand pressed firmly against her and uses the other to hold her face.

"Hang on, Nelle." He can't hear himself, but he trusts that the words are there. "You have the world to see, an entire life to live. Maybe with me, if you want. We can go back to Paris. We can adopt kids one day. Or have cats instead. And it doesn't matter where we live. Wherever you want, Nelle. Wherever you want."

He presses his lips to her cold scalp, holds her to him, and talks to her until the front door opens again.

Chapter 25

Penelope walks through the door, alone.

James's heart falls. Why hasn't she brought an ambulance, first responders, anyone who can help Nelle, who can heal her?

Penelope drapes her coat on the rack in the corner as if she has all the time in the world. Paper grocery bags hang from her arms, a head of broccoli peeking out of one, carrots another.

"Take the underwear off her, dear." Penelope blows on the kitchen counter and winces at the ensuing puff of dust. Flipping on the overhead light, she assesses the kitchen and living room with one hand on her hip, the other tucked thoughtfully beneath her chin. "Then go get dressed."

James peels the ink-crusted briefs from Nelle's chest, and a spurt of hope shoots through him. Beneath the shirt, her skin is smooth, like the bullet never touched her. Her breathing has evened, too, though she is still unconscious.

"She healed."

Penelope unfolds a rag and wipes down the counter. "They're fast like that."

He leaves Nelle sleeping against the wall to dig through his backpack on the master bed, pulling on loose jeans and a black sweater. The color will help to hide the ink stains across his torso, but it's all over his hands and face, too.

Nelle stirs when he returns. He guides her to the sofa, resting her head on his shoulder.

"In the interest of candor, Lily tried to end her own life forty-seven times," Penelope says from the kitchen. "She was brutally creative in her attempts. But as you've seen, those who are written into life can't die naturally. They're bound to their innate selves. Characters at heart, imitations of humans, with clear wants and desires and a persistence to achieve them. My husband, Samford, wrote Lily in a time of despair, and that always showed in her personality. I'm sure you witnessed her fury echoed in her son, Wallace."

"I'd argue it was more than an echo." James remembers Nelle's torture. The burning cabin. The gunshot.

Penelope wipes down the fridge handle. "When she wakes, I'll tell the full story."

While he waits, James strokes Nelle's cheek and gruffly sings. Eventually, she grumbles and blinks at him.

"Am I dead?" She touches her chest. "I heard angels singing."

"Just me," he says, relieved. "No angels."

Nelle scrabbles to her feet, ready to bolt or attack. "Where's Quill?"

"Gone."

Penelope comes around the kitchen corner, wringing a rag.

The anger-torn seams of Nelle's face split at the sight of her great-grandmother. "You *lied* to me."

Penelope sets a kettle on the gas stove, crosses to the living room, and sits in a Victorian armchair. Teacups already wait on the counter, strings hanging out.

"Likewise," she counters. "You lied about your identity the day we met."

"That was so different." James crosses his legs. "We had no malicious intent. Can you say the same? We know you've been talking to Quill."

"So you did hear yesterday."

"I'm trying to understand why you'd do this, but I can't." Nelle shrugs helplessly. "Did you know he would show up here?"

"No, I did not," Penelope says. "I'll admit, I've never cut off communication with my grandson. We talk often. Every couple of weeks or so. Throughout this summer we've spoken, but he never gave any impression that something was wrong. Didn't mention the house fire, nor you running away."

"But you knew about *me*?" Nelle asks.

James reaches for her hand.

Penelope's lips set into a grim line. "I'm sorry, Nelle, for not stepping in. I read and responded to your letters. I knew you were there, but I didn't know about the abuse. I thought he was keeping you . . . happily."

Nelle forcibly swallows, either tears or disgust. "He *wasn't*."

"I see that now."

"And I didn't send you any letters," Nelle says. "I wasn't allowed to write."

The kettle starts to howl.

"I'll get it." James goes into the kitchen, grateful to escape the ice between the women. He was teetering on the edge of distrusting Penelope, but Quill's attack pushed him over. Still he finds himself asking whether she wants milk or sugar.

"Neither," Penelope says.

James serves the cups, setting his and Nelle's on two coasters shaped like roses.

"Those letters were the one point of contact I had with you . . . I thought I knew you . . . For years, he must've been forging them." Penelope reaches across the table, hand outstretched toward Nelle. "You are a born writer, Nelle. You *deserve* to have control over your own life, as your predecessors did."

"I agree."

"I always thought you consented to being hidden. That . . . that it was your choice."

"You should have made sure." Nelle gives in and touches her hand. "But that doesn't forgive anything. Why *hide* me for twenty-one years? Didn't you think *that* was abusive?"

"I thought he taught you," Penelope says, "you know, how dangerous you are."

Nelle laughs. "Dangerous?"

James shakes his head. "She wouldn't hurt a firefly."

"Wallace didn't tell you about the consequences?"

"He told me I'd die if I wrote for myself," Nelle says.

Penelope curses Quill under her breath. "Of course he did. As I'm sure you've learned by now, you *can't* die. At least, not in that way. But what you are, the power you hold, is a danger. To loved ones. To society." She dims, reaching for her tea. "Bianca and Eleanor didn't die by a freak accident. Quill compelled the fire that took their house that night. He woke up with an idea and jotted it down, mistakenly using the ink pen filled with *his* blood. He went back to sleep, and minutes later, the house was engulfed."

Nelle's hand goes clammy in James's. He gives it a tighter squeeze. *I'm here with you.*

"You know how that story ends. They were human. He—like his mother, Lily, like you—isn't."

"So how did she die?" Nelle asks. "Lily, I mean."

"Ironically"—Penelope grimaces—"she wrote for herself. A direct command to cease existing. I can only imagine the second her pen lifted, she was gone, because all Thomas found in their house was an inkwell tipped across her hardwood desk and a black streak off the last letter she'd written . . . *g*."

"Quill told me that his mother died from a sickness."

"It is a sickness of sorts," Penelope says. "But how could we explain to people who knew her that she'd taken her life? We lied, Thomas and I together, and said she'd had a malignant brain tumor. My husband had died years earlier. With Sam gone the year before, and then Lily, it was only Wallace, his father, and me left."

James runs his thumb over the back of Nelle's hand. "I'm sorry for all your loss."

Penelope nods. "Thank you, James."

Nelle takes a prolonged sip of tea. "Your husband wasn't written into life like us?"

"No," Penelope says. "Lily was the first. Samford was an accountant, which I found boring, but there was something about him. I saw the magic. Years after we were married, I found out that his mother had experimented with spells and rituals, often using *him* as a test subject. He knew from a young age that he could write things into life, but he kept it a secret. To him, it was never a gift, but a curse. He was so scared to wield it, he barely wrote at all."

"Then how did he create Lily?" James asks.

"We tried to get pregnant for years. I was forty when I finally missed my time of the month. We went to the doctor, too scared to be hopeful, and he told us we had one." Mist blankets Penelope's eyes. "Months into the pregnancy, I lost her."

She clears her throat and continues.

"Samford wrote a poem after the death of our daughter. The first words he'd written in years. A poem about what she would have looked like. How she would've laughed. The little personality she would've had." A tear runs down her cheek. "I woke up that night and heard an infant giggling. I thought I was having a—what do they call it—a night terror. I tore down the hallway, Samford right behind me, and into the nursery that would have been little Lily's. And there she was, in the bassinet. A real baby. Hands reaching for a mother she'd never known yet somehow knew. I still had milk, so she latched on right away. She was mine. My miracle baby.

"Samford kept journals for Lily throughout her childhood. When we realized she couldn't move on her own, she had started crawling. The door was open from bringing in groceries one afternoon, and she just froze there at the threshold. For two years, we kept her inside. Then one day, she grabbed my razor in the tub and cut her thumb. Ink came out, not blood. Swirling black with the soap. Samford collected a few drops before her cut closed up. I didn't know what he was going to use them for until I was tending to the sheep the next evening and Lily came waddling out. I couldn't cut her, so he always did. I don't know how he managed. He would prick her finger with a needle, even as she screamed."

Penelope watches an osprey on the windowsill.

"When Lily was old enough to hold a pen, we taught her to write for herself. But your curse's power doesn't come from paper, it comes from blood. From *you*. Over time, Lily learned to write for herself without pen and paper. Like a muscle that takes growth and practice to function properly. The ink *inside* her grew strong enough to execute her thoughts. Lily was so adept at controlling herself without writing, the power she wielded when she *did* put pen to paper . . . Like Samford, she discovered how to use her words to create *anything*.

"And for her, that became normal, and she lived like anyone else. Until she met Thomas. Due to her mystical creation, Lily tried and tried but could never conceive. On top of that, Thomas was a serial cheater, so she was furious, foolishly in love, and desperate for a baby. So she did like her da and wrote herself one. Wallace. A couple of years later, Thomas had his hundredth affair, only to find out that the woman was pregnant. He promised to start a new family with her. Instead, he woke up a few months later to find an infant on his and Lily's doorstep. That day Lily found out about Thomas's plan to leave her, and she adopted a new son. Baby Sam, named after her da, my love, Samford. Through it all, she drove herself crazy with her writing. Her poems were fragmented, directionless, every word detrimental to her mental health. Still, she loved the high that poetry gave her."

"But if we can't procreate," Nelle says, "how did Quill have Eleanor?"

"Bianca was already pregnant when they married. Eleanor became Wallace's life and soul. He visited me once during that time, and he was happier than I've ever seen him. I thought, optimistically, that he could escape the cycle that had overtaken my husband and daughter.

"Then he called with the news of the fire. I'd dealt with grief all my life, but nothing unexpected. Samford was sick for years before he passed, and I wasn't surprised by Lily's death after her repeated suicide attempts. But what happened to Bianca and Eleanor tore out my heart.

And Wallace . . ." Penelope sips her tea. "He didn't like losing control. He learned that about himself when his brother died. So he never fell in love again, never associated with anyone else. He created you, and you were precious to him. He knew, as long as he kept his journals with your ink, that your life was insured. That you could never leave. Wallace convinced me it was all for your benefit, but I should have seen through his lies. God, he forged those letters for *years* because he didn't want me to know you."

Nelle crosses her knees. "You never tried to call? To visit?"

"He forbade it."

"And you didn't think that was strange?"

"I thought it was Wallace," Penelope says. "I will not make excuses for him—he is a bad man—but you have to understand that he was broken from the start."

"Bullshit, he isn't a *character* with his life plotted out for him." Nelle leans back into the sofa, arms crossed. "He chose what kind of person to be."

"No, he's *not* a character, but he's also not human." Penelope sets her tea down with a clink. "The sooner you understand that, the easier your life will be. What Samford's mother inflicted on him was a *curse.* It should have never happened. No one can handle that much power without hurting *many* other people."

James sits up. "You're saying Nelle should have never happened?"

"No." Penelope stares out the window at the loch dressed in morning gray. "I want you—both of you—to fully comprehend the precariousness of Nelle's situation. She comes from a line of death and struggle, most of it caused by that damned curse. You can strengthen yourself and learn how to function in the real world, but it'll be difficult. A road lined with suffering. There's only one way to end it. Quill knows it, too."

"And that way is what?" Nelle laughs coldly. "Kill myself?"

"There are alternative—"

Nelle squeezes her mug of tea. "I can't even look at you right now."

James glares on her behalf.

Penelope stands. "I've said what I came to say."

"Then you should go," Nelle says. "Thank you for the tea. We'll be out of the cottage by tomorrow."

"Nelle, I don't want to upset you. I only want you to be aware—"

"I'm well aware of what you want now, thank you." Nelle grips James's thigh. "Please go."

Penelope shuffles to the door. Before she steps out, she says, "I had someone drive your rental car up here from my house. Keys are in the kitchen drawer."

Nelle's face is dead. "Thanks."

"Find me when you're ready." The door shuts. Penelope's tiny footsteps fade on the flagstones.

At the window, Nelle watches her go, clutching the sheer curtain to her chest. Silver beads cling to her bottom lashes.

"It's not all bad news." James nudges her shoulder. "Did you hear what Penelope said about your power being a muscle? With enough practice, you'll be able to function like a normal person."

Nelle glowers out the window. "No, she's right. I'll never be a normal person. You know what Quill was, what Lily was. I don't stand a chance."

Something Penelope said circles back to his mind. *Broken from the start.* Is that Nelle? Doomed because her blood is ink and her father is a sociopath? But she is light, silver, air. He can't imagine death and destruction following in her wake. He cradles her hand like a baby bird.

"It's okay."

"I just thought she'd be . . ." Nelle shudders into his shoulder. "I knew Quill never wanted the best for me." Snot glistens under her nose. "But for a minute there, I thought Penelope really did, and I've never had that before."

James's heart breaks for Nelle. For twenty-one years she has had no one. She was alone and ridiculed and tortured by a man who should have loved her. And with Penelope, she finally thought she met family to take her in with open arms, flaws and all. For the first time in two months, homesickness pangs through James.

As Penelope disappears over the lip of the hill, Nelle shatters into tears.

Chapter 26

Light bleeds through the curtains. James doesn't pull back the scratchy comforter. Doesn't brush his teeth. Doesn't start a pot of coffee. He stares at the ceiling, imagining what it would be like to wake up in Jessie's apartment, to eat his lunch on a park bench before going to a class about literature and complex characters without stressing about those characters coming to life. He winces at the thought.

After Penelope left, Nelle turned into a ghost. James tried to scrub the ink off his body in the shower, toweled off, dressed, and found her staring out the window with a cup of tea, blond mane splattered with ink. He almost told her about NYU but decided not to. Not yet. She didn't say a word the rest of the day and kept her nose stuffed in one of the books she'd brought from Penelope's house.

He finally heard her voice at night, when she lit a candle, brushed her mouth across his, and whispered something filthy in his ear. He slid beneath the covers, happy to oblige her, but after she came on his face, while he was moving inside her, he felt uneasy.

He has never considered his time with Nelle ending, but now the thought haunts him, keeping him awake. He peels himself from bed and stumbles into the shower again, where thoughts go clear, time melts, and tears become one with the steaming torrent.

"James?" Nelle calls through the vinyl curtain.

He cuts the water off, pulls the curtain aside. Nelle sits on the bath rug beside the lip of the tub, her demeanor softening at his red, teary face.

The guilt he feels, dragging her along unaware of his wants, has reached a boiling point. He *has* to tell her, or he will hate himself forever. But he doesn't want to hurt her. He knows what she will say: *We don't need money, we'll work as we go.*

Nelle presses his cheek against her, a damp patch from his wet face forming on the faded red sweatshirt she's wearing. It's his, so it swallows her up, while her vanilla scent engulfs him.

"We should go." She kisses the top of his head.

"Go where?" His hands are trembling now. *Let's run, run, run away.* But he doesn't want to anymore, does he?

"Anywhere," she says.

Please come with me, scream her tear-filled eyes.

He watches the dripping showerhead. With every splash of cold water on his leg, he builds up courage.

"Nelle, I—"

"We can see the world together, like we planned before." She holds his bare shoulders and guides him to his feet. "We don't have to stop traveling. And now I can write for myself. Like you said, with enough practice, I might not even have to write—"

"But what if I do want to . . . stop?" James searches her face, wary of an angry response. But it falls instead, crushed. He decides to charge head-on. If he doesn't now, he will never be brave enough. "What if I told you that I want to go back to New York, and attend college there, and live there indefinitely?"

Nelle flinches. "How indefinitely?"

As he steps out of the shower and wraps a towel around his waist, James lets the last scrap of truth fly out. Bomb deployed and dropped—

"I applied to NYU," he says. For a breath, he feels relieved to have his secret lifted, but that relief dies the minute he sees the hurt on Nelle's face.

She twitches. "When?"

"I sent the application at the library in Edinburgh. I don't know why I did it, but I did. Just to see if I'd get in, I guess."

Unnervingly graceful, Nelle walks back into the bedroom and spins around at the foot of the bed, her face flushed red. She is furious, yet a smile plays on her lips. The effect, to James, is horrifyingly close to Quill.

"You could have told me . . ." She shakes her head. "Talked to me about it. I wouldn't have held you back."

James can feel the knife between her shoulder blades, the hilt in his hand. He betrayed her, and even if it won't kill her, he knows it hurts like hell.

"It's something I need to do, and I didn't know how to tell you. I"—he holds on to the bedpost to keep himself upright—"I didn't want to hurt you."

She presses her back to the wall, the farthest she can get from him. "So you're moving to New York?"

A chasm opens between them.

It's easier to hear her say it, and a part of him is glad this is happening now. Now, when she can write her for herself. Now, before he falls so in love with her that he can't recover from losing her.

"I'm not done seeing the world, James." Nelle's voice cracks. "We had a plan. You dropped out of school. We were going to travel *together*. How could you make this decision without even telling me? Until yesterday, I was dependent on you."

Defensiveness rises up in James. "I've always believed you could write for yourself. Or did you forget about the night in DC?"

She winces. "I remember."

"I can't run forever." It's hard to say what he needs to say when he can read the torment on her face. "You have a choice to make. The world or me."

He doesn't want either of them to make sacrifices. If she chooses to travel the world, he will leave for New York without her. It breaks his heart, but he has to do it. He opens his bag and pulls on a sweater and gray pants. No part of this feels like a clothing-optional conversation.

"I could give you the same ultimatum," Nelle says. "Go to New York or be with *me*."

"I ran away with you, Nelle." James buttons his pants. "I left my home, I traveled across the world, and I've shown you everything I can. But our money's basically gone, and I want to have a life now."

"And traveling with me isn't a life?"

"It's not what I want forever." The words fly hot but true. Their relationship, whatever it ends up being, will be better for it. He takes a deep breath and says the last part, the part that terrifies him. "I have enough money to buy two plane tickets . . . if you'll come with me."

"I don't want to go back with you," Nelle says. "I can't believe you'd rather live a boring, rooted life, going nowhere and doing nothing."

James sighs. "You know, Penelope has studied every aspect of your family, this cycle of writers, for decades. Maybe she's right. Maybe, by nature, it's impossible for you to be content."

When Quill crafted Nelle, after battling the grief of his lost daughter, he fashioned her out of desperation. He *wanted* a daughter more than he wanted to *love* a daughter. Because he had already loved one, and no successor could compare. That hunger, that need, that inability to sit with what is already there and be grateful . . . is that not Nelle?

She stares at him. A lingering, burning stare.

James's frustration subsides into guilt. "I'm sorry, I crossed a line."

God, he didn't mean it. He was only trying to hurt her. To hurt her for turning him down.

"I know you want to travel, but I can't afford it anymore. I *know* I want to be in New York. I need to be there. Traveling isn't what I want anymore, but you still are. Come with me, and we can start a life *together*. You are so special to me. Not because of how you were created, but because you're curious and confident and fiery and vulnerable, and I love you—"

She storms out.

He gives her a minute to cool down, then trails after her.

But the living room is empty. She is nowhere among the startling cleanliness of the place. Every surface is spotless and colorful, sunlight streaming through the windows into the cozy living room and kitchenette. A vague memory of Penelope wiping things down floats into mind.

Outside, an engine starts. James swings open the front door in time to see the back tires of the rental car spinning down the road. As the vehicle floats up the hill and out of sight, James reaches for the pendant around his neck. He squeezes the vial, still holding a few drops of Nelle's ink, and almost rips it from his neck to throw into the loch.

But he should return it to her, in person, as proof that he is not keeping it.

In the bedroom, he dumps out his backpack of dirty clothes and stuffs it full with Thomas Quill's moth-nibbled shirts and baggy pants.

When James closes the door behind him and starts down the hill, he is greeted by a cold Scottish morning. Wind hisses in a dance between brown grass and sunlight, leaves scuttling on the unpaved road. As he walks to the closest town, his destination across the Atlantic, he fights back tears, this unfamiliar misery embedded like a hatchet in his gut. More bitter than heartbreak. Hopeless without her beside him.

The gray, swallowing pain of losing a friend.

Part Three

Quills

Chapter 27

The first thing Nelle creates with her pen is a stack of money, and she spends it affluently. Wine in Greece, fairy lights in Madrid, slow boat rides in Venice. Late September is the portrait of a vengeful woman in Europe. Funneling out her ink, scribbling in her coffee- and tearstained journal, riding the high of having control over herself. Riding out her anger at James.

Nelle meets a man in a bar in Berlin, follows him back to his hotel room, and smokes her first cigarette on his balcony. Stinking of tobacco, she has sex with him. The moment he leaves her body, she feels sick. She tells herself it's from the nicotine, but she knows better.

For a few days, she spirals into a depression of drinking, day and night, bar to bar. She earns a small reputation up and down the block as the crying girl who orders pretzels and vodka. She learns to suppress her sadness. When James reenters her mind, she pushes him away with a new city, a new man who speaks no English, asks no questions, a man whose face she won't remember. She pushes James away with drinks, with dancing, with poetry, things that burn fast.

In Rome, Nelle decides to test the limits of her power. Penelope called it a curse, but Nelle hates that word. It's not a curse, it's a force. Her gift.

If Lily and Quill wrote *people* into life, what's stopping Nelle from creating whatever she desires?

So she tries. A poem about a glass of wine creates a fresh decanter of ruby red. A sonnet about a black dress, and silk wraps around her body. She wears tiny dresses out all night, moving to the sounds of club music, dancing with people she has known for mere hours, taking pills from strangers until her bones feel like glitter.

Barcelona teaches her how to summon a storm. Sitting on the lip of a dry rooftop, determined to find the limits of her power, she sets pen to paper, and as soon as the nib lifts off the page, the black-as-night clouds she described appear and begin to broil in the sky, rumbling with thunder and sheets of rain. She stands with her arms open, laughing in the downpour. Drunk on her own power.

The next morning in a hotel lobby, she watches the news on an English-language channel. Over the hammering deluge, the reporter projects, "This is the most rain Barcelona has seen in years! Last night the city put out a flash-flood warning, and this morning we have witnessed the devastating accounts of hundreds of people. Ninety-three homes have been damaged by this unprecedented storm. Over twenty lives lost so far. Today a few have been brave enough to share their story on live television for all of you."

❧

October—Africa. Nelle clutches her journal in her lap, the pages dotted with sweat. The sun is an oven lamp, the air is curdling, and everyone on the tour bus is tired and hungry. Even the lioness in the grass looks exhausted, lazily feeding on a helpless gazelle. She, too, is only violent by nature.

❧

When Nelle heard from a couple on her bus tour about a floating neighborhood in Lagos, she imagined a shaded gondola and waterways crisscrossed by quaint stone bridges. Nigeria's own little Venice. It only took the car ride from her hotel to a canoe owned by a man named Sade to realize that Makoko, this floating neighborhood, is no Venice.

The narrow waterways are lined with stilted buildings, plywood and bamboo walls topped with roofs of corrugated metal. A brother and sister watch Nelle from their porch. She waves, the lone passenger on her canoe, and they grin back. Sade steers past a woman selling fruit and nuts out of her canoe. Clouds of trash swirl in the water, but the small siblings pay it no mind as they leap off their house. Shirtless, laughing, they swim to the woman hawking her fruit.

Sade stands as he rows, his arms threaded with muscle. "Makoko is a vibrant part of Lagos, home to schools, hospitals, restaurants, markets. Some call it the world's largest floating slum, but we are not poor. See for yourself."

Nelle does. Two women take clothes off a line, the younger of the two popping the older with a shirt. The older woman laughs and pops her back. A few buildings down, a trio of children waves at Nelle. As Sade steers them past, the children dance, rolling their little hips. Another girl, no older than ten, stands on a canoe of her own, navigating by herself. Nelle can't imagine having that much agency at such a young age.

"We may not have money," Sade says, "but we have *life*."

"Everyone does seem happy."

So joyful with so little, she thinks. Maybe James was right. Maybe she is cursed to never be content.

"Makoko is a community." Sade touches a fist to his sweaty chest, the October sun beating down. "We have one heart. If we don't share it, we die."

A woman calls out from her porch, waving with both arms.

"Sade," she says. "This is your fourth tour today. It's too hot. You'll pass out without a break. I've got clean water."

At the mention of water, Nelle perks up. She feels like a dehydrated sponge.

"Ugh, fine." Sade docks the canoe alongside the woman's house. "Nelle, this is Chika. We go way back."

Chika cuts him side-eye. "What he means is he got me pregnant when we were sixteen then *left* me."

Nelle nods, unsure what to say. She writes in her journal to climb off the canoe.

"Greater forces at work, though." Chika guides them into her home. "I lost the baby two months in and got soul-tied to this asshole."

The place is small, but it has a bed, a corner for food preparation, a shelf of books. Nelle notices a table of herbs and glass jars.

"Soul-tied," Nelle says. "Is that a Nigerian belief?"

Sade huffs. "No. It's a Chika belief."

"Your *pikin* was in my womb, asshole. That brings us closer than blood." She hands Nelle a plastic bottle of water. "So what brings you to Nigeria?"

Nelle takes a greedy gulp. "Honestly, Makoko. I heard about it and had to see it for myself."

"And?" Chika grins. "Expectations met?"

"Exceeded."

"Ha! Excellent." She grabs Nelle's hand and kneads her palm, her knuckles, rolling them between her fingers. "Interesting," she murmurs. "You are interesting."

"What is she doing?" Nelle asks Sade.

He slumps back against the wall, clutching his water bottle. "Witchy shit."

When Chika opens her eyes, dark brown, framed by thick lashes, they pierce through Nelle.

"Your heart is broken."

Nelle pulls her hand back, tingling from the touch. "How do you—"

"Don't force it back together," Chika interrupts. "You're used to wounds healing fast, but this one will take time."

Sweat beads on the back of Nelle's neck. The room closes in, getting darker.

"Promise me," Chika says. "Promise me you'll give it the time it requires."

"Sure, yeah." Nelle smiles. *Please stop staring at me like you can see through me.* She holds out her pinkie. "I promise."

❧

In the dark of the night, in the bedrooms of random men, Nelle has considered using her ink to write James back into her life. She doesn't know what would happen, whether he would appear before her, or some fake version of him, only as real as a wish or a dream. Only as real as herself.

❧

Nelle is in a café in Tokyo when she moves with her mind for the first time. She picks up her drink, forgets to grab her journal from the canvas bag over her shoulder, and thinks, *Go outside*, as absently as she would think to breathe. Blood slugs through her veins, ink powering her movements, and she steps outside, into the sunlight and concrete. Easy.

For twenty-one years, she was caged. Quill broke her, locked her away, and lied to her about *everything*. All those years, she could have written for herself with no consequences. She could have learned to build that muscle, to strengthen herself, and by the time she met James, she could have already had total autonomy over her body.

What would that life have looked like? Too late now to know.

At last, she is free, and she has nowhere to go.

❧

November ends. Nelle huddles into her collar and braves the gray London street. She has no idea where in the city she is, but she doesn't care. Power thrashes like a chained tiger inside her as she stalks down the puddled sidewalk.

So adept at controlling herself now, she only needs a thought to move. And she has learned, from city to city, to create masterfully using ink and paper. A few written words, and she can conjure anything.

This is true power, she thinks. *True freedom.*

She feels so distant from the laughing Nelle that splashed in the sea with James, who screamed at Quill to burn his house down, who dipped a brush in a cup of coffee and painted a flying palomino in a single sleepless night.

A double-decker bus rolls past her, splattering gutter sludge. Her red raincoat is stained, her face dirt smeared, long hair matted. She desperately needs a bath and a hairbrush. Bubbles, candles, a book. Or even James . . .

She shakes the name away. Stupid name. *Stupid.*

A burly man barrels toward Nelle in a black suit, designer shoes splashing in a half-frozen puddle. He slams into her and she stumbles back, the air knocked from her lungs.

Without stopping, he says, under his breath, "Piece o' homeless shite."

Nelle glares after him. "Slip and break your neck, motherfucker."

The words leave her mouth with a puff of steam. Fired like a gun. Ink pumping, listening, cashing out her command.

Stop! Stop! I didn't mean—

A puddle sits in the man's path, suddenly iced over. Nelle's heart stops as the man steps on it and slips, his legs flying. His tie floats off his chest, his briefcase drops, and he falls backward.

Sometimes a thought is just a thought, Nelle lies to herself. Like she didn't feel that power course through her body, like she didn't just watch that puddle freeze.

The man hits the pavement with a crunch, and Nelle jerks away from his twisted neck, his starry eyes. She turns on her heel, sprinting in the opposite direction.

A thought is just a thought, a thought is just a thought, a thought is just a thought . . .

Chapter 28

Fat snowflakes coat the sidewalk, slicken the streets. Worker bees frantically spread across the city to cover every paved surface with salt, but despite their efforts, wrecks have been popping all morning. James stuffs his hands in his pockets and braces against the cold as he steps out of Butterfly House, his new favorite café.

He orders cappuccinos now. Upon landing in JFK in September, he asked for his usual iced latte, but when the wet condensation hit his hand, he knew he wouldn't be able to drink it. Forcing down even a swallow would have made him sick thinking of Nelle. Since starting his new life, he has only one rule: all reminders of her are banned.

He sips his cappuccino as a buzz fills his pocket.

Jessie's name pops up, along with a photograph of her wearing thin rectangular sunglasses and smoking a joint on her balcony.

"Hey, loser."

Her voice sucks him out of his day of despair. His feet are sore from standing in the cramped halls of shitty apartment buildings, holding every personal document imaginable in a manila folder, attending open house after open house, each potential listing more nightmarish than the last. There are only so many minifridges and communal bathrooms he can bear.

The pedestrian signal across the street is an orange hand, and a crowd forms to stare at it, or at their phones, waiting for it to change. A few brave souls stride across the four lanes in front of oncoming cars.

In his three months as a resident of New York, James has yet to stop traffic to reach his destination on time.

"Hey," he says. "I'm on my way. You still at the bookstore?"

"Yeah, I don't get off until four," Jessie says. "No luck?"

"Everything's so expensive." Steamed milk and espresso settle in his stomach. "And I fear working at a bookstore with a shit-ton of student debt doesn't make me a desirable tenant."

"I'll cosign with you," Jessie says. "Or stay with me. Use my spare bedroom for the next two years if you need to. Or ten. Unless I have kids, then we'll all move to a bigger place together, if you're willing or still unable to—"

"Thank you, but no," he cuts her off. "I'll be gone as soon as I score an apartment with a freezer *and* a shower."

"Well, the offer's there. Did you get your tuition worked out?"

The light changes, and the crowd shifts into motion. James crosses the street, weaving between people, smog ghosting over cars, snowflakes coming down like ash.

"Yes, the loan finally came through. It's all finalized. I have a meeting with my advisor next week to go over my schedule."

The night he received his acceptance email from NYU, he screamed and barreled into Jessie's room. She was half awake, hair a bird's nest, when she heard the news, but that didn't stop her from insisting they celebrate with ice cream from the corner store. They made whiskey floats and talked until dawn.

He pauses outside the narrow wood-paneled door to Shack O' Books. A woman walks by with her shoe-wearing dog, followed by a pair of bundled parents pushing a stroller. A suit cuts James off, booming into his phone. Behind him strides a rail-thin woman with the stature of a fashion model.

James pushes inside the store, snow blowing in with him. A bell dings its welcome note.

Jessie waves from her perch behind the vintage register. Into her phone she says, "Have fun at work!"

"Yeah." He slides onto the stool beside her. "You, too."

❦

Jessie's spare bedroom is James's now.

Despite his insistence that his stay was *temporary*, she took him antiquing for decorations, then to Pottery Barn for new bedding and sheets. Scarlet pillows on a green-and-cream patterned quilt, a knitted throw over the foot. Chestnut bookshelves filled with his favorites. The red typewriter rests on the nightstand, the typewritten copy of his novel hidden in the back of the dresser drawer. On the desk, beneath the window where he spent those weeks high on love and writing, sits a silver slab. His laptop, a magical device that has increased his productivity tenfold.

Too fast for his own liking, he has reintegrated himself back into a technological lifestyle. If society didn't require it, he would go months at a time without touching his phone. The weeks he traveled with Nelle, free from the chains of his phone, were some of the best of his life.

She left the cottage without giving him a chance to explain. To reason. Didn't bother to hear his feelings before she reacted. But he can't blame her. Like him, she knew what she wanted. And for the first time, that morning in the cottage, she had the power to leave.

He unplugs his laptop, digs his manuscript from the dresser, and takes them to the bed, exhausted from a day of walking and apartment hunting and work. The glare of the screen blinds him, so he squints as he types in his password. Jessie suggested he try transcribing *The Summer Curse*, that it would be therapeutic. He refused to let her read it, but he has told her bits and pieces. Nothing revealing about Nelle.

He plops the manuscript on his right and opens a new document on his laptop. Though it's undoubtedly a bad idea to fall down this hole, James opens page one and starts typing. As he sinks into the story, he relives those early memories of July. The honeysuckle outside Nelle's window. Fire crackling. That first taste of freedom on the highway.

It's past 3:00 a.m. when he forces himself to stop. Rereading *The Summer Curse* makes his rib cage feel like it's sinking in on itself. He ponders an alternate reality where he chose to stay with Nelle, to travel the world with no money, to live homeless wherever they went, with only enough saved up to book a flight from one city to the next.

Is that her life now? She is still alive, of course, but is she happy? *I hope she's not happy.* No, he doesn't mean that. He wants her to be happy. He just wants her to miss him like he misses her, to wonder whether she made the right decision, to twist her bedsheets up at night thinking about what went wrong and how it could have gone differently. He wants her to want to be in New York, sleeping beside him.

But that isn't who she is. She needs to fly, and James only needs to live. Nelle is a piece of fiction, a character who needs a purpose. He is only dependent on the breath in his lungs and the blood in his heart.

In the nightstand drawer, he digs past three poetry collections to find the photographs he tucked away for safekeeping.

The first is of him and Nelle in DC, smiling with their arms wrapped around each other.

Innocence, he calls it.

The second photograph hurts worse.

Him, Nelle, Jessie, and Lena, their heads hung back in laughter. Seeing Nelle back in New York, even in a photograph, is an arrow to the heart.

This one's name comes clear to him, too. *What could have been.*

He imagines Nelle on the bed with him, her head in his lap. Soft vanilla, prickly ink, the weight and warmth of her hand in his. Her laughter bubbling up, her glares, her scrappiness, her . . .

He goes to sleep thinking about everything he can never have again.

⁂

Jessie's Christmas party is a spectacle of glitter and gold. James maneuvers through the apartment with two plastic glasses of champagne. He slides around the back of the couch, cuts through a game of beer pong on the island, and says hi to some rowdy friends of Jessie's. He has barely drunk a drop, and every face he recognizes is no more than an acquaintance, so he searches for his cousin through the den of alcohol, weed, tinsel, and holiday sweaters. After scanning the apartment, he spots her out on the balcony and weasels his way through the cramped room. Jessie's leaning against the balcony's iron ledge, smoking with Lena, and accepts one of the plastic flutes.

"Your party's a hit," he says.

She blows out a plume of smoke. "Always. We were just talking about how beautiful it is out here."

"It's cold," James says.

Lena's black hair is slicked into a mass of curls. Her jaw is square, her smile wide and white, and she wears a yellow-leather trench coat over a white turtleneck and baggy jeans. Her outfit screams *fashion* while Jessie's light-up spangled Christmas sweater just screams.

Across the street, twinkly lights are strung from balcony to balcony. A family of pigeons makes a nest in the yellow crook of a windowsill. Snow tumbles from the sky, sticking like powdered sugar to the tops of trash cans.

"This is peak New York right here," says a velvety voice behind James.

He turns to see a woman in a thin white cardigan perched in the balcony shadows. She leans against the brick wall, her arms crossed, red Solo cup dangling in her hand. Her gray dress rides up to reveal a freckle on her mid-thigh. *She has to be freezing*, he thinks.

"Lucy," Jessie says, "This is my cousin James. He's starting at NYU next semester."

Lucy's stony gaze softens. He feels the urge to put on a reality TV show, make popcorn, and take an edible with her. To spiral into an all-night-long conversation, exploring each other's brains, considering each other's bodies. An urge he hasn't had since Nelle.

"I'm a student, too," she says. "Working on my MFA."

"At NYU?" James asks.

"Columbia."

"Oh, so you're *smart* smart." He laughs. *Smart* and *pretty,* he thinks.

Lucy observes him, as unreadable and dangerous as a hawk.

"So, uh . . ." Everything he can think to say seems idiotic. "What's your focus?"

Lucy tilts her cup to her lips, silver earrings dangling like tiny chandeliers. "Fiction."

"Oh, fiction," James says. "Cool. What made you choose that?"

She shrugs. "I like to lie."

Jessie squints through the foggy glass door. "Oh, honey, Ben's looking for us." She threads her fingers through Lena's and drags her inside. "I'll be right back. You two stay out here."

James lifts his hand. "Wait, Jessie—"

The glass door slides shut, cutting off the rumble of party shenanigans.

Lucy laughs. "Impressive setup."

James drains his champagne, a rush in his head, a pool of fire in his stomach.

"Sorry about that," he says. "Jessie thinks she's got a right to meddle in my life. Which, for a lot of reasons, she kind of does."

"I love that about her. She makes shit happen." Lucy tucks a light-brown strand behind her ear, showing off the glint of her earring. The curve of her tan neck. "So how long have you been in New York?"

"Only a few months," James says.

Lucy shifts off the wall to lean on the rail. No way the metal isn't ice cold, but she doesn't flinch. In the light, her dress sparkles like a trove of silver. He desperately wants to take in every inch of her, but he fixes his gaze on her azure eyes.

Being this close to her makes his lungs tighten, his heart quicken, and that feeling of desire shoves him toward a single thought, a single memory, a single person. The one he tries so hard to keep out of his head because when he thinks of her, nothing else exists.

"Is something wrong?" Lucy asks, reaching out.

Vanilla perfume clings to her sweater, choking him. He imagines Nelle's face if she saw him pursuing this other woman. How hurt would she be? What would she say? She would be devastated. So would James, if she did the same to him.

"James—"

Lucy touches his arm, but instead of comforting him, it sends a wave of anger through his body. Heat rushes from his head to his feet, and he pushes her away without thinking. She stumbles back a step, her brows furrowed as she tries to process his violent reaction.

James trembles, staring at the rug on the concrete balcony and the few dead plants still in their pots.

"I'm sorry," he says, but the words are cotton in his mouth. "So sorry."

Don't cry, he thinks. *Nelle's gone. Don't cry. You don't need her, she's a mistake, she's a mistake.* For a minute, as he sucks down the ice-flecked air, he repeats words of comfort to himself. Advice Jessie's given him. Bits of wisdom he has been gathering for months. *You're okay. Better off alone. Take this time to find yourself.*

Lucy is still there. Holding out her hand like someone trying to pet a feral cat. Her face peeks out behind two sheets of hair, showing only empathy.

"You should leave," he says. "I pushed you."

Lucy peers over the balcony railing. "Not hard enough."

He considers this surprising woman, while repeating all the reasons he needs to be single. *Career, time to find myself, getting over Nelle . . .* the list goes foggy.

"I'm not scared of you, James," she says. "I have three brothers. None of them knew how to express their emotions, so they talked with their fists."

"I'm not typically violent." James clears his throat. "Lucy, you're beautiful, you seem funny, you're obviously smart, and you're a writer, but . . . I guess Jessie didn't tell you. I just got out of a relationship. A messy one. And I'm realizing, right now, that I'm not in the mental place to start a new one. So . . . I'm sorry."

Lucy's hand stays extended between them, waiting for him.

"Didn't you hear me?" His voice breaks.

"I heard you. I'm here if you want a new friend in the city, that's all."

His eyes sting, and he thinks, *Don't cry*, but the constraint is useless. Warm tears leak down his cheeks as he takes Lucy's hand, lets her pull him closer. He's not scared of her touch anymore. No weight between them, no pressure, just the possibility of friendship. He presses into her white cardigan, breathes in her hair, finding comfort in the sturdiness of another person. Her vanilla perfume has honeysuckle notes, a bit of natural bitterness that's new to him. When they pull apart, she rubs circles on his lower back.

He wipes his frozen tears with his sleeve. A car alarm goes off down the street. Inside the apartment, the muffled noise rises into a clamor.

"Three months here and you're the nicest person I've met," he says.

Lucy leans her head on his shoulder, though they are nearly the same height. "I'm not nice."

James laughs, still snotty. "I'm sorry for crying."

"Don't be. Whatever happened between you and your ex is over now, so you need to process, and crying is step one."

"I've been trying to do that for months, but I don't even know what I need to work through, or why it all hurts so much. I hurt her. She hurt me. But the worst part is that I miss her. I don't *want* to process and move on. All I really want is to be with her again, but she's not here."

For three months, James has feared those words, thinking they would shatter atmospheres and tectonic plates, open skyscraper-swallowing sinkholes in the street, kick-start avalanches, explode dormant volcanos, push tsunamis to rise, summon meteors from the sky.

Instead, snow falls. The streetlight flickers amber.

"I can't believe I admitted that."

Lucy nudges his shoulder. "Was it hard?"

"No," he says. "Not at all."

Chapter 29

Nelle is on a plane back to New York when she has the dream, brought on by a double shot of vodka. She is surrounded by smoke. From the haze comes a rumble like hundreds of people murmuring. Two recognizable voices cleave through. Quill and Penelope, holding each other, calling out for her. She can see only their faces, distorted in pain.

Nelle snaps awake, snorting. She drifted too close to the woman on her right, who has been dutifully reading an Amish romance novel since the microwave meals were served. Nelle apologizes softly and sits upright.

Back in London, it hit her like a bus. An epiphany that plopped into her mind while she sipped a hot latte and stared out an overlarge window at a gray street.

She misses James.

She did everything she set out to do, and yet the last three months left a sour taste in her mouth. Every mystery novel, evening drive, glass of wine, and forgettable man carved her out, scooping until she was hollow. It all felt pointless without James. Who cares what that crackpot Chika said? Kissing James again would heal Nelle's heart instantly.

So she hopped on a plane to New York.

Her plan *was* to show up at Jessie's apartment and tell James that she wants him back, but now she can't stop thinking about Penelope and Quill, screaming like coyotes in her dream. Quill she couldn't care less about, but she can't shake her great-grandmother's anguished shrieking.

If James is in New York, he can wait. Nelle needs time to prepare for their reunion, anyway. Answers to his inevitable thousand questions. A pang hits her as she thinks over what *she* will ask *him*. Did he get into school? Can she read his novel? Has he started seeing someone else? She pushes the thought aside.

What if Penelope is in trouble, and Nelle's the only one who can help?

Though she hates to admit it, her great-grandmother's forewarnings have come to fruition. Wreckage follows Nelle. Flooded cities, shattered vertebrae, heartbroken men.

Even if her dream is just a dream, she needs to forgive Penelope, face to face.

The plane drops below the clouds, and Nelle presses her nose to the window. Below, James's new home sits like a city made of silver dimes, swelling into the East River. Bridges stretch across the water like spiderwebs. Nelle turns away. She doesn't want to see what she can't have.

It's torture, waiting for the jolt of the wheels hitting ground. The plane taxis to the gate, and disembarking begins. Nelle shuffles off the claustrophobic exit ramp in a line of slow-footed passengers, turns around at baggage claim, and books a seat on the next flight to Edinburgh.

She lands at midnight. Takes a cab from the airport. Dark stone houses rise like hedges on either side of the road, interspersed with parks and restaurants and cafés. Edinburgh has a coziness that other major cities lack. Shops along the street sell wool sweaters, cafés serve pots of tea and beans on toast, print shops and publishers operate from centuries-old buildings.

Her favorite parts of the city are closed at this hour, of course, and when the cab lets her out at the bus station near the city center, she discovers that there are no routes to Scourie, and none *near* Scourie, until tomorrow.

She runs back out to the street and flags down the cab before it pulls off.

"Where to now?" asks the driver.

This part she hasn't thought through at all. "Any suggestions?"

"You're asking *me*? Er, there may be a couple of small spots open still. Were you wanting more of a pub or café?"

"Café."

Nelle's eyes shut after she is buckled in. Exhausted from back-to-back transatlantic flights, the thought of coffee sends her into a dreamlike state . . . espresso, cinnamon on foam, and black, aromatic beans.

"It'll be ten minutes, all right?" says the driver as he pulls away.

She lets her forehead rest against the cool glass until her thoughts spin away.

The cab snaps its brakes. Nelle's head jerks forward, and the driver yells out a stream of curse words in a Scottish accent so thick, it's like hearing another language. The car in front of them has stopped abruptly, red taillights shining guiltily.

She peeks out the side window and sees a random Edinburgh street, the stone facades blurry in the dark. Iron railings line the balconies, window boxes full of dead things. The buildings are more uniform than in Old Town, so she judges that she is probably in the aptly named New Town, just across the North Bridge.

The cab driver points. "Under that place there is a wee spot I like. The owner's nice if you talk to him."

"Thanks." Nelle pays him and climbs onto the curb. The bottom of her camel coat hangs around her ankles, dangerously close to the puddle she's standing right in the middle of.

"Cheers." The driver wheels off.

A hot-pink poster with bold black letters catches Nelle's attention: Eye Care.

A shudder races down her spine. *You're shitting me.*

No sign for the Underground Café, but she knows the spot. *Surely it's not open this late.* She creeps down the steps, into the damp, and waits until she sees motion through the fogged window to pull open the ice-crusted door.

"Well, well, well," says a familiar voice behind the espresso machine. "If it isn't the reporter. Where's your friend?"

Nelle says nothing and slides onto a wooden stool at the end of the counter. The rest of the café is empty.

"Can I have a hot latte?" she asks. "With an extra espresso shot."

She opens her journal in her lap, shakes her pen, and writes a description of the British pound. Hears the crinkle, smells the paper, feels the smooth glossy texture. She writes down each sensation, and a little more than the amount she needs pops into her hand. Crisp. Real. She places the money on the countertop as if she pulled it from her bag.

While he counts out her change, Terry says, "How was Christmas?"

"Fine." Nelle opens her hand for the coins. Drops two pounds in his tip jar. She doesn't want to talk, doesn't care about anything but getting to Penelope's house in Scourie, ensuring that her great-grandmother is okay, and then finding James.

Terry passes her the latte in a ceramic mug. She starts to ask for a to-go cup instead when she sees that the toasted foam is swirled into a four-leaf clover, and he has placed a little spoon on the saucer by the mug.

"Thank you," she says. Steamed milk coats her throat, cut through with bitter espresso. Hints of dark chocolate, but thinner. Sharper. Tangier. The milk gives it a heavy comfort, like wool on a cold night. "This is the best coffee I've ever had."

Terry beams.

Once she is warm, she leaps. What does she have to lose, after all?

"Terry . . ." she begins. "You have a car, right?"

He frowns and scratches his scarlet beard. "I do."

"A license?"

"Yeah?" he says, a skeptical crease between his brows.

He will need more warming up before I introduce the idea of a road trip to Scourie.

Nelle drags a finger along the countertop and speaks casually. "I need to get my license replaced, and I was wondering if you knew how to do all that." She shrugs. "I have no one else to show me."

"Is your license . . . American?" he asks, frowning further.

She winces. "Never mind that. How was *your* Christmas?"

"Seen my ma." He slings a rag over his shoulder.

"Hm." Nelle sips her drink. "What's the problem?"

"I love making coffee more than money." He leans over the counter with his own mug, eyes roving across the empty tables and booths. "She thinks I'm wasting my life away. No children, no future."

Nelle takes another sip. "At least you're good at what you do."

Terry tinkers with his espresso machine. "If only she saw it like that."

"I feel you," Nelle says. "My mom . . ."

Terry flicks down his rag and wipes the counter. "Yeah?"

"Well, I never had a mom."

He sad whistles. "I'm sorry."

"And my dad . . ." Nelle realizes she has no right words to describe the man who raised her. "He's pretty awful."

"Same here," Terry says. "Yelled at me every day till I was thirteen."

"What happened?"

He cocks his head. "Well, he hit me. Then he left. Think my ma kicked him out. Never saw him again. What happened with you and your da?"

Nelle laughs and scratches her throat. Where to start? "I guess . . . well, I have a laundry list of grievances against him."

"His most recent offense?"

"He shot me."

"Oh." Terry stops wiping. "Oh shit, wow."

"It's okay, I'm fine. We're not, but . . . we never really were." The fragmented words spill out. Five months ago, she blazed out of Lincoln as fast as possible, raced through weeks and weeks of pure high, and now she's crashing.

Nelle is so lost in her head, she doesn't hear the café door open. Doesn't notice Terry sweep away to welcome the new customers. They chat for a moment, their voices garbled.

Then one voice cuts above the rest, and her instincts kick in.

Shrink, cower, obey.

Her eyes beeline to Quill, sitting beside Penelope under a soft hanging lamp. Until this moment, Nelle was still holding out hope that her dream was just a dream. She whirls back to the bar before they see her face.

Terry circles back, fiddling with the espresso machine. "You'll never guess who just walked in. *Wallace Quill.* Why'd you kids say he died? I told everyone I know the bad news."

She squeezes the edge of the countertop for support. The last time she saw Quill was in the dark of the cottage, slinging that pistol like a maniac. Seeing his profile now, under soft lighting—sharp jawline, strong nose, graying hair—is like seeing a panther in a swimming pool.

Nelle isn't naive. That bullet was never intended for her. It was James whom Quill had been set on murdering, and if she hadn't jumped in the way, he would have succeeded. James wouldn't be a forsaken lover, but a dead one.

Nelle can't die, and she is more powerful than ever.

But Penelope can. And in the dream, she was crying out for help.

"What's the matter?" Terry asks.

Nelle sips her latte to buy herself a moment to think. Then, decision made, she says, "The man in the corner booth is my father. Wallace Quill. When we told you about the obituary . . . *we* . . ." James flashes before her with every blink.

"Wallace is your *dad*?" Terry whispers. "*He* shot you?"

"An espresso," Nelle says. "I need another espresso."

Terry crafts the perfect shot of espresso, and she knocks it back. She shakes her head at the bitterness and the shock of energy. With a newfangled bravery, brought on by sheer anger at seeing *his* face again, she charges between high-top tables until she is standing before their booth.

Penelope and Quill both look up.

"You were asking for me?" she says.

"Nelle . . . I . . ." Penelope's mouth falls open. "I didn't know you were here."

Why are you still seeing Quill after he tried to kill James? she thinks, but first, she has to face her fear. She turns to Wallace Quill. Technically a father, but never to her.

His beetle-black eyes blink once. "Hi, Nellie."

"Don't call me that," she seethes, her anger fermenting into bitterness. Suddenly she feels the weight of exhaustion like a thick rope draped across her shoulders. The last thing she wants tonight is an emotionally draining confrontation.

Nelle drops down beside Penelope and thanks Terry as he brings her a cup of tea. To her amusement, he gives his old classmate Wallace a withering glare with his coffee.

"I had a dream," Nelle sighs. "Both of you were in it, and you were screaming out for me. It was too real to ignore."

Penelope and Quill flash identical expressions at each other.

"What was that?" Nelle says. "That look."

Penelope starts to inch out of the booth. "We should have this conversation somewhere more private."

"I want to have it here," Nelle says. "What is happening? Why are you two meeting in the middle of the night?"

Quill locks fingers around his mug. "Because I want to end my life."

Nelle stares at him like he struck her. She searches his aging face for an inkling of a joke, but every line reads dead serious.

"Why?" she asks.

"I shot you, Nellie."

That wretched nickname jumps off his tongue and crawls spiderlike down her spine.

"And?" She retreats to her tea for some comfort. "Neither of us can die. We both know that, so what's the big deal?"

"The big deal is that I was aiming for James," Quill says, and though his eyelid twitches on James's name—Nelle has the same reaction for different reasons—he goes on, his voice even. "I was so enraged, blinded, that I *wanted* to kill him. When the shot went off, and I saw you standing there, that bullet hole in you . . ."

He tries to hide his tears. Nelle is glad. She doesn't want to see him cry for a single fucking second. Not after the years of abuse and trauma she carries like a disease, the flashes of panic and deep-rooted self-hatred that gnaw at her soul. The constant *fear*. The numbness to pain. The need to run.

"I was relieved that it was you," Quill admits. "I regretted it as soon as the shot went off. I left thanking the heavens that I hadn't killed him, though I can't deny I still want him dead on a level I can't tame."

"And you think you should end your life because of it?" Nelle doesn't really give a shit what happens to him, as long as he never bothers her again, but she does care about her own future, and suddenly this conversation with Quill seems more like an argument with Penelope. Nelle defending her right to live, despite the debris amassing in her shadow.

"I know I should," Quill says. "It's what my mother did, when her time came."

"And you're fine with him doing this?" Nelle asks Penelope, accusatorily.

Penelope crosses her arms and shrugs. "I know the kind of person Wallace is. If he doesn't do this, he will only cause more harm to innocent people. And one of those people, eventually, will be James."

Nelle's chest pulls tighter with each word, until she snaps and says, "Stop it. Stop speaking so coldly. You did it that morning you came to the cottage. When you told me I should end my life."

"You misunderstood me," Penelope says. "I only meant to warn you that, if you find destruction trailing you like it does Wallace, like it did Lily, then you may have to alter your plan."

Nelle desperately wants to share her experiences, the horrible events she inadvertently caused across the world. People died because she couldn't control herself, couldn't keep them out of harm's way. Out of *her* way.

Pain will follow me wherever I go. The thought intrudes in her head, and she can't shake it out.

Quill sets his coffee on its saucer. "So, are we ready?"

"What, you want to end it in here?" Nelle stammers, a little too loudly. She glances over her shoulder, but Terry is preoccupied with a shelf of mugs behind the bar.

"Of course not." He drops a folded ten on the table. "But I wanted a cup of coffee before I go."

Penelope straightens the hood of her parka and clears her throat. "So, Wallace, where do you want to die?"

I suppose blunt questions run in the family, Nelle thinks, remembering a night of fireworks, her first conversation with someone other than Quill, the bees in her stomach. James. He pierces her memories of the last six months like an arrow. Where is he now? New York? Why isn't she there . . . *Why did I fly back here?*

"Calton Hill," Quill says. "Before the sun rises, so we can be alone."

The hike from Terry's café in New Town to the foot of Calton Hill is hard. Nelle trudges up the lamplit streets behind what she can't believe she thinks of as her family, wrestling with her guilty conscience. A part of her can't wait to see Quill die. Never to be scared that he is going to hurt her again. He doesn't deserve her forgiveness, and yet . . . her chest twinges like a wounded bird when she imagines him dead.

"Quill," she says.

He flinches. "Yes?"

"When the police officer came to our house, you told her that Eleanor survived. That she moved to Scotland with her grandparents after the fire. Why'd you lie?"

His mouth hardens. "The night of that fire was the worst of my life. Eleanor did die. She and Bianca both. I dragged them both out to the front yard, but it was too late. Carbon monoxide poisoning." He laughs bitterly. "I just wanted to bring my baby back." Tears choke him up, but he continues. "Eleanor's birth certificate, social security card, and passport were all I could save from the fire. I knew how my mother was created. And how she made me. So I did the same. I lied to the police officer because I'd lied to the government. Legally, Eleanor never died. Legally . . . she became you."

Nelle tries to imagine the little girl who came before her.

"Do I look like her?"

"When you were an infant, you did." Quill studies her sideways. "I had plans. I lied about her death because I wanted you to fill her place. To live in the world as Eleanor."

"But you didn't let me leave the house."

"I'll admit, I was scared for too long. But before James, I was starting to loosen up. I let you go to the library, remember? And then on the Fourth. I was testing your limits. How you responded to the world. How dangerous you could be if you weren't writing for yourself."

Nelle scoffs. "So it was never your plan to let me be free?"

"No." Quill's dark eyes fall onto her, and Nelle is not sure what he sees. Maybe shards of himself, maybe the truth of her last couple of months. "That was never my plan."

At the top of the hill, a castellated Gothic tower stands over them like a shadowy spire with a cross at the top. Down a path, the National Monument's long line of columns rises like a structure out of ancient Greece. Beyond that, the glittery city crawls to the sea. It's no Paris or New York, but from above, Edinburgh has its own starlit shimmer.

"Here?" Penelope gestures to a shaded bend in the path, where roots have grown over dead grass and lichen.

Quill shakes his head and cuts through the trees.

Nelle ducks beneath low-hanging branches, climbing over rocks and roots after him. She emerges on a stretch of grassy hill dotted with ancient stones. All of Old Town splayed out in evening blue, windows reduced to luminous or dark squares, the peak of Arthur's Seat like the hunched back of a sleeping giant.

"Right here," says Quill.

If Nelle were the one choosing to die, this place wouldn't be half bad. The wind is rough, and the air splices to the bone, but the utter freedom of the view . . .

Penelope catches up to them, impressively composed after the long hike.

"I'll only ask you this one last time, Wallace," she says. "Is this what you want?"

He looks his grandmother dead in the eye. "Yes."

"Then you know what to do."

Nelle holds her breath, confused by the feeling of gratitude that fills her. Somehow, she is a witness to this strange wrinkle in the fabric of the world. A man created by mystical means, leaving by mystical means. A balance struck. It suddenly doesn't feel wrong at all, but almost correct. Like Quill's purpose has always been to return to the liminal space from which he originates.

Wallace Quill opens a pocket-size journal, pulls a fountain pen from his coat, and writes.

He looks up, surrounded by the shadows of dawn, and meets Nelle's eye.

Then he's smoke, coiling away in the mist.

And he is gone. Really gone.

Nelle feels a twist of pain, registers where it pulses in the back of her stomach, and rationalizes it. *He's one of the few people to know I even exist.*

And she knows why he did it, knows the shattered path she herself has walked since leaving James at the cottage. The flood, the man on the sidewalk—what else did she cause without realizing? What about the men she left in the gray hours of dawn? She never followed up to check on any of them.

I've been playing with life like it's not real.

Suddenly, Nelle feels a hot queasiness. She falls to her knees in the damp grass.

Penelope floats in like a radiant angel, the sun rising behind her.

Nelle stands but immediately crumbles into her great-grandmother's embrace. She tucks her head under Penelope's chin and, blasted by wind on the hillside, tries to fight her trembling tears.

"I miss James," she says. "I really miss him."

"Do you need to do what Quill did?"

"No." Nelle can hear Penelope's heartbeat through her sweater. "Not yet."

Nelle pants and shoots awake, flipping back sheets and a comforter and a quilt. She needs her legs out, needs them, yes—she flings her limbs free and jumps off the mattress, onto the floor of the small bedroom.

A small voice calls through the wall. "You awake, dear?"

"Yes!" Nelle yells, but her voice is too raspy to carry, more of a quiet croak. She follows the smell of potatoes frying to a kitchenette attached to a small den. There is a love seat and a TV, one chair and a tasseled table lamp. A painting hangs on the wall, a stale portrait of fruit.

"Does anyone live here?" Nelle asks.

Penelope is at the stove. "Yes. Well, no. I bought it years ago as an investment when I had a bit of money. Now it's my secret hideaway. Quaint, but I love it."

Nelle stands in front of the living-room window, overlooking a street two stories below. Cobblestone puddles reflect dark, twisted clouds. People bundled in coats scurry past, carrying umbrellas.

"I love it, too," she says, admiring the bookshelves. One title stands out, the first mystery she read in New York, when she fell in love with the genre. Old feelings rush to fill her. James on the beach in France, James typing at his desk, James's tongue between her legs . . .

A familiar need for him crushes her. She wants to get on a plane as soon as possible. Back on the path she already chose. She examines her outfit. White sweater. Charcoal pants. Camel coat. Simple, sleek, casual. Good enough for a reunion.

Penelope puts two plates of potatoes, eggs, and peas on the table and sits.

Nelle joins her. "I'm going to ask you for a favor. And I know you're going to lecture me about being a danger to society, and I promise I'll take what you say into consideration, but while you're lecturing, could you drive me to the airport?"

Chapter 30

"There's something I have to do, and I just really need someone I know, even though we don't know each other that well, but someone I can call a friend, to be there with me."

James sits up in bed, phone to his ear. He normally declines calls from any number he doesn't recognize, but it was a New York area code, and his gut told him to answer. Now he tries to connect the voice to a face and comes up blank.

"I'm sorry," he says. "Who is this?"

"It's Lucy." She sounds frantic.

He sinks back against the pillows. "Oh, Lucy! Sorry, I didn't have your number saved."

She laughs, but he can tell it's forced.

"Anyway," he continues. "What were you saying?"

"I didn't know who to call, but I need help quitting my job."

"Oh." He sits up. "I don't really understand. Do you need me to meet you somewhere?"

"No—yes. Sorry. This is ridiculous, I'm a grown woman, I should be able to quit my own job without moral support."

James pulls on a long-sleeve shirt, a hoodie, a sherpa-lined denim jacket, two pairs of compression socks, then his boots. He brings his phone back to his ear like a puppet master's tugging his strings.

"Where can I meet you?" he asks.

"Coffee shop on the corner of Sixth and West Thirty-Eighth."

"Twenty minutes."

"Okay, but James . . ."

He pulls on gloves. "Yeah?"

"I was panicking, so I called the first number I could find, and I don't really have many friends in the city. So you don't have to—"

"No worries, Lucy. I'm on my way." He hangs up the phone and zips his jacket up to his chin. As an ex-Southerner, he has yet to acclimate to the cold. Before this winter, he had never seen real snow. Now he has mixed feelings about the frequent subfreezing temperatures and sunless days. On one hand, he loves how people huddle up. In shops. In cafés. On the subway. New York hibernates for winter, but it is a city of pedestrians, James included. So every day he joins the lines of New Yorkers marching the sidewalks like ants, ducking into coffee shops and excusing the six-dollar latte because, on the other hand, it is just too damn cold outside.

❧

Lucy's beneath a green-and-white striped awning. Arms crossed, cheeks red, hair tucked into a fur-lined hood. When she spots James crossing the street, her stance relaxes.

He nods in greeting, hands in pockets, shrugging off the cold. How can he play it cool, like he didn't sprint six blocks and jump a subway turnstile to meet her here in time?

"How's it going?" he asks, hoping he sounds casual.

"I want to quit my job. On the spot. No two weeks' notice."

For a moment, he is at a loss for words. She already told him this, so he has had time to stew on it. But in that time, he came up with zero advice. He can't tell her how to make such a major decision.

So he asks, "Why do you want to quit?"

"Because my boss is an utter shithead, and working there makes me feel horrible. I doubt I'll ever get promoted, and besides, I don't *want* to work there anymore. I have a different goal for my life now."

"Giving up writing?"

Lucy smiles, though he can tell she's not feeling very smiley on the inside. "The opposite, actually. I want to give my all to my MFA. Thanks to my grandpa, I have a trust fund arranged for my tuition, and I'll have a teaching assistantship as part of the program."

"So all you need to do now is quit?"

Lucy squints down the gleaming Midtown street. "Do you want to get coffee first?"

"No stalling." James shakes his head. "You got this."

She groans. "Fine."

He follows her up the street, through a throng of people rushing against them. "So where are you departing from?"

"Random House."

James wishes he had accepted the coffee so he could spew it out. Instead he just stammers, "Wh-what? Random House! That's insane. How'd you get a job there?"

"Undergrad at UPenn in English and two years of unpaid internships, then I came on as an editorial assistant. I thought I wanted to go into publishing, but I don't. Instead of promoting me to editor, they switched me over to marketing, which is . . . not my thing."

James is still mind-blown when they stop outside the Random House Tower, a silver building full of literary-minded people. He gawks up at it.

"Am I completely stupid for doing this?" she asks. "This could be a stable career, and I'm throwing it away to chase after a dream. Is that crazy?"

"Whatever your gut feels, do that."

"My gut is telling me to throw up."

"Okay, don't do that."

Lucy laughs, then groans. "I can't decide."

"At the end of the day, it's your choice," James says. "But I'll say this. For most of my life, I didn't do what I wanted. When we were kids, Jessie would climb up to the tallest tree branches, while I watched from the ground. I skipped the talent show in fifth grade after I spent weeks tinkering with my poem for it. There was this girl in high school that I wanted to ask to prom, but I chickened out and didn't go at all. I was always too scared to climb that damn tree. If you want to pursue your MFA full-time, and you feel confident that you *can*, don't hold yourself back out of fear."

Lucy takes this in with bated breath.

And James does something he would never have done a year ago. He holds her hand.

"You can do it," he says. "Whatever *it* ends up being. You can."

"Can you wait out here for me?" She's trembling, maybe from the cold.

"Of course." Whatever he had previously planned for this strange Friday morning slips his mind. "Good luck."

"Thanks." She disappears through the glass doors.

James watches the street while he waits. Nelle would love it here in the winter. She would love the cold, desperate pedestrians, the cars honking and backed up and zooming past, the black snow crushed and piled on the sides of the curbs. She would love every passing person, every stubborn little snowflake.

Nelle would love it all.

~

"No seriously, *seriously*, James is my hero!" Lucy wraps an arm around him on the couch, retelling yesterday's events to a huddle of people. James fake-laughs along. He has barely had anything to drink, far less than Lucy. He started thinking about Nelle again, knocking his celebratory mood off the rails.

A racket of confetti, champagne, twinkling decorations, sunglasses, and party hats, Jessie's New Year's Eve party is Christmas's wild sister. Drunk idiots bounce about the apartment. Too much champagne, too many shots. Lena climbs on top of the couch and dances to the pulsing music. Jessie rises to join her. Everyone seems to be having fun.

Why hasn't James partaken in any of it? He has held a flute of champagne for two hours, the liquid flat and warm now, desperate not to fall into the grave he dug himself earlier. No point in losing himself to a drunk depression, too clumsy to climb out.

"I call him up out of *nowhere*, freaking out because I'm trying to quit my job, and I tell him that I have no one else to call and don't know what to do." Lucy laughs, champagne sloshing. "Little did I know, I wasn't calling James, I was calling freaking *Superman*! He didn't even question me. In twenty minutes, he was there, calming me down." Lucy peers at him through a haze of drunken dreaminess.

"So, did you quit your job?" Lena asks.

The room leans in for her response. Lucy laughs a little. "Yes, I did."

Pride blooms in James's chest. He claps his hands, a small applause, but it catches like wildfire, and soon enough, the entire room erupts. Whoops and yells and screams.

"Fuck, yeah!"

"Good luck!"

A warm coil tightens in James's chest. *Home.*

Jessie slumps onto the couch. "Here, drink something." She offers him a shot of—he lifts it to his nose—tequila.

He hands it back. "No, thank you."

"You've been brooding all day, moping all night. You barely said a word when we were decorating the place. And you haven't drunk a drop. I don't know what's got you all down, but if you relax, you'll have fun. Don't miss out on your first New Year's Eve in New York." Then she backs off and says lowly, "But, hey, seriously, if you don't want to, it's okay."

He rolls his eyes and takes the shot. He doesn't want to be drunk, but he also doesn't want to be sober, where his dark thoughts, his doubts, stab him like swords. It's a thin line to tiptoe. Drunk, the blades on those swords dull. Harder to break skin, but if they do, they hurt so much worse.

Stinging esophagus. Saliva in his mouth, salt from the rim of the shot glass. He spits out lime pulp.

Jessie grabs the bottle of tequila and pours out another shot.

He throws it back.

She pours. He downs it. Another. Downs it. He takes the bottle from her and presses the rim to his lips, and the burning is so good because it makes him forget for a minute that he left Lincoln, that he met Nelle, that he kissed her, loved her, that he was inside her.

He's laughing now. Collapses onto the couch, rolling in a deep guffaw. Stands up, saying, "I've gotta go find Lucy," but his voice is a distant noise, like it bypassed his brain on the way to his lips.

He staggers into the kitchen.

"Lucy?"

Turns around, back into the living room, and there Lucy is, on the couch. Her face—faces—split into a laugh, and she stands up. He has her hand, he is leading her to the balcony, where he opens the glass door and pulls her outside.

"Look up there," he says, and he feels like he's yelling, but he sounds so quiet.

Only rooftops and darkness.

"Where'd all the stars go?" He chuckles. "That's what they say, right? No stars."

"Not in the city." Lucy smirks. "The light covers them up."

James frowns. *Sad.* The cold air grants him a moment of clarity. Lucy, in this moment, really *is* beautiful. Soft brown hair flowing over her slender shoulders. A gold dress that reveals long, toned legs. Sapphire eyes. Full lips.

"Hey," she says, her voice a husky wish.

He closes the gap between them and plants a warm, sloppy kiss. Her hair flows through his hand, and suddenly his lips are on her neck, and her skin is fire.

Somehow, they make it to his room, and Lucy's on his bed. He unzips her gold dress and trails his fingers down the tan curve of her back. Twisted in the sheets, he touches the wetness between her thighs. He strokes her until she's moaning. Then he's inside her, her hair twisted in his hand like a rein, breathing hard, slamming in and in and in—

Until he can't even remember Nelle's face.

Until his release shoots across the bedsheets and he collapses. Lucy settles in at his side. For the first time in months, James thinks about nothing.

∞

He wakes to a girl's face in his mind, not the girl sleeping beside him. He curses himself for that. The curtains are pulled shut, but daylight leaks through a slim crack.

Lucy's lashes flutter in her sleep, mouth parted. A wet spot of drool dots her pillow.

James shoves his legs into pajama pants and pads out of his room. From the kitchen, he smells breakfast, and his stomach drops. It is too damn early to face an interrogation from his cousin, but he can't avoid it. Jessie flips bacon strips as a pot of coffee drips on the counter.

"Bless you." He pours a cup. The bitterness pounds away the pain in his skull. He decides to bring it up first, so he can take control of the conversation. "Guess who's in my bed?"

Jessie cuts him a look. "I noticed you two disappeared before midnight and never returned."

"Yeah." James scans the room. The aftermath of the party is depressing. Glitter on the floor, lit up by the daylight through the balcony window. Cups and streamers scattered. Sticky stains on the hardwood. "Need help cleaning up?"

Jessie waves a dismissive hand. "Tomorrow. I'm going to Lena's tonight."

James glances back toward his room. "I didn't mean to do that. I didn't want to. I mean I did, obviously, it wasn't nonconsensual. But—"

"You're still not over Nelle," Jessie says. "It's okay. Sometimes you have to rebound."

"No, it's not like that," James says. "Lucy's beautiful. We have so much in common, and she's really smart, and if I were to ever be with her, well . . ." He sighs. "I didn't want it to be like that. I wanted it to be when I'm ready, and she's ready. When I'm not strung up on someone else."

"Go talk to her." Jessie hands him a full cup of coffee. "Bring her this."

James finds Lucy sitting up in bed, staring at him beneath groggy eyelids.

"Hey." He passes over the coffee. "How'd you sleep?"

"Oh, thank you." She wraps her hands around the mug. "Fine. You?"

"Yeah, good."

Lucy taps on the coffee cup, brushes back a strand of sleep-tangled hair. "Look, if last night wasn't what you wanted, that's okay. I remember what you told me on Christmas. If you want to stay friends, we can."

He wasn't expecting her to be so open to exactly what he needs.

"I never told you this, but I broke up with someone not that long ago, too," Lucy says. "His name was Noah. There was nothing really wrong, but it wasn't right. He wasn't the one."

James takes a moment to appreciate her. The whisper of wisdom behind her sharp stare. The curve of her shoulder. The tops of her breasts, dusted with freckles.

Lucy adds, "I'm sorry for being such a . . ."

"A dreamer?" James supplies.

"Yeah." A dimple creases the corner of her mouth. "I guess you could put it that way. Whoever I end up with, I *know* that I'll feel a connection eventually. Like a lock sliding into place. But I was with Noah for two years and never felt it."

"Two years," James whistles. "I'm sorry. When did you break up?"

"September."

"Really?" He sits up. "That's when Nelle and I—" His voice breaks. He should have known saying her damn name would mess him up. Not just saying it, but saying it now. "We ended in September, too, though we'd only been together since July. Still, she made me who I am today."

"She made that much of an impact?"

"She showed me the world." He stews in silence, Lucy beside him. He finds comfort in the sound of her breathing. "Friends?" he asks after a minute, hoping not to lose the only New Yorker he has had a compassionate conversation with in months. It's not that the people here are cold. They are people. Boil it down, and everyone's the same. But in New York, people are busy with plans, jobs, a forty-minute subway ride away. Nothing, no one, is ever truly convenient.

Lucy beams. "Friends."

Chapter 31

Rain slithers down the taxicab window, glass like a sheet of ice against Nelle's nose. Water pours off townhome eaves and hideous construction-site scaffolding, steam illuminated by neon lights. Midnight, but the city doesn't sleep. Umbrellas fling open and bob between cars as their windshield wipers flicker back and forth. In the building right outside the cab, three windows up, is an apartment Nelle hasn't visited in months.

She practiced her speech to James a thousand times during her *first* eight-hour flight across the Atlantic, before she went back for Penelope. Now that she is back in New York, moments away from reuniting with James, she is too damn nervous to remember a word she prepared. *Shit.* She tries to breathe. What if he's with someone else? What if he's *not*, and he still doesn't want her?

"You getting out?" The taxi driver raises his black brows.

"I am." Nelle blinks at the rain, the lights, the reflections.

He taps the electronic payment device. "You still haven't—"

She doesn't mean for the gesture to come off as rude, but she sort of flings a wad of cash at him, way more than the cost of the ride.

"Sorry about that." She kicks open the door. "Thanks for the ride."

Nelle hops over a flooded curb, the shoulders of her coat soaked through by the time she makes it to the apartment call box. She trembles and presses the 3B buzzer. Hopefully James is still an insomniac.

"Hello?" she yells into the speaker over the pouring rain. "It's Nelle. Are either of you awake?"

The building door unlocks almost immediately. Nelle's stomach drops. *This is too real.* Only the ice-cold rain coming down in sheets keeps her from sprinting down the street out of pure nervousness. She tries to remember her speech again and comes up blank.

The foyer of the building greets her like an old friend as she swings open the pine-green door. Dusty mailboxes beside a stack of packages. The shitty dome light buzzes and pops. She traveled through this room a hundred times during her stay in New York. Memories flutter past like pages of a book. James carrying that big daddy pizza box. Returning too often with coffee and fifty-cent paperbacks to add to Jessie's overflowing living room. Leaving that last day to ride to the airport, to fly to Paris, to catapult her onto the spiraling path that led her here, standing like a ghost in a poorly lit room. What if James sees her only as a relic of his past?

No more thinking. Nelle charges upstairs and knocks on 3B.

She was once so nervous to meet Jessie, to mesh with James's life, to ruin the fragile thing they'd been building. A porcelain figurine. Beautiful if handled carefully, broken if dropped. That was her alone, too. One wrong word and she starts a flash flood, a mere thought and a man's heel slips on ice.

The door opens, and Nelle sucks in a sharp breath. Holds it.

The chain snaps tight, an eye peeks through.

"Nelle?" Jessie unlocks the door and swings it open. Her hair is all natural now, frizzy and brown. "What are you doing here? Oh, you're soaked. Come in."

This place is not her home, never was, but walking in feels like returning to somewhere she wants to be.

"Tea?" Jessie crosses to the kitchen and holds up a full pot.

"Yes," Nelle says. Barely back in New York, and she is cozily drinking tea with Jessie. If she composes herself this loosely around James, she might end up spilling all her feelings to him at once, which will kill any chance of him taking her back. Because if she tells him why she feels guilty, will he see her the same?

Jessie doesn't ask before adding a dollop of almond milk and stirring it to a creamy brown. Rain types away at the windowpanes. The kitchen is otherwise quiet, lit only by the iron chandelier over the stained wooden island. It's new, probably crafted by one of Jessie's sculptor friends. They are always gifting each other pieces that other people pay tens of thousands of dollars for.

"Did I wake you up?" Nelle asks, nodding to Jessie's bathrobe.

"No, I just thought I'd spare you the sight of my tits. Lena's spending the night."

"Oh." Nelle draws back instantly. If James isn't here, and Jessie has someone staying over . . . She sets down her tea, prepared to make up an excuse to leave.

"James is out, if he's the reason you came," Jessie says. She sips her tea.

"Oh," Nelle says again. She can barely hide the disappointment that swells her chest, tinged with unexpected relief. "This late?"

"He's in Georgia, for his mom's birthday."

"Why didn't you go with him? Isn't she your aunt?"

"I try to avoid Lincoln at all costs." Jessie opens a bag of cookies. "Plus, someone's gotta pay the bills."

She dips a minicookie in her tea and sinks her teeth into the softened part. Maybe she sees Nelle ogling the bag, because she tilts it forward.

Nelle takes one, dipping it in her cup. When she nibbles, cinnamon and shortbread swirl on her tongue in a mellow concoction, and she relaxes.

Jessie folds her arms. "Why are you here, Nelle?"

"I want to see James," she admits. She opens her mouth to continue, finally remembering the speech she has practiced a thousand times, but Jessie cuts her off with the tip of an antique silver stirring spoon.

"And what do you think James is going to say?" She waves the spoon around emphatically. "Do you think he will be *glad* to see you?"

Nelle swallows, but it doesn't make the knot in her throat disappear. "I . . . I thought he might be."

"Do you not realize how upset he was after what happened between you two?"

Nelle feels her defenses snap up. Of course she understands that he was hurt, but he lied to her. He told her he would travel with her, that they could see the world together, all the while crafting a life for himself in New York and springing it on her as a fully formed plan. It still seems too coincidental that the *moment* she learned she can write for herself, he bailed.

"And he doesn't complain about this part, don't get me wrong," Jessie says, "but it pisses me off that you went and spent *all* his savings on a summer fling, just to dump his ass the minute the money ran out!" Red flushes her cheeks. She breathes in and out, her anger deflating.

Nelle is an empty shell.

Was I really too close-minded to care about him wasting his savings?

Tears burn. *How did I not see it?*

You were playing with life like it wasn't real, whispers a voice in the back of her mind.

"I'm sorry," Nelle says, and it's all she can manage. Her tears speak for themselves.

Jessie melts. "Come here."

Nelle collapses into her arms and falls apart, shuddering on Jessie's shoulder. A hand rubs her back, up and down. How could she have been so stupid for so long, running from James instead of straight at him? This is where she belongs.

"You'll be all right," Jessie says. "Do you have somewhere to stay?"

Nelle's eyes are so swollen now, she can barely see the time on the stove clock. She squints. It's almost 1:00 a.m. She pulls back and wraps her shaky fingers around the mug. A space heater in the corner puts off oven-level warmth.

"I can find a hotel," she says, and she hates how pitiful she sounds.

"Absolutely not," Jessie snaps. "You can take James's room. Bathe if you'd like, and I'll find you clothes."

Nelle follows the orders without question. She scrubs her skin until it's pink and clean, washes her hair, dries off, and puts on the clothes Jessie left folded outside the bathroom door, a frilly pajama set fit for a nineteenth-century grandmother. Nelle loves it. She is envisioning herself in the bathroom mirror, in this new life, when the door cracks open.

"You all right in here?" Jessie asks.

"Just trying to dry my hair." Nelle bunches the soaked strands in a towel, but they pull away just as dark and clumped as before. "To no avail."

"Let me help." Jessie rummages under the sink and pulls out a blow-dryer.

"I've never used that before," Nelle says.

Jessie flicks on a switch and it roars to life. "You can keep it."

Hot air blasts Nelle's head, and she leans back into the feeling, losing herself as Jessie works through her hair. The blow-dryer switches off, but before Nelle can open her eyes, she feels the bristles of a hairbrush prickling her scalp, gliding through her tangles. She watches in the mirror as her golden hair smooths out. Not quite straight, and far from curly, but voluminous.

"Much better," Jessie says. "You're welcome."

Nelle follows her into the kitchen, a bit lost as to what she should do. A creative of the night, Jessie resumes a sketch on her tablet, her pen moving furiously. The one time Nelle pulled an all-nighter for a painting, the flying palomino, it drained her dry.

She feels similarly now.

Jessie looks up. "Go get some rest."

Nelle picks up her tea. "Can I borrow a book?"

Jessie points to the shelf in the corner between the balcony windows and the TV. "That one has the kind you'll like."

"How do you know what I'll like?" Nelle drifts over to the shelf and slips out a slim volume translated from French, with a watercolor of flowers on the soft paper cover. Before she heads down the hall, she asks, "When *will* James be back?"

"What's today?"

Nelle has to think. "January eleventh."

"He will be back Friday, the thirteenth."

Nelle imagines the different ways their reunion could go. James may be furious with her. Or deeply depressed. Or apathetic. Or maybe he will want her back. Maybe he still craves her the way she does him. Maybe he misses their long conversations, their gut-stabbing laughter, their sex, the comfort and ease of being together.

She climbs under James's sheets and stares at the ceiling, listening to the noises of the street. Exhaustion hits, and she is out before she can crack the cover of the little book.

Chapter 32

Nelle sits with a coffee mug in her lap, maroon sweater swallowing her torso. For a second, James thinks he's hallucinating, but her honey eyes hold their signature sparkling wonder, and her chest rises with anticipation as he enters. His suitcase tips over.

What the fuck is Nelle doing here?

He's furious. He's elated. His heart and mind are torn, one reaching for illogical love, the other for logical anger, and coming up with a headache. His arms burn from lugging a sixty-pound suitcase, packed with his favorite books from his childhood bedroom in Lincoln, he's tired and sore from the flight, and all he wanted, five minutes ago, before he knew Nelle was here, was a long nap.

Jessie told him she would be out with Lena, so Nelle either broke in, or she has been staying here. He makes a mental note to give his cousin shit for her lack of warning.

"Hi." He stands there awkwardly, unsure what to do. Months ago, he would have called Nelle his best friend. Now she feels like a stranger.

She sets the mug on the coffee table. "Hey."

James scratches his head. "When did you . . . uh . . . get here?"

What else is there to say? He spent months trying to get over her, and he hasn't even accomplished that yet. A single slipup might set him back. He can't risk that.

Unless she is here to stay. *No.* He doesn't dare let himself think that optimistically.

"Two days ago," she says. "I came to see you. To talk and . . . apologize."

"Apologize?" James repeats. "For what?"

"For leaving you at the cottage." Nelle's voice shakes, on the verge of tears. "I basically forced you to follow me around the world, to spend all your savings, and now it's all gone, and I'm so, so sorry."

He can tell by the tremor in her throat, the shiny film over her eyes, that her apology is genuine. But the idea that she unknowingly hurt him is so far from the truth. Having his heart carved out was never her fault. His chest cracks, and he can't help the tears that spring up. He dares to sit on the couch beside her, placing a wary hand on her leg. She doesn't move away.

He wants to be angry, but his resolve melts when they touch. He wraps his arms around her, and she curls into him, folding her head under his chin.

"Nelle, listen to me." All uncertainty vanishes. "I am not mad at you. I understand why you left that day, I know why what I did hurt you, and *I'm* sorry for not telling you sooner about New York. I didn't know how to approach it, and I was scared of how you'd react."

"It's okay." Tears squeeze her voice.

James shakes his head. "I'm not done. I love you, Nelle, and I will always forgive you. You never have to ask."

Sunlight cuts in through the balcony window, the winter chill permeating through. He wraps a quilt around his shoulders, tucking them both in.

"I chose to leave Lincoln with you. Going to Charleston, to DC, to New York, to Paris, those were *our* ideas. Scotland, too. I regret none of the time I spent with you, none of the money I spent. Those memories are invaluable to me, and I loved every single one of them, *because* I was with you. I'm not the same James you met last summer. I've changed, grown. I live in New York now, can you even believe it? You don't know how grateful I am for you."

She opens her mouth, but he cuts her off.

"And one more thing." He reaches for the familiar grooves of her fingers. "I miss you."

Nelle's bottom lip quivers. "I've done some stuff, James."

"It's okay," he says. The past doesn't matter now. With nimble fingers, he tucks a blond strand behind her ear, exposing her cheekbone. "I love you. I forgive you. Always."

They are the easiest words he has ever said.

She tilts into his hand. "It's not that simple."

"It is." James leans in to kiss Nelle's neck, and the crook of her shoulder feels like home.

Her fingers find purchase in his short curls. "It's not . . ."

"It can be," he murmurs, trailing kisses to her jaw. To the corner of her mouth. Hesitating, though every molecule of his body and his growing erection all yell at him to keep going.

"Kiss me," she says. "Kiss me, James."

One kiss, and months of progress disappear. He is done for. And he will never recover.

But he wants her so bad it *hurts*.

"James," she says softly.

God, he can't resist it. A magnet tugs his lips to hers, her hands on his waist, then hot under his sweatshirt.

No holding back.

Their kiss is almost violent. Nelle twists to straddle him on the couch, and James rakes his fingers through her hair. His hands splay across her back, under her sweater. He trails one up the curve of her lower abdomen, the plane of her stomach. Gooseflesh bubbles across her skin wherever his fingertips whisper. He cups her breast while their tongues war. She bows into his touch, the pad of his thumb whispering around her swollen nipple.

"Nelle," he groans. Their tongues slip against each other, lips hungry, fingers tangled. He needs their clothes off *now*.

He lifts her from the couch, and Nelle locks her legs around him. He takes her into his room, shuts the door with his foot, and they land on the bed in a ball of giggles.

"Take my pants off," she breathes.

James kneels at the foot of the bed. His fingers find the button, and slowly, lapping up every second, he slides her zipper down. Each inch of her skin appears like jewels in a trove. Her stomach sapphire, her pink panties amethyst, her inner thighs diamonds. He tugs the denim down to her calves, her ankles, and they crumple on the floor. He finds the hem of her sweater and inches it up, revealing her breasts, her collarbones, her lightly freckled shoulders.

Sitting naked on his bed, Nelle is nearly enough to make him fall to pieces.

His removes his sweatshirt and briefs and drops onto the bed beside her, head propped on his hand. He plants a kiss on her forehead, trailing his fingers in circles around her navel, desperate to drift down. But he wants to take his time with this.

They fold into each other's naked bodies, their stormy kisses slowing to a lingering breath between their lips. Knees and noses touching. Nelle reaches down, wraps her fingers around him—James jolts at the touch—and guides him between her thighs. He groans as he inches into her warmth, unable to think past the pleasure.

Facing each other, they rock in slow, breathless, torturously tingling movements. Each plunge brings him closer to his edge. Each touch fuses them together. His lips find the slope of her neck. She cradles his shoulders, nails digging in. He has never felt so content, so happy, so—

James erupts, groaning as his legs tense, his toes curl, and his hands find momentary purchase on Nelle's ass. Their rhythm slows, like an ocean wave hitting shore, until they stop completely.

Nelle holds him while he shudders and recovers. How can this be real? He must be dreaming. *Nelle is here. This is real. Nelle is really here.* Sweat-spiraled hair falls over his forehead. He needs more of her.

"James." Nelle brushes his hair back.

He blushes. "Sorry, it's been a while, so I—"

"No," she heaves a breath. "It's perfect."

She pushes his head down in a silent order.

"Yes, ma'am." He slinks beneath the covers and plants a kiss on her ankle. Up her calf. Along her soft thigh, guiding her open again. When his lips graze her inner thigh, she gasps. Her fingers nestle in his hair as he finds her center. Languorous strokes—kissing, sucking until she is swollen—turning her body into lava.

"Yes," she murmurs, heels sliding on the sheets.

James can't help but grin at her pleasure. He focuses in, tongue flickering like fire, transporting him to another realm, a magical pocket where no barriers stand between them. No secrets, no lies, no clothes.

He pauses, his lips wet, and massages her with the pad of his fingers while he speaks.

"I *love* you," he says.

She whimpers. "I love *you*."

He brings his mouth back to her, and Nelle says his name in quick breaths while her restless hands squeeze his hair, squeeze the sheets.

"James, James, James." A wave shatters over her.

After a few sweaty, dazed moments, Nelle releases the iron vise of her thighs from his head and throws the sheets back. They lie in silence, sweat-slick bodies pressed together in the yellow daylight. Taking comfort in a realm of relaxation. Their own little cocoon.

Finally, when James's heartbeat has quieted to a dull thump in his temple, Nelle says, "Let me look at you. Let me remember this."

He sits back against the pillows while she takes him in. A smile works on his lips.

Nelle is most beautiful thing he has ever seen. Eyes that carry firefly light, spirit of a horse on the run. Dirty-blond strands fall over her collarbones. The lines of her body deserve a spot in the Louvre.

A lifetime of memories pass through James's head: Charleston's cobblestone streets, white bedsheets in DC, dancing on a rooftop in the rain, kissing on the Eiffel Tower, confessing their love on a beach in France, tracking down the cottage in Scotland. Making love for the first time. Nelle learning how to run. James learning how to fly.

"I am eternally grateful for you," he says. "You've given me so much."

Nelle runs her cool fingers through his hair. "You've given me more."

❧

James and Nelle only leave his bed for water, coffee, and a bag of grapes. Morning shadows shrink across tousled bedsheets, and he follows the path back between her thighs twice by dinnertime. Long after sunset, in the quieter hours of night, the apartment door squeaks open.

They break apart from their whispers and touches. He is immediately taken back to their last night of lovemaking. The creak in the hall that led to Quill and a gun and Nelle bleeding out all over him.

"The flashbacks are really kicking in for me right now," Nelle whispers.

"Me, too." He pulls on sweatpants. "It's just Jessie, though."

She nods. "We don't have to worry about Quill anymore."

Part of him hopes it *is* Quill that he hears through the wall, ranting about a novel-to-TV adaptation, and *not* his cousin Jessie, whom he will have to obliterate on sight for leaving Nelle here unannounced like a surprise welcome-home present.

Nelle is right on his heel as he steps into the hall.

"Would you be okay staying in here for a minute?" he asks. "I want to talk to Jessie alone."

"Yeah," Nelle says. "I'll come out when you're ready."

James strides down the hall.

Jessie and Lena are in the kitchen, standing at the island, pouring three glasses of wine.

"You're home!" Jessie squeals, grabbing another glass from the cabinet beneath the island. "Want some?"

"Please." James slides onto a stool. Outside the sweaty bedroom, his mind clears, and the reality of the past day slams into him. *Nelle is here. After months away, she's actually here.* Suddenly half his anger collapses like a pillar of sand, but on principle, he tries his best to sound angry. "I have some questions."

He chugs half the glass of wine, gagging on the dry bitterness. Lena drifts across the kitchen and leans against the fridge. She glances between the two cousins as if waiting for an explosion. Even Jessie looks like she is bracing for something.

But suddenly, James can't even fake anger.

Nelle is back, which is all he has ever wanted. She is in New York, and although he hasn't asked, he doesn't think she wants to leave. Before her return that morning, he was on a personal quest to find happiness, and he was beginning to see the light at the end of the tunnel. Now that she's back, it's like he's skipped to the end, and he's basking in the sun.

"Thank you for not telling me," James says. "I love you."

"You're not mad?" Lena asks.

Jessie blinks at him. "James, are you high?"

"If I'd known Nelle was here, I would have been stressing the whole time I was in Lincoln. Walking in and being surprised forced me to listen to my gut."

Jessie peers at him warily. "And what did your gut tell you to do?"

"She's in my bed." He fights a grin, visualizing her in his sheets.

"Well . . ." Jessie tops his glass off. "I wish I could say I kept it from you because I planned for the two of you to reunite, but honestly, I just didn't know how to bring it up."

James laughs. Jessie and Nelle—his two favorite people—are both in his life again. In his favorite city, no less. What could be better than this?

"Is this for Nelle?" He picks up the empty glass.

Jessie leans against the island. "I thought she'd want to join us."

"Is she asleep?" Lena asks, alight with curiosity.

He grins. "Nelle, come out!"

She pads down the hall in her baggy maroon sweater, legs bare, running her fingers through her bedraggled hair.

"Nice to see you again." Lena flashes the fakest of smiles. Of course James's friends and family would hold grudges against Nelle. Whether or not he spun their breakup in his favor didn't matter. He came home heartbroken, and they needed someone to point fingers at.

Nelle looks down. "I usually have pants on."

Lena and Jessie laugh, and just like that, the ice breaks.

Over the next hour, the four of them finish off two bottles of wine and order pizza as James tells the story of his visit to Lincoln. Halfway through his week in Georgia, he sat his parents down and announced that he would be attending NYU. Like he expected, they didn't understand why he wanted to leave. Why waste money on a useless degree? Why throw away thousands of dollars a month on rent? Why live in such a filthy, overcrowded, dangerous place?

Nelle's eyebrows jump up behind her wineglass. "What did you say?"

"I didn't have much *to* say," he says, catching his own sadness on the subject. Maybe his parents' lack of support cuts deeper than he thought. "I tried to explain how much I love this city, how much I like my life here, but they'll never understand. They'll never *try* to understand. So I said my piece, and then we went out for dinner. My sister was at a friend's house. It was fine."

At some point they migrate into the living room, Jessie cranks up the space heater, and they huddle around it, swapping stories about childhood, their dreams, their fascinations.

The clock slips past midnight before Jessie asks Nelle, "Are you staying in New York?"

Nelle doesn't even flinch. "Yeah, I am."

James has been too scared to ask, but hearing the words come from her lips makes his heart implode. Knowing that she will be here, that his best friend is back, that they can start their life together, he wants to scream with joy. Mornings cozied up in a snow-crusted café. Summer afternoons on Coney Island. Weekend trips up and down the East Coast. She can finally learn how to ride a horse; he has already started researching equestrian lessons in the city. His brain spins like a hamster wheel with the possibilities. The kids they will adopt. The

Brooklyn Heights town house they will raise them in. Endless nights of slow lovemaking.

"So James is a writer." Lena crosses her ankles on the coffee table. "Jessie's doing pretty damn well as an artist. I'm in law school. What's your dream, Nelle?"

The question is casual, but to James it feels like an attack. His instinct is to jump to Nelle's defense, but he holds himself back, curious. Before, her dream was to see the world, but she must have changed if she is staying in New York.

Nelle finishes her glass, sets it aside, licks her lips. "I think I want to go to college."

"Very cool," Lena says.

James stares at the frosted pane of the balcony window. Something Nelle said that morning resurfaces. *I've done some stuff.* His curiosity bites, and he almost asks her to step away with him, to confess her sins, but he restrains himself. She deserves her secrets from those months apart. Same as him.

He thinks of that drunken night with Lucy, sour bile hitting the back of his throat. Would Nelle still want him if she knew he slept with someone else two weeks ago? He feels only friendship for Lucy now, but he was attracted to her. Enough to pull her into bed, even if it was because he was drunk and missed the girl now sitting beside him.

Jessie raises her glass. "To improving ourselves, a venture I'm sure we can all work on."

Lena lifts her glass. "Except me."

When James's wine-addled head starts to loll, he excuses himself to pee. The trip to the bathroom is a nauseating blur, and when he steps back into the hall, Nelle is in front of him. Her eyelids are swollen and sleepy, and she pulls him by his collar into his room.

He protests, "Jessie and Lena—"

"Are already in bed," Nelle says, rolling onto his comforter. She plucks a book off the nightstand, but knocks out on page two, parted lips rattling an exhale.

James falls asleep happier than he has been since September.

~

Nelle dreams of the house on Blackwood Road. Clapboard siding. Tin roof. Summer insects flattened to her bedroom window. Sheer white curtains. Vials of ink. Horses prancing beyond the trees. Quill chopping wood in the smoky cold. Dust piling on canvases like snow.

She dreams of James and the night they met. The fireworks, the grill char, the sparklers, the corn dog in her throat.

She dreams of the day the police officer came. The stove's gas flame tearing her hand apart, over and over, bare palm bubbling, burning, and stitching back together.

Quill's black eyes as he poured out whiskey bottles across his study.

Fire eating bookshelves full of her lifeblood.

Scalding heat. The gnawing fear that she would disappear with those journals.

She dreams of the pain she felt as the man who raised her—who called himself her father—tried to kill her.

She dreams of acrid smoke and watchful stars, knowing that her life was changed forever as she rode away from Blackwood Road with James.

~

Nelle clutches the sheets to her chest. She's not in Lincoln, she's in New York. In Jessie's apartment. In James's bed. She is sweating, her heart racing, her skin *boiling*. Does she have a fever? A bright phantom flashes against the wall. Half asleep still, she mistakes it as a headlight cutting in through the window. But they are on the third floor.

I'm still asleep. Nelle shakes her head, frozen in fear. *This can't be real.*

Returning to New York was not a dream. Choosing to live a normal life, to search for a passion, was not a dream. Spending the day with her mouth on James was not a dream. Waking up in his bed now is not a dream.

But the angry fire consuming his desk, his laptop, the bookshelf . . . has to be.

Chapter 33

Smoke and ash sting Nelle's eyes. She sits in stunned disbelief, blinded by the fire.

The fire.

The room is on fire.

Not real.

The bedsheets catch aflame.

This is New York, Jessie's apartment, her new life with James. She is supposed to wake up, hungover, to the smell of Jessie's chocolate-chip pancakes, *not* the smell of smoke.

A scream rips the air from another room, and Nelle's blood ices over.

Real.

As if she has been floating on the ceiling, Nelle feels herself fall back into her body. With all the strength she can muster, she shoves James off the mattress. He rolls away with the blankets, collapsing on the floor with a harsh thud and a groan.

"What the—"

Fire climbs the walls, the ceiling, the floor, an unrecognizable hellscape, but James assesses the situation much faster than Nelle did, on his feet in an instant. His hand finds hers, she snatches up her canvas bag with her journal inside, and they are out the door, sprinting into the living room. Smoke clogs the room, but Nelle doesn't need air to survive. She's invincible. The others aren't.

Nelle holds the back of James's neck, pressing her forehead to his. "I can't die, but you can, so you have to get out of this building right now."

A far-off siren wails.

"But Jessie and Lena," he says. "They're back there."

"I *can't die.*" Nelle bites the words out. No time to argue with him, so she pushes him toward the apartment door and whirls back to save the others.

The flames flock to her in the narrow hall, but she runs through them, wincing at every lashing burn. It's a tunnel of fire, and she's cutting straight through. The metal doorknob to Jessie's room scalds her palm, but Nelle has no choice. Skin searing, she squeezes the knob and twists. The bedroom is engulfed in fire, opaque with smoke.

Nelle enters cautiously, unable to see farther than a few feet. Luckily, New York apartments are small, so there's not much ground to cover. She accidentally kicks something both solid and squishy and bends to feel a woman's body. Another beside it.

Oh God. She leans down, smoke stinging her tear ducts, grabs their hands, and pulls.

"Come on," she says through gritted teeth. "Come *on.*"

Jessie wheezes out a shredded cough, still somewhat conscious.

"Help me," she croaks, nudging Lena's motionless body.

Nelle scoops one arm under Lena's shoulder, and Jessie takes her other side. Lena is taller than both of them, so supporting her is an awkward act of pushing her upward between them. Together, they move to the open door and pause at the fire raging in the hall. Nelle can sprint through, but Jessie and Lena stand no chance.

"New plan," Nelle says, her voice barely a rasp. She retreats into the bedroom and hobbles with Lena and Jessie to the window, which reflects the orange firelight. Nelle's right hand fumbles around the edges for a lock until she finds the mechanism at the bottom, near the wooden sill lined with crystals. She tries to twist it free, but it's stuck.

"Is there a trick to get this open?" She grits her teeth and pulls, but Lena's weight is dragging her down.

"I never could," Jessie says. "The wood's warped."

"Can you hold her?"

Jessie struggles to keep Lena's full body upright. Nelle clutches the lock and pulls, but her grip is too weak, or the window is sealed shut, because it *just won't budge*. She cries, more from frustration now than smoke.

So she gets one night, and that's it? One night with James, with Jessie, with Lena, pretending to live this new life, and then it's all over, just like that?

Regret washes over her like acid rain, each droplet a painful reminder that none of this would have happened if she had taken Penelope's advice. She pounds her fists against the window, sobbing, trying to ignore Jessie's pleas to keep trying, keep trying, as she sags under Lena. But Nelle can't open a window that won't open. And she can't get two people safely through an apartment on fire.

Maybe James made it out.

Even with her unnatural abilities, the smoke is hurting Nelle faster than she can recover. She is too weak to stand, slipping into unconsciousness. She can't quite heal quick enough.

When a pair of arms scoop her up, when she sees, through the haze, an angel in an oxygen mask, she can't tell if it's real or a dream.

The entire building is a feast for the flames. James stands across the street, his view of the front steps obscured by a red fire truck. Everything is chaos. Firemen and police swarm the scene, along with worried pedestrians and residents. Hoses shoot thousands of gallons of water at his home. Then, illuminated by the fire inside, Nelle appears in Jessie's bedroom window like she's inside an oven, backlit by orange, banging on the glass to get out.

"She's up there!" he screams and points. *"First bedroom on the left!"*

Someone must hear him, because a pair of firefighters heads into the building. While the heartbeats pass, James waits, forced to watch Nelle's pounding against the glass, softer each time. Until she stops. Until she collapses.

She can't die, he thinks, his heart hammering. He needs to get up there. Give him a uniform, a mask, an oxygen tank, whatever they use to go in there so he can save his family. Nelle and Jessie and Lena need him.

He is about to steal a uniform and run back into the conflagration when a huddle of firefighters emerges from the building, carrying three women toward the open ambulances. James sprints. All three women have been chewed up and spat out. Their bodies are covered in ash and soot. Burns mar their arms and hands.

"Excuse me," he says, hoping the firefighter can hear him over the pandemonium of sirens and screams and the crackle of gnawing fire. "Excuse me, that's my cousin, that's my family."

He climbs into an ambulance and stands in a corner between Jessie's gurney and Nelle's spot on the bench. Lena goes to her own ambulance. The paramedics quickly check Nelle and James before rushing to Jessie.

James fumbles for Nelle's hand, crushing it between his own. "Are you hurt?"

"I was," she says. He examines her neck, her legs, her hands. No burns.

He turns to Jessie, unconscious, her clothes charred.

"She's okay." Nelle massages her throat. "Not sure about her lungs."

"Lena?" he asks, trying to keep his attention off the paramedics swarming his cousin.

Nelle shakes her head. "I don't know. She wasn't moving."

James can't find it in himself to comfort her. All his energy is gone. He's wearing a different body than he was hours ago, seeing all of this through new eyes.

The ambulance doors burst open—he didn't even know they were moving—and the paramedics rush them into the ER. James insists he doesn't need any treatment, but he is given no choice in the matter. The nurse who checks on him assesses minimal lung damage and diagnoses him with a sore throat.

"I am so deeply sorry," she says before checking Nelle's vital signs.

James's heart twists. *My home.*

When he and Nelle are permitted to visit Jessie, she is already joking about the astronomical hospital bills she will have to pay. They see Lena next. She's unconscious, but alive. The doctor says she should wake soon.

James wants to feel relieved, but he doesn't. He has crossed into a parallel dimension. He stares at the tiles of the waiting-room floor. His computer is gone to the flames. Photographs of him and Nelle. And his typewritten manuscript—the *only* copy—of *The Summer Curse*. He only ever transcribed the first chapters.

Thank God Jessie stores her art in the studio, but one silver lining doesn't make up for all they lost. Hopelessness sucks the air from James's lungs, grinds his spirit to dust. What is the point of anything when everything is gone?

But Jessie and Lena are still here, and that is a miracle in itself.

Nelle rounds the corner, wearing sweatpants from the gift shop and her maroon sweater from yesterday.

She tucks her hair behind her ears as she takes the vinyl chair beside James. "Any news?"

"Lena hasn't woken yet. Jessie's breathing is getting better."

She sighs. "That's good. Anything better is good."

"Yeah." James can't find the desire to speak, so he doesn't. He stares at the wall and the mounted TV. The news is on, an awful choice for an already grim setting, and the reporter is chatting to the camera from the still burning building on Bleecker Street. Smoke pours above the rooftops as the sun rises in a pink sky.

He wants to throw up.

"James," Nelle starts.

He peels his attention from the TV. "Yeah?"

"I need to end my life, and I want to do it in Lincoln."

If he was standing, he would double over. The idea is preposterous. "What? Why?"

Nelle takes his hand. Her thumb traces the blue veins from his knuckles to his wrist to the sleeve of his gray sweatshirt. She groans to the overhead fluorescents. "It's a long story."

James gestures to the waiting room. "Nothing but time here."

Nelle folds one knee over the other. "As you wish."

And she launches into her tale, careful with her words. Describes her terrifying power. Her practice, learning how to move with just a thought, how to conjure anything by simply writing about it with her ink.

"It's like real magic," he says.

"No." Her tone is cold. "Penelope was correct to call it a curse."

She describes the flood in Barcelona. The man who slipped and died in London. How she found Quill and Penelope in Edinburgh. How he knew, because he almost shot and killed an innocent man, that he needed to end his life. That he should never have been created in the first place. She describes the wind atop Calton Hill. How Quill was solid one second and smoke the next. And how she has to do the same. But she wants to do it in Lincoln, in the ashes of the house on Blackwood Road.

"But you've learned from your mistakes," James says. There has to be some way he can talk her out of this *insanity*. "You are more in control of your power than you've ever been, right?"

"Yeah, but—"

"So think of it as a gift," he says. He *needs* her to stay. She *said* she was going to stay. "Think of it—"

"James, stop," Nelle says. She unfolds their hands and runs her fingers through her hair. "It's not a power, it's not magic, it's not a *gift*. It's a burden I can't get rid of. Not just to myself, but to *you*. To Jessie."

"How?" he asks, incredulous. "How have you burdened any of us, Nelle? I love you. Jessie loves you. We want you with us."

"I caused the fire, James."

"You . . ." His voice dies. His brain stands still. Nelle's admission feels like some sort of sick joke. "You what?"

Tears well up in her eyes. "I didn't mean to."

Holy shit, it's not a joke.

"It was my dream," she says. "I was dreaming about the night the house on Blackwood burned down, and when I woke up, the room was on fire."

A sob rips through her, her face contorted with pain. James's heart cracks down the center. He pulls her in as she shudders, his own body racked with tears. What can he say now? It sounds like her dream *did* cause the fire. So what can he do if she wants to end her life? What if she burns down every home they ever share? God, he can't even listen to himself think.

"Maybe you can learn to control your dreams, like when you're awake, so you can sort between the thoughts that start fires and the thoughts that are just thoughts."

Nelle's finger grazes his cheekbone. "I love you." Her face crumples again. "But I can't risk you."

And there is nothing left to say.

Chapter 34

They're put up in a four-star Midtown hotel for a couple of nights, but James finds no rest. He and Nelle sleep back-to-back like in his truck bed, though their current circumstances are a far cry from last summer's carefree travels up the East Coast. Not only the street noise keeps him up; when he closes his eyes, he is back in the waiting room, Nelle telling him she has to end her life, that the fire was her fault.

Through the window, the city sparkles. Tragedies happen out there every day, people's lives irrevocably changed: a drowning, a paralyzing car wreck, an unnoticed gas leak. This time it was his tragedy. Tomorrow it will be another's.

Nelle must think he is asleep because she slowly peels back the stiff hotel sheet. At the foot of the bed, her silhouette pulls on pants, a sweater, a pair of black loafers, before tiptoeing to the door.

"Hey," he says.

She startles, her hand on the knob. She is leaving, of course, to do exactly what she promised.

James tugs on his sweater and jeans and meets her at the door.

Nelle's nostrils flare. "What are you doing?"

"You're not going alone." He says the words because he loves her, but on the inside he is fuming. How can she follow through with this? He's angry with the world, with the universe, with God for putting him in this position. For cursing her like this. *Make it go away. Make her okay.*

She sighs. "You can't stop me."

"I'm not, I—" He chokes up and shakes his head. She was *alive* during their rift last fall, yet he barely survived, even knowing he could find her if he needed to. How is he supposed to carry on if she is gone forever? But he can't argue with her choice. She is a walking bomb, and neither of them knows when she will explode again, or who will be in her blast radius when she does.

"What about Jessie and Lena?" She's grasping for anything to keep him away, but nothing will.

"I'll send a text."

"School?"

"Hasn't started yet."

"You just came back from Lincoln—"

"My mom's always happy when I visit two weekends in a row."

"But . . ." She blinks rapidly and looks down. "I think it'll be easier if I do it alone."

He tilts her chin up. Eye to eye. "After everything, don't I deserve a real goodbye?"

She sinks into him, and that's all it takes. He is going with her to Lincoln.

James calls to ask his mom to pick them up from the airport in Atlanta. Which means he has to explain, using the fewest descriptions possible, who Nelle is. *She's from Lincoln, too. She lives in New York with us.* That is all his mom needs to know about the girl he's bringing home, for the first and last time.

James spots his dad's tan Tacoma in the pickup zone, and he guides them through lanes of buses, shuttles, and cars. All his earthly possessions having burned to ash only forty-eight hours before, he and Nelle have no luggage, and it feels odd to walk around the airport empty handed.

Shit, he's nervous. The shaded windows are rolled up. He'd only just seen his mom, and they'd parted on bad terms. The story he told everyone the night of the fire was only a half-truth. Yes, he and his parents had a civilized conversation about his choices, and they had a *lot* of questions. Then they went to dinner. His dad had to leave for an early-morning conference in Macon before the check was paid, so it was James and his mom alone on the ride home from the restaurant.

She went off as soon as the truck door shut.

"What the *fuck* are you doing?" she said, the swear word clumsy in her mouth. "Don't you realize how much stress you're putting on your dad and me?"

"How?"

"Well, you'll have to take out student loans."

"I know," he said. "That's for *me* to stress about."

"But you don't understand how much of a burden it'll be. When you could go to school nearby, get a *good* degree, and graduate with no debt!"

"Don't you have student debt?" he asked.

"Yes." She blinks back tears, right on cue. "And it sucks."

"But wasn't that something you *had* to do? How can you tell me not to get student loans when you have them, too? We want different kinds of lives, and I respect that, but you don't." He'd been practicing those words, whetting them for a blow.

She was silent the rest of the way home. That drive was twenty minutes. This one will be *two hours*.

James gulps as he opens the back door for Nelle. He is clammy, shaking, a stone in his throat. He opens the passenger side, steps up into the truck, and buckles his seat belt. He checks the rearview mirror to make sure Nelle has hers on. Then he faces his mom.

"Hey, baby," she says.

The ice around his heart melts. "Hi."

They reach across the console and hug, and suddenly James is seven again. Nostalgia settles sweet in the back of his throat. He has fallen outside and scabbed his knee. She sits him on the bathroom counter, opens the medicine cabinet high above his reach, and treats him. Wipe with cold alcohol. Apply ointment. Tape on bandage. Kiss it to make it better. His mom used to be his rock.

Now that rock is Nelle. But Nelle is leaving.

Once upon a time he was that timid little boy. Now he is James Finch, New York City writer. James Finch, the friend. James Finch, the roommate. James Finch, the lover.

"Mom, this is Nelle," he says. "Nelle, this is my mom, Teresa."

"Lovely to meet you Nelle," says his mom. "Welcome to the family."

❧

The house smells like chili when they enter. His mom says it's winter food, but the fifty-degree cold feels like July to James after his first northern winter. First, he finds his dad, tugging Nelle along behind him. Despite their reason for coming back to Lincoln, he's smiling, and when he looks back he sees Nelle grinning, too.

His dad is stirring a pot in the kitchen. James circles the butcher-block island and hugs him. He is caught off guard, chili spoon in one of his hands. Peter Finch is a tall, muscular man with blue eyes and dark hair. People remark on all the traits he gave James, but James spent his teenage years counting everything he didn't get. Tree-trunk muscles, election-winning charisma, and a talent for stringed instruments.

"Uh-uh, watch out," he says over James's shoulder. "I'm gonna get chili down your back."

James laughs as he pulls away. He gestures behind him, to the girl of his dreams. His heart aches every time he dares to look at her. It twists him up like a rag to think about what she has to do.

"Dad, this is Nelle. Nelle, this is my dad, Peter."

"Nice to meet you, Mr. Finch."

"Please, just Peter."

They exchange the usual chatter, and James's attention turns upstairs.

Desperate for the quiet comfort of his books, he excuses himself. His parents have discussed converting his bedroom into a home gym, but for now, his little library is still perfectly preserved. Old childhood chapter books. Waterlogged teenage obsessions. Hardcover editions of paperbacks he already owns. A museum of his life, told through his shelves.

Floorboards shift behind him.

He expects to see Nelle, but it's his dad.

When was the last time his dad stepped foot in his bedroom? He ducks to avoid hitting his head on the sloped ceiling, then circles the haphazardly installed ceiling fan.

"So, that's uh . . . Nelle," says his dad, sticking his hands in the pockets of his khakis.

"That's Nelle," James says. "What do you think of her?"

"She's funny. Jessie told us a little. All good things." He stares the floor, the bookshelves, anywhere but his son. "She's pretty, too."

"Yeah," James says. "About everything I said the last time I was here—"

"It's all in the past."

"No, Dad, listen to me." He takes in a breath to steady himself. *Just be honest.* "I love you, and I respect your lifestyle, but I want to be a little riskier and live in an expensive city and have a flaky job. I know you don't understand that, and I know it sounds idiotic to you. Maybe it is, but when you were my age, you followed your dreams, and you never regretted it. Shouldn't I get to follow mine, too?"

His dad blinks and opens his mouth. "I . . . uh . . . I agree, yeah. I just wanted to tell you that I hope you're being safe up there. You know, it can be a dangerous place *if* you're not careful, so . . . watch out for your cousin and Nelle."

James nods.

"And . . . uh . . . just make sure you're being safe in . . . every way . . . you know . . ."

Despite being twenty-one, James's cheeks go hot when the subject of sex comes up with his parents. "Yes, I am. Always. Thanks."

His dad clears his throat. "Just making sure that you're doing . . . uh . . . everything you need to do in that department."

"I am. Promise."

"All right."

James rocks on his heels. "Where's Midi?"

"Guess."

"A friend's house."

His dad sighs. "Mandy."

"Good to know Mandy Tucker is more important than the brother she only sees twice a year," James jokes, and though sadness lingers behind the statement, he doesn't hold it against her. He is certain there have been milestones in her life that he has missed over the past six months.

But melancholy befalls his dad, weighing his shoulders down. "She does love you, James."

"I know, Dad. I know."

"We all do," his dad says. This time, he doesn't break eye contact. "You know that, right?"

"I know. I love you, too."

Nelle sits at the kitchen island, feet dangling, a mug of tea warm in her hands. A maw of sadness threatens to swallow her up. This is the life she should have: visiting Lincoln twice a year with James, getting to know his parents, sitting around on holidays and drinking tea. Nervously, she finds herself fingering the tea bag's little paper tab. The phrase printed on it distracts her: *Look how far you've come.*

"Your home is beautiful," she says to Teresa.

Teresa tastes the chili, smacks her lips, and adds a pinch of seasoning. "Thank you. We renovated a couple of years ago. It was horrifying before that."

"Well, I love what you've done. It feels like home."

Teresa puts a lid on the pot and braces herself on the island. "How's New York? Getting James to tell us anything about his life requires a full-on interrogation."

Nelle tries to hide her tears behind a grin. "It's wonderful. He really, really loves it there."

Teresa forces a smile, too. "I knew he would."

"He loves you, too, though," she says, sensing a wall of sadness. "He is so grateful for you."

"Thank you for saying that." Teresa absentmindedly wipes her hands on her pants, lets out a shaky exhalation, and cranes her neck into the hall. "Where did they disappear to?"

"I think upstairs," Nelle says.

"Would you mind running up there and telling them that dinner's ready?"

Nelle slides off her stool and starts up the creaky stairs. On her way up, she studies the wall of family photographs. Days on the beach, award ceremonies, costumes. James and Midi standing beside each other, one tall and lanky, the other short and sassy. Nelle wishes she had the chance to meet Midi before . . .

Her throat tightens. She steadies her breath and wipes her tears before climbing the rest of the stairs.

൴

After dinner, James gives Nelle the tour of his childhood bedroom. The desk with his typewriter, the window overlooking downtown Lincoln. His shelf stacked with snow globes from all the cities he has visited. He finds the crumpled letters he wrote for her last summer and smooths some of them out. *I think I'm falling in love with you. Is Quill trying to kill me? Are you both plotting my murder? Is he hurting you somehow? I'm kind of lonely, so if you want to be friends . . .*

They laugh over his letters until they are kissing over them. James cups the back of Nelle's neck and leans her down, cradling her. He kisses her soft, slow. Then he pulls away. One kiss to remember her by, ahead of whatever happens next. Tonight. In the morning. Whenever she chooses to go.

"When do you want to . . ." He trails off.

"At dawn," she says. "We should sleep soon."

James can't breathe, and the muscles behind his eyes clench. A feeling takes over his body, hot and blinding. He scrubs his tears away as quickly as they come, angry with himself, with Nelle, with God. Trembling, he pushes off the bed and paces the room. He has never felt like this. With no forethought, only fury, he kicks the bedpost.

Immediate, splitting pain. The anger dissipates. Damn, it worked. And it *hurts*. He hobbles on his foot, clenching the bedpost.

Nelle shrieks, "What the hell was that, James?"

"I'm mad," he says. "You're leaving! I know you can't help it. I *know*. But I'm still fucking upset about it."

"Well, stop," she says. "You knew not to come if you were going to have an issue with this. I have to do this, James, and you know why. You said you understood, so don't go back on your word now. And don't get in my way tomorrow."

Her voice is cold, emotionless, but James sees through her wall. If she lets it crack, then she won't be able to follow through.

He opens his mouth, but she is already leaving.

"Your mom said we have to sleep in separate rooms," Nelle says. "I'm going to Midi's. She's at a friend's house, so I hope she won't mind."

"She won't."

James watches Nelle go, hoping she will turn around one last time.

*

They drive through walls of morning mist. It blankets the town square and curls like gray snakes around the trees on either side of River Road.

The fog doesn't clear until they reach Blackwood and James takes a left. He hasn't looked at Nelle since they got into the truck. He can't even remember what she is wearing. He glances. A cream sweater and brown pants. Delicate silver earrings—must be Midi's—gleam in her lobes. When did she get her ears pierced?

James tries to drive slowly, but eventually the mailbox marked Quill rises from the trees. Now he regrets coming at all. It would have been easier to let Nelle disappear, not to witness her death. Tires grind on the gravel, stirring up dust, and he brakes halfway down the driveway.

Shit.

The house is gone. Blackened grass covered by a thousand square feet of ash. Shreds of warped tin gleam under the morning sun. Clumps of wood stand here and there, but nothing of the original structure remains upright. Nothing but the lone brick chimney watching over the destruction.

James climbs out and circles the vehicle to open Nelle's door, but she is already out. She stalks down the driveway, cutting through the yard to what was once a porch, and stops where the front door stood. She steps gingerly over the ashes, and James traces her footsteps to the center of the house, where the chimney stands.

Nelle closes her eyes. Wind sweeps through, clearing the mist, picking up swirls of ash, playing with her golden tendrils.

Strangely, James's nervousness is gone. In its place, he feels both crushing sadness and an eerie calm.

"We should've picked up coffee," Nelle says.

James laughs. "Yeah, we should've."

Nothing, absolutely *nothing* about this feels right.

"I don't want to go." She curls a finger around his. "Ask me to stay."

This is what you want! screams his gut. *Tell her to stay.* But his brain knows better.

There is a reason she bleeds ink. A reason she can't be harmed. A reason she can't die a mortal death. She is not a human. Her dying is impossible because she was never meant to exist in the first place. Some might call her a mistake, but James calls her a miracle. He doesn't tell her to stay, but he can't tell her to leave, so he lets his silent tears speak for themselves.

Nelle nods in understanding, her face crumpling.

James wraps her in his arms, lifting her off the ground as she breaks down. Her arms loop around his neck, and they kiss in the ashes of 23 Blackwood Road.

As they part, salt on their lips, James eases Nelle back to her feet.

She breaks into a teary-eyed grin. "Thanks for busting me out of this place."

He can barely see her through his bleary vision, so he reaches down and takes her hands.

"All I want to say," he says, lip trembling, "is that I love you. We got out of there *together*. I was miserable before, and no one saw that but you—*you*, Nelle, are the only reason I'm happy now. I just . . ."

Say it. Just say it.

"I want you to stay."

Nelle's forehead hits his chest.

He is running out of time to talk her out of it. To list the thousands of places she has yet to see, the experiences she has yet to have. Scuba diving and charcuterie boards and bad movies and stale chips and birthday parties and—

"Goodbye, James," Nelle whispers, her voice vibrating through his chest.

The words cleave him. He will never be whole again.

"I can't watch," he says. "I can't. It'll kill me."

Nelle's hands tighten. "Go sit in the truck and count to thirty."

She steps back, and his hand feels incomplete without hers.

"Go, James."

He soaks her in, ash flaked on her sweater, in her hair, on her nose. She reaches into her back pocket and pulls out a journal. Fighting tears and every instinct to slap that journal out of her hand, James turns his back on her.

Cursing himself, he climbs into his truck.

Count to thirty. Watching the trees, he starts. *One. Two. Three . . .*

❧

Nelle pulls the journal from her back pocket, but something else tumbles out with it. A golden locket, engraved with a rose. She excavates it from the ashes, cracks it open, and stares at the two empty ovals, like a pair of black eyes, watching her. Waiting. *Are you going to do it?* they seem to ask. *Well?* The same taunt that almost drove her to write with her own ink on a street in New York.

The truck door slams shut.

Count to thirty, she said. By then, she will be gone. Flakes of dust on the wind.

Nelle runs her thumb over the locket. Then the journal hits the ground, fountain pen beside it, glass barrel black with her ink. Wind brushes the hair from her face, giving its blessing.

Go on, be free.

❧

Thirty.

James opens the truck door, breathlessly hoping to find Nelle where he left her, already envisioning how he will sprint up to her, how good she will feel in his arms, knowing that she chose to stay. But when he steps out, she is gone.

No use fighting tears now. He braces against the chimney, hollow. The sun climbs, the sky brightens to robin's-egg blue, and then James notices it.

He kneels in the ash beside the journal, pages splayed open and—

Blank.

The pen is cast aside, ink glistening.

She didn't write it.

James looks up, left and right, spins around, but Nelle is gone.

He snatches up the journal and pen. Knowing that she is alive, that she might one day master her thoughts, that she might come back . . .

That is her parting gift.

Or maybe, he thinks as he drives away, *it's her parting curse.*

Chapter 35

James thought he would never see Nelle's face again, but there it is.

Plastered on the front cover of a magazine's Valentine's Day issue: Big City, Young Love. The photograph is of the two of them in profile, zoomed in and so clear that James can see individual follicles on his chin, gilded in low gold lamplight. Each freckle on Nelle's cheek, looking up at him as he grins, her tiny finger touching his nose. In the moment, the boop felt playful, but here it comes off as sensual. He buys a copy, then takes the L across the river.

Jessie's new Williamsburg apartment is, *temporarily*, his home address as well.

Notes from class ring through his head on the five-minute walk down Berry Street. Talia's comment about his style being too flowery for serious prose. He countered with, *What if I don't want to write serious prose?* which broke the number-one rule of Professor Gadley's workshop: unless prompted, don't speak while being critiqued. Gadley, to James's relief, didn't take issue with his writing style, but she did feel disconnected from his main character.

James punches in the door code and takes the stairs to apartment 4C. Hot sugar swirls from the kitchen to the foyer as he drops his key in the ceramic bowl by the door.

"Did you rob a bakery again?" He careens into the kitchen, which overlooks the living room, which overlooks Third Street.

"No, just your pantry." A voice floats down from the terraced second floor, footsteps ringing on the iron spiral staircase. Lucy's fuzzy socks and soft smile. "Your cinnamon's out, by the way."

James frowns. "I bought a new container last week."

"Huh." She peeks into the oven. "Not sure what happened there."

Lucy wears a thin cotton tank top and no bra. James averts his eyes before his innocent once-over becomes a stare. He hopes she wore a jacket. He forgot to bring a scarf to class, and the bottom half of his face is still numb.

"Jessie's in the shower," Lucy says.

"And Lena?"

"Also in the shower."

"Right." James laughs softly and shakes his head. "Interested in a brief trauma dump?"

She pulls up a stool. "Hit me."

The rolled-up magazine slaps the table, unfurling.

Lucy flattens it and gasps. "It's you! What the hell, James? I didn't know you were a model."

"Flattered," he says. "But no, this was a fluke candid the photographer caught. And the person I'm with is—"

"Nelle."

"Yeah." James studies the photograph. "The photographer told us he was working for a publication, but I didn't think much of it."

She sighs. "Yeah, that's depressing."

"Thanks."

"You just look so happy. She's *beautiful*. Damn."

"Yeah." James is there, drunk under rustling trees, holding Nelle for the first time, discovering that electric current between them. His heart breaks a little, all over again.

"All right, enough." Lucy sweeps up the magazine and leaves the room with it. When she returns, she takes a tray of cookies out of the oven, all twenty-four powdered in cinnamon.

"Did you throw it away?" he asks, unsure what answer he wants.

"No, it's too cool to toss out." Lucy washes her hands at the sink. "I put it somewhere safe, so you can appreciate it later, have a story to tell your kids."

"I won't tell my kids about Nelle," James says. "She's like my first novel. For *my* memory only."

The Summer Curse is an arrow to the heart. It's not the fact that he will never publish it that hurts him. Given how much more he intends to grow as a writer, he will be grateful in retrospect. What hurts is the manuscript he lost a month ago. A piece of him died alongside those typewritten pages. The fire devoured them both.

James has to ride this train of thought multiple times a day to remind himself why he needs Nelle out of his life. Why, even though he is eternally grateful that she is alive, he is equally grateful that she chose to distance herself. Living in constant fear of everything he loves disappearing wouldn't be living at all.

That said, if she showed up on his doorstep tomorrow, he would take her back in a heartbeat.

"Oh, come here." Lucy scoots beside him, lets him rest his head on her chest. Her hand soothes his hair, down the nape of his neck. He cries into her tank top.

"Sorry." He pulls back. "Sorry for crying on you."

"You can always cry on me." Lucy slides the platter of cookies toward him. "As long as I can cry on you, too."

"Right now?" He sniffles.

She crosses her ankles. "No, but when I need to."

"From here on out, my chest is reserved for your tears only."

"Thank you." Lucy napkins a cookie and holds it out to him. "Now eat this and tell me if you think there's too much cinnamon."

⁂

Nelle knows the world.

She knows heartbreak. Joy. Guilt.

And she knows she shouldn't watch, but sometimes—like tonight, Valentine's Day, when the moon is pale and the city is alive and James is cozied up on the couch next to some woman, passing popcorn with their friends, bathed in the blue-and-white light of whatever movie they are watching—part of Nelle feels like *she* should be there with him.

But she knows that she can't. *Not yet.*

For now, she stays on the rooftop across the street, bathed in artificial light.

Tomorrow Nelle will go back to Montana, to Penelope, where she can see the stars, both in the sky and on the screen. They bought a ranch out there, miles from anyone else, a self-imposed isolation. When Nelle isn't riding her palomino or painting in the forest, she and Penelope binge-watch films.

But *this* viewing is the most addictive film she has found. She shouldn't watch, but she can't resist. A Valentine's Day present to herself: *An Illegal Glimpse into My Ex-Lover's Window*. This is only the second time she has seen it, though it has only been a month since she left.

She doesn't feel bad for her voyeurism. It's almost natural, given that James and Jessie got a fourth-floor walk-up with a fishbowl window. Given that he still has a pen with her ink, and she is scared he will use it one day. Given that she still loves him.

But James is safe if she's in Montana, where she is only a danger to Penelope, her horse, and her cats. That is why she looks through his window. Not to torture herself over the life she can't have, but to reaffirm herself of the life she requires.

Peace. Quiet. Time to breathe, to sort her thoughts, to ride at breakneck speed in a saddle.

Striding down the sidewalk, Nelle feels beneath her scarf for the engraved rose on that gold locket. Cold reminder of all she has abandoned here. She clicks the locket open, dreaming of the day when two taunting black ovals don't stare back at her.

Acknowledgments

Whispers of Ink and Starlight is a novel I started six years ago in my freshman year of college. The book as it looks today is unrecognizable from its initial draft, but at its heart, the themes are the same. Melancholia. Love. Magic. So much of this novel is integrally *me*, and yet it would not exist without the support of so many.

My first thanks go to the authors and poets who taught me to dream with words, and to God, through whom I see the world.

Thank you to the editors who helped sculpt this book with their blessed red pens: Chantelle Aimée Osman, Jason Kirk, Hannah Buehler, and Selena James. For your hard work, thank you to the rest of the team at Lake Union Publishing: Jen Bentham, Rachael Clark, and Alison Impey. Mumtaz Mustafa, thank you for creating such a stunning and electrifying cover.

Thank you to Brent Taylor and the Triada team for being the best agents I could have asked for.

Thank you to the professors who helped mold my writing, Chika Unigwe, Kerry James Evans, and Laura Newbern.

Thank you to my friends, who have only ever been the most supportive, especially Zach Fleming, who read one of the earliest drafts of this book.

Thank you to my family for always believing in me. To Granna and Pappy, thank you for reading everything I write. To my parents, thank you for never telling me to get a practical job. To Aunt Stephanie, thank you for being my number one fan.

And lastly, thank you to Grace, Elsie, and Toulouse. I'd be nowhere without my girls.

About the Author

Photo © Katherine Jones

Garrett Curbow is the author of the *Daughter of Light* trilogy, which was short-listed for the Publishers Weekly Selfies Award. He lives in Savannah, Georgia. For more information, visit www.garrettcurbow.com.